Jayne Wills was born in the West Midlands, UK. She has written all her life. she worked for over 40 years as a Nurse, in the last 20 years running her own Occupational Health and Safety Consultancy. She then trained in horticulture and garden design, successfully designing a Beautiful Border for BBC Gardeners World Live.

Her first book *The Cottage* was published in 2023.

To my wonderful black Labrador, Bobby, my ever faithful companion whilst I wrote this book, assisting with some of the small characters. You left a paw print on my heart.

Jayne Wills

TIMES LIKE THESE

AUSTIN MACAULEY PUBLISHERS®

LONDON * CAMBRIDGE * NEW YORK * SHARJAH

A CIP catalogue record for this title is available from the British Library.

ISBN 9781035857913 (Paperback)
ISBN 9781035857920 (Hardback)
ISBN 9781035857937 (ePub e-book)

www.austinmacauley.com

First Published 2024
Austin Macauley Publishers Ltd®
1 Canada Square
Canary Wharf
London
E14 5AA

To my friends and family for encouragement, support and love. And for all at Austin Macauley Publishers for believing in me, thank you.

To all those NHS staff who gave time and care and lived away from their families to help people survive under extreme circumstances.

Table of Contents

Before   11

Disquiet   56

Uneasiness Spreading Like the Virus   63

Tumultuous Events   76

Hell   103

It Is the Gift of Life That Is Truly Epic   130

The Future?   215

Epilogue   259

Before

I wake with a start, sitting bolt upright, my face wet with tears; images come to me of Sam, Sam long ago and the day they told me about his death. I saw the officer and Chaplin walking up the drive... I knew immediately. I just knew. I sit back now and take deep breaths to calm my rising panic, slow the breathing Annie, slow. I manage to get the panic to subside, but my heart is still racing. I put my head in my hands and allow the tears to flow once again, the grief is still here, present as on that first day, stronger sometimes, like now, overwhelming me.

I reach for Sam's jumper, knowing I won't smell him anymore but taking comfort from the oh so familiar feel of his favourite jumper, soaking it again with my tears, at least my sobs are muffled and the children won't hear and be alarmed. The tears and sobs gradually slow. I take a breath, calming down. I wonder if this is how I'll feel forever. I can't see it changing, he was my anchor, my day and night my everything. I grieve the man before, but not the hurt after, although I think that adds to the feelings, there were so many unanswered questions though, questions rolling round my head, never spoken out loud.

A fresh sob catches in my throat and I must concentrate on my breathing again or I will fall apart. I cannot do that I have two little people dependent on me and to be strong for, if I hadn't had them and Bob the dog. I know I wouldn't be here. I would have followed Sam, the emotion consuming my whole being, overtaking rational thought.

The day is beginning, the light creeping under the blind, bird song calling out, I remember the spring Sam died, hearing the birds I railed against it, how could they be joyous when we had lost so much, when my children's world had ended.

Sam died three years ago, we knew his job was dangerous, always had, he was in the Army and died serving his country. I do not feel bitter or get embroiled in the politics, like so many people want you to. Sam and I knew what being in the Army meant, you don't go in without that knowledge, you go where you are sent. I miss him so much though, he was my best friend, we were together a long time, ten years before we had our son and only five after his birth.

When I heard the news. I wasn't ready. I wasn't ready to let him go, it was too soon, we had unfinished business. I still feel like that. The emptiness claws at me, there is a huge space inside me where Sam should be, it is constant and drags at me, drags me downwards. I fear where. I want him here beside me, holding me.

I must have dropped off to sleep, as I wake up; I hear noise downstairs and know it is Arthur our son, he is always up first, to help me get everything ready for the day ahead. He is the man of the house now, always was, as Sam was away so much.

Arthur is eight and old before his time, keeping an eye on me and his sister Molly, in charge as much as possible.

I quickly get up and shower, my whole body aching like my heart. I go downstairs and try to be myself, Bob the dog looks at me knowingly as if to say. I see what you've been through this morning, keep strong.

"Hello sweetheart," I say as breezily as I can, gently ruffling Arthur's hair, like Sam always did, Arthur's hair is brown, his lovely long dark eyelashes brushing his little freckled cheeks, too young to have had to deal with losing his dad.

"Hi Mum, I've filled the kettle, you just have to turn it on and I've got the lunch boxes out."

"That's great Arthur, toast or cereal?"

"Toast please, can I have peanut butter on it?" he asks hopefully. I smile, he's pushing it, oh why not.

"Yes, as a treat today," we put lunch together, Arthur filling the bags with fruit and the odd biscuit, we must be careful or the packed lunch police tell me off for putting bad things in the lunches. I make the sandwiches; he likes to help me and have this time with me. He likes to know what I'm doing in the day and if he is going into after school club, this time together is a comfort blanket for him, he sounds insecure and I think he is a bit, quite understandable given the circumstances. Molly joins us, and she sits and has her toast then follows Arthur outside for his kick around before school.

I take a shaky breath, it will be ok, just take each day as it comes, which is difficult as we are going away on holiday soon, which might be why I feel as I do. This will be the third summer without Sam, but we haven't been away before this. I didn't feel strong enough, in the school holidays we took day trips and had bike rides along the nearby canals. We are spending a couple of weeks in a beach hut, one my parents own, and one I have been to many times. It is situated on a gorgeous safe beach looking out to sea, a children's paradise, just sand and sea to play in.

Arthur isn't too sure about the hut, mainly because of the lack of showers and toilets in there. Molly and me feel we can cope, there are lovely facilities just behind our hut, which I suppose is nice in good weather but I am unsure if I see myself in a force eight gale, clutching a full bladder and my toilet bag running to use them.

Dad bought the hut over thirty years ago, he had it refurbished two years ago, replacing the rotten windows and doors, updating the kitchen, which was previously very basic, now having a gas cooker, fridge and new worktops, he had solar panels put in too, so electricity, to charge phones and iPads.

I start doing some of the packing on return from school drop off, everything we take must be kept to a minimum as there isn't much room in the hut. The children will have a case each, bought for them at Christmas by Mum and Dad, perhaps in the hope we might have an adventure this year, both on wheels, which is a boon as we must park quite away from the hut and catch a small train. I haven't told them that yet, as we are at fever pitch already.

Mum has leant me her box on wheels, so I can pack things to keep the children amused on wet days, and Arthur will take his football and Molly which ever doll is in favour, she is sporty too and loves to play football with her older brother. Having organised as much as I can I take some tea out into the garden, still feeling shaky from last night, trying to be strong, looking round the garden I remember the picture Sam took of me and gave me for my birthday, the picture had been taken on a warmish end of November day and I had put some shorts on and was digging, when he gave it to me he said, "Remember you are strong, this is to remind you every day."

I laughed and said, "you silly man," the gesture a sticking plaster on a new wound, but that was the last time I saw him, and I realised after he died that he had been showing me the future, to be strong. I had often wondered if he knew somehow, but I'm being fanciful.

It is so hard though. I didn't lean on Sam, but we were a couple in everything, we balanced each other. I feel like I am off balance all of the time. It isn't that I don't love the children. I do with all my heart but Sam was everything, he was a solid part of our unit, and with him gone I feel that our square of four is missing a side, and that we are all going to fall out, I feel I have fallen, am falling without him, even with everything that happened latterly.

After putting in some much-needed gardening and checking on some of my garden customers who I do some chores for I shower and walk down the hill to collect the children. We are lucky we live in a village with a small school, both the children love it and have done well considering the difficulties they have had to bear, Sam and I bought an old police house the year after we met, it had started as a police house then been converted to a station, so we have spent quite a bit of time and money making it habitable. The house is quite elevated, we have a lovely large wrap around garden, with a gate at the bottom of the drive to stop footballs escaping.

Molly finishes ten minutes before Arthur, but she is always last out of class, walking along day dreaming, usually without some piece of her school uniform, forgotten, left inside, ties, cardigans, lunch box. She doesn't so much walk though, but skips or hops, which never fails to make me smile, Mum says I was just the same at that age.

Arthur emerges from school virtually as he went in, tie in place and immaculate except for his shoes being scuffed from playing football. As we walk up the hill, he tells me he had to stand up in assembly this morning. I groan inwardly, thinking he had been in trouble. I should know better, he won an award today for standing up to some bullies, who were being rude to a little boy in his class who must wear very thick glasses.

He asks if we can get it framed and put it next to Daddy's medals and pictures on the wall. We keep a rogue's gallery of pictures on the stairwell, you can stop and look at the pictures, Sam and us, Sam on parades and with his buddies, remembering him, but we are starting to put our own pictures up now, trying to build a future without him.

As I finish the tea for the children the phone goes, it is my friend Sue. She works in personnel for a large logistics company and is often working away, she's home and wants to pop in this evening for a catch up. I agree as we are away ourselves soon, it will be nice to chat to an adult and face to face, as much as I love the children, adult company is good for you and it can be quite lonely.

The children go off to bed after baths and stories and another chat about the beach hut. I know from experience that Molly is likely to be down at least once, but Arthur will sleep soundly.

Later I hear the gate go and open the door to Sue, she is the opposite to me, tall and leggy and blonde, but both the same age, 42, we had contemplated a joint fortieth but with Sam not being there I felt it would be a dampener on her celebrations, and I had no stomach to celebrate myself.

Although it is lovely to see Sue and other friends. I find now I don't want to go over and over how I feel, initially I did and cried with them, well those that understood anyway, so many people can't deal with grief. Now if I feel low. I prefer to be low on my own, trying to gain some control, dealing with it without other people's interference. I know Sue feels I should share, but not right now, and some things I cannot share, yet. Or at all. I am not sure.

We do have a good catch up and mainly discuss her waning love life, she lives here in the village but it isn't easy meeting someone when she travels so much. I invite Sue to the local pub for the harvest auction later in the year, we laugh at how our lives had changed from going into the city for a night out to going out to the village local.

The following morning as I'm making beds and tidying up. I remember last night's conversations with Sue, we did have a bit of a laugh, reminiscing about school, we have known each other since childhood. She asked if I was going back into Nursing. I gave up my job within three months of Sam's death. I was a sister in an inner-city A/E department, it was a job I loved. I went part time after I had the children and juggled everything and managed well. I had some time off after Sam died and contemplated going back but my empathy button wasn't working and I knew my concentration was poor, so I resigned. I didn't want to end my career making a mistake. I also wanted time to grieve and support the children. I had to be both parents for them.

Thinking about it now and what I replied to Sue. I doubt I will ever go back. I changed dramatically when I was told about Sam. I don't think I will ever be that person again, and it works with me being here, it gives the children stability, when I made the original decision, it was like a weight lifted from my shoulders, financially I could just about cope, the only thing, which Sue pointed out last night was that I missed the company and laughs I'd had at work. But we have made a new life, a different one and in a sense what choice did I have.

With time at home. I started gardening. I realised how bad ours looked and I just poured myself into it, it helped me grieve, it decreased my anxiety being outside so much, it made me plan, something I did subconsciously, as I didn't want to plan my life, not without Sam, but planning the garden felt right. The hard work helped me sleep. I had been so emotionally exhausted prior to that and couldn't sleep.

I put in raised beds, with Dad's help, and started growing some crops, minor successes followed with radishes and some early potatoes, but also some failures, but that's gardening. I also planted a lot of flowering plants, to lighten the darkness that crept upon me. Dave, my brother, helped a lot too, not a gardener himself he would do the heavy jobs, like removing old woody shrubs, he was just there, not saying much, just being around.

The children became interested too, and so we would go out and water and check how everything was coming on, it was our time and it was something new for all of us, it definitely helped us all that first summer. I found that gardening gave me some peace.

We have come on leaps and bounds since then, it seems that the whole family realise how good it is for us, so presents are all gardening orientated, from bare rooted raspberry canes for me, to garden tools for the children and even a short kitchen garden course for me.

That took a lot of courage to attend but I did and learnt a lot. Gardening meant I was using my hands and creating new life, then one or two neighbours who couldn't do their own gardens asked if I would help, which I was happy to do, initially I was just happy helping out, but some insisted on paying me, and I then started doing more, so this has grown. I also joined the local gardening club, egged on by Iris, who is a force of nature and who must be obeyed. She works in the local shop just to keep herself out of the house now her husband Ted is retired, she has babysat the children for me and Sam in the past, Ted is a great friend and so knowledgeable about gardens and chairman of the club and the allotment association. Sam would be laughing at all of this. "You live on the edge girl," he would have said.

I have attended some of the meetings, which take place in the village hall, but don't join everyone in the local pub afterwards. I have gained some confidence doing all of this, but am not quite ready to spread my wings too much.

Iris looks after the children when I go to the gardening club, the children adore her as she spoils them rotten, she is so sharp too, she never misses a thing, and loves a bit of a gossip, she usually turns up early, to keep me up to date, she is a demon on Facebook and knows everything that is going on locally.

Ted is going to keep an eye on the garden and produce for me, not necessarily a good idea going away at such a busy time, but Ted will be great. We have far more produce on the go this year, runner beans, peas, courgettes, salad leaves, tomatoes. I had them in grow bags last year, and had to net them as someone was pinching them, Bob the dog took a liking for small cherry tomatoes, he is good at keeping the rabbits away though, but not the mice, as they seem to enjoy a lot of crops, the children have enjoyed it all too, picking and eating fresh foods.

I've told Ted to help himself when he is around as there is no point crops rotting unpicked.

Thinking about everything and organising the holiday has probably produced my wobble, it is overwhelming sometimes, coping with everything on my own, but it is important for the children to have some normality and this holiday will be that for them.

We are on our way to the south coast, the pretty way, as Mum always called it, through the Cotswolds and over Salisbury Plain. I hope for Arthur's sake there is a helicopter or tank to be seen there. We have left very early, Arthur in the front, and Molly and Bob in the back, Bob has his car harness on and is quite happy looking out of the window. We stop a couple of times for Bob, and for the children to stretch their legs, and the inevitable snacks.

Excitement was at fever pitch last night, luckily worn out they slept well. When we started off, I told them about the train at the end, so many questions about what it would look like and how we get on it and what about the luggage. Answers when we get there.

Parked up, ticket for car and train purchased, luggage being pulled by us all and there is the ubiquitous train, a lovely bright red with its luggage wagon at the back. Arthur is beyond excited, he helps the driver put our luggage away and then has to choose which of the carriages to sit in, the first obviously, behind the engine and facing forwards, Bob sits on the floor and the chains are put across the little doorways, with a ding on the bell we are off, as we climb out of the car park area, we can see the beautiful nature reserve and as the children point out the sea, you can see the incredible curve of the sandspit with all the pretty coloured huts glinting in the sun, it looks idyllic, the sea is quite calm and we can see boats gently keeping to the speed limit going out through the harbour and the estuary to sea.

Through a lovely wooded area bordering the harbour and we are there, we collect our luggage and make our way along the path and water's edge, huts to our right and the harbour to our left.

"Which way do we go, Mum?" Arthur in charge likes to be at the front.

"Straight up to the café and shop and turn right then left Arthur," he strides off pulling his case, and holding Bob's lead, we have to stop though to look at the sea taxi coming in to moor and discharge its passengers.

"We can explore later guys, let's go find our hut."

As we move up by the side of the café, we can see the sea on the other side, and the wonderful beaches. I stop this time to take it in, but have to quickly keep up with the children, as they are asking which is our hut and checking them all out. And there it is, set well back from the path, and slightly elevated, pale blue with white paint on windows and doors. I point it out and luggage is abandoned in the sand as the children and Bob run towards it.

"Come on Mummy, we're dying to see inside, aren't we, Molls?"

"Yessss, quick Mum, unlock the door," says a bouncing Molly.

Once I have dropped my bags and found the key. I open the central double doors and let them in, it looks lovely inside, it is tiny, but ample, a sofa bed is on either side of the doors as you go in with lovely beach hut patterned covers and the same is mirrored with the curtains at the windows, all neatly tied back maximising the light and views.

As I turn and look outside. I realise how lucky we are, we can see the beach, and Dad has put two wind breaks parallel in front of the hut, marking out a play area for the children. The decking is deep enough for a table and chairs now the doors are secured back.

"Mum look at our bedroom," shouts an over excited Molly. Following their voices, I move to a small room on the right at the back. I think room is too excessive a description for what is basically a cupboard with two miniscule bunk beds with a rug in front of them, but it's their space and so important, it has a concertina door to maximise the space. The bunk beds are on the right of the area, with a ladder to climb to the top bunk, Arthur is obviously on that already.

"Do you like it?" silly question really when I can see their smiling happy faces, Molly is lying on the bottom bunk shoes kicked off, hands behind her head, like she's in heaven.

I leave them to it, and go back and grab the discarded luggage, then return with the cool box to the kitchen area, the hut is only about sixteen feet square, beside the bedroom area is the kitchen, a very narrow breakfast bar separates the kitchen from the living area, along the left hand wall is a worktop with the cooker and a fridge below, and a small sink, Mum has left a vase of flowers cut from her garden on the breakfast bar, they had wanted us to go to see them as they only live in the New Forest, but as they go away to Canada later today, I felt it was too much for them.

There is a note, telling me to have a lovely time and that the children's spare bikes are in the store cupboard on the deck behind the hut, along with beers for visitors, they are so kind, Arthur and Molly will be able to ride their bikes on the tarmac road in front of the huts to their hearts content, and no traffic too.

"Come on you two, get your cases and we can put our stuff away and go and explore," as I open the fridge, I find it well stocked, what is Mum like, just as I am making room for our food Arthur comes out of their room.

"Mum, we have to decide which bed you are sleeping in," I doubt I will have any say in this, and there is only a choice of two.

"I think the one on the right, then I can see you from my bed, what do you think Molly, shall we get on our beds to check, and you lie on yours, Mummy," so we all do that and yes, they can see me, which is good and reassuring for them. I show them how they can hang some of their clothes on pegs on the wall facing their beds and show them the drawer under the bed too. I will tidy their things myself, but they have suddenly found two new buckets and spades. I wonder who left them those? They want to go onto the sand in front of the hut, so I unpack.

As I sort everything out, I can see them happily trying to make small sandcastles with their new buckets, Bob sitting on the top step keeping an eye on his "pups," we've only had him 18 months, he was a rescue dog, a border terrier, he's only three and is devoted to the children. They've long sleeve tops on at present but I must make sure they have some sun protection on, especially Molly as she is fair like Sam, whereas Arthur is darker like me, but still some factor 50 for them both. I go and check the store cupboard to see what else is in there, bikes, parasol, chair seats and barbeque and coals, I've done a couple of barbeques so might fancy doing one here too, might be nice to do one tonight.

I get changed and then get them some drinks and biscuits, which we eat on the deck, we sit in silence as they recharge their batteries, knowing that silence won't last for long, and yes questions pour out, so to answer most of them I get them ready for an explore, all kitted out and hut locked up, we make our way towards the estuary, seeing the boats making their way out to sea.

As it's July, the huts are mostly open and busy, the beach in front of the huts is made of smaller beaches, with boulders dividing them up, placed to help prevent erosion.

"Mum, can we go to the beach soon and into the sea?" Arthur asks.

"Yes, love, let's give Bob a walk and then we can," we continue on to the estuary, and over on the other side all you can see are families crab fishing, Arthur and Molly are fascinated, poor crabs they must spend the holiday being caught, put in a bucket for the day then thrown back only to be caught again the next day, very ground hog. Obviously, they want to have a go, but am hoping it's an activity that Dave might like to organise, he's coming down soon for a week or so.

Walk sorted I decide to take a small picnic down to the sand, even though the hut is nearby. As I am doing this the serious business of toilets raises its ugly head. I take them out the back of the hut and a couple of huts behind us is the toilet block, Arthur is relatively happy especially as he sees the sign 'loo of the year 2023' and they are clean, spotless in fact.

Costumes on, lathered up with sun protection, food and drink for all and we make our way to the beach, Bob in tow, he will sit with me on the rug, he's not a big lover of water is our Bob, doesn't like to get his paws wet, and not fond of rain either.

"Mum, do you think Bob would like to go for a swim in the sea?" Arthur asks hopefully.

"I shouldn't think so love, if he doesn't like water, he's not going to like the sea, but you can always see if he follows you in."

"Ok," he seems happy with that.

We settle ourselves on a lovely patch of dry sand with some dunes behind us, now the fun begins sand in everything. The children run down the gentle sloping beach to the sea, "To check the temperature," Arthur says.

I sit watching them with Bob, wisely staying away from the water. I put his corkscrew tie in and put up the small parasol to keep the sun off him.

Arthur shouts and gives me the thumbs up; the temperature is obviously suitable for him. I lie back propping myself on my elbows, the sand is lovely and soft I push my feet into it, there is something quite childlike in having bare feet in cold sand, enjoyable. Sam would have loved this for the children. I think, as I do my breath catches in my throat. I have to swallow hard to control the urge to cry, it isn't always on cold wet dank days that I feel like this. I think of what he would have enjoyed, what he's missing, like now seeing his children enjoying simple pleasures, behind my sunglasses my eyes are filling with tears, come on Annie get a grip. Bob rests his chin on my leg, knowing, making me feel worse, taking a deep breath I stand up and pat Bob on the head.

"Wait here Bob," trying to focus and make sure the children don't see me upset I walk slowly down towards them, "Is it warm you two?"

"Mummy," they both shout, I stick my toe in the sea, not too bad.

"Mummy we are sitting and letting the waves wash over our legs, you sit down," Molly tugs at my hand. I sit down next to them, it would take a bigger wave than these to wash over my legs I think, although I have lost a lot of weight over the recent years, we are only in the shallows.

"Shall we go a bit deeper and you can have a swim, Arthur?" he can swim well, no armbands required, Molly isn't so good or confident, she likes to sit on the edge of the pool if we go swimming splashing her feet and sometimes sitting on the steps, not scared just watching. We wade in, me holding Molly's hand, Arthur gently swims near us.

"Do you want me to hold you and you can have a float, Molly?"

"Yes, but don't let me go Mummy, Daddy always held me tight," and he did, although she was only a toddler but she remembers it, so I hold her and she slowly relaxes, and lets her legs kick out a bit.

"Way to go, Molls," Arthur says circling around us, bobbing up and down with the waves, "I'm hungry now Mum," no surprise there then, my son is virtually two hourly fed, even at eight, it's the school routine really with breaks. I stand Molly up who also wants food, she does like to mirror her brother and looks up to him so much.

As we dry off, Arthur pours a drink for Bob and we settle for our lunch, watching the other beach activities.

"Mum I'm going to make a sand castle in a bit, a big one with water around it."

"In a moat love."

"Yes, that's it just like a real castle."

"I'll carry the water for you Arthur."

"Thanks Molly, you can collect stones and shells too for me to decorate it."

"Ok," they run off to begin their excavation as I sit and watch with Bob.

We cram most activities into that first day, including a kick around for the children with the football. The showers were a bit of a palaver, with Arthur using the men's toilets while Molly and I sit patiently waiting for him and then him waiting outside for us, which worried me a bit, well a lot. It was something I hadn't thought about how helpful having another parent or person with you is, especially a male one for Arthur.

We have our barbeque and after another round of toilet visits, they go to bed, I've learnt quite a lot today, mainly how daunting it is with only me to look after them, although I know this, at home its different, after a quick tidy up I go and sit on the deck, all around are groups of people, families, couples, enjoying the barmy evening, barbeques are still alight, huts are decked out in light and tables lit by candles.

I now cannot wait for Dave to come down as I feel a bit lonely and overwhelmed, he has kindly taken a week off to join us. I wish it was tomorrow he was coming not five days' time. It will be good for all of us. Bob hops up onto the seat next to me and I gently stroke his ears, it was the Chaplin who suggested we got a dog, it would be a different focus, for all of us, and Bob has helped tremendously. I can ramble away to him and feel better if I have vented, he was also a good excuse to avoid people, "Got to go the dog needs a wee," is a frequent statement, or was in the early days, when I didn't want to talk, it is amazing how many people don't know what to say to you, so Bob was good at manoeuvring me out of situations.

It is the firsts that have been the worst, first Christmas without him, first anniversary of his death, and I am now realising first holiday. We never went away without Sam, we always had holidays that coincided with his leave, we did everything together, perhaps we knew our time was limited. It took me a while to realise Sam wasn't coming home. I just expected him to walk in the door with his usual sunny grin… My phone vibrates in my pocket interrupting my maudlin thoughts, its Dave.

"Hello little sis, how are you coping on your own, are the children in bed?" he asks chirpy as always.

"Yes, they zonked out ages ago. I think I will be joining them soon, it's all this sea air, and all the activities." I go on to tell him what we have done today.

"Are you ok you sound a bit down?"

"I'm ok it's been a long day. I think I under estimated how much I have to do being on my own, simple things like Arthur having to use the men's showers and me and Molly having to use the ladies', but I'll cope don't worry," I say not quite believing it myself.

"I do worry, and you will cope, you can always let Arthur use the ladies' showers, people would understand," but would Arthur I think, Dave carries on, "I'll be there in a couple of days, so do simple things around the hut, they can play in the sand in front of the hut and ride their bikes up and down the track, we can do trips when I get there."

"Yes, perhaps I tackled too much today."

"I've no doubt sis, Mum and Dad caught their flight, so they are somewhere over the Atlantic now. I spoke to them earlier and she asked me to bring some food down with me."

"What's she like, there is enough food here to feed a proverbial Army, let alone one adult and two children, I'll let you know if I have any shortages," I reply laughing.

"She enjoys fussing even from far away, hey do you remember the Abbots?" he asks.

"Of course, I do," Dave went to school with Matt Abbott, he lived locally at Ash Farm, when he left school he went onto agricultural college, but didn't like it and upped and joined the Parachute Regiment, we used to see quite a bit of Matt when he was back on leave, he would always hook up with Dave when on leave, and I lived with Dave for a while so saw him then, he met Sam and they got on well. "I've seen Matt a few times in passing since Sam's memorial service, his mother died earlier in the year. I didn't go to the funeral but wrote him a letter. I wonder how he has coped with his father and the farm, as his mum did everything, looking after his dad and running the farm."

"Well, I spoke to Matt yesterday, his father has had to go into a home, the carers they had couldn't cope with his father's Alzheimer's, and weren't live in, since his mother died his father has deteriorated a lot."

"Oh. I am so sorry to hear that Dave, how's Matt about it all, it's difficult dealing with all this if he was away, although I expect the Regiment gave him compassionate leave."

"He's not good, but I hadn't realised he's come out of the Paras."

"You're joking, was it to look after his father?"

"Not completely, although there was an element of that, he wanted to come back and take over the farm, he said he's been thinking about it for ages, then his mother's death put the seal on it, he just needed to complete his twenty years, better for his pension, but he didn't think his father would deteriorate so quickly. I think he regrets not just leaving as soon as his mother died, as his father wasn't too bad then."

"Oh, poor old Matt. I can't see him running the farm though, it was never his thing, was it?"

"I know you could have knocked me over with a feather when he told me, he's changed, he's lost a few good friends over the years, and he feels he wants to put down roots and do something with the legacy his parents created, his mother left the farm in good order apparently, and the farm manager is very competent and has kept it going well. So, he's working with him and looking to diversify a bit to keep cash coming in."

"Good for Matt, I'll give him a call when we get back."

"You'll see him sooner than you think. I told him I was coming down here and he sounded interested so I invited him to join us, don't panic he going to stay up the road with his cousin Theo," Dave knows me well I was at that point trying to work out how you get five people into four very small beds, and I remember Matt being a good six foot tall and a larger model than would fit into these beds comfortably.

"That's great Dave, it will be lovely to see him again, we will be quite a party then."

Dave says good night and I quickly let Bob out the back, when he returns, I lock all the doors and make a dash for the loos myself. I scuttle back in checking all is well. I make up my bed and see Bob settled on his rug, the gentle sound of the waves lulls me to sleep.

We get into a nice routine over the next couple of days of play and lazing around, the children are enjoying their freedom and have begun to make one or two friends, usually all joining in for a kick of a football, they've had bike rides with me and Bob walking along side, and loads of swims.

As for me I'm looking forward to Dave coming down today, to share some of the responsibility, at 11 he texts to say he's half an hour away. I gather the children and Bob, Dave is going to park on the other side of the estuary, which gives us a chance to use the sea taxi.

As we wait for the boat I think about Dave, he has been an absolute rock for me, we were always close, but he has been there for me so much. He's in the police force, now a Sergeant, paper pushing he says, but he still enjoys the job. He's had a few relationships and one marriage that didn't work out, he doesn't want to be pinned down, his ex said he's as slippery as a bar of soap. I'd like to see him settled, he's so good with the children, it would be lovely to see him as a dad.

We get on the boat and head over to the other side of the estuary, the children are enjoying themselves, it's only a five-minute ride parallel to the sandspit, we try to spot the back of our hut, before we know it, we are standing at the edge of the car park looking for Dave's car. I spot him parking and holding the children's hands walk over. As he gets out, both the children run up for a hug.

"You all look well, has it been good weather?"

Before I can answer, "We've been swimming every day," says Arthur.

"And I can float on my back with Mummy holding me," pipes up Molly.

"Way to go Molls, has Bob been in the sea," Dave knows all about Bob's aversion to water.

"No," Arthur shakes his head looking at Bob sadly.

Eventually we get back to the hut, drinks all round, and a beer for Dave, the children have decided they want a swim before we have any lunch, so are getting changed, at lightning speed. Leaving Bob to watch through the hut window we amble down to the water, it's another beautiful day, the water has heated up with the sun over the last few days, Dave paddles with beer in hand.

"Uncle Dave, will you hold me in the water?" Molly asks.

"I'll look after your beer for you."

"No doubt there won't be much left when you give it back," he says wading into the water, he holds Molly under her arms and lets her float, she's starting to do some kicks now, her confidence improving. I think about her comment, how Daddy always held her tight. I wonder if her reluctance to swim is linked to Sam's death. I smile as Arthur is swimming around them both and waving at me too.

Later with showers over, a much easier process with Dave sorting Arthur out, and a happier Arthur. We have a barbeque and the children start to wilt; bedtime has arrived. While Dave tells them a short story. I take Bob for a walk around the block. As I get back I can see Dave sitting on the deck on the phone, he hands me a glass of wine.

"That was Matt, he's coming down to Theo's late tomorrow night and will come across on Saturday."

"Oh, that's good it will be great to catch up with him."

"He's using Theo's small boat and he will moor it in front of the café, easier than parking the car, Theo's going to put in a couple of life jackets for Arthur and Molly if they want a trip."

"Oh, that's so kind, I'm sure they will."

"How are you, sis?"

"I'm ok, it's not been a bad week, it's lovely seeing the children enjoy themselves and be carefree."

"Well, I'm here to help now, have either of them mentioned Sam?"

I think back to my conversation with Molly a few days ago, "Yes, Molly asked me when Daddy was coming down."

"I wondered if she would as she hasn't really grasped Sam's never coming back."

"No, I don't think she has, but she will in time," Dave squeezes my hand. "I know he's not coming back Dave, that he's dead, but coming here I sort of expect to see him. I suppose it's because we are somewhere different, I've thought about him so much and how he would have loved to see Arthur and Molly doing all of this, having this opportunity. I suppose it's opened up the wound a bit, at home I'm in my comfort zone."

"This has moved the horizons for you Annie, broadened them."

"I've had time to think, and I want to open up more, do more things, perhaps get more gardening opportunities in, meet more people," saying this I feel that I am trying to forget Sam, guilt ripples through me. "I have kept people at a distance as I didn't want them to see me falling apart, it was bad enough in front of you and Mum and Dad."

"We didn't mind sis, so you are looking forward a bit, which is good, have you thought about you and," Dave pauses, "Someone else?"

"No," I'm stunned he's said this, "I definitely haven't and I don't want to go there, Sam was," she pauses. "Uhm everything."

Dave starts to interrupt, "No let me go on. I can't visualise myself with anyone else, in every way, physically and emotionally."

"What about the children, do you think they might need that role model?"

This conversation is going into areas I don't want to go into, part of me had raised the same question, but it felt too raw to question it too deeply.

26

"I don't know Dave I think I'm doing fairly well, it's too early to think about all of that."

"Sorry sis. I didn't mean to upset you. I just thought you deserve more, more love in your lifetime, and Sam would want you to be happy."

"Sam didn't deserve to die, but he did, and perhaps I had so much love in our time together that it was a lifetime of love," but was it, inside I ask was it love on both sides, something no one knows about, changing the subject, I ask Dave about his love life, turning the tables.

"Yes, been seeing a woman called Melinda, for once I'm doing the chasing, she's independent, quite in control of her life, we get on well."

"Good, it will do you good to do some of the running instead of women falling at your feet."

"I'll take the children crabbing tomorrow, get some lines and bait, and while we are over there I can spot where the best fishing is."

"Are you going to try and catch some sea bass then?"

"Yes, I'll give it a go, the rods are under the hut, if I catch some, we can barbeque them later."

"You're optimistic," or is that cocky. I think. But my brother being my brother did catch some sea bass and after a full day the next day, we barbequed them and had a great time.

Saturday morning and I walk up to the car park to renew my ticket with Bob, Dave is going to take the children for breakfast in the café and wait for Matt to arrive. The walk is lovely along the side of the harbour and then under the trees with a gentle breeze blowing, my hair ruffled from the wind, I get the train back, and notice how tanned I'm looking. I actually feel chilled this morning, its having Dave here to share with.

As I walk up to the café, I can see Arthur talking to two men. I can see its Matt, he hasn't changed much, over six foot tall, broad and muscular, close cropped brown hair. I assume the other man must be Matt's cousin Theo, he is dark haired, smaller and a slighter build, he's in the family business, they have a restaurant down here.

Arthur spots me, "Mummy come and have breakfast, we've waited for you, and Uncle Dave is paying," I don't think everyone in the cafe quite caught that. I smile and look up into the pale blue eyes of Matt.

He puts his hand on my shoulder and kisses my cheek, then introduces me to Theo. They both follow me into the café, "I've ordered breakfast for everyone, bacon butties all round, but porridge for Arthur and Molly," Dave says smiling.

I settle Bob under the table, we are in the outer area with great views over the harbour and the boats, with dogs allowed.

"We aren't having porridge we are having butties too," says an indignant Arthur.

"He's joking, Arthur, Uncle Dave told me," Molly says trying to pacify him.

"Snitch," Dave says chucking Molly under the chin.

"Well, I'm starving," I say as the order arrives, there is a lot of banter, particularly between Matt and Dave. I look at Arthur, his eyes shining and even joining in himself, lapping up the male company.

"So, Arthur are you and Molly going to be my first passengers?" Matt asks, "We can go up river, as the tide is going out it's a bit lively by the estuary," he turns to me to reassure me, he has his sunglasses pushed onto the top of his head. I notice dark rings under his eyes, he looks tired and a bit care worn.

"I thought it was only the marines that went on water. I thought you 'poopers' stayed well clear of water," says Dave teasing Matt.

"I make exceptions, but at least I'm doing a proper job not pushing paper," everyone laughs.

"It's a tractor now for you, isn't it?"

"Yeh yeh, you'll be thinking up farmer jokes before we know it," they'll be play fighting next, I think. Boys.

We go out to admire the boys toys, boat and jet ski. I hadn't realised Theo had come over on that, his wet suit lying on the top, the boat is a small rigid inflatable boat, or RIB as Arthur explains to me, Matt gets the lifejackets out and starts to put them on the children.

"Are you joining us Annie?" he asks.

"No, I'll stay here and watch," not too keen on being on water, the sea taxi was my only concession.

"I hear you always fancied going on a jet ski, Annie," Theo says.

"That was years ago, how... Dave?" I shake my head at my brother.

"You'll enjoy it, I'll take you out a bit later on."

It looks like I don't have much choice, as far as I'm concerned it is still "on water," whether it is a boat or a jet ski, my younger self wouldn't have minded but my confidence now isn't what it was, "Oh thanks Theo, but don't go to any trouble."

"No trouble at all Annie."

Dave and Theo push the boat off and the children sit there good as gold, waving, as the RIB glides up river keeping within the buoys.

"You take Bob back, I'll stay here, they're in good hands," Dave squeezes my hand.

Knowing they are, I go back to the hut, to tidy up and sweep the floor of the ever-present sand, as I'm finishing Arthur and Molly come running up the steps.

"I want to be a sailor Mum. I loved it."

"What about you Molly?"

"We saw lots of birds and fishes and some big boats parked."

"Moored Molly," the sailor corrects her, "Shall we go and tell the others and have a kick around?" and with that they are gone to see their friends.

"Coffee or tea or something else guys?" as the three men approach and come into the hut, suddenly the hut feels very small. I shoo them onto the deck and get the drinks.

"We'll do that jet ski trip in a minute, Annie," Theo says. I grimace and Matt and Dave laugh.

"Annie isn't a good sailor, she loves looking at the sea but isn't good on it," Dave is enjoying this. I will have to find a way to get him back.

"Annie, take no notice, the jet ski is different," Theo adds smoothly, and he is smooth lounging in the chair, and yes looking me up and down, not too comfortable with that.

Oh well better change and get this ride over with. I put my cossie on in the children's room and a t shirt on top. I assume no wet suit for me.

"Right, I'm ready," I announce as if I'm going to the guillotine.

"Annie, you make it sound like a chore not some fun," Theo says putting his arm round my shoulders and propelling me down the steps.

Dave locks up and they all follow us to the jet ski. I wade out a couple of feet to the jet ski putting my life jacket on, Theo lifts me onto the jet ski, his hands a little higher up my waist than is necessary I think. I sit down and take my flip flops off and throw then at Dave, trying to stop him laughing. I turn and look back at them as we gently start moving. Arthur is giving me his thumbs up and Molly is sitting on Matt's shoulders waving.

"Annie, get closer to me and put your arms around my waist, just slip them under my life jacket it will be easier and hold on tight," his silky-smooth voice commands me. I think I'm not putting my arms or hands under his life jacket, well at least I can't get too close as I have my life jacket on.

Dave and Matt and the children are walking along the path following us along the water's edge.

"Does he have to be so close to Annie, and did he have to put his hands under her life jacket to pick her up?" Matt says through clenched teeth.

"Why," Dave stops and asks him.

"Oh, no reason," Matt replies walking on.

"Yeh sure, don't kid a kidder mate, you always did like Annie. I grew up with you remember."

"Whatever," he replies.

We start to move out to the open sea, bouncing on the water, I'm thinking what on earth am I doing here, oh my god, oh my god, fear ripples through me. I realise I don't feel sick and yes. I am enjoying myself, we go out a little way from the coast then come back into the beach in front of the hut, taking my life jacket off, I gently slide into the water, and do feel exhilarated, as I'm walking out of the water, jet ski moored, Theo comes up behind me and gives me a hug.

"Oh, thanks Theo it was good."

The others are approaching, Dave glances at Matt, and sees a scowl on his face replacing the look of joy that was on his face when he saw Annie come out of the water.

"I think I need a shower," I say walking towards them.

Matt has to hold his breath and look away, as Annie's t shirt is clinging to her like another skin, and he knew what he would like to do in that shower with her, deep breath, Matt, he tells himself, she looks so attractive her auburn hair curly and longer than it used to be, she's slim but curvy he thinks, in all the right places, with lovely legs, for all to see in her swimsuit.

"I'll get the children some lunch," Dave says approaching the hut.

"Ok won't be long," I grab a towel and some clothes from the drawer under my bed and scoot out the back of the hut, as I come back down to earth I think how much fun it was, although not sure I would do it again, not with that particular driver, he's quite familiar I think to myself and shiver, not from the cold and not excitement either.

It's been a busy few days, lots of activities for all of us, the children are so happy with Dave here, and company from Matt and Theo, although Theo has returned to work but has promised to pop over some evenings, he has monopolised me a bit, just when I'd have liked to chat to Matt. As I'm thinking this. I see Matt mooring the RIB in front of the café.

"Hi," I shout and walk over to him with Bob, Matt bends and kisses Annie's cheek, gently touching her shoulder as he does.

"Where are the others?"

"Dave has taken Molly and Arthur crab fishing again, so I thought I'd walk Bob, do you fancy a coffee."

"Yes, that would be great," we walk into the café and get a seat at the front, Bob settles under the table and we order coffee, and bacon sandwich for Matt.

"Hungry?"

"Yes, no food at Theo's, he tends to eat at work and I haven't had a chance to buy in anything in the last couple of days," his bacon sandwich comes and he tucks in.

"We haven't had much of a chance to catch up since you've been here, sorry."

"No problem, Annie, there's been a lot going on and always someone wanting your attention," he smiles and I wonder if he meant Theo, as he has been a bit of a shadow.

"I was sorry to hear about your father, Matt, how is he doing now, have you thought much about the farm?"

"He's ok, doesn't really know what's going on or who I am," his voice thick with emotion. I reach over and hold his hand, "I think with Mum not being around at the farm, her death being so sudden and him not understanding, then with strangers in, the carers, his dementia just accelerated quickly." He visibly shakes himself, "But I have to get on with everything now, having this break away has put things into perspective for me. I only wish I could have come back sooner for them."

"Matt don't beat yourself up, you came back as quickly as you could."

"Yeh," he doesn't look convinced, "To be honest I was glad to be coming out, so much has happened to friends and obviously family that it didn't feel the same anymore," finishing his sandwich, he takes a mouthful of coffee as if to steady himself. I look into his eyes and see that tiredness again before he drops his head.

"I've quite a lot of plans for the farm, Don who has been running it for Mum has worked wonders, we are mixed in that there is arable, potatoes, maize and rape seed, and we have cattle, sheep and chickens. So quite a lot to do, but Mum had started to convert the barns by the river for holiday accommodation, what with the fishing rights, I think it is a sure winner, I'm also selling two rundown cottages for conversion on the far side of the farm, which will give me the money back the farm has spent on the barns, just ploughing the money back in to the farm. I'm also hoping to convert a barn out at the top of the farm by the Eastlands Road to make a farm shop and possibly a café, in the future, just to increase revenue."

"Wow loads of plans, are you keeping the house?" I ask, the farmhouse is old eighteenth or nineteenth century, three storeys with beautiful gardens including a sunken garden, which was his mother's pride and joy.

"Oh god yes. I may rattle around in it and it might need serious modernising but I couldn't think of selling that."

"Do you remember school holidays when we used to come round, the fun we had." I don't know how Matt is going to cope as it is so different from the Armed Forces, but farming is in his blood.

"Yes, we had some great times, you should bring the children up when we all get back, you've done a great job with them Annie, Molly is gorgeous," just like her mother, Matt thinks, "And Arthur is such a scream, and so good natured, especially with Molly."

"Thank you, Matt. I love them dearly," I feel a lump in my throat with his complement, "It would be good to come and explore, they would love the farm as we did when we were there."

"Did I hear Dave say you are doing some gardening jobs?" He asks.

"Yes. I love it so much, it has helped me so much recently, I'm doing quite a few gardens now, but I am also exploring the possibility of expanding my produce growing, as I have given some of my produce to a few locals, and the Bugle pub. I just thought it might be a good business, but where to extend the garden, you can't sell if you grow on an allotment, so that's not an option. I have to give this a bit more thought, but I know a couple of places are desperate for fresh local produce with no miles attached to satisfy their green credentials…"

As I'm talking, I spot the children and Dave coming off the sea taxi, looking happy, obviously crabbing had gone down well.

Conversation over for now, Matt thinks her produce might fit well in to his plans for a farm shop, he pays and we amble back to the hut meeting the others as they reach the shore, we sit on the deck as the children zoom off to tell their friends about their crabbing exploits, as I'm relaxing, suddenly there's a cry from Molly as she runs towards us.

"Arthur's gone," Dave jumps down to the sand and scoops her up, my heart is pounding.

"What do you mean sweetheart?" He asks calmly.

"He was here then he was gone. I can't find him anywhere, I've looked," Molly is in tears now. I jump up, but Dave completely takes over, he can see the panic rising in me, he's frightened I might spook Molly, he needs to find out more information, and is worried my reaction might stop her.

"It's ok, Molly come with me and we'll see if we can find him, he won't have gone far, where were you when you lost him, stay here Annie, just in case he comes back, I've got my phone, Matt check behind the hut."

"He never leaves me, he's always there, he always tells me if he is going somewhere so I can go with him," Molly sobs in Dave's arms, Matt squeezes my hand as he goes through the hut. I look all around, shaking with fear, my hands are tingling. I take some deep breathes. I saw him not many moments ago, he was playing football just up the path, and he gave me his usual thumbs up. I can see other parents joining in now, oh my god where is he.

Then suddenly there's a whoop from one of the neighbours, Bob starts barking. I hadn't realised he was standing watching with me, just as Dave comes into view with Arthur and Molly, it was literally only minutes but the fear is overwhelming. I feel guilty that I was so useless, but overjoyed now. I jump down off the deck and go and hug them both, they're eating ice creams.

"It's alright Annie, Arthur went to the loo and then used his pocket money to get him and Molly an ice cream. I haven't told him off just gently said he needs to tell us where he is going at all times," Dave quietly tells me.

I don't know how I'm standing up; the fear and relief are mixing to make me feel weak, a part of me knows I am over reacting that my feelings are out of proportion, but I guard the children, protect them. I can't lose again. Somehow I manage to go up into the hut and sit on one of their bunk beds, my legs giving way.

"I'll go Dave, stay with the children," Matt walks through to the room closing the concertina door behind him.

"I couldn't bear to lose anyone again," I sob, "I just want everything to be normal. I don't want this anxiety and fear all the time. I don't want to feel upset, close to tears, why did he go and die, leave us, leave us without him, we miss him so much," I try to draw a breath, Matt pulls me towards him. I cry onto his shoulder and feel his arms wrap around me, "I feel guilty about so much, guilty I want a normal life, guilty when I can't cope, guilty because we didn't talk, being strong is so hard all of the time, he was a good man," she hesitates. "But I want everything to be as it was."

"It can't be Annie," he quietly says, he doesn't understand what she meant about not talking, as far as he knew they were the closest couple out, there's something more there and her hesitation too.

"I know. I do know. I wish it though. I hate all the emotion running through me, it feels like it will be forever with me. I want to be happy. I want the children to be happy, then I feel bad that I should want to be happy without Sam. I feel such regret…" she pauses, on the cusp of saying more, more depth, "Guilty… at what I've thought, what I want. I want to live, but I am in this cycle of happy, guilt, regret, happy guilt…"

"Sam would want you to be happy Annie. I know it sounds trite, but you shouldn't feel guilty when you are happy. I know it's easy for me to say, you knew him better than I did, but I am sure he would want you to be moving forward, it's a slow process, it's gradual, you have done so much and on your own, everything at home, your gardening, your aspirations for the future, and coming here, has been huge for you, you've ventured out in to the big wide world, but this has shaken those emotions up again."

"Perhaps you are at a crossroads, Annie, trying to move forward on a path but taking some steps back and unsure which route to take. He will always be with you Annie, those memories of your lives together will always be there, no matter where you are, what path your life takes, you must remember that and try to put another foot on that path."

As Matt is talking my crying is stopping, and I'm breathing easier, he talks quietly, reassuring me, his right hand is holding my head into my shoulder. I feel calmer, his words sinking into me, making sense. As if he senses that Annie is calmer, he gently brushes the hair out of her eyes and lifts her head slightly. She manages a weak smile, and puts her head back on his shoulder.

Whether it is the physical contact, being held, that helps me, perhaps I've kept myself closed down to others, not wanting to have hugs and dissolve, and say more than I want. But Matt's arms help to right the balance that has been missing, as he gently strokes my hair. I can feel myself drifting to sleep.

Matt feels Annie's breathing gradually change, and he looks down at her, she is sleeping, he lets her go, with regret, and lies her on the bunk, pulling a cover over her, and quietly leaves the room, a huge weight dragging at his emotions. He stands still for a moment, he can't get Annie out of his mind, the feel of her in his arms was so right but so wrong when she was distraught. He bends his head, he realises he has it bad, still, all he wanted to do was smother her with kisses and more… yet he felt daunted by her obvious feelings for Sam, at that point, it seemed insurmountable to him, but he could not understand some of her words, had there been a problem, he was not sure.

Could he just be there for her without wanting to crush her body to him and love her, he didn't know, he'd have to try, did he have any other option?

It is good to be home, ok I'm back in my comfort zone again but I feel I have changed, taken a step on that path, Matt's words have stopped with me. I do feel I am at a crossroads. Having time to think that first week we were away about what I want to do, my ideas about growing more produce, has galvanised me into action, his words have helped to give me a new found confidence, it would mean some extra income. I wouldn't be so reliant on Mum and Dad for extras, although there will be initial outlays.

I'm fairly sure there's a market in the area for what I want to do, I've looked at what I could grow and what would sell well, and Matt's idea of a farm shop might mean I can supply him too, but where to grow it? As I'm standing looking over the garden, on a slightly wet day. I think of Matt, we're all going up to the farm at the weekend for a barbeque, Theo is coming up, personally I'm not sure I'm looking forward to that bit, he was a bit too touchy feely with me on holiday and has been phoning quite a lot, don't know what I did to warrant all that attention.

We haven't heard from Matt, when I mentioned it to Dave, he seemed really surprised. I must give Matt a buzz to see what he needs food wise for Sunday, Dave's coming too with Melinda, it will be nice to finally meet her.

I start weeding the beds, the children are watching some cartoons, Arthur is happy now toilet and bathing facilities are back up to standard, so am I to be honest. He's been moaning about all of the salads we have been having, we had a glut of rocket and lettuce, he likes his hot food, he says he is putting in a written complaint, no doubt writing it as we speak. I dig up some potatoes, he can have his hot food tonight, pork steaks, potatoes and for Molly and me ratatouille, for Arthur peas. That will tick some boxes for him.

I straighten up thinking of what Matt said to me, those words. I look at our house I always thought I couldn't move from here, not that I'm thinking of doing that, but talking to Matt I realise those memories I thought were wrapped up here, would be with me anyway, anywhere and forever, no bricks and mortar is going to alter that fact. Matt. I must give him a ring. I go in to warm up and make a cuppa and ring him.

Matt stands by the phone listening to Annie's voice fill the hall, he must have been outside when she rang, he curses, he would have liked the opportunity to talk to her, but couldn't quite pick up the phone and ring her himself, why Matt? Because he now knows the depth of his feelings for her, but he feels there is little hope of her reciprocating those feelings, even though he could sense some issues between her and Sam from the past, she is still very much grieving.

The couple of days before they all left, she treated him like the others, Dave and Theo, she wasn't rude or cold, she just didn't appear to see him other than a friend, and his thoughts were not of a friend. He knew Theo was interested in Annie, they were like two bees buzzing around a flower, only this beautiful flower did not have a clue, she was oblivious to the feelings of at least one of the two bees, if not both.

Matt sighed and walked back into the kitchen, he rested his back against the range, he had mixed feelings about Sunday, mainly because he would have preferred it to be just him and Annie, yet he hadn't instigated that, or him Annie and the children, yet again he hadn't phoned. But hey that wasn't going to happen, he'd better phone and sort out the arrangements.

Arrangements made, he broods again, could he cope with just being a friend, well he's had to for many, many years. But his feelings had intensified recently and those feeling couldn't wait, but he knew that's what he had to do.

Arthur and Molly leap out of the car as soon as we park in the yard at the farm. I go and close the gate, and we then go round the side of the house towards the front garden, me carrying cool bags and them running on ahead. I linger by the sunken garden to my left and the warm walls of the old kitchen garden. I stop and feel the solid walls, put my hand flat on the brick, it seems to emanate something.

I catch up with everyone on the lawn, Matt has tables and chairs set out at the end of the garden, the view from there is spectacular, the river winds gently below, through the countryside and green fields dotted with cattle and sheep. Both the children are hugging Matt, Molly took a real shine to him on holiday, he was so good and patient with her, even helping her swim, he bought her some arm bands and she started doing a few strokes.

Arthur leaps from Matt to Dave, who is standing next to a strikingly attractive blonde woman, with the shortest skirt I think I've ever seen, with long legs that Theo is currently admiring while Dave is monopolised with Arthur, Melinda, I take it, what a tableau.

Suddenly Matt looks up and sees Annie, beautiful in a jersey wrap dress, strappy and mid-calf length the colour complementing her green eyes, falling over her curves, the breeze lifting the skirt where it wraps around, showing enough to make you wonder what was underneath, sexy but not overtly so, unlike Melinda who left nothing to the imagination, Annie tanned and with sunglasses pushed back on her auburn hair, now slightly streaked from the sun a smile lighting her face, for him Matt hoped, Matt couldn't take his eyes off her, the heat burning through him.

I meet his gaze, wow, what was that? I swallow, carrying all this stuff I must be out of breath, but something took my breath away. Matt comes over and pecks me on the cheek, he smells of fresh air and lemons, suddenly that is replaced by an over ambitious aftershave on an over ambitious man. Theo moves in for a bone crunching hug, running his hands over my bare arms and shoulders. I manage to out manoeuvre him and excuse myself saying I must put the raspberry roulade in the fridge.

Dave follows me through to the house that I know so well, and by the look of it very little has changed in the intervening years, lounge on the left with a huge fireplace where we sat and played board games on wet days, dining room on the right, then Matt's father's study, looking out over the farm, the kitchen overlooking the sunken garden and walled garden on one side and the pond on the other, yes as Matt said it needs a bit of updating, but still a good home.

"You ran off. I was going to introduce you to Melinda."

"Sorry… Uhm just wanted to get this in the fridge."

"Yes, and the rest, Theo coming on a bit strong?"

Shaking my head I say, "It's a bit too much Dave what with the calls as well."

"What calls?" Dave asks concerned.

"He phones all the time, usually when the children have gone to bed, but why?"

"Annie you are an attractive vivacious woman that's why," he says incredulous.

"I'm not and I'm not interested."

"Chill little sis, just take the compliments, I'll tell him to step back a bit."

"You don't need to protect me, Dave. I can sort myself out here."

"Protecting you is my job sis, come on I'll introduce you to Melinda."

I'm introduced to Melinda and chat briefly, she does seem more interested in the men rather than me, so I go over to Matt and see if he needs anything, Arthur and Molly are chasing round the garden happy.

"Are you ok, need anything, do you want a beer," seeing his empty bottle.

"I'd love one Annie, the cool box there has some in, help yourself."

"I'm driving, though I do fancy a glass of wine."

"Leave your car here, Dave will take you all home."

I settle near him with a glass of cold white wine, just generally chatting, is it eating in the fresh air that makes food taste so good, or the company I wonder later, even though Theo has been trying his hardest with either me or Melinda.

"Matt, can we go and look in the river for fish," food and silence over I think as Arthur continues, "Uncle Dave said there were lots of different ones."

"Yes, of course Arthur, we'll all go as you shouldn't go down there on your own, I'll show you all the first finished barn while we are down there."

"I'll put the rest of this food in the kitchen, then catch you all up," I turn to see a flash of something cross Matt's face, regret?

To be honest I wanted to have a moment to myself, the children are running on ahead with Dave, so I have ten minutes. I come out of the back door of the house and walk over to the sunken garden, it's beautiful with a small circular mill stone spouting water, the sound calming the area, the scent from the flowers is a heady experience, roses, Dahlia's, and echinacea, one of my favourites, Matt's mother was a good gardener and someone has nurtured her garden well.

As I admire the climbers on the wall I see a gate, pushing it open into the walled garden I am greeted by the opposite of the sunken garden, it is a mess, overgrown plants and weeds, the large greenhouse against the wall has some broken panes with the wood in places looking rotten, inside is choked with weeds too.

The garden is big, with red brick walls that feel warm to the touch. I touch the inside wall as I did outside, something transmits to me, it is so sheltered in here, outside there was a gentle breeze, but not in here. You can just make out the original layout with raised beds, not made of wood like mine but the same red brick. I bend and wipe some dirt off the floor, which is a herringbone brick path, beautiful workmanship.

I stand in the centre and turn slowly taking everything in, like life has suddenly paused. I look at it all, Matt's mother's work gone to waste. A seed of an idea that was sown a few days ago is germinating, would it work? Could I do it, but mostly would Matt let me? I can hear voices, the children chattering on their way back up the hill. I slip through the gate and into the sunken garden. I see a shadow pass across the kitchen window, Matt I wonder?

I don't get to see Matt until later in the week, we collected my car the next day but Matt wasn't about, and I had the children with me, and I did want to chat to him on my own. I left a message thanking him for Sunday and saying if it was ok could I pop up on Thursday afternoon, the children are going to a friend's from school. Modern life being what it is Matt phoned back and got my voicemail too, and said he would be around Thursday afternoon.

I park up and shut the gate again, nip into the kitchen and call Matt, but he must be on the farm somewhere his car is here though. While I wait for him. I thought I'd go and have a good look in the walled garden, this time though I had a pad and pencil with me. The last few days I've jotted down ideas and plans but I need to draw the existing garden and see what's available.

I sit on a bench at the far end of the garden away from the house, and look at the garden properly, the history here is amazing, all the people who have gardened, walked these paths, the atmosphere is incredible, magical she thinks, calming too, she sees there are six long narrow raised beds, wide enough for good planting but not too wide so you have to stand in the bed to work, paths around them mean easier access, at the centre of the beds is a trough and tap, I'll try that in a minute I think, along the right wall is the large half brick greenhouse topped off by glass and abutting the outside wall, there are further beds along the far end towards the house and two along the right and left walls.

I stand and start walking down the garden, it hits me the enormity of the task, if we go ahead, not just clearing out the whole area of weeds and plant debris, but digging over every bed, mulching to put nutrients back into it, heaven knows the last time that was done.

39

I turn and walk back looking into the greenhouse. I won't go in I'll wait until Matt is here. I look in through the grime, on the back wall through the tall weeds are what looks like fruit trees, this must be the south facing wall. I try the tap and it works, so that is positive. I walk back towards the small gate I came in, there is a bed with more fruit trees, espaliered apple. I lean over and try to work out what type, there is some fruit too, small but certainly promising.

"Scrumping Annie?" a voice behind me says. I topple slightly and Matt catches me, lifting me down like I was light as a feather, which I'm not, he puts me down directly in front of him.

"Oh, you made me jump," I say sounding flustered, which I am, "I didn't hear you come in," I take a step back out of his arms.

"Sorry. I came in by the top gate, you can't see it well as its covered in wisteria," I turn to where he points, it's by a covered area for tools I just make out the gates. I wondered how to get wheelbarrows etc in, now I know.

"How did you know I was in here?"

"I saw you when I came back in to change and went upstairs, the bedroom windows overlook the garden," he'd watched her from his bedroom window, slim and fit in cut off shorts and clinging T shirt, she so didn't know the effect she had on him or anyone. "How long have you been here?"

"Not long."

"So, what do you think, now you have had longer to look around."

"You saw me then on Sunday being nosey?" he nods, "It must have been fantastic in the past and then when your mother gardened here, it would take a lot of work to get it back to how it was, uhm if you wanted to that is. Can we look in the greenhouse?"

"Sure, it looks quite sound, a bit of rot, but not extensive, it is a shame it looks like the inside of an old shed not a lovely greenhouse."

"That looks like a peach tree in there."

"It is. I remember Mum growing peaches, sending me out to pick some for tea, so what's the interest Annie?"

"Umm well... I've had an idea, you don't have to agree, it's only my thoughts at the moment."

"Come on," he walks to the bench and we sit down, "Spit it out."

"When we were away, you implied I was at a cross roads and I think I am, which started me thinking about what I wanted, one thing I love is gardening. I find it peaceful and fulfilling. I love to grow produce, the allotment idea is out as you know, as I want to sell produce and be less reliant on Mum and Dad, so I thought of doing vegetable boxes, and selling produce to local businesses, you mentioned opening a farm shop. Perhaps I could supply some of your produce too, not that I would charge, you." She runs out of steam, looks up at him and continues, "I was going to mention it, my ideas on just the produce growing last Sunday to get everyone's thoughts, but it wasn't the right time. And…"

"What?"

"I saw in here as you know, and my ideas sort of took off, perhaps this could be where I site the market garden, well that's what I thought," I gabble as he sits quietly. "It all depends on what you think, what needs doing, how it would work, if I could do it."

"Oh, I think you could do it, Annie. I think you could do anything you put your mind to." He stops leans his elbows on his knees and looks at the garden taking in all the chaos and mess, "it would be lovely to see it how it was, it would be a good memorial for Mum too, but it's been a difficult few years for you Annie. I don't want to encourage you to do something that might set you back."

"I want to do it Matt. I want to stand on my own feet more, not have to be reliant on others, the holiday although not easy taught me a lot, you helped me lighten the burden, helped me to look at taking steps forward, this beautiful place made my ideas more real."

"Ok Annie, we'll have to do some planning and see what needs doing, the greenhouse needs some repairs," he starts.

"What I don't want Matt is you taking on more. I know what needs doing and I can set out a plan of work, get a written agreement. I want to pay rent for here too," he puts a finger over my lips to stop me talking, a little ripple goes through me.

"Part of our agreement will be to share the work, so yes do a plan of work and then we can work out who can clean, dig over, replace panes etc, Don can have a look at the greenhouse. I think there's a heating system, and a watering system, although the pipes inside might have perished as they will be rubber hosing."

"When did you become so masterful?" I say holding his hand down from my face.

He didn't reply but appreciated the connection between them however brief, she gently took her hand away.

"I am paying rent," I say forcefully.

41

"You won't."

"I will on principle as I would have had to pay if I was using land elsewhere," thinking he is not going to win this argument.

"One penny a year then."

"Oh, you are infuriating," he raises his eyebrows waiting for an answer, "Alright one penny a year it is," I put my hand out and we shake on it. I then check in my pocket for money, none, "I'll drop it off then."

"I won't rent it out to anyone in the meantime, so now I know why you wanted to pop up, here's me thinking it was me you wanted to see."

"It is as well."

"Yes, sure Annie, you're only after my garden," he laughs, then suddenly gets serious, "Or is it Theo you're interested in?"

"No, no way," I say shaking my head, "I don't know what came over him on holiday particularly…"

"And the hug on Sunday?"

"He's very attentive… goodness knows why."

"He fancies the pants off you Annie."

"Oh, don't be silly Matt, you're wrong there."

"Right, open your eyes Annie Davis and look at yourself, see yourself as others do, you're a very attractive woman."

"I'm not doing anything to encourage him, Matt."

"I know you're not sweetheart, you are just being you."

She stands suddenly and walks down the garden, Matt shakes his head knowing she has not got a clue how her cute little self affects the men she comes into contact with, including himself. Matt follows Annie.

"Mum used to grow on ground behind the walled garden, she used a couple of polytunnels to extend the growing season out of the garden, although the plastic will have deteriorated the hoops are still stored in a barn, if you want, we can resurrect them for more growing space, come on I'll show you," he indicates the gates and she follows him through.

"Matt I'm sorry. I just find all this talk about me a little unnerving."

"Annie chill, lets stick to the job in hand then."

Behind the walled garden is quite a substantial plot, "I think this would be ideal if you are happy for me to resurrect it Matt, the poly tunnel helps to reduce carbon footprint as well, which is important for some of the farm shops, and if the plastic is still around, I can contact someone to recycle it, it all needs digging over though."

"I think it will need rotavating Annie, it's too much to dig over by hand, we'll leave the original paths in though, so the poly tunnels are accessible."

Blimey I feel like a child in a sweet shop, as I turn and look down the slope at the end, there are fruit trees. I walk to the end of the plot.

"I don't remember an orchard before Matt."

"You probably never came out this far we tended to stay around the house and then the top end of the farm."

"There's loads of fruit," I reach up and gently twist the stalk on a lovely red and green apple. I take a bite, "So sweet, try it Matt," I pass the apple over.

Matt hesitates, and feels this is a bit Adam and Eve, but nonetheless takes the apple, and agrees.

"What are you going to do with the apples that are ripe now Matt, and it looks like you have more that will be ready later in the season, these must be a Worcester variety, a discovery I think."

"Well Don's wife helps herself but I have to say I don't think the last couple of years they've been picked, which is sacrilege really."

"What about if I take a basket of fruit down to potential customers, like the farm shops, to get them generally interested in our, oh I mean your produce, not charge them just highlight what could be available in the future and…" He gently puts his hands on her shoulders to quieten her.

"Annie, these are your ideas and I am happy for it to be yours, ok I can see that look in your eyes again," he lifts his hands as if in surrender. "It's your project and if the apples help to highlight what can be sold to them in the future that's fine, my farm shop isn't up and running yet so they would only go to waste."

We start to walk back towards the farm house, "Ok I'll come and pick them tomorrow, no don't argue, is it alright if I bring the children, we'll only be up by the orchard, then I can take a couple of baskets off with us, I'll email my ideas and plans for the walled garden over tonight," as I turn, I see Dave walking over, he's obviously on duty as he's in uniform. I hope nothing is wrong.

"Hi sis, what are you doing up here?"

"Annie is going to rent the walled garden and a plot to start her market garden business," Matt says before I can get a word in. "And before you say anything Dave her rent is a penny a year, although she hasn't paid yet."

"Is everything ok Dave."

"Yes, no worries sis, thought I'd catch up with Matt, are you off."

"Yes, I've got to pick up the children, they're playing with friends at the moment, I'll see you tomorrow, Matt," with that I walk back to the car, cheerfully contemplating the future.

"So how are you going to cope with Annie being here all the time Matt?"

"That obvious, is it? I don't know Dave, it's tearing me apart as it is," Matt stands watching Annie walk away his hand gently stroking his chin in thought, "But I will do my best for her, I'd rather she was up here renting some land from me, than being conned by someone."

"Ok mate," Dave pats him on the shoulder, he's seen how much Annie means to Matt, and he feels he would be good for her, but it has to be in her own time, "Well the competition is out of the way now."

"What?" Matt turns to look at his friend, and realises unlike Annie that Dave looks distant. "What's the matter, Dave?"

"Theo and Melinda are an item."

"You're joking."

"No, she phoned me and told me, early days for them, but good luck is what I say, and good riddance. I thought something might happen, Melinda wasn't one for monogamy, and they were all over each other on Sunday. I know perhaps I got what I deserve as I have messed around before in relationships," he shrugs, although inside he is hurt. In one way, Matt is glad Theo isn't around, but in another he is upset for Dave, wait until he speaks to Theo, cousin or no cousin he's going to have his say.

"Now back to Annie, no I don't want to say any more about them," he shakes his head to stop Matt talking more on the subject, "I just wanted you to know face to face about the situation. Back to Annie, she had that look in her eye that Sam would say you can't argue with, so she can be a whirlwind when she wants to be and there is no stopping her. I think this will do her good, but I don't want her taking on too much."

"I've said that to her Dave. I said I'm happy for her to go ahead as long as it doesn't set her back in any way, and that's all any of us can do, isn't it? And believe me I've seen the look too."

They both laugh and turn to walk back to the farmhouse, Matt updating Dave of Annie's plans.

The next day, with only a couple of days until school goes back, we go up to the farm to pick the apples, or should I say, me and Molly do, Arthur is running around the orchard pointing out farm activity. "There's a tractor, do you think it's Matt? Oh, look sheep and cows, Mum, and Don's dogs," on it goes, I'm picking and Molly is gently placing the fruit in baskets, after I explained to her about not bruising the fruit, as we are part way through Matt appears on the quad bike, offering to take Arthur off our hands, he puts a small helmet on him and they depart for pastures new!

The next day having successfully got interest from the farm shops about the produce and the gift of the apples I am blanching and freezing runner beans from my garden when Molly runs in.

"Mummy Arthur says he's running away from home to be a farmer, and he's packed a case and is going now," these last few words are said with a slightly raised voice, which gets my attention. We go into the hall as Arthur descends the stairs banging his suitcase down each stair, with his rucksack on his back, he's off then I think.

"What's going on Arthur."

"Mum, you can't stop me, I've phoned Matt and told him I'm coming over on the bus and I'm going to live with him and be a farmer. I told Uncle Dave too; he said I should speak to you."

"What did Matt have to say?" Poor Matt I think, there's certainly been a lot of phoning going on.

"He said he'd phone you," as Arthur says this the phone rings, "There he is."

"Right, you stay here young man, or there will be trouble, Bob guard the door," Bob barks. I know Arthur he'll be down that drive quicker than you can say farmer Giles. I go through to the kitchen and pick up the phone.

"Annie it's Matt, Arthur just phoned me…"

"I know I'm sorry. I just found out, don't panic you aren't gaining a farmer, I'll sort it out, he's packed already and was just off."

"What's he like, no hassle, let me know how it goes, and if he wants to come up to the farm any time, that's fine."

"OK, thanks bye Matt."

"Right," I say hands on hips and meaning business, "Let's sit down and talk this through," an hour later they are both sitting in the lounge, watching television munching on pizza, their favourite, Bob in attendance. Having unpacked Arthur's case. I phone Matt to explain.

"Sorry about that, he's sitting eating his favourite pizza with Molly now, all part of the delicate negotiations to stop him becoming a farmer."

"What started it all, well silly question he was very keen the other day."

"Since we came back yesterday, he put a plough on the back of his bike, well tied some wood to it, he's been ploughing up and down the lawn, then I found him sowing seeds he said, luckily they were sweets and Bob followed him eating them, he was also trying to get Bob to be a sheep dog rounding up his toys, but Bob just ran off with which ever toy he fancied," all I can hear down the phone is Matt laughing.

"There's never a dull moment at your place, Annie."

"I know. I promised him another farm visit, if that's alright, perhaps show him the cows up close. I don't think he would enjoy the smell and pooing aspect, being Mr Meticulous."

"Yes, that's fine, just let me know," he rings off. I check they are still where they are supposed to be, they are, he'd only packed pants and socks so that wouldn't have got him very far, we had a talk and I pointed out that if he was a farmer, he would be too busy for school, which hits home as he loves school, and he's in Mr Thomas's class this year, he's the only male teacher at the school and the boys always look forward to his class, because rumour has it when he takes the register in the morning, when your name is called out you have to say Aye-Aye Captain, which goes back to Arthur's previous career as a sailor.

I also told them to ask me to use the phone not to use the extension in my bedroom, if Arthur does go up to the farm one Saturday, I can take Molly shopping. She's been so good this holiday, she's so placid, don't know where she gets that from, she's growing fast, another birthday Sam missed, he is in my thoughts, what with planning the garden, he would have listened and given good advice. I do miss him, but somehow the ache isn't as raw, perhaps it is being busier. I don't know.

The next day children safely ensconced in school Ted and I drive up to the farm, Ted has offered to help me with the garden once he heard about it, he said it was a brilliant idea and would be good in the long term. Dragging the spades and forks out of the boot, we walk over to the garden, Ted taking in the sunken garden and planting as we go, the sooner we get the tool area fixed then I can leave some tools here, although Matt has put some of his mum's stuff for me to use, as we go in Matt is there and I introduce them.

"Pleased to meet you, Matt, I've always wanted to see your mother's garden, she used to enter the local annual vegetable show, years ago though."

"Did she," we both reply.

"Yes, she was always very successful and won the overall cup one year, she had a clean sweep in every category."

"Wow," says Matt. "Do you know I think there was a photograph of that somewhere, I'll have to unearth it. I've found a couple of spare wheelbarrows Annie, so you won't have to bring your own up, Don and I are going to have a go at the greenhouse while you're here, so if there is anything worth salvaging you and Ted can identify them, like some of the pots, we've made safe the panes and wood already."

"Matt, you didn't have to do that I know it's a busy time for you and me and Ted could empty it."

"No, you couldn't I know you and spiders from when we were kids, so I've saved you there," he says smiling.

"Yes, you're right thanks Matt, oh here's my first years rent," I hand over a small frame with a shiny penny in it. I cleaned it up in brown sauce and we wrote underneath love from us all, "You can have one of these every year, unless you want it un framed to spend," I laugh.

Matt looks totally taken aback, he looks touched and leans over and gives me a quick hug, he's forgotten kindness and thoughtfulness, it seeps into him, "It'll take pride of place in the office, thanks Annie."

As Matt walks off me and Ted look around planning our days' work, we pick a couple of raised beds and start digging, clearing the years of weeds, Don's going to burn the stuff as you couldn't put it on the compost, so we fill the barrows and take them off to where the fire will be, it's getting warm. I take off my long-sleeved T shirt and just work with my strappy one on. After doing three barrow loads each, I go into the kitchen to make tea for everyone, although all I want is water.

Matt and Don are making good progress too as I give everyone their drinks I have a look inside the greenhouse, you can see benches on the glass side and a bed on the wall side where the fruit was growing, I'm hoping the benches aren't rotten as we don't need to incur costs replacing them. I nip back to the car to get the biscuits I bought with me for everyone.

Ted watches Matt, he has not taken his eyes off Annie the whole time he's been here, he's looking over making sure she's alright every few minutes, Ted wonders if Annie is aware how Matt feels, it is obvious to everyone, but he doubts Annie notices somehow, as Annie comes back in to the garden Matt's eyes light up.

"What did you think of my plan of work and the planting plan, Matt?"

"It looks good to me Annie, you've a lot of work to get it up and running though."

"I know, once we get the beds cleared and mulched. I can get started, I'll put in some crops like onion sets and spring cabbage in the next few weeks and sow some seeds in the greenhouse, like baby spinach and salad leaves. I've been putting in my orders already. I need to get some labels and twine and seed trays, although I have a few this is going to be on a larger scale, I've got to check what quantities I need for supply, but I'll look into that."

"What are you going to call the business Annie?"

"Well, it's here at the farm so Ash Farm produce or vegetables. Don't know yet, don't you want it named after the farm are you worried it won't be a success?"

"No of course not I just thought it should identify you in some way, Annie's kitchen garden at Ash Farm."

"That's a bit of a mouthful, isn't it?"

"Well, something along those lines."

"I'll have a think," I've managed to clear one full bed, and am starting on another, Ted is having a look at one of the long beds where the fruit trees are.

"Annie. I think a lot of these are okay, they'll need pruning but we might get some fruit next year, it's worth a try," I wander over.

"How come there's no evidence of fruit on some of them now, is it diseased?"

"No. I should think a good frost got the flowers earlier in the year, and I doubt there was any protection on them, which we will have to do, although it's lovely and warm in here and the walls act like heaters frost can still be a problem, these are different varieties from those you mentioned in the orchard, and plums too."

By three o'clock, we've cleared the six main beds and getting on well on the long beds, Don's gone off to light a fire for all the debris, and him and Matt have put a lot of terracotta pots out of the greenhouse to be washed. I can do that tomorrow, I think, as I am on my own, and am going to wash down the panes inside and out too.

Later, children fed and bathed and now gloriously asleep. I catch up with Dave. I already spoke to him about Melinda and Theo, and said exactly what I thought, but he's been quite sanguine about it all, and doesn't outwardly seem too bothered, but I know my brother it will have hurt, not wanting to rub salt into the wound I don't mention it again. Instead. I update him on today's progress, which I did with Dad earlier too, they are both saying I shouldn't do too much, but this has grabbed me in a way I can't explain, it's breathed life into me, given me something I didn't know I was missing, and working in that beautiful garden too, who wouldn't be inspired.

"I'm worried Matt is giving me too much of his time, he has so much going on, I don't want him to think he has to help," Dave thinks Matt is only too willing to help if it means seeing Annie.

"He wouldn't think that Annie, what does Ted think about the garden?"

"He thinks the garden is wonderful and a great idea, but a lot of work, he's keen to help out, I'll have to think about a wage at some point if he does a lot."

"Pay him in Olde Speckled Hen for now, he'd love that."

"That's a good idea, I'll get some cans for him, which reminds me are you coming to the produce auction at the Bugle?" Following the produce show the produce is auctioned for charity, I've never been before but I felt it would be good to support Ted. "I know Ted was talking to Matt about it, and Sue's going to try and make it too, it should be fun."

"Well, I'm really worried about you now Annie if that is your idea of fun, but hey why not, count me in."

I get into a pattern over the next few days, dropping the children at school and going up to the farm, Iris has said she would be happy to collect the children any time, but I want to try and do it myself, at the end of the day that was part of the reason for giving up work, having time with them.

It's a nice warm early September day, I've washed the pots and they are all drying, the beds look lovely now clear and with mulch in, Iris has found me an extendable mop, that can do the panes easily and then I can wash down with the hose to wash the soap and disinfectant off. I am enjoying myself being so fully occupied, and with plants on my mind I am not dwelling on the past.

After an hour or so I sit with a flask of tea and dry out, it's so sheltered and peaceful in here, it settles me. I feel some balance returning to my being. I start thinking about the farm and wonder how the barns for holiday accommodation are getting on. I know Iris is doing all the curtains for them, she can turn her hand to most things, so they must be near completion. If I get time, I must walk down and have a look. I haven't seen an awful lot of Matt these last few days, it was originally pencilled in for Arthur to come up to the farm at the weekend, me and Molly can do our shopping and then when we collect Arthur, we can have a look at the barns.

Better get on. I stand and stretch as Matt walks in, he stops momentarily, she doesn't see him straight away and it gives him a chance to drink her in, the sight of her takes his breath away, her T shirt clinging to every curve, her flat stomach just visible, he remembers holding her on holiday, the contours of her body next to his, he just wanted her so much, hold her, he couldn't then, he couldn't take advantage of her grief, but god seeing her all the time and not having more than friendship was driving him crazy.

Yet having her on the farm has helped him in some ways, his nightmares had reduced, he had been having terrible ones from the final days of his service, death and explosions just ripped through his mind, he had hoped they would go once he was home, but stress piled on to stress had made them worse, having Annie on the farm had helped, just her presence sort of reassured him, he didn't understand it himself but if he was able to get some sleep…

He felt conflicted, he wanted her around, but wanted her so much it hurt being near her, he'd phoned Dave and asked him what to do, Dave felt he should show his hand, but Matt was afraid he would frighten her off, or worse she would reject him and that he couldn't take.

"Oh hello, how long have you been there?" Annie asks, jolting Matt out of his day dreams.

"Not long," Matt walks up to Annie, she goes on tip toes and gives him a kiss on the cheek, placing her hand on his upper arm, his strong muscular arm felt good under her slight hand.

"Sorry I'm still filthy and soaking from washing down the greenhouse."

"You look fine," and she did to him.

"I don't," I look into his eyes they hold my gaze for a spilt second, and in that moment. I feel something flare inside me, it's like a flame trying to light a pilot light, my pilot light, then it's gone. As I look at Matt closer. I can see dark smudges under those so blue eyes.

"You look tired out, Matt, what is it?" she asks tenderly.

"Dad isn't too good, he is deteriorating fast now, he doesn't recognise me at all when I go in, and he doesn't know much of what is going on around him, the home phoned to say he has a chest infection too now, so am going in shortly."

"Oh Matt, I'm so sorry," she rests her hand on Matt's arm again, something flares again, she shakes her head what is the matter with me, perhaps I've a touch of the sun.

To break what is obvious tension that Matt can feel from Annie, although he is unsure what the cause is, it wouldn't occur to him that she had some feelings for him, "I found some of Mum's things," he points to the wooden box he has put down on the edge of one of the raised beds, it's an old-fashioned wooden fruit box, wooden slats, similar to one my grandmother had veg delivered in, which sparks something in my mind.

"Matt these are great," Annie says peering into the box, there are slate plant labels, metal sticks with hooks to hand the labels on, twine, three balls of it, and in good condition, an old garden line and pegs, and a dibber for making small holes for seeds or seedlings, "Everything is wonderful Matt, the labels will give the garden a traditional look, which I would like to retain if you are ok with that."

"Of course, I am Annie, this is your garden now, there is probably loads more stuff lying round some of the out houses, so help yourself to anything. I know you like traditional and older things."

"Like you Matt?" I get a smile out of him, he is a few years older than me and we always used to tease each other about it, "Are you coming to the produce auction tonight?"

"To tell you the truth Annie. I had completely forgotten what with everything going on with Dad."

"I'd love you to come, but I understand if you can't, if you do decide to why don't you come and have tea with me and the children first, they would love to see you, just let me know, I'm here till just before three."

"I'll see how things go, I'll let you know in a bit."

After Matt goes, I sit down on a wall. I suddenly feel emotional. I can sense something more with Matt, not just his father though that is bad enough, he looks so tired. I wonder if he's having disrupted sleep, with all the postings he had and then coming back to loss and stress it wouldn't surprise me, Sam occasionally had disrupted sleep, usually on initial return from deployment, but a few days back in the family and they reduced, but Matt doesn't have family around him. As I'm wiping down the benches in the greenhouse and putting some of the pots now dry, back in, Matt pops his head in and says he will come if it is ok. I reassure him it is and tea is only chilli, to come any time, but I am dishing up at six.

It's fever pitch when I tell the children Matt is coming for tea, as soon as he arrives the children drag him outside, while I sort out the chilli, of course burger for Arthur. I left some of the mince out of the chilli to make it for him. They all troop back in. I think there's been a plough inspection by all accounts.

"That's a great plough Arthur has there, the rollers are a bit different though," he says smiling, he's leaning on one of the worktops, he's wearing combats and a dark fitted T shirt, Annie glances at him and looks away quickly.

"How do you mean?" I'm a bit lost, last time I looked the plough was made of wood.

"Arthur has modified it, he said. I hope you don't need your rollers for your hair in a hurry," he is now laughing.

"Arthur what's going on here then?" firstly I don't use rollers and secondly. I don't want Matt thinking I do, and thirdly whose are they?

"Iris gave them to Molly for her dolls, so I thought I would put them on my plough, Molly didn't mind."

"Got the picture Matt. I don't wear rollers," I say serving the food, grinning.

"That's your story, Annie. I have this image of you getting the children's breakfast with your rollers in and a cigarette hanging out of your mouth."

"Very funny, now eat up you rabble or the dog will be eating it for you," laughter emanating from everyone.

As we are finishing and the food silence is over Arthur asks if it is ok for him to go to the farm on Saturday, which was arranged anyway, but instead of shopping Molly wants to go too.

"If it's not too much for you Matt, are you sure."

"Yes, no worries, we'll walk the farm a bit and look at the different animals and perhaps get some eggs from the hens," there's a whoop from two children, in the midst of the chaos Iris arrives to babysit.

"Hello my lovelies how are you two today, and who's this fine young man then?" I thought she was talking about Arthur, but then realised she meant Matt, which makes me giggle.

"This is Matt, Iris, from Ash Farm."

"Pleased to meet you at last, thanks for your order for curtains, Don has been sorting it out. I hope you aren't working Annie too hard up there. I did a spot of cleaning for your mum in the past and that garden is huge," Iris knows everything. I see her giving Matt the once over, he looks smart tonight. I look again, he's lost some weight but still fills the T shirt, my breath catches, honestly Annie get a grip.

I quickly dash upstairs to change. I had a shower earlier just need to put my glad rags on, which of course are jeans and a top, a pale pink cardigan with a vest top underneath.

"Sorry to keep you Matt," I needn't have worried Iris has him sitting at the table interrogating him by the looks of it, "Bye then you two, be good for Iris. I won't be late Iris."

"Don't worry love take your time," not that she will, Iris thinks, and with such a lovely young man too, Ted's right, he's smitten. I only hope our Annie sees it soon, or she might be too late.

"Your face," I say laughing as we walk up the hill, "You looked like a rabbit caught in the head lights, with Iris talking to you."

"At me more like, telling me to look after you and not work you too hard, no matter what I said she wouldn't have it you are working for yourself, she asked me my marital status too, what's that got to do with anything?"

"Iris likes to gossip," she's a bit naughty asking that I think.

When we reach the pub it's standing room only, but I see Sue has grabbed some seats and Dave's at the bar, Matt checks what I want to drink and I go and join Sue, I'm so pleased to see her especially as she tells me she has a new job and it's local, it will be lovely catching up with her more now.

"Hi little sis, you look lovely tonight, positively glowing."

"Yes, you do Annie," Matt looks at her glowing skin, nicely tanned, appreciating all of her, she smiles shyly at him.

The evening was a success for the auction. I somehow ended up with a bag of windfalls, as if there aren't enough apples at the farm, Sue has them for her mum to make chutney with, we have a good laugh, it is good to catch up with Dave we natter away. I notice Matt getting on well with Sue, something rips through me, jealousy, surely not. I jump up to get a round of drinks for everyone. Matt follows to help me.

Sue shuffles up to sit by Dave, "So how long has Matt had the hots for Annie?"

"Years, well before Sam came along, is it that obvious?"

"Yes."

"He's beside himself with it. I have told him he ought to tell her as she hasn't got a clue, he's worried how it will go though. Personally. I think she would be good with Matt; he is so calm and thoughtful. I know it's been hard for her, well that's an understatement, she did say on holiday that she couldn't contemplate a relationship in any way, but I feel she has moved forward since then."

"I can see and hear a change in her, and for the better, she is close to Matt. I think just give it time, for them both. Did Annie tell you I have a job locally now."

"Yes, she did, less travel for you, it would be good to catch up," he looks at her and sees her, which is strange as he has known her years, but something opens his eyes, wow he thinks, "Do you fancy dinner one night?"

"Yes, do you know that would be really good Dave," Sue smiles, lighting up her whole face.

I have dropped the children off with Matt and pop back home to clear my own garden, firstly I must dig up some leeks, cauliflowers and courgettes and some salad. I have approached two local pubs who do food, and promised them some produce from my garden as a taster. I pack them into some more veg boxes I found at the farm, feeling they would be great in the long run for our veg boxes and Matt could always use these in the farm shop to stock produce, it would look traditional.

I've some jobs to do at the garden too. I want to take some photos, to show the garden going through transformation, perhaps even for a website in the long run, en route I drop the veg boxes off and am just about to get in the car, when my phone goes, it's Dave.

"Hi sis, good night last night, wasn't it?"

"Blimey I thought it was a bit dull for you."

"No. I enjoyed it, perhaps my perspectives are changing."

"You mean gone are the clubbing nights or noisy bars, and now local pub," which she thought mirrored what she and Sue had said.

"Yes, something like that, you looked like you enjoyed yourself too."

"I did. I didn't realise I knew so many people in the village, it was lovely and friendly. I felt comfortable in there and confident," changing the subject I say to Dave, "Uhm I do like Matt," I say hesitatingly, "But I worry I like him because he reminds me of Sam, their Army backgrounds…" before I can finish Dave butts in.

"Annie you couldn't get two people less alike than Sam and Matt. I know there is a similarity in that they were both in the military, but your," he was going to say attraction, but stopped himself, "Liking of Matt is because of his character, Sam was all guns blazing, wanting to achieve all the time, driven, you both set yourself big goals, take the house for a start, what a mess that was when you bought it, but you both made it happen and quickly. Matt is a quieter man who looks steadily at things before making a decision, he plans at an even controlled pace, especially when he has a lot on. Neither character is wrong or right just different, different people Annie."

Dave thinks that with Matt life would be calmer more balanced for Annie, although she says she hasn't had balance since Sam died, he feels that is predominately loss, "Don't overthink things you have a lot on with the new business, just take each day as it comes, and take Matt's help where he offers it, just enjoy the company," and he hopes grow from it.

"I know in some respects he's like another brother," as soon as I said it. I knew it was untrue, things and feelings are creeping up on me, and those aren't sisterly. I brush them away quickly, not wanting to voice what is happening.

Dave thinks poor Matt, if that's how she sees him he'd curl up if he heard that.

Disquiet

The following couple of months are busy, Mum and Dad came up for half term and took the children to various places enabling me to do more in the garden and get my planning down for the business to, Ted has been invaluable and is appreciating his payment in beer, he's up with me today and has some young strawberry plants he's raised from this year's runners to start our indoor fruit bed off, am going to put in Loganberry and Raspberry canes in the outside bed next month, we are adding blackberry bushes and gooseberries inside the walled garden, although there are some fruit bushes in the orchard already.

Half way through the week it will be the anniversary of Sam's birthday. I usually meet his uncle at the grave and put some flowers there for him, Sam lost his parents when he was six, and was raised by his Grandparents and his uncle Stewart, his parents were killed in a car crash, and despite that he had a lovely childhood and was very close to his uncle, his Grandparents died about ten years ago, we saw a lot of his uncle and I have kept in touch since, he is such a character, he travels a lot on his old Triumph motorbike even managing trips over to France, he keeps in touch by letter, no email for Stewart. Arthur is incredulous about this, but saying that he loves getting Stewart's post cards from all over the country and Europe.

The children have gone out with Mum and Dad. I collect the flowers I have put together from my garden and walk down the road to the church and cemetery; his grave is at the back with views over the river. I am early and sit on the bench thinking about him, my thoughts are interrupted as Stewart arrives.

"Darling girl, how are you?" he gives me a kiss on both cheeks then holds me back at arm length, "You look good Annie, all this gardening is working it's magic on you."

"Thank you, Stewart, no bike today?"

"No had to give the old girl up I'm afraid. I was having difficulty getting on and off safely, just a bit of arthritis I'm told, but I have got the old Morris out of moth balls, so similar age to the bike, no modern cars."

We sit together on the bench contemplating Sam, talking quietly about the children and how he would have loved to see them flourish.

"I sense a slight change in you Annie. I think your market garden is helping your confidence and you are looking forward again, you've talked about Matt who owns the farm and how helpful he is…"

I go to interrupt. "No let me continue dearest girl, you mustn't hold Sam up as a paragon of virtue and mark everyone you meet against him and his character, as you know he wasn't perfect, he had flaws."

In that instant, I knew Stewart was referring to Sam's affair, it must have shown on my face as Stewart continued.

"Yes, he told me Annie. I was as shocked as you no doubt were. I think part of Sam's character was moulded in the loss of his parents, he wanted to achieve so much, it was as if he was in a hurry, wanted to do so much before he became the same age that his parents died, which he did, then I think he felt he was invincible, losing friends and being in war zones but coming out unscathed. And I think that affair was part of that, he was thinking look at me, everything around me survives, so I'll do this and it will be fine."

I swallow, my throat dry, it was all very well knowing he had an affair, but it was hard knowing someone else knew, Stewart knew. I thought I was the only one. Stewart takes my hand, gently squeezing it to reassure me.

"He had a difficult tour, and yes he did let himself down he knew it, it ate him up."

"I know Stewart," we sit quietly, then Stewart gets up to leave,

"I will drop you a line in the next couple of weeks," with that, he walks away after a hug.

I sit back down on the bench, winded, it takes me back to it all, it was 3 months before he died, as soon as he walked in the door I knew. I don't know how I knew but I did, it was as if he reeked of guilt, like a perfume, a woman's perfume. He looked me in the eye and confessed, just someone he met in a bar, when in Cyprus on his way back to England. It rocked my foundations. Everything crumbled for me, the love and security that had been so strong was dust.

Knowing Stewart was aware of it left me cold, perhaps he was trying to show me that Sam wasn't perfect, who is? But I knew that. I had to live with that after he died, and perhaps that knowledge being in me made the grief worse, only I knew that he was a man with flaws, which was hard, but a good man, was he? And one who was a good father, yes, he was. I couldn't share though. I just couldn't tell anyone.

But we didn't have time to ask the questions, discuss the events that had unfolded. One of those questions was why, was I not enough, it undermined me so much, we had been so close, a tight unit, for him to hurt me, and I was horrendously hurt, all of that kept rolling around my head, then his death, the loss, for the children and me, even though hurt. I still had loss.

Something in me shifted as if Stewart's words had opened up a new hurt, a new wound, that I didn't need, no it wasn't a hurt, it was an ache, in my heart, that needed love and a future, something better than having this hurt wrapping itself around me.

I of course bury myself in the garden and preparation for Christmas, the children were immersed in this as school was just starting rehearsals for their Christmas activities. I decided to have a houseful on the day as I needed the planning distraction.

Dave and Sue seem to have settled into a good relationship. I was flabbergasted to begin with, they are attached at the hip, everywhere one goes so does the other, now though I am so pleased. I had never put them together as a couple, but Dave has changed. I did give him a warning not to hurt my friend though, so they are joining us for Christmas, and I have asked Matt too. Mum and Dad are staying at home this year.

As December continues. I receive a worrying email from an old friend, we worked together for many years, he did Orthopaedics and ended up a consultant, on a trip home he fell in love and decided he would stay living and working there, eventually getting a good job. Home was China for Mark Woo, and now he had two children, it was lovely to hear how his family were getting on, but part of his email told me about a new virus, a serious respiratory virus, he initially linked it to SARS, but said it was different, he said a lot, "It's going explosive Annie, many are dying and have been for some time, and that includes medics, they say it is just a flu virus, but why are hospital staff dying?"

I felt sick. I closed his email and checked about SARS, but that died out I think. I was the infection control lead at my last job, and had a good smattering

58

of knowledge on the subject, what I read in Mark's email left me feeling very, very uneasy. I would just keep an eye on things and not worry anyone.

The week before Christmas Matt's father died, he phoned me. I went straight up to see him, he was sad but felt relief that his misery, his father's, not his own, was over, and perhaps he would see his beloved wife again, he did manage to arrange a funeral, between Christmas and New Year, which Dave and I promised to attend.

Christmas was good despite the disquiet I felt and some darkness and storm clouds around us, the children had a brilliant time, too many presents and too much chocolate, Iris and Ted popped in for a lunchtime drink on the day too, Iris bringing loads of mince pies for us. I am hopeless at pastry, she also made some apple ones for Arthur, as he hates mincemeat, he was overjoyed. Matt relaxed but looked sad, part of me wanted to wrap him up and take away his worries, my nurturing part I assumed as I looked at him on the day.

I did look at what was happening across the world, and what I saw worried me even more, the World Health Organisation had put themselves onto an emergency footing for dealing with major disease, seeing that hospital being built in China in ten days seriously scared me at what it meant, this is as dangerous and explosive as Mark said. Was it coming our way, that's what made it scarier still?

With the children back to school after the Christmas holidays I decided to go up to the garden and start sowing crops in the greenhouse. I had so much to get on with, at least it would take my mind off everything including Uncle Stewart's revelation, which I haven't really processed, Ted was joining me later in the week to give a big push so we had seedlings ready to put out.

Following a morning of hard work. I sit for a quick cuppa, warming my hands on the mug. I had started taking my own flask of tea with me so I wouldn't disturb Matt, thinking about him I must have conjured him up as he walked into the garden just then.

"Hi, how's it all going Annie?" he sat down on the wall next to me.

"Ok I suppose, just sowing loads of seeds to get our crops going," Annie's voice is unusually flat, Matt takes her hand, which starts tears welling up for her.

"What is it, Annie?"

"I'm sorry it's nothing really. I just feel uneasy about things that's all. I have no right to feel off, you just lost your father, Matt, I'm sorry."

"Stop saying you're sorry and talk to me."

"I'm worried about this virus in China, well there's cases outside China now and deaths, its spreading, it's frightening. I think I just feel a bit vulnerable. I don't think I have got over what Sam's uncle Stewart said to me too..." I trail off, realising I haven't discussed what he said with anyone, and haven't told anyone about Sam's affair.

"What do you mean, you saw him months ago, did he upset you in some way? You should have said something to me or Dave," Matt looks with concern at Annie, and although she had been looking better and was more her old bouncy self, he suddenly realises with everything that had been going on it hadn't clicked, he hadn't noticed that bounce for a while, "Come on talk to me Annie, or do you want me to call Dave if you can't say whatever it is to me."

"No, I'd rather talk to you, it's just I never realised Stewart new about Sam's affair," oh my god I've said it out loud.

"Wait what, he had an affair," anger courses through him at both Sam for what he did and his uncle for telling her he knew now, what was the point in that, he puts her mug down and takes both of her hands willing her to speak, he looks at her with shock.

"I am not sure why Stewart told me he knew, whether it was to make me see that Sam wasn't a saint and not to hold him up as a paragon of virtue, perhaps he was getting me to see I need a future, to move on. I don't know. But the darkness after his death enveloped me having to act and hide so much." I feel the warmth of Matt's hands reassuring me to continue, so I tell him everything, all of it, emptying the years of pain, as I finish, I say, "I don't know to this day how I knew but I did."

"Guilt is a very powerful emotion Annie, the strongest emotion, perhaps Sam was unable to hide that and you read it."

"I feel ashamed, and feel I'm at fault, even though I know deep down I'm not, but don't feel pity for me Matt, I'd hate that."

"I don't Annie, none of it is your fault either. I feel Sam was an idiot to do that to the most precious gift he'd ever been given," I look up into his eyes, he looks at me and gently cups my chin and gives me a fleeting kiss, so light that I'm unsure if he did kiss me, but she saw his eyes darken as he looked at her.

"I better get on," I say jumping up, breaking away from my past, as Matt grabs my arm, his touch like electricity.

"I'm glad you told me, trusted me with this." With that he walks away just turning to give me a reassuring smile as he opens the gate.

I let out the breath I didn't know I'd been holding, you could be trapped by those eyes I think, the startling blueness, their depth. I wonder at my feelings, I'm glad I told Matt, it sort of helps, we all have faults, and although Sam's was huge, it needed to be said.

As she sits there, she looks at her wedding ring, she had worn it faithfully all this time, never questioning the wearing of the symbol, a habit, and what did it symbolise? Something that was broken something that might have either repaired or never ever mended, she didn't know, it was impossible to speculate on it all, with events that followed.

Listening to Matt and his look when she told him about Sam's affair made her realise what he had said was right, she was a precious gift and for whatever reason Sam had run rough shod over that gift. He had sucked everything they had out of her in that moment, like emptying her body of oxygen, and then it felt like it happened again with Stewart, to think Sam had told him this very personal incident in their lives but never discussed it with her, apart from his initial words.

She had mulled all this over in the last couple of months, never telling anyone and felt further betrayal, she looked down at her ring, and took it off, she knew now it was time, she could make the excuse that with gardening and hand washing she had left it off, but she knew deep inside it was the right thing to do, she didn't need excuses to herself or others to confirm that. When she got back to the house, she just left it on the dresser, not in sight but there.

Matt walks at a fast pace up to the top barn to make sure he knows what needs doing, all the time fury bubbling inside him at what Annie just told him, he just can't comprehend why Sam would do that, whether he felt he was invincible or in fear as Annie said, that didn't excuse his behaviour, how Annie accepted his behaviour showed Matt how much she thought of him, or was it because of the children... He didn't know, he couldn't ask, the only light for him was that Sam's uncle was trying to get her to move on, he hated to see her so vulnerable again though. He stands in the centre of the barn, his head full of all that he has heard, he doesn't see how well the space works, how the shelves are ready for produce, how good the area looks, as he finally opens his eyes to everything, he knows he will ensure Annie's produce takes pride of place in his farm shop when open. He shakes his head at the enormity of Sam's affair, Annie had carried all of this herself without telling anyone, he felt so much for her, not pity as she mentioned but so overwhelmed at her strength. And he realised that had been what she hung back saying at the beach hut, it made sense now. He reluctantly concludes to himself how much more he feels for her, how her hurt hurts him.

Uneasiness
Spreading Like the Virus

February comes in wet, and with virus storm clouds circling, getting closer, a public health emergency was declared by the World Health Organisation, cruise ships are quarantined, and there is a death in Europe, then why are school skiing trips going ahead. I feel that all I'm doing is looking over my shoulder to make sure this virus hasn't caught up with us yet, we can all feel it, this fear, its palpable, watching the news all the time, making sure you know what is coming, new data is emerging hourly, adding to the fear, how could young people die? I think of Mark in China and wonder at how some medics are dying too, it is so frightening. The awful thing is you know it's there but you can't see it. People liken it to the war, but you knew your enemy, we don't. We haven't got a clue, an invisible evil, that can get anyone.

I try to concentrate on the garden and use it as a beacon, sort out plans with buyers and hope we can move forward with it all. In amongst all of this was my birthday, but I didn't feel like celebrating anything, and dismissed it to everyone, except the children and we just had birthday cake and cards, anything else could wait I thought.

I see Matt often, since I told him about Sam, there is something new found, something difficult to put my finger on, when we meet, he always touches me, not in the way Theo did, which was like he was trespassing, intrusive and very disconcerting, but a gentle touch of my shoulder or hand, comforting and reassuring, but it awakens something in me, my pilot light is lit but a low flame. I feel different. Matt stating, I was a precious gift rocked me too, was I? I never felt like that, ever, there wasn't time to think back then either. I just drove on after finding out, the children so important.

Matt has asked me to go and look at the holiday barns with him later. I am making the most of Iris picking the children up today and am putting some extra time in, but the light is just beginning to go when he meets up with me outside the garden, I've put my things in the car and cleaned up a bit, we walk down past the front garden and along towards the bigger barn, this one is full height, with a lower section at the side.

"What do you think?" he asks opening the main door in to the newly completed barn, warm air coming towards them keeping the barn aired.

"Oh, it's lovely. I love the colours, it's like you're bringing the countryside in," she walks over to the double glass doors at the end of the barn. "And the view down to the river is lovely, did you choose all this?"

"Are you doubting my interior design skills Annie?" he says teasing her.

"Well…"

"Yes, and no, Iris produced the curtains, and I liked the colour, then I remembered a heather tweed pattern on a friend's sofa, one his own company made, so I approached him. I also wanted a corner sofa, so you could see the view," he points towards the windows, "Watch the TV and make the most of the heat from the log burner in the corner," he looks over to the fire and rug in front of it, he knew all he wanted was to make love to Annie in front of that fire the room dark, her body lit by firelight, when he looks up Annie has wandered over to look at a mirror near the open plan kitchen, he follows her and stands behind her.

"This was in the house I remember it," Annie looks into the mirror, with Matt behind her, she sees the raw feelings in his eyes, reflected in the mirror as he looked at her, it made her catch her breath, her hand going to her mouth and something pooled inside her slipping down to her pelvis, he moved closer to her, gently resting his strong hands on her shoulders, rubbing them with his thumbs, all the time looking at her in the mirror, he slows his moves as if she was a startled animal ready to run.

He lowers his head and kisses the back of her neck, gently stroking his hands down her arms, she relaxed back against him, hope flared in him like the heat he felt for her. Slowly he turned her round until she was in front of him, held against him, she moved her hands up his arms feeling his muscles, the strength of him, he looks in her eyes and sees them darken, he strokes her jaw with his thumb, running it over her lips, she kisses it, he holds her face and lowers his head to her mouth, gently opening waiting lips with his tongue, she responds as he kisses her deeply, she wraps her arms around his neck as he runs his hands down her body, feeling her curves resting one hand in the small of her back pulling her into him.

64

"Oh Matt," she groaned into his mouth, that word suddenly bringing her to her senses, she begun to pull away, but he held her close, looking down at her.

"It's alright Annie," he said into her soft curly hair, kissing her jaw and rubbing his fingers over her cheeks, as tears started to fall.

"Shush, what's the matter sweetheart?" he held her, not regretting the kisses or anything, hoping she didn't either, "I want you Annie. I want to feel every bit of you, explore you, and I want you to want me to."

"I do," she stumbles over her words.

"Are you frightened?" she nods, "You want me too don't you," she nods again, "Let's just take it easy, sit down and have a chat, we don't need to rush anything."

"Matt. I feel so much for you. I want an us, but yes I am frightened," she reaches for him and kisses him deeply, he pulls her over onto his lap and they just sit there holding each other, knowing that they feel the same, as dusk falls, he cups her head and begins to kiss her, feeling her responding once more, they shift to lying on the sofa, their bodies moulding as one, they begin to take their clothes off, they are naked, he leans on his elbow looking at her body, drinking it in, he starts to kiss down her body, occasionally going back to engross himself in her lips, all the time her hands feel the strength of his body, holding his shoulders, touching his head as he kisses further down her body, the sensations in her explosive. As he kisses her mouth again his tongue probing in to her as if he's inside her already. She feels the sensations rising inside her, the feelings in her body take her away, they are locked together finding their rhythm, his idea of taking it slow goes out of the window as they both move quicker and quicker, need taking over, she gets higher and higher, over the edge and takes him with her.

Holding her, Matt can't quite believe what's just happened, he looks into her eyes as they gradually open, he is so relieved he doesn't see regret, he sees something he has wanted to see for so long.

"Oh Matt," she strokes his face as he pulls a throw off the back of the sofa over them to keep warm, although the heat between them is likely to start a fire, he thinks. He holds her close, and feels her begin to get up, "Be still Annie, the children are with Iris, it's just us."

That's what worries her, us, she's never felt like this before, the longing, the emotions at his touch, she shivers at the thought, but good shivers, as they gently start to kiss each other again, Matt says, "Look at me Annie, open your eyes, know it's me."

"Oh, I know it's you Matt, oh god I do," their rhythm becomes faster, together, joined, both racing towards oblivion, no words spilt from their mouths as they reached their goal eyes locked deep with lust.

Later Matt walked Annie back to her car, holding her round the waist close to him, he had worried she might regret this but as they dressed, they held onto one another, no shyness between them and she kissed him again with a longing he had only dreamed about.

As Matt looks across the fields the next day, seeing but not seeing, he rubs his chin deep in thought, he's supposed to be looking at where the fields were flooded, instead he's thinking of Annie, the hours in the barn imprinted on his mind, he can feel every minute and he knows Annie does too. He saw her earlier, he saw the heat in her eyes when she looked at him, her face lit up, he would have taken full advantage of her there and then but he didn't feel Ted would have been too pleased, while he was digging.

Coming too he realised as he looked at the field that he's lost a lot of the barley crop due to continued soaking of the field, the river at the far end of the farm didn't usually flood, but this wasn't a usual year, he'd have to plough and re-sow, he saw Don wandering over and they discussed what needed to be done.

By just after lunch, he had completed a million and one jobs and updated his accounts in the office, he stretched in his seat, looking out over the small pond to the side of the house, as he did hands covered his eyes.

"Guess who?" she breathed into his ear, he hadn't needed to hear her voice to know those hands, the hands that had touched every part of him.

He swivelled his chair round and came face to face with her amazing body, even clad in layers of clothes, because he now knew what was underneath, he stood and kissed her, she responded as his hand held the back of her head.

"Matt, I came to talk," Oh god no, he thought, he wanted to kiss any words away.

"We don't need to talk," he looked at her, "Ok perhaps we do, you don't have any second thoughts about what happened do you darling?" suddenly all his earlier confidence was seeping away.

She laid her head on his chest, "No Matt, no regrets nothing like that. I admit to some mixed feelings, about the past, but it felt so right with you Matt," she lifted her head and kissed him, opening her mouth with longing, she couldn't believe any of this, she felt he ought to know her thoughts, "I didn't sleep last night going over and over everything, waiting for guilt to come creeping in, or remorse, waiting for tears, but all I felt was how right it had been," he pulled her close to him, what she didn't say was the only thing that disturbed her was that she'd never felt like this before, his gentle sexy loving had overwhelmed her senses.

"I want you Matt."

"I want you too Annie," pushing his hands under her layers and finding that delicious warm skin.

"But I don't want snatched minutes."

"Neither do I, but we'll work it out," he pulled her against him, his hand wandering over her hip and cupping her body to him, he suddenly lifted her.

"What are you doing?"

"Taking you to bed."

"Matt no."

"Don't you want to?"

"Yes. I do."

He slid her out of his arms in his bedroom, starting to take her clothes off, watching her eyes darken as he peeled each layer away.

"If I'd known we'd be doing this I'd have left my thermals off."

They landed on the bed laughing, she moved on to him and started to kiss the mouth that she'd thought of all night, later they lay with limbs entangled, the cold of the room seeping into their heated bodies.

"Bloody hell Matt," she raised herself up to look at his face, "Don't give me that smouldering look Matt Abbot with those come to bed eyes, you are a bad influence," she teased.

He grabbed her and pulled her in closer, savouring every moment, "I've come to bed eyes, have I?"

"Definitely. I was just passing and going to say hello."

"Yeh, yeh sure sweetheart."

"It's your hot bod, it's hard to resist."

"Hot bod, eh? Well, if we stay here something else will be hard."

"Matt!" I say blushing.

"How can you blush after all we've done?"

She rises and sits on the edge of the bed her legs hanging over, Matt sits behind her his legs either side of her, holding her close, she leans into him.

"I'll have to go I have to pick up Arthur and Molly," he holds her tightly arms wrapped around her, although she loves her children dearly to have this for herself is incredible, to feel all this just for her.

"Don't overthink Annie, we'll take everything a step at a time," she turns slightly in his arms looking at him, and voices what she was thinking.

"To have this for me Matt is incredible, just for me, because I'm me, not a mother, not a widow, just me. I haven't felt like a person, an attractive person for so, so long, uhm, I'm not very good at this," he frowns. "Talking about what we've done, words can't say how you've made me feel." He pulls her to him.

"Life is becoming frightening Matt, in the big wide world."

"I've got your back Annie," he grins, "Literally sweetheart."

"I know now."

"Don't wiggle that gorgeous bottom of yours or I'll have to haul you back into bed," he laughs and kisses her shoulders and across her neck. Oh god I want him so much, the lust is pulling me to him again. I must go though. I move out of the warmth of his arms and start to get dressed, he joins her and when dressed they walk downstairs.

He holds her briefly, "Don't be frightened, don't worry, this is the beginning of a lot of change Annie, not just for us, but for the country and the world, we'll get through it."

As Annie leaves Matt is not sure his words are adequate, the virus is spreading across Europe, some parts of Italy are in lockdown now, the fear is like a stormy atmosphere all around them, he feels the shutting of schools, limiting contact somehow, is going to happen to them too.

Lying in bed that night after talking quietly to Matt, she remembers the last two days as if in a dream, she is wary about giving so much of herself, but the release of her feelings was, as she told Matt, incredible. Nagging at the back of her mind is some self-preservation, she doesn't want to get hurt, but then who does, you have to try to live life, and perhaps she had avoided life, she doesn't think though that Matt would hurt her.

Annie sleeps deeply and untroubled and wakes with a new spark, smiling and happy, though when she takes the children to school, the murmurs of uncertainty and yes fear is there, it's all everyone can talk about only once the children are in school though.

Before going to the farm where she has to plant and not get distracted, she has to pop some eggs into Iris, these eggs Iris asks her for two days ago, she was so stunned with Matt in the barn that when she got home, she had forgotten them, she remembers Iris looking at her quizzically, and wondered if she had "I've just had amazing sex," written on her forehead. She had also forgotten to give them to Ted yesterday, when he left early, she drops them off and hurries to the farm.

As she goes Iris turns to Ted, "Well something is definitely going on she has a smile as wide as Cheddar Gorge, and I'm guessing a certain farmer has put that smile on her face."

"I think you're right there, when we bumped into Matt yesterday, they just looked at each other all dreamy like."

"You never said."

"I don't tell you everything."

Concentrate Annie, concentrate, you have so much to plant, just keep reciting the jobs over and over or you'll run over to the house and into Matt's arms. I turn on the radio in the greenhouse, it's warmer while planting today. I have a dance to some music, the Beach Boys "don't worry baby everything will turn out right," smiling I plant up carrots and French beans, and salad leaves, in the garden I dig over the beds to prepare, there is some spring broccoli to harvest too, I'll leave one in the kitchen for Matt, any excuse Annie.

As I'm finishing up thinking about Matt. I think it would be nice to spend an evening together cook for him, here would be preferable, as I'd just like the opportunity to get to know him more and I know Arthur and Molly would monopolise him, and this early in our, well whatever it is, it would be good occasionally to see him on my own. I could wear something nice not work clothes and layers of thermals. I phone Iris and ask if she can baby sit tomorrow, and then text Matt and say I'll cook for him tomorrow night at his if he wants me too.

I push the phone into my pocket as Matt opens the gate and comes in, just looking at him takes my breath away at what he can make me feel. I wonder at how something can develop from just friends being around you for years to this searing heat I feel. We both halt and stare at each other, knowing how it develops every time we see each other, he strides towards me and gathers me in his arms and kisses me deeply.

"Do you know what I want to do to you?"

"Well bearing in mind the last two times I've seen you. I can make a guess, but not here," I say shyly.

"Oh Annie, that is like red rag to a bull saying that, you know me," he shakes his head and picks me up pushing me against the wall, kissing me, flattening me. I can feel how aroused he is and can't help myself the lust coursing through my veins my whole body. He stops and puts me down, my legs nearly giving way.

"Better not, eh?" he says and I slap his arm. "Sorry did you want me to carry on?" he says smiling down at me.

"Matt," I lay my head on his chest getting my breathing together again, this is so powerful, and he knows that too, as he lifts my head and looks at me.

"Bed?"

We somehow make it upstairs, the tension between us monumental. I tell him I've never experienced this before as we lie down afterwards, he looks pleased and begins to kiss me again, taking me high so quickly with his lips his touch and all of him.

I eventually get home, collect the children, and start the evening of food, reading and baths for them both, they are both excited about Iris coming round tomorrow, Matt agreed it would be good to have some time together, chat over food. I haven't said what I'm doing to the children just been a bit vague about seeing Sue, and the same was said to Iris too.

Once the children are in bed I settle down in the lounge, having this power of feelings surging through me has meant I haven't concentrated on anything, the news flickers and I read the strap lines, the news beginning to permeate my dazed mind. I found Arthur singing happy birthday earlier while washing his hands, he told me that is what they had been taught in school, it means they spend the right amount of time hand washing, to ensure they are protected against the virus, that really scared me, my children are learning something to keep a deadly virus at bay.

As I'm absorbing everything. I hear a knock at the door, Dave.

"Hi, was I expecting you?" he shakes his head and then behind him is Matt.

"Can we come in Annie we need to have a quick chat," he whispers, he knows Arthur has got hearing like a bat. We all go into the kitchen and close the door, and sit round the table, this is beginning to worry me now.

"The Prime Minister spoke today about the crisis, following on from the World Health Organisation declaring this virus a pandemic, he said it was the worst public health crisis for a generation, he spoke about losing loved ones before their time," silence fills the room, words unsaid, fear creeping in, cold running through their veins, not believing this could happen in their lifetime, it feels so unreal, like a film playing out, a horror film.

"Everything is changing, and it's changing fast, faster than a lot of people thought, there's talk of shielding the vulnerable as you know, from what I've heard at work, Officers with long term illnesses are going home for up to three months," I gasp at this, that long. "It won't be over in weeks; this is going to be with us for months. I think we will be going into lockdown soon; we will have to stay in our own homes, we won't be able to go out except for essentials like food and medicine, not see other people, it will be difficult for you with the children and your business too."

"If I have to be at home with Molly and Arthur, how are we going to carry on the produce business? I suppose that doesn't matter its health that matters," I hang my head worry running through me again. Matt takes my hand.

"Matt and I have been talking, all his bookings are likely to be cancelled for the barns, he can carry on with the farm with Don, but we don't know what all this is going to bring Annie, what worries both of us is that we might not be able to see each other and support each other, you and the children particularly."

"We'll be ok," I say not really believing this.

"No. I think you should move onto the farm…" Matt doesn't finish as Annie interrupts him.

"What no way Matt, I'm not ready for that it's too soon."

Matt gently puts his finger to her lips and they just look at each other the heat coursing between them, both remembering, he lowers his hand and holds both of hers tenderly, stroking them.

Dave looks at them and frowns, feeling he's missed an episode here and lost track of the story, something has obviously happened between them, looking at them he can see it now, Sue always said he missed things, well he'd caught up now and quickly, you couldn't miss this development.

Matt speaks, "Dave and I feel you should move with the children in to the big barn," he stills and looks at her, a look passes between them. He continues, "You can carry on with the market garden, whatever happens food will be needed, I'm not sure yet in what way, schools will shut and the children can be with you, and I'll be on the farm too, you'll be safe," his paramount thought.

He sees her independent spirit struggle about needing help, also, he sees the slight panic returning to her, he wants the newly confident sexy woman back, but realises what an upheaval all of this is going to be, her hands shaking Matt stills them with his, helping her, he speaks.

"The market garden might be so important to locals, we can't let all of the newly planted produce go to waste, the children will be protected and secure at the farm, and so will you Annie," they continue to talk and it washes over me, as I think I realise it is the only solution. I can tend the garden and still look after the children, it won't be easy, and it will take a lot of planning.

"I never saw the bedrooms, what are they like," suddenly realising why I didn't see them, we never got that far, Matt gives me one of his looks, which helps.

I don't go up to the farm the next morning. I have so much to think about and I didn't sleep at all last night, just worrying about everything, Dad phoned me this morning after the school run, Dave had spoken to him yesterday, he agrees with Dave and Matt it will probably be the best solution, he was also extremely worried about me having limited support, Dave would be working and also high-risk with his job. Emotion grips my insides as I realise, I won't see Mum and Dad, and how will they cope with everything they are not old, but it just feels so frightening, them being so far away too.

We discuss Dave's other dilemma, he told me last night that he had wanted to ask Sue to move in with him, until all of this came up that was what they had planned, but Sue has quite severe asthma, and he and her were worried that if he continued to work, which he will, he could potentially bring the virus into the house, risking her health and possibly life, as the virus appears to be respiratory linked.

I'm still going up to Matt's later, Iris is going to come round and pick them up from school. I have told her and Ted what we propose and they agree it is the only solution. I want to look at the barn and get an idea what will be needed and then stay and see Matt for something to eat, he said he'd cook. I don't think I could have contemplated cooking, my head feels full of so much fear, for everyone.

We've decided not to tell the children yet, and to leave it as late as possible, although that won't be easy as there will be so much upheaval, and a lot can't be done at the very last minute.

I shower and change. I wouldn't normally be in leggings and a nice jumper to go up to the farm, but am fed up with jeans and layers, and I am having dinner with Matt. So, for my trip down to the barns I put my wellies on and walk down the track, Matt has put in a separate entrance and track for the barns so visitors aren't coming through the yard and near the house.

I walk up to the barn and open the door, Matt has left it unlocked, toeing off my boots. I obviously remember the open plan living room, and look at the sofa, a breath catching in my throat, it seems so long ago, an age when words like lockdown were remote, yet not so long ago. I turn and look at the kitchen, there is an electric range cooker, more than enough for us, an island, and fridge, dishwasher and washing machine, all built in, a small room to the right of the front door houses, the boiler and a small freezer.

I can probably put any large amounts of frozen food into the freezer up at the house. Matt had ordered a full kitchen equipment pack for all the barns but has cancelled two of those at the present, the packs include plates, cutlery, bowls and pans, so I won't have to bring too much, just favourite knives and whatever I use often.

In front of the island are two stools, and then a table and chairs, which sits behind one part of the sofa. I walk over to the door in the far wall, and walk into a light corridor, and find three good bedrooms off it, there is one en suite and a bathroom. There is one that is a twin bedroom, normally Arthur and Molly have their own rooms but I feel under these extenuating circumstances they will be better and happy sharing a bedroom.

Daylight begins to fade as I make my way up to the walled garden. I just want to check how everything is doing and check if anything needs watering, then tomorrow Ted is coming up for the day, which will give me time at home. He says he wants to make the most of his visit, as he's heard talk that over 70s will have to be at home, and non-essential travel banned he wouldn't be able to come over, when he told me that I welled up for them both two more people so vulnerable, two good friends.

Everything checked I walk back to my car and slip off my boots and old mac and slip into some animal print flatties and throw a shawl round my neck. I run my fingers through my hair and put some lippy on. I feel a bit nervous. I don't know why, it's as if it's a first date, oh grow up Annie, what you and Matt have been up to, this can't possibly be called a first date.

I let myself in the back door smiling at my thoughts, Matt straightens up and closes the oven door and turns and sees Annie, he drinks her in, she looks lovely tonight, a fitted red jumper clings to all the right places and he sees her shapely legs, not clad in jeans for once, he knows what he wants to do tonight and eating isn't top of the agenda. The only thing that stalls him is her pale face and the dark rings under her eyes, he moves towards her and takes her in his arms, holding her close and giving her all his strength in that hug. They look into each other's eyes; he makes a decision.

"Right, come through to the lounge, I've lit the fire and we can sit and have a drink and wait for the food to cook," he knows tonight is about comfort not the hot sex of the last few days, he leads her down the hall and sits her down on the sofa, in front of the fire. He sits next to her and holds her close, just kissing the top of her head and rocking her gently.

"You look worried sweetheart, talk to me."

"God where to start, it's frightening, it feels so unreal, not how we live, only going out for essential items, it can overwhelm you if you think too much, and I have, but something good," she takes a deep breath the fear making her feel anxious. "The barn is ideal, it's lovely and would suit me Arthur and Molly perfectly. I think I'll put them in the twin bedroom together. I think under the circumstances it would help them. Dad phoned and he agrees about the move it is the best solution, it's the only one Matt. I'm sorry I jumped down your throat last night when you started suggesting this."

"Annie it's fine I know what you were thinking, it is early days for us." He kisses her softly, lingering on her mouth, Annie responds feeling some of her worries melting away with the feel of him. She holds his head to deepen the kiss, pulling him to her, Matt realises that control is overrated and the thought of comfort flies away as he lowers her to the floor in front of the fire.

"Annie," his voice is rough, "Do you want this. I thought it might be better to talk."

"Matt. I want you more than you'll ever know," she needs that comfort that loving, a life raft in a stormy sea, she strokes his face, Matt thinks of the precious gift he has in his arms and knows he will never let her go or let her down.

Later after what Matt felt was the most incredible experience of his life, they hold each other, the need in them both tonight was so intense it heightened their feelings, Annie gets her breath back and puts her arms around Matt, over his chest and looks at his face.

"I've… I've never felt like that before, ever." To reinforce this, she bends over putting light feather kisses up his jaw. "Do you think it is so intense because of the turmoil around us?"

"No sweetheart I think it would be the same, fabulous hot sex," he smiles, although as he says it, he knows what they felt tonight was deeper somehow. She was burrowing into his heart, and he hoped she would stay there forever.

"I'd better get us something to eat," he says moving reluctantly, "Ok in here on laps?"

"Yes," I start to gather my clothes up and put them on, my legs like jelly and my head dizzy from the effects of him. I look up at him and his eyes are fused on me, how can I want more after what just happened. I step towards him again, and bury my body in his arms and breath in the smell of him. A small part of me knows how few of these moments we are going to have over the weeks and months to come. The storm clouds are getting lower and closer, the change to all our lives is not something we can undo all we can do is make the best of it to help to save lives. I think. But I'm lucky at least I can see Matt. I feel so much for Dave and Sue, particularly Sue who will be on her own, as Dave will have his work colleagues.

I sit cross legged eating the delicious meal, "Beef bourguignon, my favourite, do you know I can't remember the last time anyone cooked for me, the barbeques on holiday don't count, this is delicious," he watches her and wonders at her relationship with Sam, it looked pretty good from the outside but he feels that there was a lot of give from one side, and one side only, he knows that is not how any relationship with them would be.

Later after food and quiet talk, reassurance from Matt and some lowering of her anxiety, especially with the love he gives her, "I'd better go."

"Stay."

"I wish I could."

"But what would we do all night if you did?" Matt asks innocently though his voice is rough from lust building up again, he really doesn't want her to go, like Annie he knows these moments are precious and to be savoured, they hug and, he leads her out to her car after a lingering kiss he waves as she goes down the track and home. He shuts the gate, he thinks about the events around them and feels a cold hand gripping his heart, his only hope being that they will get through this unscathed, them as a couple can feel their way later.

Tumultuous Events

Friday the 13th sees me packing like a demon, we've decided that me and the children need to move this weekend, it isn't ideal, in that it is so quick but Dave says events are going to move faster than any of us thought. The one big problem is I won't be able to lead the children gently into this, it will be abrupt, but they are both resilient and they know changes are coming, they are asking questions all of the time, all I can do is reassure them. We will have a chat about it tonight and make it like an adventure, like our holiday last summer, that now feels years ago. Part of me wants to savour the growing ties with Matt and the incredible sex, he's so strong, so calm, such a lovely man, I've loaded three boxes into the car, when the man himself arrives in his four-door pickup truck.

"Morning," he grabs me for a kiss, he looks down at me. "Are you ok?"

"As ok as I'm going to be in this situation, I've managed to pack most of the clothes we'll need and emptied a lot of ingredients and tins out of the kitchen cupboards, I've put the boxes in my car but the cases are in the hall, I'll pull the bikes out of the shed too…"

"Slow down, we can get this done, we don't have to move furniture, it is just every day essential," he puts a hand on my arm to steady me, he's right of course, less rushing will get everything done. We pack both vehicles with all but the bare essentials for home tonight, I've put bags of linen and towels in too and we drive up to the farm, going in the barns entrance.

The area to park in is in front of the kitchen window, as I get out of the car I see Iris inside, "I didn't know Iris was coming up today,"

"Yes, she wanted to put voiles up in the bedrooms, whatever they are," he picks up some of the cases and bags and goes round the side into the entrance. I follow wheeling two cases, as I round the corner I stop and walk to the patio overlooking the river, I'm startled to see Don rolling out some fencing. Matt moves up behind me, his hand on my back.

"What's this?" I ask.

"We thought you better have a fenced off area so Bob could go out and not wander and it will be an area for Arthur to play his beloved footie, Bob shouldn't be able to get through the post and wire stock fence, it will give you peace of mind too in that the children can't run down to the river."

"Matt that is so thoughtful. I will be setting some rules for those two I can tell you," the fencing wraps around a large grassy area and along towards the main door as we unload the car. I get a call from the school. I had left a message this morning for the head teacher. I wanted to outline what we are doing and that the children will be in school until whatever happens, she feels lockdown is coming very soon too, she is putting together home learning ideas and some on the school website too.

"I've put one of the tables and chairs into the walled garden so that when you are working in there the children can sit and work or play at the table, when we go back to yours, I'll grab that parasol too." It is warm today, and the forecast is for more warm weather too. "I think the children's bikes and any outdoor toys will have to go into one of the outhouses or the walled garden store, there's no storage down here."

As Matt walks up the hill with the bikes, Don finishes the fence, a small gate by the front door means we are dog and child proof he says, Don has had some upheaval too, his wife Sally has some underlying health problems and as people like Sally and the elderly seem to be most vulnerable to the disease, she has moved into the annex at her daughters house and their son Phil, has come to live with his dad and help on the farm, Don told Matt that he hoped Phil would be a help but being as he worked in a bar he wasn't so sure, it is company for Don though.

I go back inside and finish filling the cupboards in the kitchen, then put the new crockery and cutlery into the dishwasher to make sure it's clean.

"Well, that's me done," Iris says making me jump.

"I'd forgotten you were here, sorry Iris, and sorry I forgot to bring the kettle on the first run, we'll get it when we go back."

"Well, I'm off." Ted parked the car at the top, she takes a deep breath and gives me a look. I know that look, it is "I am going to interfere whether you like it or not" look. Oh what now.

"I'm so glad you and Matt are getting together, it's a big step living with someone again. I can see how attracted you both are anyone could see it, I'm pleased for you, don't know why you're not living in the big house though…" and no doubt she could have said a lot more but I stop her.

"Iris. I am not living with Matt. I am here to run the business and keep it going so we can supply as much food as possible, and Matt and I are only friends." I feel disloyal to Matt saying that, but I need to protect me and the children from gossip and today is not the day to say I am in a relationship with Matt, when the most important people don't know.

"Annie. I don't mean anything by it. I just noticed that's all, I'm sorry I got the wrong end of the stick," we say our goodbyes and she walks up the hill. I see her stop to talk to Matt on his way back. I put all the boxes back outside throwing them down to repack at the house. I am so torn and cross. I love Iris to bits but I had enough talk about me when Sam died to dislike it immensely.

I throw another box out the door, just as Matt comes in, "Hey be careful," as I walk past him and towards the back of the barn and garden, "What's got into you?" He follows me, "Iris just said she thought she had upset you, what is it?"

"She said she could see how involved we were and even that we had moved in together," I fume.

"Come here and sit down," he holds his hand out to me. I sit at the picnic table but don't take his hand, "Is it so terrible if someone sees how much we mean to each other? Yes, she got it wrong about us living together but Annie we both have smiles on our faces in this terrible time. I don't know about you but it certainly helps me to keep going, and I'm hurt you could say we are just friends, yes, she told me." He walks away around the side of the barn.

I put my head in my hands. I am so protective of everything so worried about what people think, it is stupid, and to think I was worried about me being hurt and yet I have hurt the one person who doesn't deserve it. I run round the corner and collide with him coming the other way.

"I'm sorry," nearly in tears, "You are the last person in the whole world I'd hurt, and I have, it was all the gossip when Sam died, the speculation about who I would see in the following years, a small village, the questions constantly. I became protective, mainly for the children, and it stays with you, please forgive me," he just stands in front of me as I wring my hands in distress, no, please don't shut me out I think struggling and just looking at him.

"I'm finding all this change disturbing, I've lived in that house a long time I've taken whatever life threw at me there, to have to step completely out of that comfort zone is unnerving and at such pace, but it doesn't excuse my treatment of you," there is another reason I was jumpy and unnerved, but I feel I am using something to excuse my behaviour that I shouldn't.

"Annie. I don't know what we have, 'Us,' it is a fledgling, it is early for 'us,' and everything around us is moving at pace, we both have to make changes to our lives that could affect the other, we have to get through this together, if you don't want that you have to say," he stops talking and looks at me, his eyes sad.

"You have made me feel emotion I have never experienced in my life before Matt, it is all whirling in my head and mixed in with the past and all of this change, but it's no excuse for me saying we were just friends, you are much more to me and I will stand up and say that to anyone who asks, you have broken through my protective shell, quite a feat, and I want to feel everything with you again and again. I want us to carry on and be together," I look at him and inside I am pleading with him, willing him to forgive.

They both reach out at the same time, her hand coming toward his as he takes a step forward, they hold each other for the longest time, then she tentatively lifts her head up and stands on tiptoes to begin to kiss him her arms around his neck, he responds, as she opens her eyes, she sees his eyes glitter with unshed tears. For the first time she sees how much she means to Matt, and feels something shift in her, she realises for him it isn't about the hot sex but something far deeper, this moment is a revelation and game changing. He said she was a precious gift, but she realises he is the precious gift for her.

"We have a lot to do," he says.

"I know…"

"Do I hear a hesitation? Is it outdoor sex then?" he says knowing it will embarrass her.

"Alright then," as she says it, she sees Matt look incredulous. "Only joking," she says as he picks her up in his strong arms, "No Matt, we can't I didn't mean it."

He lowers her down to the ground his arms around her waist, "But we could carry this on inside, couldn't we, good make up sex."

"Is that like hot sex, but hotter," she laughs, as they trail into the barn together, both thinking it might be some time before they have the space and time to do this.

He makes love to her, it is the only way Matt could describe what happened, the sex was tender, unhurried, although they hadn't got all the time in the world, and magical. Not wild, but it seemed to cement them together, to bind them inextricably. The changing world around them strengthening their attraction, the depth of their feelings. The love healing the hurt of earlier, and making it disappear, afterwards they lie on the bed holding onto each other so no one could tear them apart.

"What time is it?" Annie suddenly asks.

"It's ok I texted Dave earlier to pick up the children if he could and he agreed, he's going to bring them up in a bit to see around and have a chat, you put some pizzas in the freezer didn't you, well we can christen the oven, now we've christened the bed," he quips. "You're ok with me making that decision aren't you."

"Of course, it's ok, we are us," I smile, "If Iris could see us now," we laugh together, "Better get dressed then," she says reluctantly.

"We could have a shower first," Matt raises his eyebrows suggestively.

"What are you like, no, or should I say not yet," as I jump up, he grabs me around the waist and lovingly kisses me once again.

"I will hold you to that promise."

I finish tidying the kitchen and putting as much away as possible, the beds can wait to be made tomorrow. As I do, Dave arrives with Arthur and Molly, they had nipped home and he found some clothes for them to change into, quite a haphazard look, but I don't think there was much choice as I have most things here.

"Hello you two," I go outside and hug them both, and show them round into the garden, there's a football on the lawn that Matt must have put there, they both charge down to have a kick around.

"Everything ok?" Dave asks, reaching over and squeezing my hand.

"Yes, so much to do so much change," I sound shaky, "But I'm alright Dave, we have no choice here, we have to get on and do what's best, I'll just get some cold drinks for the children, are you staying for pizza?"

"No, I'm on duty later, doing some nights, but I'll speak to you tomorrow, hope it goes well." With that, he hugs me and goes back to his car.

"Molly, Arthur come and sit down," I call after getting them a drink each, they run up and sit on the steps down to the grass from the patio.

"I've got something to tell you and it's really exciting…"

"Are we going to the beach hut for the holidays?" Arthur says hugging Molly to him, they both pump the air with their hands.

"No, but wait," as they look disappointed, "We are going to come and live here on the farm for a while, to help Matt…"

"Does he want me to learn to drive the quad bike Mum. I can herd the cattle and the sheep."

"We'll see what jobs he needs us to do. I have to do the garden, so you can both help me plant seeds and water and everything, you will be able to feed the chickens and collect the eggs," Arthur looks ecstatic, Molly less so.

"But what about school Mummy?" she asks worried.

"Well, you will carry on at school, I've spoken to Mrs Markham, but I know the teachers have told you all about the virus, because they taught you how long to wash your hands for, didn't they?" they nod.

"It may be that we have some longer school holidays coming up because we have to be safe and not get poorly," they seem to have taken this in.

"Are we going to live at the house?" Molly again.

"No, we're going to live here," I say pointing behind me to the barn, they obviously look surprised, "We'll have a look in a minute, but Matt has put a fence up for you both to play on the lawn, you can play footie Arthur and no kicking the ball over the fence."

I think that is a hopeless statement on my part as the fence is only four feet high, "The fence is for Bob too, so he doesn't go onto the farm, shall we go inside and have a look?" Holding each of them we walk round to go in the main door. I show them the open plan kitchen and living room.

"Where's Bob's bed going to go Mum?" Arthur asks, as I am about to reply he and Molly both consider the problem looking round the room and then deciding he can have his bed in front of the radiator, and can still see out of the glass doors. I just hope there aren't too many rabbits hopping past and him charging up to the windows every few minutes.

"What's really exciting is your bedroom," I have put a few of their things in there, a small table and two chairs that has been in the shed, and with a quick clean, gives them a little desk in their bedroom, and some of their toys are there too. "What will be good is both of you sharing, like you did at the hut," sudden inspiration, "But not bunk beds," I said quickly before Arthur could get a word in.

Opening the door. I see Iris has changed the curtains to some small dog patterned ones, that is so kind and makes it more special for them. I turn and look at them, hoping everything will be ok. I shouldn't have worried.

"Which bed Molls?" they stand considering, the two twin beds sit either side of the window, with two bedside cabinets between the beds, note to me, bring the bedside lights over.

"I like that one, can I put some of my pictures on the wall Mummy, and the one of Daddy?"

"Yes, of course Molly."

"Hey Molls we'll bring some from the hall too, and my certificate." I think of Sam resonating here, but leave it for now. I leave them to plan and go to put the oven on as Matt comes in with his arms full of pizzas.

"How's it gone?" he asks dumping the boxes onto the island.

I smile and nod my head to the bedroom where serious planning can be heard, "I likened sharing to the beach hut and they are more than happy, a few questions from Molly, more than Arthur, but ok, I'll tell them in a minute we are moving tomorrow."

They run in then whooping at seeing Matt.

"Can I learn to drive the quad bike Matt and help you on the farm?"

"Oh, forgot to mention that, Arthur wants to learn to drive the quad bike." I think get out of that one Matt Abbot, raising my eyebrows at him and smiling.

"Well Arthur that's great to offer to help. I will find you both jobs, we'll have to leave learning to drive the quad for a while though Arthur, you need to get a bit older," he sees Arthur's disappointment, "But you can come with me whenever we have time."

"Shall we go for a kick about Molls?"

As they run outside. I shout "pizza in 15 minutes," Arthur gives me the thumbs up as they go.

"Well, that seems to have gone ok," Matt says hugging me to him, "What do you think?"

"Yes, I think it has. I feel we'll be happy here, they've lovely space to play in and," I don't get to finish as they come running in, out of breath Arthur asks, "Is Matt going to live with us Mum?"

Oh. I didn't think they would ask that one, "No, he'll be up at his house, but we'll see him a lot." Matt is just standing there taking it all in smiling.

"But won't Matt be lonely on his own?" Molly asks always concerned for others. I need to grip this before it escalates, but Matt sits them down at the table and talks quietly to them about keeping the farm safe and it's the best place as he's got his office up at the house and his computers, and from there he can see all of the farm, as he continues to reassure them I place a plate of pizza slices on the table and squeeze his shoulder, he's doing a good job, something else shifts in me, as I appreciate his kindness to my two lovely children.

I thought I had taken nearly everything yesterday, but there is so much more today, Matt's had a new smart TV delivered, meaning we can access the internet which will be important for home schooling, we can piggy back on his broadband too. Kettle, mustn't forget that, radio, last tools out of the shed, luckily, I don't need much in the way of shopping, we have meat in the freezer at the farm, eggs on tap and growing produce, I'm so glad we don't have to shop it's chaos, people are panic buying, Dave told me that some were fighting over products, the favourite being toilet rolls, what do they think the infection is?

He said one of his mates had to break up this fight and watching was a family of four adults with four full trollies, mostly toilet rolls, ridiculous. Dave also reassured me about one of my many worries. I was unhappy about leaving the house empty, for security and a house needs to be lived in I think, but someone at work, a guy called Tim, is going to move in, his daughter has complex health problems and is to be shielded, but he has to work, and didn't want to possibly give her the virus, so he felt it was the best option for him, the poor family. I realise how lucky I am.

I feel guilty though, as looking at all the images of how hard Nursing and Medical staff are working around the world and I have some of those skills. I did look at going back and the children having to go into school as I would be a key worker but the only school would be 20 miles away, not one they had been to and certainly not in the village, Mrs Markham was disappointed the village school couldn't do this, but she hadn't staff to help, and then the option Matt and Dave presented was the only one really. I would be helping with food production and on days I wasn't in the garden I would help where I could on the farm.

I think that is it, Matt has put the child seats in his car and I'm left to make sure it is clean for Tim. As I lock the front door, I look at the house, memories flooding through me, memories that will always be with me, never forgotten.

At last, we are settled, it feels like trying to get a pint into a half pint pot to be honest, the pristine barn looks busier and fuller, and a bit like home, clothes all put away into wardrobes and wellies by the front door in different sizes.

"I'll go now Annie," Matt says.

"You're going?" I can't believe it; he has been with me every step of the way.

"Yes, I'll leave you in peace and you can…"

"But," he silences me with a kiss.

"I need to get some jobs done and the children need your time." I know this but part of me was hoping he'd have food with us this evening, he sees my disappointment.

"You don't want me here all the time Annie, it's your home."

I do though. I think and then say, "Am I leaning on you too much, Matt?"

"Annie sweetheart you can lean on me all you want and preferably naked," she slaps him gently and holds onto his arm, as he wraps his arms around her, "No you're not leaning on me Annie, you're an incredibly strong woman and you will manage well, come on we'll all walk up together, you have to water and check things in the greenhouse, I'm around Annie but I don't want to crowd you."

"You're not Matt, we're all in this together as you said, it's lovely having you here, even…"

"Even what," he says in my ear, knowing what I'm about to say, as he feels it too.

"You know."

"Yes, I do, even though I can't drag you to bed for hot sex," he softly kisses me, the longing within us both, "Come on children await us."

We gather the children from the back garden and all amble up towards the gardens, while the children tell Matt about all the plant labels they wrote for me, and show him. I water in the greenhouse, we haven't been able to replace the hosing that perished as yet, another job on the list, but I can use the hose from the tap so it's no great hardship just takes longer, everything finished we close up the greenhouse as it's just beginning to get dark, the clocks must change soon and we'll have lighter evenings.

The children run down the hill as I say goodnight to Matt, I'll see him tomorrow as he's coming for lunch. I turn and wave to him, the longing in the pit of my stomach. That night I take stock, no one has mentioned today, and neither did I, that it was the anniversary of Sam's death, which would have made my outburst yesterday explainable with Iris and Matt, but for some reason, I didn't think it appropriate to say, perhaps as I am so close to Matt now, while rushing to and from the village I took some flowers to the grave, and I will speak to the children, but there has been so much disruption that I don't want to add more to their little lives.

With the children playing outside, I'm prepping Sunday lunch, and have the luxury of the radio on. I forgot that being open plan life will be noisier, so I catch up on the news. I still as I hear that Spain are now in lockdown, it takes my breath away they have severe restrictions, it's rolling our way, that is the feeling I've had the whole time, like an avalanche you can't out run, it's inextricably approaching, my heart rate rises with all of this, it is so close, terrifyingly so.

I switch to music to lighten the mood. I make a pineapple upside down cake for pudding, both the pineapple and golden syrup found at the back of one of the house cupboards, no waste here. I look up from washing up and look out of the window, the kitchen window looks out over the farm up towards the house, standing solid in the cushion of the green of the farm, shining in the beautiful weather. I spot Matt walking down the hill. I drink him in. I can't believe until the last few weeks I never noticed him, his powerful strength and physique, he's so attractive, great shoulders and abs I think, god stop lusting after him girl and get a grip.

The children must have seen him too, as I hear them shout his name and good, they have stayed this side of the fence and gate, rule number one. The three of them walk in and it's all questions, questions about the farm from Arthur, Molly just basks in the boy's company and is happy listening. We have a lovely lunch, perhaps one of the last Sundays without restrictions.

The children go to school the next day, new changes emerge later that day, with worrying talk of health systems being overwhelmed, a request for manufacturing to support the supply of ventilators, that sent cold shivers down my back, don't we have enough, they have obviously looked at Spain and Italy, it puts fear into your heart. Commands like no non-essential travel, keep away from others, avoid pubs, clubs and theatres, indication that we are moving towards a lockdown.

I just have to carry on and make sure that I can produce brilliant vegetables, fruit and salad, as it's been warm much of what I started off is coming on leaps and bounds. I plant tomatoes, chillies, and sweet peppers in the greenhouse, then prepare beds for sowing lettuces, radishes and leeks. I go round the back of the walled garden to check the contents of the polytunnels, all is well there and I do some weeding. I finish off behind there where I saw a load of rhubarb growing, it is already mulched but I want to give it some general fertiliser, we'll be able to pick some soon, it's a large patch and looks quite established. I'll call one of the farm shops later to see if they want some, life is so uncertain though.

As I'm standing looking towards the orchard. I hear steps behind me and am enveloped in strong arms and warm breath on my neck, heat rises through me, Matt turns me round in the protection of his arms and hungrily kisses me, no words are necessary to convey how we both feel, our bodies are fused together, the kiss melting my insides and I know for Matt too.

"Have you had lunch?" he asks.

"How can you think of lunch when you are kissing me like that and I can barely concentrate," he raises his eyebrows in a question, "No I haven't."

"I am a man with dual appetites, come on," he leads me further up behind the walled garden to an old open fronted summer house, and on the table in the centre is a plate of sandwiches and cold drinks, and her favourite millionaire shortbread.

"Did you do this?" he nods, "When did you find time in your busy schedule."

"It's only sarnies Annie," he laughs, but for me it's the thought that so counts, in that moment I realise how little thought Sam gave me, it was the same when Matt cooked for me, Sam would never have done something like that, Sam would never have remembered I loved millionaire shortbread. I suppose in a relationship you accept what's there and enjoy other things together, but I know I need the things Matt gives me. And I thought they were so alike, how wrong could I have been.

Matt looks at Annie, he wonders what's going through her head right now, she looked stunned that he would do this, however simple he thinks the gesture is, its enormous to her, perhaps it's a gesture she didn't see very often.

She sits on one of the chairs looking out over the back of the farm, holding his hand as she eats.

"What's going through your head sweetheart?" he asks gently rubbing his thumb over hers.

"Sam would never have remembered I loved this," pointing to the shortbread, "I feel disloyal saying that, he was kind," I say determinedly.

"You're not being disloyal, we're all different Annie. I listened that's all."

"No, it's more, you are so generous with everything, your time, your love, for us all. I suppose it's your attention to detail, Sam always seemed in a hurry, looking for the next thing, renovating the house, getting a bike and being the best, entering triathlons, pushing himself, and yes sometimes to the detriment of me and the children, perhaps I didn't see it until now." He pulls her over on to his lap and holds her, she kisses him with such warmth and tenderness, Matt feels emotion well in him, not heat, although that is there constantly when around her, something else, something he has never felt before.

As they sit there it hits him that he loves her, he knew he had feelings for her but the emotions stir within him, he is overcome with how he feels, he never knew all of this could be so good, he'd had relationships before, many short, and with sex, but not like he had with Annie, in such a short time the feelings ran deeper between them, heightening the sex, love, making it so incredible. He hugged her to him knowing they would not have many more moments together once school closed.

Later that afternoon Matt goes into town to the appointment he arranged that morning, Geoff his solicitor had been on at him to make a will ever since his mother then father died, they had discussed it that morning and his wishes, he asks for it to be hurried through so he could sign it that afternoon. Geoff had briefly gone over the fact that his mother had signed over the farm to him over eight years ago, that had been when his father had developed some minor memory loss, they had visited Geoff, signed the Lasting Power Of Attorney, giving his mum management of all finances then Matt had been latterly asked to sign one in terms of his mother, he'd never had to use it, as his mother had managed everything until her untimely death.

It meant though in the event of his father's death there was no inheritance tax issues, as Matt had owned the farm for so long, against his better judgement at the time, but he could see his mother had been given good advice.

The only other issue apart from who should inherit was Don, he and his wife lived in one of the cottages on the farm, Matt had already removed the rent for Don, but now in his will he wanted him to have the cottage as his. Everything signed he returned to the farm and finished some more jobs and walked down to the barn to see how the children's day had gone and any news on closures, the children are outside at the back when Matt walks into the barn, he reaches for Annie and hugs her.

"Ok?" he asks as she rests her head on his chest.

"No. I shouldn't watch the daily briefing, Italy now have over 1800 deaths with the highest death rate in a day there and Spain deaths have doubled in a day, it is overwhelming their health systems, they can't cope, will we? The government said we might have to go further with the measures and fast. It is so close Matt it is really scary now, lockdown is coming, at the school gate none of us wanted to get near other people, you can see fear every time you look at someone, one or two had masks on, it is not something I would have ever thought of seeing in our own country."

"Do you want to take the children out of school early?"

I had thought about this, it's trying to do the best for them, "I don't know. I don't think so, they say children are less likely to get the virus, but it's about whether they are super spreaders like with flu, there is so much we don't know, and it's being in close contact with the parents. But," I steady myself, his strength giving me stability, "We want normality as long as possible, what do you think?"

"Yes, but don't hesitate if you think the risk has gone up, we will be ok here, we have everything, we can school the children, they can be in the walled garden, they can be involved, and we have each other for support, did you speak to your parents?"

"I did, Mum is very anxious, she had a bad experience shopping, people acting like animals fighting, she won't go again, Dad says they have all they need, but how long will any lockdown last? It could be months, looking at the rest of the world. But he reassured me as much as possible."

Matt didn't say anything, Annie's father had phoned him today when he was out, it was about reassuring each other, he wanted Matt to look after Annie and ensure she knew her parents were safe and not to worry about them, and Matt wanted to reassure them that he would look after their daughter and grandchildren, he told them that once school was closed, he would set up some Facetime or Skype so they could see them all.

The week rolled on with words bouncing around them, dangerous, so infectious, drastic measures, worst public health crisis in a generation, social distancing, a marathon not a sprint, travel restrictions, vulnerable people, Annie thought about the charity who had made her vegetable boxes all young adults with educational needs, requiring stability in their lives but now at home, without the contact of their peers and mentors, her heart went out to them and she realised once again how lucky they were on the farm.

On the Thursday after dropping the children at school, they all now knew schools would close the following day, just talking to one or two teachers made her sit up and make sure she had everything the children would need. She felt she was running all the time, there seemed to be so much to do, the growing in the polytunnels because of the good weather was accelerating, she would have at least lettuces and spinach and a good deal more next week.

The work in the gardens hadn't changed too much, weeding, planting, watering, nurturing as much as possible, it took her mind off the impending doom on the horizon, her only worry was ensuring people got to eat the produce and she was gradually working on that, one of the farm shop owners said food shops were likely to stay open in any lockdown, but who really knew at this stage.

She hadn't seen much of Matt in the last few days, he was as busy as her, lambing was in full flow, they had caught fleeting glimpses of each other, she'd told him about schools closing. She took a drink from her bottle, and went to fill the watering can from the water butt attached to the greenhouse guttering, they had put this in a couple of months ago, until the tank below the greenhouse could be looked at there wasn't much option, there wasn't a huge amount of water in it, as rain had been scarce recently, but it was nice to use rain water where possible, but not for the seedlings, she was watering in the greenhouse when Matt came in, he gives her a hug.

"You've been busy. I saw you doing your nurse's walk earlier," he grins at her.

"What nurse's walk?"

"The one where you are virtually running."

"Nurses don't run, when I was training, I was told off for running, so like every other nurse I developed a quick walk," she smiles up at him, "I'm frightened Matt."

"I know sweetheart, we all are, we just have to take everything a day at a time. I don't see how we can plan ahead in any way now; we'll be ok here we have everything we need, just keep working, it's coming our way, and there's nothing we can do about it, except stay home and hope it keeps the numbers down," he holds me in his arms giving his strength to me.

After our quick catch up I go into the sunken garden to weed and dead head to keep it vaguely in check, Don is busy elsewhere so I've said I'll maintain it, he or Phil were going to run the mower over the other garden. I said don't bother, does it matter if the lawn grows tall, as long as we can keep the farm and produce going that's the important thing. They are re-sowing the barley today, which is an extra job. When I get a moment. I want to throw some wild flower seeds on that lawn I think, it will prevent the men thinking about mowing if it's all flowers later in the year.

"Did I tell you those shorts look good on you, especially with the walking boots and thick sock," Matt comes up behind me and gives my rear a cheeky slap.

"Well better the boots than a fork through my foot, I'm starved have you got any food in your kitchen?"

"Oh, I thought you were hungry for me, and yes, come on I'll make a sandwich," he says as I rest my tools in the wheelbarrow and follow him over the yard to the house. I take my boots off and wash my hands for the millionth time. As I look up drying my hands. I see Matt looking at me, the look melts my insides. I throw down the towel and walk over to him, putting my hands round his neck, he lifts me and kisses me with the hunger I feel.

"I know we haven't got time but I want you so much Annie," his words carry me to all the wonderful places he has taken me with his raw emotion and love making. We kiss deeply, Matt holding me firmly against him, my feet off the ground. I wrap my legs around his waist my hands in his hair, the way he makes me feel empowers me. I lower myself to the floor still kissing. I feel his strength, his muscles tense through his t shirt, all the farm work and his previous work developing those muscles, his physical strength matches his mental strength. Slowly we move towards the lounge, lunch forgotten for now, our passion so great, so overwhelming for us both, the emotion is huge, as we finish, I realise I am crying.

"Annie, did I hurt you, what's wrong?"

"Nothing," I sniff, "It was just so beautiful, you make me feel so much, feelings I didn't know existed. I just want you all the time, oh Matt." He holds her to him, revelling in her words, smiling into her hair, content, even with the world in turmoil around them, this was something to hang onto.

They dress, occasionally holding each other, to bind them together, if what they'd both experienced wasn't already doing that. Matt puts together a sandwich for Annie, and she takes it and rushes off to the poly tunnels, they are due to see each other later, with Matt coming down to eat with the children.

Annie nibbles at the sandwich, she goes over what they had, what they'd just done, the loving. It wasn't easy to admit how she felt, she worried it was because of the precarious situation everyone found themselves in, but deep inside she knew it wasn't. Her feelings frightened her, she wanted to tell him how she felt but something held her back, was it guilt, was it fear of losing again, or was it once said it couldn't be taken back. She could see how Matt felt, she could see it in his eyes, it wasn't the physical aspect of their, well, relationship, it was actions, looks, tenderness. Love?

Hours later showered, children picked up and starting on making something to eat Matt walked into the barn, they exchanged the tenderest of looks, then Matt started.

"Oh. I haven't missed someone's birthday, have I?" as Arthur and Molly's voices could be heard singing happy birthday.

"No," I say smiling.

"Have they got a friend over whose birthday it is?"

"No," deciding to put him out of his misery, "They've been taught to sing that when washing their hands," he looked confused, "The tune is the right length to hand wash to, to ensure they do it properly, to save lives."

"You're enjoying my confusion," he gives me a hug as the children run into the room.

"Were you going to kiss Mum, because you can and I saw you the other day. I told Uncle Dave…" Arthur says hurriedly.

"And when did you tell Uncle Dave?"

"He phoned him when you were hanging the washing out," Molly says smiling.

"Thanks Molls," Arthur says resigned to being told off.

"Now what have I said about using a phone when I'm not here, that's right, you're not too, now sit down and I'll sort food out." I didn't tackle the kiss issue but will have a chat later, not that I think they shouldn't know we like each other. I can see Matt is dying to laugh, and I am too.

After we've eaten, Arthur and Molly take Bob outside in the garden, "So when do you think he saw us?" Matt asks.

I turn and point towards the double glass doors, "You know Arthur he is a nosey whatsit, probably like now when he was outside, it isn't an issue Matt."

"I know, it's just he's so honest isn't he, he makes me laugh with what he comes out with," we both lean on the island watching them throw a rubber bone for Bob.

"Last day at school tomorrow, lockdown is nearly upon us, the death rate is so high already, they are urging people not to go around to family for Mother's Day, imagine the infection spread if they did, our NHS is wonderful but it would be overwhelmed if we don't do as we are told." Matt puts his arm around her shoulders, he feels so much for her, it feels wrong to feel this happy in this dreadful situation, but you have to make the most of every minute, even when it comes at a critical time for the country, he remembers his grandmother telling him about how she met her husband during the war, the feeling that life was too short and to enjoy it and make every moment special, as you didn't know how long you had. He felt that applied now.

Home schooling begins, we've had two days already, thank goodness for people like Joe Wickes, he is a fitness guy and his PE sessions for children have begun on day one of no school, that keeps these two occupied for 30 minutes every morning, it gives me time to do any accounts, and work out what we are doing for work and school. Luckily there is a lot online from the school, so I tap into that and do a plan for the week, some of which can be done at the table in the walled garden, allowing me to carry on working, I'm also going to get them to start a garden each. I've prepared two small patches in one of the long beds for them to plant seeds, label them and watch them grow.

I try to keep the children up to date on what is happening, but shield them from the worst, they need to know why there is change, we have started emailing some of their friends, and as parents we exchange ideas and support each other.

Mum is going to set them some English projects, as she was a lecturer at a University in English I hope it isn't too hard, but I shouldn't have worried, she's come up with some lovely ideas, them writing stories, she has given them story lines too, she's also going to supervise some lessons with them via Skype on my tablet, while I'm gardening, and little quizzes too, she's going to do Skype every other day at about 3, to end the school day. When we go up to the walled garden in the first week. I tend to take a lunch with us, and then after lunch they read for half an hour with me. It gives us all a good chill.

I'm becoming addicted to the daily briefings now. I just put it on my tablet, while I am cooking, the children at that time are usually playing outside or in their room. I am upset when I see two NHS staff have died, doctors, and I remember Mark Woo and hope he is well. I remind myself to email him later, how many deaths will there be, Italy is escalating fast even with lockdown and Spain.

The farm shops are looking at social distancing in their premises, and are going to advertise to say they have local produce, we are permitted to go out for food but infrequently, so they are doing produce boxes, which I am contributing too, Matt will drop off the produce for collection at the bottom of the drive.

There is talk of building a new purpose-built hospital in London, it is so scary, and the call for businesses to help supply ventilators and ventilator parts, the problem is we have become so reliant on manufacture outside of our country. I think this may change so much in our country, and I hope for the better.

I'm woken by Bob barking furiously in the lounge and then the children scream as a light is shone through the bedroom windows. I jump out of bed and run to them, picking up my phone as I go from the bedside table, Bob is still barking. I gather them to me. I can hear engines roaring and lights are still shining through the curtains. I take the children in to the lounge, there's banging on the doors now. I quickly phone Dave and tell him what is going on, am about to try Matt when a face appears at the strip of window by the front door, in that split second, I put a name to the face. I pull the children and Bob behind the sofa and tell them to stay there.

Voices shout, "We know you're in there…" along with so many swear words I worry even more for the children. I run to the door picking up one of my boots from by the door, as someone hammers on it again, I open it abruptly, sending the person spinning towards me. I push him back with the boot in my hand and he topples over the fence.

"Owen Samuels, you little—" I stop myself swearing, "What the hell are you doing here, you know me, what's this all about."

"Go back to the town," shouts one and another says, "Holiday makers."

"I live in your village. I am here working to produce food for the likes of your parents, the police are aware I am here. I am not on holiday," I shout over the noise from their quad bikes, as I do so I see Matt running down the hill and a police car coming from the lower gate.

One of them spits at me, shouting "I've got the virus, I've got the virus," but I am quick and slam the door shut. I can see through the side window two police officers hurl themselves at a couple of the lads, they tell Matt to stay back. Another car arrives and I see Dave get out, I run over to the children and hold them tight, reassuring them all the time. Bob runs over to the door and is barking and growling at it, trying to go and have his say.

Matt comes in, switches the light on and see us huddled by the sofa, he comes over and holds the children now crying with the fright, we both talk quietly to them telling them it is all over.

"Come on, sit at the bar and I'll get you both hot chocolate," Arthur is asking if they are coming back, he looks fearful. I am angry now. I can see Matt is too. Mugs in hand they start to calm down a bit, then Dave comes in staying by the door, he's joined the angry club too. I can see he is finding it hard to control his temper.

"What were they thinking?" Matt asks.

"They weren't thinking Matt, there isn't a brain between them, they had seen on Face Book that some second home owners were allowing people to stay in holiday accommodation during lockdown, so they thought they'd be clever and come to your barns, which they had heard about in the village as holiday lets."

I indicate the children and he stops saying too much, and in response to Arthur's worried question about them coming back he says, "No Arthur they won't be coming back, they've all been arrested and are on their way to the cells for the night, we are taking the quad bikes too, we might have to leave them to be picked up tomorrow if that's ok, Matt?" he nods, "They must have ridden them on the road to get here, so they won't be getting them back in a hurry."

Molly is leaning on me and I can feel her slipping off to sleep. I go to pick her up but Matt does and takes her through to the bedroom. I take Arthur's hand and encourage him to go back to bed, he is still a bit wary, but eventually is happy when I move Bob's bed into their bedroom for the night, we leave a night light on and the door open.

As I come back in, I'm shaking, with anger and shock. I tell Dave what the one lad said, he goes outside to radio it through, that will be an extra charge, he says, it is the new sport lying about the virus and spitting, but mostly at the police. For me I hope he was lying about having the virus. I get paper towels, bleach spray and gloves and wipe the door bagging everything up even the gloves and wash my hands.

I rest my head on Matt as his arms come round me, "I just can't believe it," I say, "Why, this is day one, what goes through their heads? That Owen Samuels has always been trouble."

Dave walks back in and stays by the door, "Some of it is fear Annie, fear of the unknown."

"But we are all in fear Dave. I don't know how you do it."

"You shouldn't have opened the door Annie, anything could have happened," Matt says.

"I recognised him, and he might be trouble but he's a coward," I look at them both, "I know. I won't open the door if anything ever happened again."

"Did they come in the bottom gate Dave?"

"Yes, looks like it."

"Right, I'll double check security tomorrow. I think I might start shutting and locking the two lower gates in the lane, it's a pain for us in terms of the farm as we have to unlock them if we are working in the fields on the other side of the road but it's worth it for peace of mind."

"I doubt this will happen again mate, but yes extra security will help the children too, just bear in mind the tips are shut we've had fly tipping flagged as a possible issue, so the extra security might help that too. Are the children ok Annie, are you?"

"Yes, I'll check on them again in a minute, and I'm ok just cross now. I think I'll make a cup of tea, do either of you want one?"

"Yes, please love, do you want me to stay over?" Matt asks, and earns himself a look from Dave.

"No tea for me Annie, I've got to get back, Matt can you help me drop these quads over to beyond the gate."

"Put these gloves on," I throw Matt some latex gloves from the cupboard, Dave is wearing some anyway. Matt follows Dave outside while I check the children before making a drink.

"How are you two getting on? I haven't had a chance to speak to you since they moved in."

"We're getting on well Dave," he smiles and nods as if to himself, "But staying over isn't something I'd normally do because of the children, if I do tonight it will be on the sofa, it's not fair on the children."

"That's fine I understand, look after her Matt, she might appear strong but she isn't always, don't hurt her mate."

"Oh god Dave, I won't hurt her, I'm in love with her," Dave looks surprised but then why he thinks, because he knows how Matt has felt for years.

"Does she know?"

"We have very strong feelings for each other, but no I haven't told her yet, it's early days but it feels intense and…"

"Whoa. I don't want to hear any details of my sisters love life," he lifts his hand as if to fend off Matt, but smiles, "You are good for her I can hear it in her voice when we've spoken and I think she's good for you, let's get these bikes off your land," they ride them over to the gate and Matt waits to lock it on his side as Dave goes back for his car, "Right stay safe and look out for them all," with that Dave drives off and Matt locks up and walks back to the barn.

I get back into the kitchen as Matt comes in. I left the two of them asleep with Bob on listening watch.

"Do you want me to stay?" I nod, "I'll light the wood burner and we can sit on the sofa, as I don't think you want to sleep tonight, ok? I've locked the gate and I'll get Don to lock the two lower ones tomorrow."

"Do you want some tea, mine's gone cold, and how about some toast."

"Sounds good to me love," he bends and puts a light to the paper and wood already in the wood burner. I turn the main lights off and just leave the lamps on, we sit on the sofa eating our toast and drinking tea, both lost in thought. We then chat about the farm and the gardens, keeping it light, there's no noise from the children's bedroom, they are both sleeping sound with their guard dog. Matt talks about lambing and how it is going, the strain on the three of them hard, but he says the wonders of those lambs makes it bearable.

"We're going to let some of the older lambs and their mothers out tomorrow, oh I mean today," as dawn begins to creep over the sky, "We'll do it about lunchtime so bring the children up, it will take their minds off what happened, and I'll get Don to pop down and mend the fence." The fence took a bit of a pounding from the quad bikes last night too, as did we all.

"Yes, that'll be good," we just hold each other close, recovering from the events. I still feel shaky, Matt's phone gets a text, he pulls it out of his pocket and looks at the message.

"Phil needs me, he's got a breach birth and finding it difficult," he kisses me lightly on the lips and looks into my eyes, "I was frightened to death last night Annie. I was worried they would hurt you or the children. I feel I've let you down not protecting you all better, I'm sorry love."

"Matt, you have always done the best you can, you can't legislate for people like that, don't apologise, there is nothing to apologise for."

"I couldn't bear it if something happened to you," he holds her face in his hands and just looks into her eyes, she looks back absorbing the love she can see, she takes a deep breath holding back tears.

"I couldn't bear it if anything happened to you too Matt," she wants to say the words that are bubbling under the surface, how much she cares.

As Matt leaves, I think I'll take a shower before the children wake. I check on them first and they are both sound asleep still, in the shower I let the tears fall, feeling safe to let them out, the shock and fear mingling with the feeling of frustration that I couldn't tell him I love him. Showered, I walk into the children's bedroom and two little heads are poking out from under their duvet covers.

"Hello you two," I sit on the edge of Molly's bed, "Is it breakfast in bed then you sleepy heads," they both cheer, "Stay here I'll put the toast on and let Bob out, peanut butter for you Arthur, what do you want on yours, Molly?"

"Can I have peanut butter too Mummy?"

"Yes, of course," I swiftly remove Bob, and let him out mindful the fence is down in places. I return with toast and drinks and they sit up for their breakfasts.

"Mum did Bob sleep here all night?"

"Yes, he did, he's a good boy," Bob has followed the smell of toast and is now hoping for scraps.

"Mummy are those men going to come back?"

"No Molly, Uncle Dave has sorted them out and Matt and Don are locking all of the gates now, so no one can ever get in," I can see them both thinking about it all, I'm going to have to keep an eye on them and make sure we talk as much as possible I don't want them worrying and not speaking about it.

"We're going to do PE with Joe, then some lessons, and at lunchtime we are going up to the fields the other side of the house to see the lambs go out to play, that should be good," I say smiling at them both, they both look suitably impressed.

While they are getting dressed. I hear the tractor outside and see Don sorting the fencing out, I wave and ask him if he wants a drink, he shakes his head and gets on, I'm hoping he will be finished by the time they emerge. I had been worried about taking them past the fence, bringing the fright of last night back.

After PE with Joe, we walk up the hill to the walled garden and I settle them down at the table and chairs, they both have school work to do with drawings for Molly to complete, so a bag of paper and colouring pens accompanied us, along with some lunch for later. I would have stayed down in the barn but the weather is hot and the greenhouse needed to be opened and the poly tunnel doors. I work away, talking to the children as I do, pleased with the growing, there are even shoots on the peach tree in the greenhouse, Don and I pruned all the fruit trees in late winter, with the warm weather the orchard will look lovely soon I think, bursting in to life.

With one child either side of me, we walk up to one of the barns, where lambing has been taking place, on the other side and slightly higher up is the field they are going out into, all this walking is working wonders for my thighs I think, I've a cool bag on my shoulder so if Matt or either of the others wants some food I have supplies, the children haven't mentioned last night since we've been out.

We arrive, and Matt releases the mothers and their lambs and they run up the path to the field, the sheep dogs keeping a watchful eye on them, as the gate is closed, Arthur and Molly run up to it and look at the little bleating lambs, with their mothers calling them.

"Mummy can I have a lamb?"

"Well Molly they like to be with their mummies, so probably not, but you can come up and look at them with me or Matt."

"Mum why can't Bob be a sheepdog, he'd be good," Arthur asks me. I look at Matt for an answer, which he supplies.

"Sheepdogs are usually collie dogs Arthur; they are specialists at looking after the sheep. I don't think Bob is quite tall enough either." We sit them on a low wall, where they can see the sheep, and I give them some lunch and for me and Matt, only some cheese rolls, but it will keep everyone going, with fruit.

"Everything ok?" Matt asks.

"Yes, a few questions first thing but nothing since, but we'll see how bedtime goes," I reply leaning on him. I am beginning to miss the sleep of last night.

"We've sorted the gates, and I've asked Phil to check all perimeter fences and any gates and make it all secure."

"Don's done the fence at the barn. I was worried about going out and them seeing it down."

"I asked him to do that as a priority."

"Thanks love," he gently rubs my shoulder, reassuring me, the children are totally absorbed in the lambs, lunch finished they walk up and down the fence looking at them, marvelling at them bouncing and frolicking now they are outside.

"How did that breach go?"

"It was a bit of a struggle but we sorted it, Dave phoned, they've posted something on the Force Facebook page about the incident, not naming the farm but highlighting the stupidity of it, they have told the press about the spitting, he said another officer had been spat at the same night and has had to isolate, what low life," he kisses my head wondering at people and what goes through their heads.

The days carry on with a similar routine, although no more sheep trips till the weekend, the children were a bit worried about going to bed that first night, but I just tried to give them confidence that nothing is going to happen. I do allow Bob to sleep in there again. I get the feeling this could be permanent, but if it helps the children I don't mind.

I eventually catch up with Matt at the weekend. I haven't slept well, it's all very well telling the children it will be alright, but I woke at any small sound for the last few nights, we've spoken on the phone though. The children are running up and down the lawn kicking a ball about and I'm sitting with a mug of tea in hand on the patio, when Matt appears, I'm so glad to see him. I jump up and give him a hug.

"Hello sweetheart," he engulfs me with his arms. I feel his strong muscles folding around me, a sudden surge of lust warms me, not quite appropriate I think with the children around, but I know he feels it too as he gives me one of his smouldering looks, then releases me to walk over to Molly and Arthur, who both hug him.

"I'll get some drinks. I made chocolate chip cookies earlier, I'll bring some out," not sleeping means I'm up very early, and cooking helps calm me, only thing is I'm having my elevenses at 9. I walk through to the kitchen, and put drinks and cookies on a tray and go back out, by now Matt is sitting and watching as the children run around generally teasing Bob.

"So, Bob's got a permanent job as night watchman now has, he?" Matt asks.

"Yes, and I must check that Arthur doesn't put him on the bed though, but I've a feeling I might be on a losing battle with that one. But if it makes them feel safe. I have no problem with it," I put the drinks down and Matt takes my hand, just looking in my eyes. His strength gives me strength, we chat for a while, then Matt says he'll take the children up to the sheep while I do any jobs in the garden, then he's in the lambing shed for a few hours.

I manage to do loads on the garden, replanting some seedlings but leaving them in the greenhouse as the weather is cooler, and by the look of next week even more so. I found some old long metal cloches, and used some of the plastic from the old poly tunnel to cover them, so am using them to cover some of my seedlings that I planted out in the garden the week before, although the garden is warmer than outside, you can still get frost damage.

Don did manage to repair the heating system in the greenhouse so, if necessary. I can put that on, if the temperature drops a lot. As I collect the children, Matt tells me the PM had tested positive to COVID-19, he's still managing the country though.

We are only going into week two of lockdown, the phone is a godsend, at the barn there is only my mobile so I have to be on top of ensuring it has a full battery all of the time. I get calls, texts and face time calls, which is a boost for all of us. There is plenty coming from the school, there is a lot online too, on nature, stories for bedtime, and of course PE, they love it, watching every day. I'm making the beds as Arthur runs in.

"Mum where's my spiderman outfit? Joe couldn't do PE today so spiderman is doing it," he rifles through a drawer and drags out a load of T shirts including spiderman and runs back into the lounge. I follow to see spiderman taking PE, with a Joe voice. I laugh. Later in the day, I marvel at the extreme contrast between that and the fact a hospital has been completed in London called the Nightingale, will it be enough, can our systems cope? The wonder of childhood hopefully protecting them from the brutal truth and horrors of this world, our world now.

Dave phones later, he sounds a bit down and is worried about Sue, it must be so hard for her being on her own, she is still working but at home, so has some contact, and we speak as often as we can. To ease the tension. I get the usual banter from him, asking me how well I knew Florence Nightingale when I was a student nurse, he's lucky he's not nearby or he might get a bucket of something thrown over him, from a distance of course, which I tell him.

As we speak I say I fully expect an address from the Queen soon, to prove what an unholy mess we're in, and no sooner do I say that out loud than we get her address, she was wonderful and so many people watched, "We will succeed," and if she had anything to do with it we will, and she says "we'll meet again," this makes me cry as does the song every time I hear it, but it is so strong for our times now.

Easter is looming, not a term I would usually use for it, but after a cool week it looks like the weather will be warmer. I feel anxious that people will go out increasing the infection rate, as it is we learn London hospitals are at peak, deaths rising minute by minute, heaping horror on horror, the briefings remain addictive though, just watching quietly on my tablet, trying not to alert the children to all of the trauma, but they have their news and it is put well what is happening, we talk about it as much as they want. Voices are getting louder about issues such as care home deaths. I know it isn't easy to grasp the figures there, but looking at Spain where there have been multiple deaths in care homes, even some abandoned, you feel death numbers will rise here.

What plays on my mind the most was an article I read about Ebola virus in Africa more people died from other causes there than Ebola, because people were frightened to go to hospitals and put up with pain and illness ultimately dying from cancers and heart disease. I hope that isn't to be reflected here. I need to limit my reading and watching of news it can take you over very quickly, Mum and I discuss this in one of her many calls, you need to know what is happening and what is happening close to you, but not every news channel.

She is sewing again and enjoying doing something, she is making scrubs bags so that staff can put dirty scrubs straight into a bag and then into a machine at home, not handling them, around the village where they live everyone is doing their bit, you realise then that good does out weight bad, thinking of those louts the other night.

The Tuesday after Easter sees me in the garden checking plants as we had frost last night, it is a bright clear morning and jumpers are needed, the children are walking around looking at plants and reading labels, a task I have given them, they draw some of the leaves in their note books as it isn't warm enough to sit for long. We decide to wander up to the sheep fields where we see Don and Matt. The children go to the fence and peer at the new lambs, pointing at ones they think they have seen before.

"Look I don't know if you two want an hour or so on your own. I know it is a struggle, but I can take them for a walk and we can go down to the pond and see the ducklings on the island," I look at Matt to see what he thinks, as we are in a sense one family on the farm, there is not an issue with Don being with the children and me and Matt, "Only the wife thought it would be nice for you to have a bit of time occasionally."

"That's very kind Don, if you're sure, it would be good to catch up without little ears picking everything up," Matt says.

"No problem," so we tell them Don is going to take them to the pond in a bit and we walk down towards the house.

"Do you think he knows what we might get up to?" I ask going bright red. Matt pulls me to him and laughs.

"You're blushing Annie, and I hope he hasn't read my mind it is not something that should be seen, other than by you," he releases me and we try to walk not run.

As we get into the kitchen, he pulls me to him in the deepest of kisses, locked together, where I'd like to stay forever, his hands run up and down my body, gently cupping my bottom and pulling me into him, "So what were you thinking?" I ask barely getting my words out.

"Wait and see," he groans into my mouth, and gently pushes me towards the stairs and the bedroom, as we get there the kisses grow more passionate and desperate for each other. I can feel myself melting under his kisses, passion overcomes us both. I cry out his name, he clutches me to him, then I collapse onto his tense shoulders, licking them, salty from heat and sweat, the taste of him, he holds me so tightly it's as if we want to become one.

"Have we got time to go again he whispers near my ear," we both laugh and that breaks the tension of what has surpassed anything we have done before. The way he makes me feel I want him time and again, just to have that tenderness and passion and heat, is incredible, and the love, it feels incredibly intimate.

I look up and look into his eyes. I see what I feel mirrored there, it steadies my breathing and I hold his face kissing his lips, his eyes and down his jaw, in awe of everything he gives to me. Showing how much I love him. I then just rest my forehead against his.

"We'd better get dressed," he says reluctantly, feeling the warmth of her body on him, what he wouldn't give to spend nights with that body next to him.

Matt goes to collect the children and I go to sort out the inevitable food, that punctuates the day at regular intervals. I stop and watch them coming down the hill, this man has got under my skin so quickly. I feel I have it bad, how has he gone from friend to lover in such a short time, but it isn't just the sex, which is off the scale, it's so much more, my emotions feel so involved with his, so close, nothing like this has happened before.

Hell

All around I can see nature coming to life. I look up and see the clear skies, no vapour trails. I hope when all this is over the world nurtures what we are seeing now, it's been a busy week but it is good to enjoy what is around us, I've hardly seen Matt this week, on Sunday he had to go and help Fred Blount on the next farm with a difficult calf birth. I was a bit reluctant to let him, but they all help each other virus or no virus he said, afterwards he said he would just keep at a distance until he was sure that he hadn't been exposed to anything, to make sure we were safe.

I've opened the greenhouse vents and doors as it is warm and we walk back to the barn to have some lunch, the children were painting pictures today as it is still holidays. The table is just outside the front door now so I can see them while I get lunch. I have the radio on and am singing to a new song, just then my phone rings, it's Don.

"Hi Don, how…" I begin but he interrupts me.

"I can't get hold of Matt. I've tried ringing and he's not answering. I knocked on the door and no answer, but it was locked and I haven't got a key," I think no he didn't reply to my text from earlier. I thought he must be on the farm out of signal, "The thing is, Annie, he told me last night he didn't feel well, he was coughing and he sounded strange." I feel like someone has poured iced water over me. I go cold. I clutch the side of the worktop to steady myself my legs jelly.

"I've got a key, I'll go up," I turn off the call and grab some drinks and a couple of puzzle books, throw them into my rucksack, I'll have to take the children with me, quickly summing up how I can do this. I get the keys and call the children.

"We've got to go up to the farm Arthur, Molly, quickly," I manage to lock the door, my hands shaking, and attach the lead to Bob. I can leave them in the sunken garden, Bob will be with them. I walk as quickly as I can up to the farm, the children are ok. I think they can sense something is wrong, but sit quietly with Bob as I rush to the farmhouse and manage to unlock the door. I step into the kitchen and Matt is in a chair but he's sprawled across the table top, head on his arms.

"Matt," I take a step in, he just manages to lift his head slightly, his arm outstretched his hand stopping me.

"No, don't come… I think I have the virus," he can barely get his words out, I look at him, he is short of breath, trying to gulp air in, he's sweating profusely too, his face so flushed, yet his colour is terrible, bluish, dark shadows under his eyes, the effort to say what he did leaves him exhausted and he collapses onto the table.

Fear grips me. I never understood that term, but now I know, someone is holding my heart in a vice, ice running through my veins. I feel sick and every muscle is taut, my hands are clutched at my sides my knuckles white. Adrenaline rushes through me waking me into action, it has only been seconds but it felt like a lifetime looking at him. I get my phone out of my pocket and dial 999. I rush to the steps, just checking the children are still where I left them, they are, Arthur gives me his thumbs up.

As I finish the call I go back inside, "Matt I've called for an ambulance, you'll be alright darling, stay with us, I'm going to phone Don to open the lower gates, and I'll just go and open the top ones for the ambulance," he doesn't move apart from his chest, his breathing worse, trying desperately to drag air into his lungs.

I run down through the yard and phone Don, "Don he's really ill," struggling to say the words. I hear Don swear, "I've had to call an ambulance, can you unlock the bottom gates, I'll do the top ones."

"Oh god Annie of course I will, he should never have gone over to Fred's. I told him not to, I'll call them later, thank god he stayed away from all of us and the children, I'm off, I'll let you know of any problems," with that he was gone. I unlock the top gates and push them back securing them with the bricks used, so the ambulance can get in the yard, as I do, the song I had been listening to comes back to me.

"In times like these … all about love, the love I feel, love, love and I haven't told him," it goes over and over in my head, tears well in my eyes and my throat feels blocked. I get to the kitchen and check on Matt, he hasn't moved at all.

I must speak to the children and I run over to them, Bob barks as I approach.

"Arthur, Molly, Matt isn't very well," before I can say I've called an ambulance, Arthur interrupts me, clutching at my hand.

"Has Matt got the pandemic?" I can hear the fear in his voice.

"He's certainly poorly darling, but I've had to call an ambulance and we'll see what they have to say," I can hear sirens from the main road. I hope it's for here. I hold them both, "We have to be brave and give all our strength to Matt to get better, stay here as I think that's the ambulance coming up to the yard," I hug them both and run to the yard.

The crew jump out, I stay back, they are kitted up in visors, gowns, and gloves. I tell them the history, and that Matt has no underlying health problems, but even saying that I know that doesn't make you immune to this illness, it gets the fit and the young. I don't know how I'm calmly relating to them his symptoms; they go into the house and I just have to wait. I walk to the steps to watch, even with visors on I see a look pass between them. I put my head in my hands, god help him I think, one of the crew comes towards me and I back out letting him get on with his job, he brings a stretcher to the kitchen steps then lifts it up into the kitchen.

I walk away and look at the children, they are just sitting. I can feel the anxiety radiating off them. I just shout some reassurance. It takes some time for them to stabilise Matt, and then they are coming out with him on a stretcher, my heart breaks, the tears now flowing down my face for him.

As they begin to load him. I go as near as I can, "Matt, I love you. I love you Matt, please hear me, we all need you home. I love you Matt," I turn to the paramedic, "Please tell him for me," I plead, she nods, she has my contact details as I am next of kin.

I know I can't go with him; no one is allowed to do that anymore; I've seen relatives on television saying how dreadful it is to see the ambulance with their loved one in it go to hospital without them. I know now how they felt. I feel as if they are tearing my heart out. They shut the doors and go back down the track. I feel like lying on the floor and crying for ever, cursing myself for not telling him how I felt before, our love torn from us. I lock the back door, putting hand sanitiser on my hands, then quickly secure the gates and go to the children, both are now crying. I can hear the ambulance sirens as they hit the main road, oh god, oh god. We just huddle. I can't help crying now too.

"Will he come back?" Molly whispers.

"Yes, he will darling," I hope, oh god I hope so.

"Daddy didn't," they both look at me.

"Daddy was at war," this is a war, are we going to win any battles, we need to win Matt's battle, "Matt is going to come back and when he does, we are going to help him get well again."

"Didn't we help Daddy?" Arthur asks.

"Yes, a lot of people helped Daddy, but horrible people had hurt him and no matter how everybody tried they couldn't get him better."

"But we're going to get Matt better, aren't we?"

"Yes, Arthur we are," I crush them to me with my arms wrapped around them, my arms have to be the strong ones now. I say a silent prayer to any god up there to help Matt.

We walk down the hill to the barn and I sit them down on their beanbags and give them some food, bits to tempt them, Bob sits with them, my phone rings then. I nearly have heart failure but it's Dave. He knows because Don phoned him, but he'd only just picked up the message, he was beside himself for not being here with us, and he wanted to come over and support us. I told him no, to be honest I couldn't talk about any of it, and I just said I'd be in touch.

Then later, the call came I'd been dreading, the hospital. I go outside the barn and lean on the wall.

"Annie, Annie Davis?"

"Yes, that's me."

"You're down as next of kin for Matt Abbot," my heart nearly stops, and I slide down the wall dropping to the floor as my legs give way.

"Annie, it's Francesca Smith, we worked together," I murmur something, "I'm looking after Matt. I work in ITU at the moment."

"How is he?" I barely manage to ask.

"He's very poorly Annie, we have had to sedate and ventilate him, the infection has caused a lot of damage to his lungs so we are breathing for him, but you know about ventilators anyway Annie, but you need to know that the immune system which fights illness, with this virus it does damage to the body, for instance lung damage," is she saying that has what has happened with Matt already? Fran goes on to tell me what they have done and what they will be doing. I begin to breath, "You and Matt are together, Annie?"

"Yes. I run a market garden from here, and we are… together, and he has no other family, he lost both his parents, me and the children live in a barn on his farm, so I can carry on food production, oh Fran. I can't believe it," I sob.

"Annie, we will do our complete and utter best for him, but you must be in no doubt he is very ill. I will speak to you as much as possible also one of the Consultants John Peebles will phone too, we want to keep you up to speed on everything."

"Do you talk to the patients Fran?"

"Yes, love you know we all do."

"Will you tell him over and over how much I love him, and how he is needed here, please. I can't really say any more, words just... I feel numb."

"I'm here Annie, and yes as you know we do talk to the patients, conscious or not, now is there anyone with you apart from the children."

"No. I told my brother Dave not to come, there is help on the farm, the farm manager and his son, but I'm on my own with the children and I have the market garden to run..." My words just slow to a halt.

"OK I will keep in touch, not just for Matt," she rings off. I lean on the wall and try to get myself together, the only way I will get through this is to keep busy I think, make sure I can keep these businesses going, so there is something for Matt when he comes home and he will.

I've seen the impact of this disease in the news, how being ventilated affects them, how they have to keep turning the patients as the lungs are so inadequate. I have to keep going and not think about this too much, little knowledge is a dangerous thing, trouble is I have a lot of knowledge, and that is not good either.

I wipe my face and go back into the barn, the children are still sitting nibbling food, oblivious to the dramatic news I received. I manage to get through the rest of the day and bath them and put them to bed. I haven't told them about Matt being ventilated as I don't think they need that, but tell them he is in the hospital now and being looked after.

I text Mum and Sue who have both tried to phone. I tell them I can't speak at the moment. I want to get myself together before I do, they send love, Mum wanting to come up, but no she mustn't. I text Don an update too and say we will meet up tomorrow. I don't go to bed I just sit on the sofa wrapped in a throw and think of Matt, all our loving, and how much I now realise he means to me; it is a love that is so deep, it is a different type of love to the one I had with Sam. There is nothing to compare, it is just that different.

As I sit drinking tea. I think about how we are going to get through this, as dawn breaks, I take my tea and sit at the table outside looking at the beauty around me, hearing the bird song and smelling the hawthorn blossom on the hedges nearby, accentuated by the lack of pollution and noise, all of this continues to make the break in my heart bigger, all of this is Matt. I couldn't believe last summer when he said he was taking over the farm. I didn't think it fitted him, but being near him and working with him and being here. I know it does, this feeling begins to creep into my wounded heart and puts a temporary dressing on it as I sit and breath, breath I think, Matt breath and come back to all of this, to us. Even with no sleep I begin to have some clarity to my thoughts. I must keep all of this going for him, for us. I am not letting this man go. I am going to manage for both of us.

I go and shower and dress and decide on my first steps. I need to sort his house out, it needs a deep clean because of the virus, but also when he comes home it has to be clean, tidy and ready for him, if I can get a lot done today. I can then concentrate the next couple of days on the garden and produce. I have promised some salad and other items for the farm shops at the beginning of next week, the children can play in the garden at the front of the house where we had the barbeque. Matt had put up an old swing ball game for them, which they haven't had time to use, Bob can come up with them too, as long as they keep the gate shut. I can leave the front door of the house open and they can shout me if they need anything.

Plan sorted at least in my head, the children wander in to the kitchen and I sort breakfast out and we talk about Matt, and how he will be doing, and how much he loves them both. As they are munching their cereal. I make their beds and get out their clothes. As they get dressed. I put together all the cleaning things I'll need. I know there is cleaning fluids up at the house but I want my bleach sprays and wipes so I can wipe down hard surfaces first.

The children are happy when they see the swing ball. I put my bag by the front door and zoom round and go in through the kitchen putting my gloves on as I open the door, my breath catches in my mouth as I see some of the wrappings on the floor of the equipment and drugs they used on Matt. I visualise him collapsed on that table. I shake myself and head for the front door, opening it, letting air in. I get the cleaning stuff and head upstairs, all the while checking the children are ok out there.

I go into his bedroom, the memories flood in, good ones, brilliant ones. I want to sit and wallow in them, remember my wonderful Matt, the man I love. I think I'm going to have to block those for now or I won't get anything done. I won't survive, think about the beautiful times later Annie, get on. I strip the bed and go down and find the washing machine, it's in one of the rooms off a corridor from the kitchen, blimey I didn't know they still did top loader machines, then I realise it is an original, oh well. I put everything in and put it on, crossing my fingers.

I run back upstairs and start wiping all hard surfaces down, opening windows, letting the warm spring air in. I tackle the bathroom next, piling towels on the landing floor. I clean that room to within an inch of its life, open the window as I will be overcome by fumes of bleach if I'm not careful. I hang the first wash out on the line in the garden where the children are, I've washed my hands so much, as I change my gloves repeatedly. I give them some drinks and biscuits and we sit for a while, they want to colour their colouring books for a bit so they stay at the bench table, although a school day it will do them good to do what makes them happy.

I begin the hard surfaces down stairs now, door handles, light switches, you name it. I know how long it can live on these surfaces. I look at the sofa and throws and cushions on there, the covers and throws will need washing I strip them off, it looks like Matt slept in here, it takes my breath away, he couldn't get up the stairs, carry on Annie. I make my way to the kitchen, carrying the washing, which I dump by the machine, then I clear the detritus on the floor first and bag it, hard surfaces next, filling the dishwasher with plates and cutlery left on the draining board and any at the front of cupboards, am I going over the top I think, possibly, probably, but it has to be ready for him when he comes back.

I force the anxious bubble down, towels finished and in the drier I am pleased to see is new. I put the sofa covers in the wash next. I hope this machine can take all of this, then I tackle the fridge, empty most of the contents into a bin and then walk outside to the bins with all the rubbish. As I do. I see Don coming over on the quad. I must look in a state as he stops abruptly and asks if I'm ok.

"Yes, thanks Don, I've cleaned the house through, well, I mean I've washed down hard surfaces and done the washing any vacuuming can wait. I just have to mop the kitchen floor. I want it all ready for when Matt comes home," I see him look at me as if I am half or all mad, "He will come home, Don."

"I know he will Annie, he is a strong man," we talk briefly about what work is ongoing and what I can do. I leave him to his jobs and go through the kitchen and along the hall. I can see the children sitting at the table colouring. I just have a couple more jobs, then I will be giving them quality time.

I go into Matt's study. I use the wipes to do some hard surfaces then clean the laptop and keyboard. I know at some point I am going to have to check emails and look at accounts, as I look down I see a picture of me, it must have been taken on holiday as behind me are Dave and Arthur fishing, and Molly is in front of me, leaning back into to my arms, we are both laughing at Matt, yes I remember now he took the photo, we had some fun that day with the boys fishing, fancy him printing that out and keeping it from back then. It stuns me a bit, did he have feelings for me then, or did he only print it out recently I wonder. I will ask him. I will.

I wonder where he keeps his passwords, then I realise the post it notes stuck to the lamp are the passwords, what is he like. I think, shaking my head, and the very faintest of smiles touches my lips, those lips that he devoured time and again.

I lock up and we go back to the barn for some lunch and quality time, we'll walk up later and put the washing away and shut the windows, when I go to water. Don had opened the greenhouse and poly tunnels for me earlier.

I kept my phone with me all the time, frightened I might miss a call. I put it on charge, then we sit at the table outside by the door, the children happily eating, which seems to be a favourite pastime. I look at my hands they are red raw from hand washing. I just look at them. I wonder about the look Don gave me, am I going back? I start to shake. I put my mug down quickly before I spill my tea.

No, I don't want to go to that dark place again, but is there a choice. I feel it overwhelming me, when Sam died I, well. I lost it. I grieved the man he was before, the hurt afterwards adding to that grief. I used up every ounce of energy, cleaning, washing. I just had excess nervous energy. I couldn't sleep, couldn't eat. I just ran, was driven. I was always driven with Sam, but it felt like someone had given me something, then I hit a brick wall and collapsed, by that time Mum and Dad were there and caught me, figuratively speaking, the GP gave me something to calm me and I spent days in bed.

I don't want to go back there, the darkness, the anxiety, Matt has helped me so much, calmed me, balanced me. I look again at my hands, it has been less than 24 hours, am I becoming her again?

"Here you are Mummy," I turn and look at Molly, "Here's your hand cream," she hands me the tube of hand cream I keep in the kitchen; she sits down and watches as I put some on my hands, smiling at me, my heart going out to her kindness, and to her thoughtful act, she carries on nibbling her chocolate chip cookie, oblivious to the raw feeling inside me too, hand cream won't help that.

I am not going back. I am not the woman I was with Sam, life was slower with Matt, he supported all I did and me, we were always busy but his calm manner helped me. I want to be that me again, he was so good with the children, listening and spending time with them. I know I have to work hard but I can't fall here, there is only me, for them as much as for him. I need to get up every day and live, and ensure they live the right life too, be clear headed, get everything ready for Matt, do the best for the farm and garden, it has to shine for him, reflecting my love for him.

When he comes home, there will be a long road ahead for us. I know that. I have to have strength for two, but I look at the children and think, no four.

I try a bit of lunch, make another cup of tea, wrapping my hands around the mug. I felt chilled earlier even though it is a warm day, but I'm warming up now. Although I wish I could have held Matt and kissed him when I found him. I realise he was protecting me and the children, keeping away from all of us since he went over to the farm was a good but difficult decision. What if I became ill, how would we manage, who would look after the children? Mum and Dad couldn't come up, Dad is over 70 for one thing, and has had heart surgery, so is vulnerable, and it would break the rules we have been given. It would have to be Dave.

As if reading my mind Dave phones and says he's coming over, we have a heated discussion about this and in the end, I say we'll meet him at the farm entrance gate. I have a quick shower, then I kit the children out for a bike ride down there, the bikes being on the garden not up at the house thank goodness, it will do them good. I had picked up Matt's farm keys earlier so I could open the gates without asking Don.

I was reluctant to see Dave as I always felt he could read me like a book and presently, I'm not a good book to be thumbing through. I also don't really feel like talking, but I know him, he'll climb every gate and end up on my doorstep. We will socially distance. I shake my head at that. I could become so angry with Matt's neighbour, but I let others deal with it. I know Don has had words with him, one of them was infected but they didn't realise, and they needed help, what else could they do.

The children are excited about the ride. I walk along with Bob on his lead, we get to the first gate and unlock it and then just close it behind us, we go down the track, the hedges full of nesting birds. I can hear Arthur telling Molly about the birds, Matt gave him a book on birds recently and he marked those that he would see on the farm, so he is into it big time. We get through gate two and amble down and at the bottom see Dave parked on the other side of the gate, off duty for once.

As I see him. I think how I could do with a hug, my body is aching for strong arms to wrap around me, to take everything away, as I think of strong arms Matt flashes through my mind, those strong arms that hold me and keep me safe.

The children race up to the gate, shout hello, then turn and race back up the track giving me and Dave a chance to talk.

"You look terrible," I pale even more at his bluntness, what does he expect? "I guess you didn't get much sleep?"

"I didn't go to bed. I just sat on the sofa," I was afraid I might miss a call, "I'll try tonight," I tell him what I did this morning, trying to put some lift into my flat voice. I see the worried look he gives me, and then I mention the photo in Matt's office, "I wonder when he printed it out Dave?"

"I'd say straight after the holidays."

"No, all that time ago," I am so surprised.

"Matt has had feelings for you for a long time Annie," I must have looked aghast, for a long time? "You know he loves you?"

"He's not said…" but a spark lights in me, giving me a lift.

"He told me the other night, reassuring me how he felt, he thinks the world of you."

Tears course down my face, "As they put him in the ambulance, I told him I loved him. I hope he heard me."

"Look I'm sorry this is happening again…"

"No, I'm not going there Dave, he will come back," I change the direction of the conversation, "The nurse looking after him is Fran Smith, remember I worked with her in A/E."

"I vaguely remember her."

"I've told her that every time she is with Matt and talking to him to tell him how much I love him and need him back with us."

"I wish I could hug you sis." I want that so much too. We just stare at each other both with tears flowing now.

"I'll be alright Dave. I definitely had a wobbly this morning, but I'm not going back there," I say with finality, "Do you understand?"

He nods, "I've just got to keep busy but in a realistic way, there is so much to do, but I will enjoy what has to be done, my main aim is to be a good parent to the children and get everything ready for Matt to come home," we say our goodbyes, me wiping my face on my sleeve, the children are still racing up and down so I make my way up to them.

Dave watches her go walking disconsolately up the track and his heart bleeds for her, he leans on the car head on his arms, he can't believe this is happening, Matt is a fit healthy man, it is so overwhelmingly unfair, he wishes there was something he could do, he waits until they have gone through the last gate, he gets in his car and decides on a few things, firstly he needs to speak to his parents, what she won't need is what he nearly did and that is give her reminders of losing Sam, linking the two events, Annie he feels is just holding it together, so to keep it light, not to go over the past, text and still help with home schooling.

Next, he's going to speak to Don on the phone and see what practical things he could help with, perhaps delivering the produce for them. And finally, he's going to ring his boss and make sure that patrols just keep an extra eye on the farm for security, he knows it won't be an issue as they tend to drive around the area frequently anyway, but it would give him peace of mind.

They drop the bikes back and walk up to the house, the bikes are better at the barn but will have to go in the spare bedroom if it rains. She puts the sheets in the house, hanging the covers on the overhead pulley drier, she closes all the windows, she will come in and vacuum next week, she picks up Matt's laptop and phone, the chargers and passwords, she picks up the picture Matt took of her and Molly and puts it with everything else, it will be something she will want to see every minute of every day, showing her how this man loved her from afar.

When they get back to the barn, the children settle down to some television and she contemplates food, she has enough eggs to sink a battle ship and potatoes, so she starts to make a Spanish omelette and will put salad with it, just then her phone rings, she sees it's the hospital, withheld number, she grabs it and goes outside, round the front of the barn.

"Annie it's Fran," she takes me through how Matt is and then passes me over to the consultant, he is good and sounds determined and his voice gives me confidence, he talks about a long road for Matt, how very poorly he is, how they are obviously focused on his acute respiratory failure, but also aware of the need to help the heart deliver blood to other organs, he chats about what those drugs are that will help him and what might be the pathway forward for Matt, but he reiterates that the pathway can change daily and even hourly, depending on his condition and whether other factors come in to play.

I ask what those could be, he talks about his kidney function and heart, he says it is a rapidly evolving picture, with little comprehensive data to work with. I think he is only young how can this thing do this to my big strong man. John the consultant also says this is a long haul, leaving me in no doubt.

"Annie," I get put back to Fran. I feel over taken by all the information, even though I worked in A/E I knew what the work entailed in critical care units, but being on the receiving end as a relative and with this deadly virus, it is different, all my knowledge flies out of the window, and because of the stress concentration does too, so I try to note down all they tell me straight afterwards, to look at it and think more clearly later.

"We will call you daily about this time, it might not always be me, we only talk to one relative, and you can pass on the information yourself to any other relatives," well I think there is only me, "We are getting some phones and iPads so we can relay messages to our patients, as it is so hard without relatives here for them. As soon as I have one for Matt, I want you to put some messages on, and we'll play them for him. I tell him all the time about you and how much you love him. I also tell him some tales of you and I in A/E, just to help him."

"Thanks Fran. I should have put his phone with him, you are so kind, I'll speak to you soon."

"Annie don't beat yourself up about things, we have phones so don't worry on that score."

Only day two I think, this is going to be a long journey from what they are saying, the adrenaline courses through me at each call, then disappears and that's when I feel like I could just collapse.

Fran had sent me, or someone anyway, a good information PDF, so informative, it guided me through various things, including how to talk to the children about Matt, and although he isn't a relative he is very special to them and they need to know, it says to be clear and straight forward with them, to speak to them when we are doing a happy activity together, the information also said to start a diary for when Matt comes out of hospital, showing all we have done and linking into events. I think about this while I'm cooking and feel that Arthur and Molly should contribute to this, in fact knowing those two they will do it all.

I get through tea, baths and bedtime stories, the children have obviously been talking about Matt as they tell me they want to do some pictures for him and make a card, telling him to get well soon. So that's what we plan for the morning. I do go to bed, and collapse into a dream filled sleep, my phone in my hand, the picture Matt took propped up on the bedside table.

The weekend flies by with jobs, fun for the children including making cards for Matt, while they are doing that I start to tell them plainly how Matt is and how he has a machine helping him to breath, they ask a few questions, which I answer as best I can, then I suggest we start a diary for Matt, to tell him what we've been doing, they love that, and I think it will help them to focus on him coming home, keep hoping Annie.

I will find some paper, I'm sure I have a pad up at the garden we can use, they can draw pictures too in the diary. Fran also reiterated what is in the information PDF, and that is don't look at social media too much, limit news and what you read on the internet, which I do anyway.

With all of this I am also checking what needs picking for the farm shops tomorrow. Don't know how I am going to do that with the children in tow, it isn't really fair to do that first thing to them, before home schooling, but I don't have much choice.

Dave rings, "I'm going to come up to the farm and do your picking tomorrow," is he a mind reader?

"You?"

"What's the matter with me doing it?"

"Dave, you don't know one end of a lettuce from another."

"Well, you're going to have to teach me then, I've been thinking about it and spoke to Sue, how were you going to do it with the children?" I'm quiet, "Right email me what needs picking, send a few photos so I know what is needed and any You Tube videos that might be helpful," love him to bits but there's more work there than me doing the picking, but for the children it would be good not to go up there.

"Ok I'll get it all together."

"I'll pick, put it in to those boxes you use and take them down to the farm shops, I've spoken to Don and he's going to unlock the gates so I can get up easily. I won't be seeing anyone, I'll wipe clean any tools I use or handles I touch, and if it all helps you and the children, then that's what we're going to do, if there is anything complicated in the future, we can cross that one when we come to it, but you can't do it all Annie."

"Yes, I know, you're right, we're going to take Bob for a slightly damp walk in a bit and I'll photograph what needs to be picked, and say where in the garden or poly tunnels, I'll make sure the boxes are accessible too, then after this first time you should be ok with most things. Thanks Dave. I really appreciate it."

The death toll is over 20,000 now, should we have gone into lockdown earlier, would it have made a difference, I'm sure someone will say one way or another in the future. Matt remains the same, although they have slightly changed some treatment, he is still ventilated. I visualise him on the bed with all the tubes, it doesn't take much imagination, as we see pictures all the time on the news, but it is scary when you know someone you love is there, and without you. I just keep repeating breath Matt, and come home, choking back tears.

When John the consultant phoned earlier, he asks me if I would be willing to put Matt forward to participate in a trial, a drug trial, what they call a randomised control trial, some getting no drugs, a control group, other cases getting unproven drugs, he allowed me time to think it through. I checked about the type of trial, he had said that it was being rolled out through over a 170 hospitals and was set up via Oxford University, what could I say, if it gave Matt a chance and helped others then I was willing to put him forward, it was a decision that whirled around my head for days and worried me that I might have put him at risk, but John was so reassuring that I felt his confidence, those getting the drugs were picked at random, so he might not have anything different.

I'm so glad Dave is doing the picking, it took quite a few emails and conversations to be clear what he had to do, he had already spoken to the farm shops, so they knew it would be him delivering. It is a relief, so the children can start this new school week after Matt's hospitalisation with a good routine. I've paperwork to do and I need to go through emails on Matt's laptop, so am here for them all day. I will try and do this most of the week, the weather forecast is not too good, rain, which the garden will appreciate. I can just go up after school and check, and they can have a run, in wellies and jackets.

As the week goes on. I get calls from the hospital every day and speak to Fran quite a bit, she has given me a number to phone to record a message for Matt, that was hard. I didn't want him to hear me upset, but wanted to tell him how much I loved him, the next one I will get the children to speak too.

Arthur does watch some of the news, and he is so impressed with Captain Tom Moore, he reached his 100th birthday that week, Arthur wants to do something himself, he knows he did his 100-lap challenge for the NHS and the nurses.

"What do you want to do Arthur?"

"I'm going to walk to the gate and back every day after school," he's obviously thought this through.

"What about the 2.6 challenge, you could do the trip to the gate 26 times," we look up the 2.6 challenge on the internet and he chooses his charity, he knows how much the NHS needs money but looking at the other charities who will be losing money, particularly with no fund raising like from the London Marathon, he chooses Help for Heroes, which leaves me with a lump in my throat.

The walk to the gate is about 400 meters, he wants to walk there and back every day after school, as we talk about it, he thinks he could do the walk twice, so he could get to his 26 in 13 days, so he's set himself a target.

"Mum when I reach my target Matt might be home," I wish and hope, as his enthusiasm grips us all. Molly asks me for her pocket money and promptly gives it to Arthur. Mum and Dad are involved too and Dave has told his mates at work, we will be keeping an eye on his Just Giving page.

After the walk up and down the road, we wander up the hill, to check all produce, when I begin thinking about something Fran said, how difficult it is getting food, I'm wondering if Nick at the Bugle would be interested in supplying some meals for the NHS staff. I can give him some produce. I have early carrots and onions, and potatoes stored from last year, he could do shepherds pies. I'll give him a ring later.

I might get Sue involved as Dave says she is feeling isolated, she had problems with her neighbours in the warm weather the woman next door spent hours outside on her phone on speaker phone, so poor Sue either had to listen to the woman's conversations or go indoors, Dave got her some noise cancelling head phones, but as Sue said the good part about being outside at the moment is to hear the bird song and the new silence.

Sue knows Nick at the Bugle so she has given him a ring, she also thought about doing something for the police, as they are in the same boat finishing shifts and no food available, and probably not thought about at all, she is also helping to galvanise a few friends into some baking as well, she's also phoned the local care home and said we'd include them in any food parcels, Nick is going to pick up the baking before he distributes food, Don left the veg for him by the bottom gate. I think this has helped Nick too as he was going stir crazy, he said, so I can leave it to them all to sort now. I just provide what I can.

Matt is holding his own they say, we are in to day 10 since his hospitalisation, when the children have gone to bed, I indulge in time thinking about everything that has happened with us, how quickly we went from friends to lovers, and what lovers, and then to something more personal, loving. I try so hard to keep it together, but some nights it is too much and I do cry for him, thinking of him, so poorly, without me by his side. I just want to hold him and urge him to get better. I feel he would with my arms wrapped around him. I hope he hears my messages and I hope it brings him back to us.

The children's schooling is doing well, they are both bright, Molly had been a bit behind in her class, originally the teachers thought it was because of the loss of Sam and the effect on my life and in turn the children. She has blossomed in the last year, so they were probably correct. Arthur likes the routine of schooling, and I'm glad we have that, it might be that some days I still have to take them up to the garden, but even then, they have work to get on with.

They are making a card a day for Matt, and now have them on string on the wall in their bedroom, so we can count how many days he's been away from us. They want to photograph them and put them on the iPad so he can see, when he wakes up Molly says. They have taken over the diary, which I thought they would, telling him about Arthur's 2.6 challenge and his fund raising, Molly tells him about her cake making and how she is going to make a big cake for when he comes home, it has been good to do this. I don't contribute to their diary, but I do start one myself, telling him how I feel.

It's the week approaching VE day, I'm worried about it, like I was at Easter, but now people are beginning to flout the regulations as it has been a long time on lockdown, for me I don't know if I ever want to go out again. I fear people will mix and then the figures will go even higher, we have the highest death toll in Europe. I agree with the deputy chief medical officer, when she just hung her head and said the toll was too many. The weather is getting warmer too. I have spoken about VE day to the children and explained it all to them.

Mum has as well and set them a project, which included for Molly making bunting, thanks Mum as if I haven't got enough to do, I now have to find some material, preferably red white and blue. I know Matt's mum liked to sew, we go up to the house and I find her box of materials and sewing things. I find some different colours and put them aside to take down with us, not a job I'm looking forward to as I can't sew. But I'm sure I can cut out some triangles.

Mum and Dad have been good, they have spoken to the children and are continuing to do some home schooling with them, but we only text about Matt. I am pleased as I find it hard to talk about him, our love is quite new and I want to talk to him about it before I talk too much to others.

Dave is coming up regularly to harvest produce for the farm shops, and I am planting out plugs from seeds that have come on in the greenhouse, and then planting more seeds, like leeks, courgettes. I check on the fruit trees in the garden and put some fleece over them, as a frost is forecast that night, Arthur is doing his project about VE day, he is writing a story about the celebrations, he even asks Dad what he remembered, as Dad wasn't born then it wasn't a huge amount but he did remember stories his mum told him about a street party and bunting, but Arthur was happy and was looking up pictures with me later. I don't think Dad was too happy at being cast at such an old age.

Molly and I are trying to make bunting, Sue thought it hilarious that I was doing something that involved sewing, as she knew my skills didn't lie in that direction, but me and Molly make a good job, we used some pinking scissors from Matt's mum's sewing box to cut out the triangles, and I then stapled the triangles onto binding tape, so we could hang it from the down pipes and along over the windows, we also managed to put some along the fence by the table.

Molly wanted to make some cupcakes for our party, there is only the three of us but she is insisting it is a party. I find some sausages in the house freezer and make sausages on sticks and go retro with cheese and pineapple too. I will need to get Dave to drop some everyday shopping off for me, as am scraping the bottom of the barrel a bit. I have meat and salad and eggs, but not things for the children like the odd crisp or some ham, I'll text him later.

All through all of this, I never stop thinking about Matt, how he is, hoping he is improving with every minute of the day. I want to be there but I can't, how must that feel for him? I am not back to the dark days of years ago, but I do feel that anxiety all the time, just bubbling underneath, waiting for me to lower my guard and get in deeper, but I seem to manage it somehow, and keep the darkness away. I am sleeping a bit better, but wake early, worrying.

Arthur wants to stand for the two minutes silence, so we put the television on and see people all over the country observing the silence and remembering those lost. I think many people are also thinking of those lost now, the NHS workers and carers and bus drivers, the list goes on, all exposed doing their jobs, but without those who died during the war we wouldn't have today. We see the fly past of the spitfire on the television for Captain Tom.

"Mum, can we go and see a spitfire soon?" Arthur asks.

"Yes, of course, once everything is back open," I think the air museum not far from here has one and other aircraft, that will be a nice treat, and a challenge.

We have our tea party, sitting at the table by the front door, the children have enjoyed the day. I feel it is a shame we aren't in the old house and we could see friends in the distance, but then I think I would be too anxious to be near anyone, and both the children talk about social distancing, and say we couldn't have a party with friends Mum, as if I'm daft.

Arthur manages to do his walk up and down twice today, and he wants to do the same over the weekend, if he does that, he will have reached his 26, his fund raising has gone very well, Dave's mates put in £200 and various other people including his dear old Mum, have given and he has a current total of £453. He's talking of carrying on to raise more.

I watch the Queen's speech and her words 'never give up, never despair' resonate for today. Perhaps the Queen's words helped us all. I put them in a message to Matt that will be played to him, the children join me chorusing 'We'll Meet Again', they so want to talk to him and see him, but they know he is sleeping to try to get himself better, and know the doctors and nurses are with him and give him stuff to help him sleep.

Then I get a call that brings me to my knees, with relief. The staff have been slightly lightening his sedation, trying to wean him off the ventilator, they say he is beginning to respond. I am so happy and relieved, but the consultant says don't celebrate yet there is a long way to go, he says they will tell me progress and phone as things change, hopefully I think, for the better. As I sit on the sofa where my legs gave way, Arthur and Molly come up to me and I tell them some positive news for once, but I try to temper it with caution.

I want to know minute by minute progress, but know that is impossible, the nurse-to-patient ratio has been revised, gone from 1 to 1, to 1 to 3, they are so busy. I just pray now he starts responding, that his brain gets the commands and he comes out of the induced coma and starts to breath independently. I feel sick, it is still such a long way to go. Open your eyes Matt, breath, come home, that is my mantra, along with my heartfelt love.

Amidst the slightly improving news life here carries on, home schooling, the day beginning with PE with Joe, now part of the household, then a day of school work, work books and projects. I go through all the incoming mail for Matt, divert some things to Don, he and I catch up on the phone, setting out what needs doing, he and Phil are working hard, he's pleased his son has stepped up to the plate.

As the school day is nearly finished for the day, Dave phoned, catching us before Arthur goes out to increase his 26.

"Hi sis. I got your text," I texted him last night with the news about Matt, again making sure that he realises that it is very early days, and could go slowly or return to heavier sedation, "We were busy last night so didn't get a chance to phone you."

"That's ok. I understand and I got your text anyway, is it getting busier then?"

"Yes, the VE day celebrations started the idiots off, and we had to break up quite a few street parties."

"Are you ok Dave?" I ask concerned as he sounds a bit fed up.

"Yes, you have to be don't you. I am enjoying this gardening lark though."

"What gardening? you're picking produce, not planting or hoeing, but still very important," I say reassuring him. I don't want my picker disappearing.

"I know, but I just like doing something completely different, it helps in this time."

"Do you want me to give you some other tasks then?" I think he won't as he has always steered away from gardening, he did help me with some of the big tasks at my house, but that was about all, his garden is all hard landscaping, not plants.

"Yes, that would be good," well you could knock me over with a feather, "I know you are speechless aren't you, but I just think it gives you thinking time and to be in that garden, even in the rain, because of the age of the garden and the walls you feel you are in a different world, and we could all do with being somewhere else. I find it really helps."

"I know, those storm clouds that were gathering all those months ago, are still over us, you still feel the pressure of them, that just about anything can happen to any of us."

"Look it's everything. Matt, you, the children, Sue, sometimes it gets to you, and I know it does to you too. So, having those hours in the garden helps, and if I can lighten your load I will."

121

"Thanks Dave I'll look at what extra you can do."

As we walk to the gate and back recording Arthur's miles for his continuing challenge. I mull over the conversation with Dave, he moved the conversation away from the root cause of his change on gardening, he did say some things were getting to him. I can understand how difficult the job is, and not having Sue to be with must be so hard for him, in fact for them both, but I feel a shift in him, he's never been a planner just taken each day as it came, he loved the job when he was in the firearms unit, but he went for promotion and ended up in a station away from that. I thought he was ok with it, but perhaps I'm wrong. I will have to have another chat with him.

We go and check the garden, it is cooler this week, in fact I think there is a frost in a day or so. I will put some fleece on anything tender, and keep the poly tunnel doors closed as well. I pick some spinach and decide to make a mild curry, they both love curry, yes even Arthur. I have some coriander and I think I saw some poppadum's' in the cupboard, so that will keep them both happy.

While I'm cooking. I think about the unit lightening Matt's sedation, they phoned earlier and said he had opened his eyes, Fran had played our messages to him, she said he was a little more alert. I can't help but think ahead, and although the consultant said don't celebrate yet, I'm not doing that but I am thinking about practicalities. I of course look up and read articles from reliable sources on after care, they talk about having to learn to walk again, and swallow and how having lain down for weeks just sitting up can cause dizziness, there is so much it feels daunting and I'm not the patient.

The next evening, I go up to the house with the children, it is lighter now so after Arthur's walk, they can play with the swing ball, though it is a little cooler. I go in to the house through the front door and go upstairs, it's a huge house with three floors, on the first floor where Matt's bedroom is there are two bathrooms, oldish but workable. As I walk down the stairs I turn back and look at how steep they are, then I walk into the lounge, thinking, then I go and sit on the porch step watching the children, they come over as soon as they see me.

"What you thinking Mum?" Arthur asks.

"I've been thinking about when Matt is well enough to come home, we don't know when that will be yet though, but it is important to plan, what do you both think," they sit either side of me nodding, "We'll have to decide where he can sleep, it might not be easy for Matt to climb the stairs when he first comes home."

"Why?" Molly asks.

"When you've been in bed for a while your legs are weak, so it might be better if he had a bed down here in the lounge, but no bathroom down here though," Arthur stands up in front of me hands on hips.

"Mummy, Matt has to live with us," he says.

"Yes, Mummy, you can't let him live here on his own," well I wasn't going to leave him to his own devises I think, "There's loads of room and no stairs in the barn," Molly says with Arthur nodding.

"We can look after him, that's what we thought isn't it, Molls?" they've been planning, "And we can help make him better," they obviously have thought about this and related it to their dad, and what we discussed when Matt went into hospital.

They are correct, he obviously can't be here on his own. I had thought we could move up here, but we still have the stairs issue and no bathroom down here, but I'm sure the hospital will be asking these questions before discharge, and the house wouldn't tick the boxes.

"You're both right he has to come and live with us in the barn," they whoop and run off for another swing ball game. How lovely to be able to move on from a problem to swing ball. I think. The barn is the best place for all of us, we can help to get him better there, so with a bit of hope in my heart we go off to the garden to water, Arthur and Molly have watering cans of their own and water the beds I started for them. I make sure everything is protected for the frost, but most of the produce is fine. I just put some fleece over the fruit trees in the garden, and shut the greenhouse.

I text Dave as he is picking tomorrow and tell him what is expected at the farm shops, and ask him to remove the fleece for me, he has a few other jobs as well, as I'm doing that Sue phones.

"Hi, how are you?" She asks, "What do you think about the schools going back?"

"Are they?" How had I missed that? "Do you know Sue I haven't seen the briefings for a couple of days and haven't heard the news on the radio either."

She updates me, how we are no longer "stay at home," but "stay alert," and that reception, year 1 and year 6 are going back. My anxiety starts to ramp up, and when she says, it is only England. I find it quite unbelievable. I know the idea for school is as Sue says not until June, but still. And talk of face covering in certain places, it just doesn't feel like our country somehow. I know people talk of the new normal, but it is a worrying new normal.

"Good news about Matt Annie."

"Well certainly baby steps. I don't want to get my hopes up too much but he has opened his eyes and that's progress." I tell her about my plans to have him at the barn, "Is Dave ok, only I get the feeling he's not telling me something, and enjoying the garden is just not him at all?"

"Well, he's been unhappy at work for some time, and he has done his thirty years so he could retire if he wanted to. I think when he went over the thirty, he started thinking of the future, yes, I know he isn't a planner, but we had planned to live together and talked about where he and I would go from there, work has changed for him, he knows he couldn't leave now, but getting into the garden and doing something different is putting life into perspective and allowing him to think of a different future."

I'm about to ask what future, and does it involve gardening or is the gardening just giving him time to think, when Molly comes through to the lounge, so I hang up and take her back to bed, she's fine but does wake sometimes, with a cuddle she just goes back off to sleep. I can't imagine sending her back to school as she would be year 1. So much to think about, I yawn and feel suddenly very tired, I'll think about all of this tomorrow, and hope Matt's baby steps are advancing. I look at the picture he took of me and Molly by my bed and wish him my love, breath darling.

Everything appears a little brighter this morning, the weather is sunny although cool, but everywhere I look outside looks lovely, it catches at my heart, this is all because of the news that Matt is moving to high dependency today, he's been sleeping a lot and can swallow, his tube is out too, he has taken some sips of drinks. I can't wait to see him. I sit at the table outside as the children do some schoolwork, a smile just coming to my lips, he is also beginning to sit up, but as I found out that is quite difficult for the patient.

Dave has been able to sow some produce for me, as I can't take the children up as it is a bit too cool to sit at the table in the garden, although it is going to get warmer at the weekend, so I can have a good session then, he has got into all aspects of the garden, I've been watering though in the evening. I hadn't realised Dave had done over thirty years in the job. I suppose he was a cadet so that must add to his years' service. I wonder what he wants to do after, whenever that is.

Matt is on the ward. I have had calls from John the consultant taking me through all they are doing, he talks about future issues, such as critical care acquired weakness, which he says is more prevalent in COVID-19 patients, not from research but anecdotal, he also mentions extreme fatigue, he outlines the occupational therapist work and dietician for the immediate future, they will talk to me about everything else later. I am also told about communicating with Matt, he might be slower, might have some initial confusion, to keep everything factual, and to try not to interrupt him, as it might take him off his train of thought. I have a call about his discharge, not that it is now. I am pulled back, but they need me to know what to expect and to talk about his living accommodation.

They say Matt is very weak, he could be susceptible to infection. I explain that we have in effect been isolating here, that since lockdown I have not been in close contact with anyone, and neither have the children, which is a positive. His physical recovery could take three to six months, he may need nutrition support. I should be prepared for emotional and psychological after effects, there could be persistent psychological difficulties. I talk through some of his possible post trauma symptoms from his work in the past, which he did in quiet moments talk to me about, and ultimately, he might have ongoing physical symptoms or weakness, possibly from his lungs. It is overwhelming.

Fran texts me, and although she is not looking after Matt now has arranged a video call with Matt, and she tells me the time. I feel that this first time I ought to do this on my own, so at the time given I park the children in front of the swing ball and just walk out of the garden still being able to see the children and take the call.

What did I say I can't wait to see him? The call was a huge shock. I try to bear in mind the poor quality of the call screen but even so I am shocked, he just whispers as he can't speak properly yet, he looks ten or even twenty years older, his face has shrunk, his eyes aren't the usual blue, they are dull. It takes all my will power to not break down, to act normally, not to show him how shocked I am.

He whispers, "I… love… you… Annie," this seems to wipe him out, he looks exhausted so I quickly say.

"I love you so much Matt. I can't put into words how I feel for you, keep taking those baby steps darling, come back to me, to us. I want you back here, back home with us." The nurse ends the call and I just continue looking at the phone in absolute disbelief. I exhale. I feel so unsettled by the call, so upset.

With all the calls over the last couple of days and the video call. I am on automatic pilot, water garden, cook, baths, stories, bed. After that I do what I haven't for some time and that is pour myself a glass of wine. I sit with the log burner on, taking all this in, it is daunting, but we can do it. I just can't get my head around how he looked. I remember our passion, our first time, on this very sofa, in this barn. I remember every part of him, his muscles his strength, looking at his face alone I know that is all gone, for now I think. I hope, for now.

I will hold him through sleepless nights. I will help him in every way possible to get through this. Nurture him with our love, help him build his strength up, but mostly just be there for him. I didn't think too much about where he was going to sleep, just in the barn, but perhaps a tiny part of me was considering the children in any decision, and although they are important in this, fundamental, Matt I think has to be the priority here. I have no doubt if I say to Arthur and Molly he will sleep with me, they will look at me as if to say we knew that anyway.

Two days later, there is another video call, this time the children are with me. I had explained that when Matt comes home, we need to feed him up as he has lost weight, so that when they see him it won't be too much of a shock. I don't know why I worry as those two are so resilient and generally say what they think anyway. He looks slightly improved less exhausted but you can still see he is tired, his head looks too heavy for his body as he leans on the pillows, "Hello you two how are you?" he says slowly.

"We're good Matt, we have done you loads of cards and written a diary haven't we Molls," she just nods, "Your hairs grown really long, I'll tell you don't let Mummy cut it, see my fringe Matt, she made a right mess of that, all I can say is I'm glad I'm not at school," with that indignity I wrestle the phone off them and scoot them away. I do hear a giggle from Matt, and a bigger laugh from one of the nurses.

"Sorry about that you know what he's like," I pause to wait for Matt to reply if he wants to, he doesn't at that point, "We'll see you tomorrow," I can't believe he will be here tomorrow, he doesn't look well enough, but I will get him there.

"They don't want us at the hospital. I think they explained to you, so will see you when you get back, stay well," he just nods and I think I see his eyes glaze with tears, the call is cut off.

Because we have been in isolation they feel it will be better for us not to go to the hospital, possibly putting us in danger of contracting the virus somewhere, it means extra protection for Matt, but I would have loved to have collected him, Fran is going to film him coming out, and the children have used the bunting from VE day and put it out the front of the barn, apparently it all feels overwhelming to Matt the consultant told me.

While the children do PE, and before they start schooling, which they both thought should be cancelled today because Matt is coming home. I change the sheets and put extra pillows on the bed, so he is able to sit up supported if necessary. I managed to get Don to bring a wing backed chair down from the house and had it put in the bedroom, he bought it in via the patio doors at the end of the bedroom, the doors give a view of the patio, lawn and river. I thought if he had a chair there if he didn't want the bustle of the lounge he could sit and chill.

Matt will have exercises to do, to build up body mass, particularly for his legs, but he will get tired, so I want this room to be comfortable and so different from the hospital. I nip out the main door and pick some wild flowers and put them in the room too.

Don has been on gate duty, Fran sent me the film of him coming out of the ward, bells rang and the staff all clapped him. I could see even from a distance he was moved, so was I, the tears run down my face. I rub them away. I feel nervous but so looking forward to seeing him, I'm nervous as there is a long way to go down his recovery path.

Dave and I have spoken frequently this week, he can't believe everything I tell him, about recovery about how he will be fatigued, weakness, and on and on. I realised that Matt had to have clothes at the hospital to come home with and also what would fit him now? Dave said he always wore his T shirts too tight anyway, so they should still fit. I said that was muscle, his reply was 'show off'. I can see banter will help Matt, humour has always been part of military and police life. Dave ordered some T shirts, boxers and cargo shorts and trousers for him, he left most up in the garden for me and then sorted out getting some stuff up to the ward for Matt, I've bought down some jumpers and fleeces for him from the house and other bits.

Dave has also put forward a huge proposition, on the day Matt came out of critical care he phoned me. I knew something had been playing on his mind.

"Hi sis, glad things are moving forward I got your message. I want to have a chat with you, and really it should be with Matt too, but obviously I can't do that."

"What is it?" I ask worried, what now?

"It's nothing to worry about, it is positive, well I think it is. I have given notice at work, in fact I did that a week or so ago," I am quiet with shock, "I wanted to finish and retire before all this started and felt I couldn't let the Force down at such an awful time, but others have gone and I feel now I have given a lot and supported them during all of this, my boss was fine with it, so I have a couple of days to go, as I only have to give a months' notice and I have some leave due, you're quiet?"

"I'm so surprised Dave I don't know what to say."

"Well don't say any more, as I have a proposition for you, and Matt, you are going to need extra help up at the farm and garden as you will be supporting Matt and you don't know how that will pan out yet, what he will need. So, I would like to cover all your jobs, wait—" as I go to interrupt, "What I will need to do is isolate from you all for up to 14 days, so I can have eventual contact with you all and Sue, who is important here too."

"How will you do that?"

"I'm coming to that sis. I wondered if I could move into one of the other barns, temporarily, work in the garden get this produce out, the farm shops will be happy with more produce, and I have chatted to Don and he will drop off produce. When I am sure I am no risk to Sue I would like her to move up here too. I don't want to put off moving our relationship on to the next step, we all know life is too short Annie," he pauses. "I've really learnt that, and before you question me about my gardening ability. I have been watching some programmes on YouTube and the iPlayer, I've been reading lots too, so I know about growing and the various processes, well a bit. I would like to do a course some time…" His voice peters out.

"Gosh Dave, what a huge amount to take in," I don't know where to begin, but he is right how am I going to keep the garden going and just at the peak time. I don't know, but my priority is Matt, and I feel certainly for the next few weeks I will be predominately by his side, or cooking tempting food, "You are right about the garden, but don't change your life just to help us."

"Sis, I'm being selfish here too. I want to do this. I feel that my mind has cleared doing this gardening, or picking, it has helped me realise I want something else, it might be temporary and if it can be of advantage to you, Matt and the children, then great, if it takes the weight off your shoulders again great, but it also means if I isolate here, I can have Sue here."

"Look Dave. I can see where you are coming from, but it is huge, empty houses, mine will be just like that soon, moving, learning something new, and, oh I don't know, sorry if I'm putting obstacles in your way."

"Annie. I have thought this through I have thought of nothing else ever since Matt was hospitalised. I want out, and if in wanting that I can help everyone, then great. I have spoken to Dad and he feels even if it is for a couple of months then it will be an advantage for everyone, as for houses, it is the least of our worries. I know lock down is easing, but Matt is vulnerable, and I can't leave Sue out of this anymore."

My head is over loaded with all of this, but I just say, "Go ahead Dave, move up, it will be like some bloody commune," I say shaking my head, but inside there is an element of relief. I do mull it over, more problems, or are they? I must think clearly here, difficult as with Matt's illness I have had some concentration problems, and anxiety continues to bubble, just about kept at bay. It is Matt's farm, not mine, but Matt would be happy with any decision I take. I know he would, and if it is ultimately a decision that would help us and continue to bring money in and much-needed produce out, then it's a good one.

Dave doesn't want to leave Sue on her own any more, he could self-isolate and then have her round at home but what would he do, he couldn't work then, and we don't know how long the vulnerable must stay at home, he wants to help his family in time of need, except I hadn't realised I needed it. I have just about managed to keep everything going, with Dave picking and doing odd jobs, I've planted and watered, and taken the children with me, but I don't know what having Matt at home will entail.

I phone Dave back, and we talk practicalities, yes there is furniture in the one barn and curtains, but nothing else, he feels that is not an issue. I wonder to myself if he has already packed, Dave also reminds me that Ted might have been able to help once things lift, but Iris fell and fractured her hip, so he will have to support her as much as possible.

It Is the Gift of Life That Is Truly Epic

As I stand out the front and wait for Matt to come home. I think on all of my calls with Dave, he has been here five days now, he must have had everything packed as after our call he moved in. I do chuckle about that, from a man who never planned anything, he has seriously stepped up a gear, and organised himself. I get the feeling Sue had verbal input and directed him, but he is so genuine and so desperate to want to do this. I have seen him about in the distance. I sent him my original plans for the garden and planting plan for the season. I can't wait to share more with him now. I have told the children about Dave coming here and living in the barn, they both understand about social distancing now, it is amazing how those two words are now a part of our way of life, and I think probably for a long time to come.

I look up and see Dave at the top of the hill, waving, Don opens the gate and a patient services ambulance drives down the track. I call the children out; they have put some triangles from the bunting on sticks and begin to wave them cheering as the doors open. I am so overcome with emotion. I didn't think I would see this day, and I know "don't celebrate yet" still rings in my mind, but he is here. I run up to the ambulance and as Matt is helped down the stairs I step toward him, he slightly lifts his arms and I walk into them.

"Oh Matt," one of his hands comes up and just touches my arm. I realise I am also supporting him, as he isn't steady on his feet. "Come on let's get you inside, Arthur and Molly just walk ahead of us, make sure Bob is on his bed too," they are so excited. I don't want Matt tripping over them or Bob.

"Annie," his voice is still hoarse, but louder than a whisper now, "I'm glad to be home sweetheart, with you," he looks down at me as I help him walk, and I see a slight light in his eyes, glad he is here. We go into the barn and I help him to sit on the sofa, supported by cushions, the children are talking nineteen to the dozen. I have to slow them down, just then there is a knock at the door. I go and see who it is, it's Don.

"I'll water Annie, but will take the children with me, if you want, it will give Matt time to settle in, I've texted Dave to tell him and he will stay down in his barn," I was so relieved again, it will be good to have time with Matt to see what he needs, and what he could do.

"Don thank you so much, Arthur, Molly we're going to give Matt some time to get sorted so Don's going to take you to water your plots, come on," they turn and say goodbye to Matt, at least Matt has some time to settle in.

"We're going to get you better Matt," Molly says, "I'll pick some spinach Mum, Don can show me, we can have curry."

"Ok off you go," I see them walk up the hill with Don and walk and sit with Matt, "Oh my darling," I just curl my legs up and gently hold his hand. I place it against my face and look up into those eyes. He smiles. I see a glimpse of the old Matt in that smile, but it looks forced, as if it is an effort to do anything.

"I thought it would be good to be down here, rather than in the house, would you like a shower, to try to get rid of the hospital smell," I smile, "Dave hated that when I used to come home from work, do you remember," he smiles and grips my hand.

"I would like a bath," he says slowly, "But I don't think I could get out, so it will have to be a shower, and here's me in the past dreaming of getting you into the shower," an ironic chuckle. For me I am so glad he can remember. I was afraid he might not recall everything, but perhaps he won't, at least he's remembered some of what we shared.

"Baby steps Matt, I'm here for you. I want to help you get completely better, do you then want to rest in bed, or come out here for a while."

"I feel drained Annie. I can't tell you how much just doing a few things gets me."

"Come on, the longer you sit here the more tired you'll feel," I help him up and we walk slowly to the bottom bedroom. I take him in and then we go into the en suite, he sits on the stool I put in there and he started taking his things off and stands to go in the shower, he just manages to support himself in there, perhaps it should have put a stool in the shower too, but I don't want to undermine him and make him less than he is, but as he comes out I wrap a towel around him and he sits heavily. I get another towel and gently dry his body and his hair, as I do this, he lifts his arms and puts them round me, laying his head on my chest. I feel him relax against me, and I just hold him, not wanting to hurt him, his body so sensitive after what it has gone through. I know the nerve endings are sensitive to touch and feel of clothes. I go and get a clean T shirt and boxers, that I already washed to make them soft for him. I put some cream on his dry arms and on his face and lips.

I then help him walk into the bedroom. I had to help him off the stool too, he sits on the edge of the bed, and I fold his legs onto the bed, and pull the soft duvet over him, he sinks into the pillows, a breath coming out of him, which sound as if everything was too much for him. I just kiss his forehead and sit on the bed.

"Isn't this your room?" I can barely hear him.

"It's our room," he looks at me, "I am not going to leave you on your own Matt, if you wake, I'm here if you need anything. I want to hold you so you relax and get better, and no smouldering looks I have too much to do," I try to lighten all of this and am rewarded as I get a smile back and a nod and I see his eyes close.

I go into the lounge to get him a drink, and reach the worktop for support. I let the tears flow, he's so weak, so changed. I only seem to get a glimpse of the Matt I knew, perhaps I'm expecting too much, he's only been home a short time, they did warn me it is going to be a long journey. Then my phone goes, Dave.

"How's it going? It was good of Don to take the children for a while it gives you both a bit of time," he must have heard me sniff, "Are you crying…"

"Yes, but I'm ok, he's so weak Dave and different."

"I saw him walk to the barn, he was definitely leaning on you, where is Matt now?"

"He's had a shower, and then went to bed, just the slightest task exhausts him. I just have to think he's alive and he's here, we'll get through this." I pull myself together and get some homemade lemonade, sweet and syrupy for Matt as his mouth and lips are so dry, and take it through to the bedroom. I sit on the bed and he lifts his hand to my face rubbing my cheek with his thumb.

"Don't cry Annie. I can't bear it, and don't say you haven't been," he opens his eyes.

"Oh, sweetheart come here," he pulls me into him and I rest my head on his chest, he kisses my hair, we stay like that and I feel him relax and his breathing deepens. I could stay like this forever, his arms gently resting on me, they may not be strong yet but they will be. I rest his arms down and get up, he is still sleeping.

As I walk into the lounge Don is leaving the children by the gate, they come in and as good as she said Molly gives me the spinach she has picked, so curry again, I've made some celery soup for Matt. I know it is his favourite, I've put cream in it to help build him up. I will give him a small portion. I talk to the children before I start cooking, we are going to be quiet. I explain that Matt is very tired, and by getting some rest and sleep it will help him get better, they ask if before bed they can go and see him and start to read their diary to him. I say yes if he's awake, but remember how I read to you at night, "Softly," Molly says, and I nod. I know she can do that not so sure about Arthur though.

I have a quick shower in the main bathroom, so as not to wake Matt. I remember glancing at him in the shower, he looks so wasted but I'll feed him up gradually. I get some clothes out of the airing cupboard and start on the curry, the spinach Molls picked goes with some I picked the other day, her handful wouldn't be quite enough, but she is a good girl, while that is simmering, I nip and see how Matt is. I'm so surprised he's standing leaning on the wing chair by the double doors, open, and is watching the children have a quick kick around.

Matt looks at the depth of colour in the grass and the sky, he breaths in the air and feels it is sweet, fragranced, alive with life, he can't believe he is alive too, he turns as he hears her come through, "I am supposed to exercise a bit they said, they don't want me developing any blood clots and it's good to get these legs moving slightly. I can't stand for long but it is nice to try," I go over and stand by him, he sits in the chair, "I'm alive Annie," I crouch down and rest my hand on his, watching the children run off excess energy.

"I know Matt and I thank every god you are," we just take in the moment and hold hands I feel if I can hold him. I will help him mend.

"Arthur and Molly want to come and read you a bit of their diary before bed time, the hospital suggested we as a family write down everything that has happened while you have been in hospital and as you know my two, they did it themselves. Is it ok if they do?"

"Of course, they can, is it my bedtime or theirs though?" he smiles at that, and moves his hand entwining his fingers through mine.

"Are you hungry?" he pulls a face, no then, "I've made some celery soup for you, it might tempt you and waken those taste buds up. But don't if you aren't hungry."

"You remembered."

"Of course," I rest my head on his hand.

"I can't see Arthur eating that," he knows my son too well.

133

"We've got curry," but Arthur being Arthur will have poppadum's, not a rice fan, for me and Molly rice. It's only mild but they love it, even Arthur, "Shall I bring you a bit of soup?"

"Yes, I'll try some."

I get a small bowl with some soft bread. I spread that with butter so it can slip down easily and not be dry, he does eat some of the soup, and then goes and gets into bed, he collapses back on the pillows. I leave him with a kiss on his head and go to sort out the children and me. I realise I haven't eaten all day, just cups of tea.

Later, jobs done I feel shattered and want to go to bed. I left a low bedside light on earlier in our bedroom, so I wouldn't disturb Matt when I came to bed. I quickly put my shorts pyjamas on in the main bathroom.

"You've lost some weight too," I look up and see Matt is awake as I walk in the room. "Been doing your nurses walk at pace since I've been away."

"Yes, you know me, no running but fast walking, do you want me to move any pillows for you, is it too high to sleep with?"

"Just move one will you love. I don't want to be too low."

"Are you worried about your breathing, it's fine now darling," I reassure him, it is obviously a worry for him. I take one pillow away and make him comfortable, then I slip into bed on the other side, sit and face him, just looking at him. I feel completely overwhelmed having him home and here with me. I can feel tears choking at the back of my throat, but I don't want to cry, so try to hold them back.

"Do you remember the last time?" He asks.

"Of course, I do. I remember every time."

"As we lay there afterwards. I thought, what I wouldn't give to have nights with your body next to mine. I now have that and can't do anything about it," he sounds chocked, so I hold his hand and bring it to my lips, he adds, "Be careful what you wish for, they say."

"Baby steps Matt, we have each other, and I will be with you every one of those steps," he groans and I see tears on his cheeks. I brush them away and snuggle closer to him. I hold him as best I can without leaning on him too much, he seems so vulnerable so broken, so fragile. He cries softly for a while, with me whispering reassurance and love. It just breaks me, but my face stays dry for him, to give him some strength. Eventually Matt falls asleep. I lie down close to him, my hand resting on his arm, so that if he moves. I will know.

Light shines through the gap in the curtains, Matt is still asleep, his breathing even. I look at the clock, five o'clock. I can hear the birds in the distance. I lie on my side looking at Matt, thinking, this is the first time I have slept through in so long, but I know I would have woken if he had moved, his tears just broke my heart, the fractures were beginning to heal over, but his tears rent them open. I see how long a journey we have, and how I need to help him physically and mentally.

I move quietly around the room collecting some clothes and go into the other bathroom and shower. I add some of my clothes to the washing machine with Matt's and make a tea. I sit outside by the door and take in the farm and river, it looks beautiful, there is still little traffic noise even though people who can't work from home have been lately encouraged to go to work. I loved the complete peace. I didn't love what caused it though, the numbers dead are so high I feel devastated for those who lost loved ones.

I say a prayer of thanks for having Matt home, but I'm under no illusion that he could relapse and that is my main job to get him better. I don't know what that better will be, at the moment I can't see him doing much but we have to take each day as it comes. There are so many things I need to tell Matt but I feel it is too soon, it might overtax his thoughts to know all the news, might add an element of confusion, that is why the diary is a gentle introduction to life as well as a history.

A text comes in on my phone from Fran, asking if I'm up. I text back and she phones.

"I know you are an early riser, how is Matt and importantly you too?"

"Well, he's exhausted all of the time, a simple task just does him in, and I don't mean he's been ploughing a field I mean taking a shower walking a few feet, eating some soup."

"It's a devastating disease Annie, we don't know enough about the virus itself let alone what happens afterwards, as I know you will have been saying, baby steps."

"Yes, I have, we've talked a little bit, but nothing taxing. I let him talk if he wants to, there has been quite a lot of change on the farm and garden but it can wait. I haven't even thought about Molly and going back to school."

"Do you want to talk about it?"

"Yes, that'd be good, what I'm thinking as she is year one, she should be going back 1 June, but with Matt here, I'm reluctant to send her back. I don't think she will be missing anything too much, but also Arthur would miss having her here, as his class isn't back in at that stage. I think stability for both of them is important. I will no doubt get a call from her form teacher or head teacher and I will voice what I'm telling you."

"I think for someone who hasn't had time to think too much you've made a good and sound decision, you said to me how fond the children are of Matt and I think keeping him safe will be something they will completely understand."

"You are right, and yes they are fond of him, particularly Molly, although she was a toddler when Sam died, she did and does remember him, and has felt close to Matt, so to tear her away even for one day a week wouldn't be fair all round and that's without the infection risk."

We finish off and I start to gather breakfast together, although it is cloudy today it is warm but I quite fancy real porridge, so set to the task. I had found some oats when we moved, the rhythm of stirring and looking out the window continue to calm me, sitting outside helped. I don't feel anxious, there was an element of anxiety yesterday, but having slept next to Matt I feel calmer. I think about Sam and realise I haven't thought about him in some time, other priorities I suppose. I wake the children and they come through for their breakfast, while they eat that I check on Matt, he is sitting with his legs over the edge of the bed, he looks like he is contemplating a marathon, not a possible trip to the bathroom.

"Are you ok?" I kneel in front of him, resting my hands on his knees.

"Yes. I slept well, just trying to get the body together for activity," he grins, "Just the bathroom on this occasion though," I stand and he grabs me to him, breathing me in. I look down at his face and see a little more light in his eyes. I help him up and he walks tentatively into the bathroom. I open the curtains and straighten the bed.

"Do you want some breakfast?" I ask Matt as he comes back, "Or do you want a shower first."

"I'll have some breakfast, but not much and then contemplate a shower."

"I made some porridge, the real stuff your mum and mine would make," as I say that I realise I haven't spoken to Mum and Dad for a few days, but am sure Dave will be updating them, "I just fancied some myself," I go through and stir the porridge and tell the children to wash and get dressed.

"Don't forget teeth too," I say as I go into the bedroom.

"Were you talking to me, because that sounds like your severe voice?"

"Very funny, just chivvying them along otherwise they will never be ready for PE and home schooling." I give Matt a small bowl of porridge with some golden syrup on it, and put a half mug of tea on the cabinet, "The tea isn't too hot. I think that's what the dietician said."

I stand and look out of the window, a bowl of the same for me. I eat it slowly and turn to him. I thought I would if I could have some with him, as eating on your own can be unsettling. I know it is only day two, or one and a half, but do as I mean to go on is my saying. Even though he looks so different, is so different, just sleeping by him last night has made me realise how attracted I am to him, inappropriate as I feel any physical relationship is a long way off, but it doesn't stop me loving him. As I say that to myself, I think I haven't told him how much I love him since he got home. I know I said it on the phone messages and when he first came out of critical care, but will he remember.

"What are you mithering about, standing there. I can see you know, even ill, ok? I know you, Annie."

I walk over and put my bowl down, "I love you do you know that. I said it every day in messages to you. I said it every day here. I shouted to you as they took you away to hospital how much I love you. You do know, don't you?" I sit on the edge of the bed. I take his bowl as he's finished and set it down. He holds my gaze, locked together again, "I know. I can see it in everything you do for me Annie, but most of all I can sense it in your touch, your looks, I'm worried though, you don't need an invalid."

"Firstly you are not an invalid, you have had a terrible virus and will come out the other end of this, it is only the second day you have been out of hospital, Matt nearly a month ago you were ventilated and your life," I was going to say hung in the balance but I don't think that is good, as elements of anxiety are definitely here for him, "Your life wasn't your own, a machine was breathing for you and you had many NHS staff caring for you, so don't say that."

"What was secondly? You said firstly, so what was secondly?"

"For an invalid you've got a lot of questions," I smile, "Ok so, secondly. I am never letting you go, you are my world, my everything, we'll get through this Matt, don't doubt that love. I regret not telling you how I felt when you went into hospital, then Dave told me how you had said you loved me, and I wished we had talked."

"I want what we had, Annie," he holds me to him.

"We will Matt, but slowly. I am so glad you are home, you're helping me already," he looks at me doubtfully, "I slept all night last night for the first time since you were taken ill. I need you Matt, when you went into hospital. I realised how much you helped and supported me and loved me. I found it daunting to manage without you and I can't get through all we have to do without you, however well you are, you are there for me and I need you, do you hear me."

"I do and I love you too Annie. I had so many scary dreams and I have so many strange insecurities. I suppose it's having been so ill, so long in an induced coma."

"It is Matt and it will make life difficult for you sometimes, but we are here for you, now we should hug and not talk so much, it's difficult love when you have been sedated to get your head around conversations. I'm just going to start the children's PE session off, and I will come and give you a hand showering and change the bed I think."

The day goes on with all the usual activities, interspersed with helping Matt, he gets out of bed in the afternoon and put on cargo shorts and wants to sit with the windows open, he pales, even more, at me putting a throw over his legs. I know it is fairly warm but I don't want him catching cold. I decide to mention Dave, and just briefly tell him what is going on, then I text Dave and suggest he comes down and sits in the garden with Matt inside the doors, he can tell Matt his thoughts and what he proposed, it will do both of them good, but I warned him to be brief.

While they do that. I check the children are getting on with projects. I think I can fit in a call to Mum before we go for Arthur's walk, he has done double his predicted 2.6 challenge and wants to go onto treble. I know he wants to tell Matt about it soon too.

After the challenge for the day, me, Arthur and Molly walk up to the garden as Matt and Dave are still talking I want to look at my pet project and check all is well, not that I doubt Dave, he has had enough emails from me telling him what needs doing, but it's lovely to be back in here, the children run around and show me their plots, they both have radishes coming through and some cut and come again lettuce showing. I pick some strawberries, these are early this year because of the beautiful weather we have been having.

As we go down to the barn, Dave waves, he and Matt have obviously finished their chat. I think Matt will be exhausted with all this conversation. I am having doubts about telling Dave to come over. The children go and get their bikes out and want to ride up and down the road to the gate, they know they can't go anywhere else.

I go and check on Matt, he's lying on top of the bed, eyes closed, as I go to leave him, he speaks, "Annie."

"You're awake. I hope all of this hasn't worn you out today?"

"No, it was good to catch up with Dave, but he can talk the hind legs off a donkey. I have to say I did zone out once or twice."

"I told him to keep it brief, hold on," I get up and walk to the side window and check on the children, "Arthur and Molls are riding their bikes up and down to the gates. I just want to make sure they aren't going off piste, no they are fine," I sit with him holding his hand, he reaches up and strokes my face, "I better sort food out."

"Have you eaten today?" Matt asks, "Anything since porridge, bet you haven't," I think and then admit that I haven't, "No, there hasn't been time. I did nibble some carrot batons the kids had for lunch," he raises his eyebrows to me, "Alright I know pot and kettle, I'll have something in a bit with the children, what do you fancy?"

"Apart from you?"

"Yes, apart from me. I was going to make a creamy pasta sauce for you and me. I don't think chicken goujons floats your boat."

"Sounds good, have you got any juice or something like that?" He hates having to ask Annie for anything but he feels so incapable and so exhausted, as much as he likes Dave all of that fried his brain, he sees his Annie so busy she doesn't need the added pressure of him.

"Right. I am reading your brain now. I will get you a drink and it is no problem. I should have left you a jug, also having Dave on the farm has reduced my work by nearly a 100%, and for me it is lovely cooking for us, you and me."

"Ok, I'll shut up."

I go and get a fruit smoothie from the fridge and put it in a glass for him, while he drinks that I prepare tea. I so look forward to sharing a table with Matt and eating together, it will be some time. I look in on him, and he's sleeping again. I shower, sort the children's food out, bath them and then put them to bed and read to them, Matt was still asleep so they couldn't read to him their diary, they are disappointed but I tell them it is half term next week so no school, they will be able to share with Matt different things at different times during the day when he's not asleep or resting.

I stand having a bowl of pasta leaning on the island, Matt is still asleep. I hope he's alright, I'll give him one of the high protein drinks they recommended, so at least he'll have had something. I decide to chat to Molly tomorrow about school, as I expect a call on the last day of term from one of the teachers to see if she is going back. I hear something and realise it's the wind and rain, this was forecast, and the winds are going to be higher tomorrow. I shut all the windows and go into Matt. Light from outside streams in, he has his eyes open and reaches his hand out to me.

"Hello sleepy head, did my brother wear you out?" he just nods, "I thought you might like a hot chocolate drink." I go and get him a drink giving him an opportunity to use the bathroom. I let Bob out, he came round the patio earlier and went and sat with Matt. I was worried where he was but he had jumped up and was on Matt's lap while he talked to Dave.

I shut curtains, it's getting dark now, Bob goes into the children's room where his bed is for nighttime. Then I take a drink through for Matt. I get into bed next to him, while he drinks his drink, "Talk to me."

"Haven't you had enough talking already today?"

"I want to hear you."

"Don't tell me I lull you off to sleep," I smile at him and turn to him. "Ok then," I tell him a few things the children have been doing over the last few weeks, little tales they won't tell him themselves, they can tell him about his cards and Arthur's challenge, he finishes his drink and strokes my face, leaning in to kiss me on the lips, but he just touches the corner of my mouth. I look into his eyes and I see sadness.

"Matt don't be sad, we are here together, and it will be alright, we have each other and the children."

"Mum and Dad wanted me to go with them," he says. I catch my breath, is he confused, his parents are both dead. I still, waiting to hear what he says next, "But you kept saying you needed me. I told them I had to help you…" He tails off. I shuffle closer to him and I put my hands on his arms to reassure him, he continues, "When I woke all I could see was them, they were beckoning to me. I was able to tell one of the nurses, she explained it would have been a dream while I was under sedation, and she told me that you had sent messages they told me what you said, how much you loved me and that you needed me, then they played messages from you to me, she said my brain had connected the two, but I wonder if I was so close to dying it was them there waiting for me, virtually saying we are here and it's ok, but you pulled me back Annie, that's what I think."

"Oh Matt, you were very poorly sweetheart with the virus, and under sedation, with so many drugs coursing through your body, you would have had dreams, nightmares, and sometimes they do come back to you afterwards," I remember a story of a man who had a cardiac arrest and could see the team working on him, he was above them looking down, as if he had died and was waiting there to see what happened, if they got him back to life, so anything is possible. I wonder if Matt's dream was something like that, he was on the cusp and had his dead parents encouraging him one way and me the other, it leaves me cold.

"I'm not sure it was a dream, Annie."

"It is good to talk about what you saw, Matt, talking gives you perspective, it is also important to know you are here, you have come out of that terrible time," all I can think is thank goodness I told the nurses to tell him I loved him and needed him, and the messages reinforced that. I just want to wrap him up in my arms and make the bad things go away. I rest my head on his chest as he strokes my back. I don't think there are any words that can take what he saw and said away, just a reassuring presence.

The next morning Matt lies there listening to life going on in the barn, greetings as the children get up, the smell of toast cooking, Annie laughing, no doubt at something Arthur has said, a bark from Bob, then a greeting as he comes in from outside. Matt listened and was transported back to childhood, when he had been in bed ill with some childhood ailment, he could hear his mother downstairs, the smell of bacon cooking and his father coming in for breakfast following an early start on the farm, then he heard the woofing of the dogs, and them hurtling upstairs to see him, jumping on the bed, good memories, he knew he had to make some more with Annie, Arthur and Molly.

Matt feels he needs to try and try hard, no matter what, he takes himself into the shower and then gets dressed, he sees his face in the mirror and it shocks him, but he had to push on, he needs a shave and a haircut, but he will take Arthur's advice and will not ask Annie to do it. He walks through into the open plan living room, suddenly all goes quiet as the impact of him standing there dawns on them all. Bob runs up to him followed by Arthur and Molly who puts her hand in his and draws him to the table to sit for breakfast. Annie just comes up and wraps her arms around him, he knows she's crying as his shirt feels wet, but knows she won't show the children.

"So, porridge is it for everyone," he says and smiles as the children sit down too.

"No way Matt, we have toast, we don't like porridge, Mum's has lumps in it too."

"Well thank you for that Arthur," Annie says, reeling at the vision of Matt up, "Finish that toast or it will be porridge, lumps and all," she's praying this isn't too much, but thinks even for a few minutes it will be good for him.

Matt looks at Annie and behind her sees through the window, "It's getting windy out there," the trees are rocking alarmingly.

"It is forecast for high winds today, Dave texted to say Don and him are checking the farm and gardens to make sure everything is tethered down, we don't need any flying debris."

"Some of the older trees might take a pounding as they are in full leaf."

Annie sits down, "Do you really want my porridge?"

"Definitely," he says earning him a look from Arthur as if to say big mistake, Matt does chuckle, it is difficult to take everything in but he tries his best, his head feels full of cotton wool. Annie puts a bowl down in front of him and gets one for herself, telling the children to get ready for PE and school, with loads of moans from them. She rests her hand on Matt's arm.

"Are you ok?"

He turns and looks in her eyes, just holding the look between them, a look that says it all, full of love, "Little steps, Annie. I decided I needed to take some this morning. I might have to lie down shortly but I wanted to do something I decide to do, not be dictated to by this illness," he picks up his spoon and tries his porridge. "This is good contrary to the review from Arthur. I always loved golden syrup; Mum used to make steamed syrup pudding for Sunday lunch."

"Yes. I remember my mum doing the same. I might make that this weekend, haven't done a steamed pudding for ages," light conversation going to and fro between them, some control, making something simple, huge for Matt, some normality in the world he's been forced into.

As Annie clears up after breakfast, she smiles to herself, Matt coming into the lounge earlier was a shock, but ultimately a good one, and a move he needed to make himself, getting some control back, before he went back for a rest, she straightened the bed and tidied up, thinking about his words last night, they had deeply disturbed her, and she knew she would have to mention them to Fran or to John the consultant, he was very poorly, possibly then near death, that frightens her, but she has to think that he's here, he's back with them.

I get the expected call from school mid-morning, and speak to Molly's form teacher, she fully understood my reasoning behind not sending her in, and would continue to support her at home, it would have only been one day a week as trying to socially distance a class of over twenty all together in the small school would have been impossible. I did speak to Molly earlier and explain about going back, to see what she thought, she said she wanted to stay at home with Matt and Arthur.

The winds are getting stronger. I walk down to the gate with Arthur and Molly, so Arthur can do his challenge, no Bob though, he has attached himself to Matt, which I think is positive, there is nothing more soothing than having a dog by your side, it is very calming gently stroking one, and Bob seems to think that being on the bed is his mission, so I have put a throw on there for his visits. As we walk back up towards the barn my phone rings. I sit out on the chairs as Arthur and Molly check to see if Matt is awake, they want to tell him about Arthur's challenge.

It is John the consultant, part of critical care follow up, we talk about Matt's health, whether he will need physiotherapy, John says the dietician will give me a ring early next week again. I am giving him food that will boost energy, muscles and immunity, but a call would be welcome. I tell him how Matt got up and joined us for breakfast, he felt that was a good sign, and also that Matt knows his limitations. I also told him about Matt's 'dream'.

"Yes, Annie. I have heard of people who have been unconscious talking in similar ways, it is the combination as you said of drugs, but also, we don't know for sure what being on the brink of death can produce mentally, what people see, what's out there, but Matt does need to talk, if you feel it is too much and that he needs any psychological support you will have to let me know. I think it is also important to bear in mind his history and the possibility of post trauma symptoms, by the sound of it that isn't an issue now, but it is early days. Ultimately Annie I am pleased with his progress, has he mentioned any specific pain or had any reoccurrence of fever?"

"No, he hasn't told me of any pain, his muscles are weak though, and I haven't noticed a fever."

143

"How are you?" I talk about me for a bit, but I feel overwhelmingly that having him home can only be positive, no matter what is thrown my way. As I end the call, I sniff. I can smell burning, which is strange. I can't see anything. I go inside but it isn't here. I go through to the bedroom, where the children are sitting at the bottom of the bed and talking, softly I note, to Matt, no bouncing, just nice calm, Matt looks tired. I think this morning was his own challenge, plenty more of those. I go to Matt and rest on the edge of the bed taking his hand.

"How are we all doing in here then?" I get a chorus of greats, "Oh well I'll sort food out then," Matt keeps my hand in his gripping my fingers, entwining them in his, he smiles, and I realise how important moments like this are for him and all of us. I just sit and listen to the children, and feel Matt's hand loosen its grip on mine. I shush the children as he has gone to sleep, and tell them quietly to go to the lounge, Bob stays.

As I am serving tea for the children Dave phones, "There's a big fire in Old Hall Forest in the distance," I go to the patio door and see smoke swirling round, quite far off though, "Apparently it was started by someone who lit a camp fire and it's obviously been whipped up by the winds," the poplar trees down by the road in the valley are bent double with the wind. I think what idiots, and the poor firemen having to deal with it.

"There's no problem for us, is there Dave?"

"No Annie, I'm thinking is this what we can expect for bank holiday week, now people can drive any distance for exercise and see someone from another house outside. I bet the Forest will be heaving."

"Well luckily it's not your problem now ex-police sergeant," I say.

Dave ends the call chuckling to himself, it's hard to kick the old work habits, but he's trying and trying very hard. He heads back up to the walled garden, he's picked up a can of lager to enjoy in the calm of the garden while he waters. Anyone knowing him would not be able to believe how changed he is in a matter of weeks. As he gets the hose out to use he can't believe it himself, he realises how unhappy he's been for a long time, he'd drifted since his early glory days, living the life dictated by his job, and probably out of habit, not planning and not looking beyond work, that was until he met Sue, they hadn't known each other long when he understood his life had to change to be with her, he didn't want yet another relationship going south because he wasn't there or was constantly stressed and doing overtime, too busy cultivating the next relationship while still being on the current one, something now he realised was shallow and beneath him, made him sick for his previous behaviour.

The chance to help Annie and pick the produce gave him the pleasure he hadn't had, gave him a new purpose, he and Sue had enjoyed the few months they had together before lockdown and he knew as she did that, she would have moved in with him if it hadn't been so difficult with her health and his work, they had discussed the future and even about him finishing, she didn't need to shield but she was vulnerable because of asthma.

He had racked his brains trying to work out a way to live with Sue, every time he spoke to her in the weeks following lockdown he could hear her distress, she was a gregarious person, she enjoyed work and the colleagues she worked with, and that part of her he connected with, they had such fun, it made him realise that many of his relationships had been shallow, Mellissa a case in point. Then helping in the garden had granted him the purpose he needed, he wanted to do more, learn more and he found it so good, he didn't feel stressed, he took time to do the jobs, coming up when he was still working very early before his early shifts and after shifts. He felt better in himself, no headaches, he was eating better and drinking less, it took away his stress, and he wanted to do it full time, he and Sue discussed his 'epiphany' as she called it, and talked about looking to buy somewhere related to garden work or nursery work in the future, but that didn't solve his worry about Sue.

Matt being in critical care deeply affected how he looked at work and dealing with people, their laissez faire attitude about the virus begun to wear on him, thinking they were invincible in the face of the pandemic, spitting on his colleagues, and he had to stop himself from doing something that would lose him his job, while picking and following his talk with Sue, he realised he could help more at the garden and he could with careful planning and if Annie and Matt approved, live in one of the barns with Sue, he talked to her about this, making sure her asthma wouldn't be affected by a move to the farm, so he set the wheels in motion, he knew if he carried on he would go over the edge, fail and loose so much and be no use to anyone.

He kept counting the days, not long now, five days before Sue could come, and he had completed his isolating, he sat on one of the raised beds and took stock, he was pleased how well the garden was coming on, there was a lot of produce for the farm shops, who were doing a roaring trade now, with negotiation from Don he had managed to get their eggs in the shops too, he felt that one day they might be able to do their own veg boxes, in alliance with Matt's shop.

He had seen Annie's plans and that was one of her ideas, a good one he thought, he had to get the poly tunnels watered, thinking of watering he was going to look at the system in the greenhouse, and see if he could get that working again, especially as it used rain water, he also wanted to see if he could get piped water into the poly tunnels, water wasn't a problem at present on the farm, as they had their own reservoir, which Don was using to water other crops, perhaps a portable water container near the poly tunnels using rain water from the reservoir.

As he went out, he could see smoke still coming from the Forest, but not as ferocious as earlier, by all accounts it was several fires. As he watered, he checked for pests and anything that might ruin their harvest, he knew what would be in the boxes to the farms tomorrow, he had never been an early riser except being forced to for shift work, but now he relished being up picking and getting the produce to Don to go to the farm shops, it was responsibility but good responsibility.

Finishing he looked out over the farm, down to the river and barns and realised what a good idea Matt had about the barns, how popular it would be with the fishing fraternity, when all this was over. Particularly the two-bedroom barns. Thinking of Matt he knew they had a long way to go for him to be anywhere near how he was prior to all of this, he had been such a vital man, now he looked a shadow, but if anyone could get him through he knew Annie could, his worry was for her though, she kept a lot hidden, he could read her, although he did admit to Sue he missed the Matt and Annie situation initially, but it was difficult to read her from afar at the moment, she had told him about Matt's "dream," he didn't comment just allowed her the opportunity to speak, but he felt that Matt had been on the brink at that point, near death. He fervently hoped that he wouldn't have to go back in at any stage, as he had heard this was a possibility with some cases.

Dave had started his own gardening journal, so he knew what he had planted and where, although he labelled everything, noting it down helped to get his head around what else he needed to do, he wanted to plant out the runner and French beans, but needed to put together some support for them, a wigwam of sticks would be good, but he would have a look in the out houses, he had found all sorts of things in those, that saved money and time. He gave Don a ring and asks his advice about the watering system under the greenhouse, Don said there was a tank, which was fed from the guttering on the large greenhouse, currently going into a water butt, he thought the hose inside had perished too, but he would check.

After his picking tomorrow, he'd sow in the greenhouse as although warm there were still winds, and as the week got hotter, he wouldn't want to be in there. He had a long chat with Sue on Face Time, she looked better already knowing they would be together, he still felt they ought to distance from Matt, more than 2 meters, as although both of them would be fine in terms of COVID-19 infection risk, he wouldn't like to pass anything on to Matt with his reduced immunity.

Matt felt exhausted, he slept fitfully last night, every time he opened his eyes though he knew Annie woke, as she sort his hand reassuring him of her presence, when he slept, he had dreams, worries and flashbacks gone when he opened his eyes, flying away with her touch.

Knowing Matt had a poor night I make sure he doesn't contemplate a shower or getting up for breakfast, he might be weaker with his tiredness, I'm very early the children not up yet, so I make him a tea and go into him, he has dark shadows under his eyes this morning, his eyes open as he hears me walk in. I put our teas on the bed side table. I lean into him and kiss him lightly on the lips, as I sit his hand rests on my bare leg. I am still wearing my pyjamas; he circles his thumb on my leg. We look into each other's eyes both thinking of different times, it's the first time he has felt her warm skin other than her hand, he cherishes the moment, it gives him impetus to push on and heal, he knows what he wants more than anything and that is time with Annie, the times they had before.

"Bad night?"

"You know you were with me all the way."

"Do you want your tea?"

"No," I look surprised, "I want you, but…"

"Matt we will. I want you too. I look at you and feel…"

"What?"

"Everything, do you know you have shown me so much, shown me a part of myself I didn't know, you know all of me Matt, you have made me experience highs I've never had," she shuffles closer to him, putting her head on his chest, hearing his heart beat, she even feels it rise with her words, "You have let me be me, without asking for any return on your investment, you know me better than anyone and in such a short time. I love you so much."

Matt hearing her words feels so pleased, he must try to banish the self-doubts about Sam, her words are like a balm to him but still he has questions.

"Why?"

"Why what?" I lift my head and look into his eyes.

"Why did you forgive him the affair?"

"Oh Matt," I go round to the other side of the bed and get in, snuggling up to him under the duvet, the wind rising outside, the cloudy morning giving some intimacy to the moment. I look into his eyes and realise he needs to know more than I told him, his illness undermining his normal level headedness.

"Whenever Sam was on leave it seemed to race past, this one particularly so, it was as if he didn't want to be on his own with me this last time, we never discussed the affair apart from that initial conversation, and it was very brief. I rationalised it all later. I felt so raw. I just wanted normality. I didn't want the children upset; was that why I didn't raise it. I think so, was I running away from the truth too. I don't know, once he went away on tour, you know it wouldn't be a subject to speak about. I did love him, but in the last few months I've realised it was a different love to what we have, he wouldn't remember things like you, he never did gestures, like treating me to millionaire shortbread," he smiles. "He wouldn't have known that detail, I'm not trying to put him down, but what I had with him was different to what we have."

I want Matt to know how different, but am careful he is the father of my children, "I didn't forgive him. I just carried on for the children, he felt terrible for what he did, as Stewart told me, but he never said sorry to me, and that hurt, would we have carried on being married. I don't know, that option wasn't available, it was taken out of my hands by circumstances. What I do know is that our love Matt is wonderful, passionate, and very deep, it's in here," I touch my heart and place his hand over mine, "It's not going anywhere, our relationship was fledgling as you said to me, but was abruptly halted, both of us wanting more, but unable to, yet."

"I love you, I'm sorry for asking you," I place a finger over his lips, something he's done to me.

"Shush, you are right to ask. I know too that what you have been through will put all sorts of things into your head. I understand that, we are bonded together by every kiss every touch, remember that my darling. When I told you about the affair, you said to me that I was the most precious gift Sam had ever been given," Matt nods, "Those were your words, and they meant so much to me."

It's still early and all our words have tired us both out, I lie close to him and feel his hand gently rubbing my back, through the silk then under it on my skin, that feeling is so intimate, so caring. I know he feels bad not being able to be my hot sexy man, we have each other and with strength that will come. I eventually get up and leave Matt asleep, have a quick shower and discover Arthur in the lounge, quietly watching the television.

"Hello, you," I go over and give him a hug, "How are you my gorgeous boy," I sit next to him.

"Mum, do you think Matt will be able to go on the quad to look around the farm, he should see how much everyone has done, it would be good for him," I think that is an idea, "And I could go on it with him," are there's the crux of the issue.

Smiling down at him. I say, "That is a very good idea Arthur, but not just yet, you are right Matt does need to see the farm, but he hasn't quite got the strength to sit on the quad yet, but when he does, he will want you with him for definite," that gets a smile, "So breakfast. I think I'm going to do scrambled egg for everyone, do you want some too, and toast."

"Yes, please, I'll go and tell Molls." With that, he's off. I start cooking. Matt has a long way to go I think before getting on a quad, but more worrying is his insecurity. I try to work through it as I am cooking, we all feel a bit like that after a bad night's sleep and if we have been ill too, that adds to it, but what Matt has been through will obviously manifest itself into many different post viral symptoms, this being one.

Before I put the eggs on. I check if Matt wants some breakfast, he's sitting up in bed, looking out towards the river.

"Do you want some breakfast, our tea is long gone cold," I smile at him and see some lightness in his eyes. I hope our talk helped him.

"Too busy snuggling under the duvet, and yes please," he smiles at her. All I want is to get back into bed with him and hold him and make him better. I take a deep breath and hold back any tears that threaten. As I finish cooking the eggs. I plate it all up and decide we could have a carpet picnic with Matt, Bob will hoover up if there any spillages. I just check if Matt is up for it, he is.

"Ok you two we are going to eat with Matt, come on," I take a tray with everything on through and settle them down leaning on the wall, give Matt his and I sit on the chair, "I thought it would be good for us all to eat together again."

"I texted Uncle Dave," Arthur says. I hope he hasn't invited him for breakfast too, and where is my phone. "I thought he might have a better idea than the quad,"

I explain Arthur's idea to Matt.

"Hey Arthur that is a brilliant idea and we will do it but not yet, what do you think Dave will come up with?"

"He said a golf buggy or you could have a trip in the land rover, but Mum would have to drive so that might not be too good."

"Oh thanks, Dave and Arthur, I'm a good driver, even double declutching the old landy I'll have you know," this banter goes on through our scrambled egg, making a lovely atmosphere.

The children go off and get changed, although windy they want to go and have a kick around, and later Arthur wants to finish his challenge, he's told Matt all about it and has raised over £500 now, part of him he says wants to continue, but school have given them a new challenge, to make and write cards for all the residents at the two homes near the village, as they aren't having visitors the head teacher thought it would be good for them and also with half term it would be good for the children too, both Molly and Arthur are excited about this.

I go back into Matt and supervise his shower, although not telling him that's what I'm doing, I'm just keeping an eye on him, it gives me the opportunity to change the bed again, Matt gets dressed and wants to sit in the chair, he can do some exercises there. I have put a radio in the bedroom, it has a remote so Matt can change channels and volume. Eventually I get the washing done and put out, although it might end up back in the village as it is still windy, but warm. I opened the one patio door and secured it back so Matt can hear us outside. I look up and he is standing in the window, he is tall but being thinner he looks taller somehow, or is he just standing up straight. I go over to him; he leans down and kisses my head.

"Do you want a short walk?"

"Yeh, I'll give it a go," he steps the one step down and slowly moves over the patio, with me by his side, Arthur whoops and Molly runs over to him giving his legs a gentle hug then runs off again. We walk slowly across the patio, it is so quiet, all you can hear apart from my two, is the birdsong, sparrows in the hedges near the river, the river gently flowing below. Matt looks up at the sky, although a bit cloudy there are no vapour trails.

"It's so clear without the pollution, it's lovely, do you know I think in some ways I prefer being down here, so close to the river, the house is great don't get me wrong, and my family home, but this is new with fresh memories, although…" he looks at her, "We had one or two good memories up there didn't we," we smile knowingly at each other, as we hear the quad coming round to the fence, Dave, and new toy.

"Here's renaissance man," I joke, with Dave still on the quad and engine going I say to Matt, "I can't believe the change in Dave, can you?" Matt shakes his head.

"Morning," he shouts, "How are you all today, good to see you out Matt, I've been sowing in the greenhouse this morning, just popped back for some late brekkie, are you cooking lunch tomorrow, do you need some vegetable or anything from the garden," this from a man who rarely cooked anything that didn't come from a tin or pack, fresh was foreign to him. I love it, and have to hold off the giggles.

"Yes. I thought I'd do roast beef, as long as it is tender for Matt, and yes to vegetables, whatever you think, do you want me to plate up a meal for you Dave?"

"That would be good, I'll drop the veg down in the morning, and collect lunch later, we could do with a chat this week to look at increasing planting and sowing as the farm shops are keen for more, what do you think?"

"Yes, any day suits me."

"Ok how about coffee time Tuesday, will bring my own, oh Don has had a quick check of some of the trees, he said there are some branches down but not too much, see you later," with a wave he's off.

"He is changed, he looks so happy too, never seen him like this, is it Sue or life?" Matt asks.

"I think both, Sue said he realised how his life had been empty and shallow, he drifted and let good life pass him by, I'm so pleased for them, do you know I would never have put them together. I think part of me thought he might hurt her, but she is the best thing that's happened to him. And he's loving the outdoors, which is the huge shock, Mum can't quite believe it, so we need to take some photos to prove it to her. Are you ok with Sue coming to the farm to live for now?"

"Yes, definitely, it means they can live together, and we all need to grab some happiness in this terrible time," I see him shiver slightly.

"Come on this wind is a bit cool," we go in, and I ask the children to read their diaries to Matt, who's back on the bed now, as I want to nip up to the freezer at the house and also if I can get it out of the ground, bring the swing ball down for them.

I walk up the hill, the wind blowing, but not as strong as yesterday. I know Dave is at the barn so take an opportunity to go into the garden, it looks lovely, he's doing such a good job, I'm really proud of him. We do need to increase production, it will be good to have a chat with him about that, life feels quite small at times. I get a joint out of the freezer and check the house is ok. I go into the front garden and collect the swing ball. I just get it out of the ground, then pick some flowers for the barn. I think I must pick some for Sue when she arrives.

It is slightly warmer and Matt is able to sit out for short periods, getting some sun, he is watching the children play swing ball, although Annie had pushed the spike into the ground, he could see it wasn't deep enough, but the ground is so hard she couldn't have pushed it in any deeper, he knew he couldn't do it either, he hung his head feeling useless, he had felt a small improvement and yes it was only four days since he had been home, but he was inpatient.

"Oh hell," he gets up with difficulty and goes to the swing ball, Annie had seen him through the window, his head hung, she could see his struggle with wanting to help and not being able to, then he jumps up she stops herself running outside to help, he is trying to push the spike in, telling the children to stop a minute, he does get it a little deeper, she sees him walk back towards the bedroom doors, rubbing his arms. What could she do, she knew he was pushing himself, he needed to rest for a good part of the day, that was what John the consultant had said.

She goes through the barn to their bedroom, he is slumped on the bed, he feels a wreck, his mouth is so dry, he can't kiss Annie, he has no appetite, even for all the lovely food Annie produces, he has no energy, just trying to push that spike in took everything, he feels defeated by it all. He hears Annie and tries to get up and pretend nothing is wrong.

"Lie down and rest, Matt."

"Why what's the point, I'm not getting any better," she sees the defeat and sadness in his eyes.

"Yes, you are, it is going to be so slow darling, you have only been out four days, Matt you were very, very ill, four days is nothing."

"I can't even kiss you," he lies back on the pillow, moisture evident in his eyes. She takes his face in her hands and gently kisses him, his jaw, his eyes and the corner of his mouth, she knows his mouth and lips are dry and sore. He looks deep into her eyes and sees love, he feels so bad about all of this, useless.

"Yes, you can, just gently kiss my lips. I will get you back to super kisser, you have to trust us all darling, we can make it," he lightly kisses her lips, and presses his forehead to hers, she is still holding his face and stroking his tears away, "You have got to be patient you know; we will do this."

She sits on the edge of the bed and leans on his chest, his arms go round her, "Take all my strength and we can be as we were, but let it happen, don't fight against the progress however slow, you know you felt slightly better today, that's good isn't it, and don't say it isn't enough, it is, baby steps, Matt." They stay like that for a while, lost in their own thoughts.

"Sorry," he says quietly.

"No don't apologise, you didn't ask for this, but we have got to get through the best we can, please never apologise," she begs him.

"It's so difficult Annie, it's not me. I feel wrong emotions, insecure and that is what is hard. I feel I am surplus to requirements in every way."

"Oh god you are not. I couldn't be here without you, please don't leave me, don't think this, it is breaking my heart. We just have to try darling and take strength from each other, you are my rock." He sees tears in her eyes now, and feels awful, but her words reassured him, why does he feel this emotional, not only physically drained but mentally all the time. He voices this to her.

"John said this is normal Matt, well it is normal for being ventilated but what they can't say is what effects the virus will have on top of that, so we just have to roll with the punches, let me get us a drink, the children are happy out there, back in a minute."

She swallows back her own emotions, feeling she has to be strong, and yet his words have caused more fractures of her heart, this vital man, her vital man, looking up, swallowing, trying to push the tears back, deep breaths, strength Annie. She goes back in to the bedroom, and gives Matt the honey and lemon drink, he has been using some glycerine swabs to help his mouth, she rubs some Vaseline lip salve into his lips too, and sits at the bottom of the bed, leaning against the bedstead.

"Do you want to try some cheesecake without the biscuits," she stands and gives him a spoon and her plate, and he has a few mouthfuls.

"I was thinking you know Dave wants to chat about the garden and increasing production. I think we should both see him, if you feel up to his long windedness," I smile at him, "I don't know the farm as well as you and you might know of further areas we can use, what do you think," she holds her breath, as this thought had come to her mind, she felt it might help Matt with confidence, being part of everything.

"Yes, that would work, he won't be coming in though?"

"No, come rain or shine he can sit outside the patio doors, yes we have quite a bit to think about," she continues to talk about the garden and what Dave has been doing, bringing Matt into the plans.

As I prepare Sunday lunch, Dave pops down with some veg for me. I go out to him and we have a catch up. I tell him I want Matt as part of our chat about the garden, he was fine with it and agreed Matt would know more than us.

"Are you ok," he pointedly looked at her.

"It had been a bit of a roller coaster to be honest, Matt has not only physical weakness but mentally it is taking its toll on him. He just needs a lot of reassurance Dave, he's been through so much, and they aren't sure how this virus is going to affect people afterwards, what will be left. You would be the same, he is inpatient, he wants life back. But I'm ok as long as he is here."

"Give me a ring if you need anything or want a chat, I'll pick up lunch later."

"Ok, oh Dave will you make sure Mum and Dad know everything," he gives me a thumbs up as he scoots off.

Matt decided to eat with us, he had stayed longer in bed this morning, just listening to the radio. I made sure the children left him alone to his thoughts. I have been in and out with drinks. I made some more lemonade earlier, nice and sweet and gave him some warm, his mouth is improving bit by bit, just being hydrated will eventually help. He is doing some exercises to help strengthen his legs and arms, but just on the bed, that is another long journey. I remember his powerful strong arms, built from years in the Forces and all the hard work on the farm.

The weather is warming up, Sunday was nice but a bit cloudy, lunch was good, Matt enjoyed it and ate sparingly, although the steamed syrup pudding and custard went down well. Tuesday has dawned bright and clear, the skies cloudless and seeming so far away, so blue.

I get a call from John that morning. I update him on Matt's, well, progress, although it is hard to see too much, but John is pleased, he tells me about other patients in terms of after effects and I know he will pass on Matt's symptoms and progress to help all of the patients recovering, he shows concerns about his emotions, and suggested he have a chat with him, he won't say anything to Matt about what we have said just let Matt talk about how he is in his own words, so I take the phone through to Matt, he is sitting by the patio door. I leave them to it, only going back when I guess the call has finished. I don't ask him about it, and leave him to update me as he wishes, giving him some control over his life.

The children are going to cycle up and down the track, we sit on the patio under a parasol that has materialised, Dave presumably, he sits on the lawn away from us, he can see the children and they dart up to the fence and shout at him frequently interrupting out chat, but that is family life, Matt is a modicum brighter today, but still very weary, I've asked Dave to keep it as brief as possible.

"So, it's doing well then Dave?" Matt asks.

"Yes, we are supplying a lot of produce now, lettuce, rocket, radishes, spring onions, calabrese, to name but a few, early potatoes, but we can't compete on those as our levels are quite low, with the greenhouse starting everything off and the warm weather before we are quite ahead, eggs too now, Don was looking at getting some meat in, but he wants to speak to you about that, as it needs some conversations and negotiating," he opens his journal and sets out all the sowing he's been doing, and what is going well in the poly tunnels.

"Strawberries are good and I have been able to supply quite a few punnets for them, they are big and sweet too, I'm told that as they are locally grown, people are very keen."

Matt takes it all in and comments on some aspects, he's pleased it is doing well and particularly as it was named for Ash Farm, a good memorial for his parents.

"I think your original plan for veg boxes and even setting up something from here is a brilliant idea and definitely something for the future, as more people want local and want to know the exact place it is from. I think this has changed slightly with lockdown."

"Thanks Dave, it's something to take forward for the future."

"What we need is some more areas to increase production, we can have more poly tunnels if necessary, although they are unsightly, they do encourage growth.

The orchard is doing fine. I know Annie and Don did necessary pruning and we have loads of blossom, which I believe is good isn't it."

Matt smiles and agrees it is, "Dave you are such a surprise. I can't get used to it, this enthusiasm, well done mate, it all sounds great. I think you could go further above the orchard. You know where the summer house is, well to the right there is an area Mum thought of using for potatoes to be honest, but it could be rotavated or dug over, and used for more varied production, we could do with looking it over."

"Well, I've taken delivery of a golf buggy, I've cleaned it and it is currently charging up in one of the barns near the house, but I'm not sure how stable it is off road, and I wouldn't like you turning it over Matt, not dissing you're driving, just the actual vehicle," he gives Matt a smile. "So, I could go up in the next day or so and video it and we can have a chat about it, then if things improve all round, I might be able to take you up or you can drive yourself in the next couple of weeks, what do you think mate?"

I looked at Matt worried he might feel the reminder about his illness was raw and reinforced that he couldn't do everything, but he nodded and spoke.

"Dave, I think that's a great idea. I haven't got the strength yet, and there's no reason why you can't video it and we can look at it afterwards, although I look forward to using the buggy, and no doubt Arthur will too, is it two- or four-seater?"

"Four of course, as if I could leave those two out of it."

We talk some more about plans and Dave talks about his excitement with Sue coming day after tomorrow. As Dave goes the children park up and come over to us, no doubt hungry and thirsty, so I go in and make them some lunch, Matt goes for a lie down, but he has a look about him that makes me feel it was good for him to be involved. I think about that summerhouse, and what an incredible view it has over the farm and valley, it was where Matt's gestures made me wake up more to him.

As Dave drives off, he feels good about the chat, and decides to go up to the summerhouse, he hasn't been up there before, he's seen it in the distance when he was in the orchard, but not close too. It looks lovely although in need of a lick of paint, he turns and the view is breath taking, he goes up behind it and takes out his phone to start videoing the ground, it's quite substantial, and flat. He feels it might be just right, then on the far side he sees that there is good access too, leading back down to the house and barns, and the road looks in quite good condition, so Matt might be able to get up here at some point.

As he goes back, he passes the summerhouse again, a seed of an idea playing around in his head, a surprise for someone new to the farm, yes it might work, he nods to himself and with that goes back to his barn to get a bit of lunch before carrying on with his jobs.

Matt feels some pleasure from seeing Dave and talking about the gardens and business, he still feels tired though after even a short conversation, and it is difficult to absorb it all. His talk with John was good, the man is so sound and level, he gave Matt such confidence, he knows Annie does too, but it's different, he spoke to him about everything, his dreams, his flash backs, his physical ability or lack of, he even mentioned a relationship with Annie, and John was positive, and said as he recovered, he felt everything else would. But Matt had to take it slowly, rushing might mean further illness, setbacks. As he thought of Annie, he drifted off to sleep again, thinking positive thoughts.

As I make some burgers for the children for later and chilli for us. I think of the slow releasing of lockdown, it does worry me, this week being warm and half term means people are out and about, being able to drive any distance for exercise, that means travel, beaches are full, areas with few critical care beds are being swamped, luckily Wales is still in lockdown and Scotland so they are protected, but not the south west. The rate for new infections remains high, and as for the deaths, over 37,000 now, it is shocking, it brings me to Matt, how I could have lost him. I know John is worried about the lasting effects on him and others, and the possibility of relapse.

Matt hasn't discussed his talk with John but he has seemed slightly improved. I wonder if John's words to Matt have helped him in some way, but whether it is a coincidence or the words, Matt is more positive, not necessarily hugely better but there is positivity and a lightness to him.

It has been a week since he came home, he still needs to rest a lot but has managed some limited exercise, although I am trying to improve his health with all my cooking, good rich sauces and soups, and smoothies, and fresh produce, he doesn't look like he has put much weight on. I haven't got any scales so it is difficult to determine, it is how he looks and if his clothes still hang off him, which they do even the new ones Dave got. I feel he might be thinking eat, sleep, repeat, but if it helps, good.

The weather being warm the children wanted a barbeque, firstly, we didn't bring one with us and secondly. I don't fancy using one, and I don't want Matt to feel he should cook either. So indoor barbeque, I've put some potatoes in to bake and am going to slice them when cooked and just put them back in the oven to crisp up with dips, Matt and I can have rice with our chilli, I've got a couple of sausages out too.

I know Molly and Bryan love them, I'm hoping we can eat outside and Matt can join us, he has sat out once or twice with us and is now watching the swing ball competition. I'm going to take a quick shower before it gets busy in the catering department and I'm going to dig out a dress I'm fed up with jeans, shorts and cut offs.

Matt walks back in from the patio, feeling tired, he goes into the bathroom, not realising Annie was in the shower, he stops and looks at her, drinking in every curve, he may not be able to do anything about his feelings yet but he can certainly appreciate her. She switches the shower off and with water in her eyes opens the glass door and reaches for a towel, Matt picks up the towel and wraps it around her, making her jump, before he can stop himself, he kisses her wet lips, opening them with his mouth, kissing her deeply, something igniting in him.

He wipes the water off her face, "You are so beautiful," he kisses her again, his tongue probing her mouth, "This is a promise."

"Of what?" her eyes shining looking up at him.

"Of more to come."

"I don't doubt it," she says as he gently dries her body, then he has to sit, energy gone. She kneels in front of him, and leans into him holding him tightly, he holds her aware she is naked underneath the towel, his imagination is trying to kick start the rest of his body, but not yet.

"That's the first time I've seen you naked since I've been here," Annie looks surprised. "You always have your pyjamas on in bed, and get dressed elsewhere," he says with regret.

"Necessity really. I don't want to wake you rummaging for clothes in drawers, and a necessity with Arthur and Molly if they needed me," she knows it is more about her and Matt.

"Don't hide from me. I can cope with seeing your beautiful body day in day out you know, we will get back to what we had Annie, what we had was huge, passionate and awesome. I want that to continue, and want it to become so much more."

"So do I. I think it will be even better Matt," he kisses her again, gently, lovingly. They enjoy those minutes together, the present haunting their past, although they want to get back to the past, they both know that theirs will be a different present and future. Reluctantly I go through and get changed as Matt comes back in slowly.

"Are we dressing for dinner?" he sits on the edge of the bed, pleased with how he felt but shaking his head at how it takes so much out of him. So very pleased his mouth and lips have healed, and he was able to give her the kiss he had wanted to give her from the moment he arrived home.

"I am always wearing jeans or cut offs, so I thought a dress would be good for a change, it will be good to sit outside and enjoy the warmth," she looks at him, "It's only a sundress."

"It's not the dress its whose wearing it," he says.

"Come on and sit outside and I'll put the food on, I'm cooking it indoors, and then bring it out."

"I'll have a shower first, no you don't have to supervise, which I know you've been doing. I will just take it easy, ok? I know I am tired but I want to feel fresher and then sit outside with you all for something to eat." I nod and leave him to it. I don't want him to lose any independence and obviously he has been aware I was checking on him. I worry he might fall or something. But I must give him some space.

Half an hour later we are all eating when Dave texts, he has had an order delivered and is going to drop our food off by the gate, more to clean I think, he's certainly stocking up for when Sue comes. I have a feeling we will hear a champagne cork or two popping off tomorrow, he also adds would Matt mind if he took Sue up to the summerhouse and have something to eat up there tomorrow. I mention it to Matt, and he smiles and says it's a magical place and yes of course he can, we lock eyes momentarily.

That night in bed I note that Matt still likes to sleep with a few pillows propping him up, he is still anxious about his breathing, so I lie against his side, he wraps an arm over my shoulders, as I press into his side, we talk, about everything, he is amazed at the events that have happened while he was in a coma, although the children's diaries don't say everything that was on the news Arthur had picked up some things, he knew about the number of infections and how bad London was. Matt can't get his head around the deaths. I think that adds to his anxiety too, and it certainly does to mine.

Then we just talk about us, how everything moved so fast, we talk about the picture I found in his office, and he tells me how long he has had feelings for me, it shocks me, so many years ago. I remember we had a party, Dave and I, and Matt was there he said that when he came home next, he wanted to ask me something, we weren't romantically together then, or at any time till now. I say to Matt so what happened you never did talk to me, and all he said was, Sam. He regretted not saying anything before he left, but life has a way of taking charge.

"Matt, we can't change that, as you know, but oh I am glad I have you now," with that he leans down and she looks up into his eyes, they glow for the first real time, they kiss each other, saying goodnight. Matt lies there with Annie pressed against him, he is beginning to feel some normality, he runs his hand over her warm flesh remembering and with that thought feels himself relax.

"Mummy," I hear a shout, which wakes me, in fact wakes both of us. I look at the clock and realise it's after 8. I look at Matt we have both slept, well I hope he did and I didn't not wake.

"Did you sleep?"

"Yes, deeply and no dreams. I feel ok too, not so exhausted as usual."

"I better get cracking, as I have no doubt that Sue won't be leaving it too late to come up to her new home, I'm just having a shower Arthur I won't be long."

I hear him shout ok, showered and dressed I go into the lounge, they are both dressed too, amazing, they are also sorting flags out, like they did for Matt.

Dave walks down to the first gates, he has the keys from Don and is so excited he can't open the locks, what an idiot, as he gets into the lane he can see Sue's car on the other side of the bottom gate, his heart kicks in, he walks down quickly and instead of unlocking the gate he climbs over and grabs her to him, both of them wrapping their arms around each other, Sue crying into his arms, and he knows he made the right decision and how all of this time has affected her, his lovely Sue.

"Oh god Sue. I can't believe it. I have counted down every bloody day, and it's happening, come on, let's get you onto the farm," he unlocks the gate all the while holding her hand, Sue is overwhelmed, she keeps shaking her head and tears run down her face, Dave jumps into her very full car and she gets into the passenger seat, they make their way up through gates, locking them afterwards, he drives her to her new home, such pleasure inside him words can't form, he just looks across at her and she at him, now both smiling.

As they pass the big barn, Annie, Matt, Arthur and Molly are out, the children waving flags and smiles all round, Matt is leaning on the barn wall, but he too is smiling a big smile, Dave stops the packed car, and opens the window, Sue opens the door and stands on the sill and shouts hello and waves, everyone looks so pleased and happy. As they move off, Sue looks at Dave and says, "Matt looks terrible."

"He looks a bit better to be honest, but still a shadow of his former self."

"God help us all Dave," she puts her hands to her face in distress, "I can't believe what has been thrown at us, it is too much some days to take in," he grabs one of her hands and kisses it.

"We'll be ok love, you're here now, we can get through this together, and help Annie and Matt as much as possible," he drives her car up to the second barn, "Well this unpacking is going to take some time, you didn't need to bring everything including the kitchen sink. I already have one," Dave says lightening the mood.

They spend the day getting to know one another again, yes unpacking, and settling in too, the months apart begin to dim and Sue starts to relax into her new home, she walks round with wonder, drinking in the view down to the river and the beautiful barn, smaller than the one Annie and Matt live in but no less comfortable and now homely with a few added touches of her own.

"I love it all, this room being open plan is great, is the other barn like this?"

"Yes, just bigger, and obviously lower down, right do you want to explore. I have to water and then I thought as it is such a lovely evening we could eat up at a summerhouse above the garden," he picks up a cool box clinking with promise, and holds out his hand to Sue.

They walk up to the garden and poly tunnels, Sue like Dave is amazed by the walled garden, it is the brickwork and the pathways all in brick too, she is also impressed with the amount of produce growing, she helps Dave with watering as best she can, as he points out the different plants. Eventually they walk up to the summerhouse, the table and chairs are out the front, a beautiful completely private place. He smiles, no doubt Matt and Annie have been up here in the past too, he turns Sue to look at the view, the sky feels so big on this clear late spring evening, bird song ringing out.

"Being here seems unreal, it feels a million miles from pandemics, news, death and illness. I can see why you love it, Dave."

"It doesn't mean you forget what's happening, it sharpens it to be honest, it makes me more determined to build something, make sure we provide food for the community, even if I am only the caretaker of the gardens and produce."

"Do you think Matt will be well enough to go back to farming, and running two businesses?"

"That I don't know. I don't think anyone does, and from what Annie says even the consultant is unclear at present, it is all so new," he wraps his arms around her as they look out across the farm and valley, "It feels wrong to celebrate, but I think we should try."

"Yes," she turns around to face him, "A small celebration of us and a toast to better health for Matt."

Annie is waiting for Bob to do his night time wee, and is looking up towards the house and beyond, the evening is warm, it feels like summer, she isn't a jealous person, but there is a small hint of envy, she knows Sue and Dave are up at the summerhouse, she remembers her and Matt having lunch up there, his thoughtfulness and kindness, there has been a slight change between them, in a positive way, she feels less a carer and more his partner, perhaps shedding some of her protection helped.

Subconsciously she hadn't wanted to show Matt how she was unchanged, hence her dash to get dressed anywhere but in the bedroom, although she tries to rationalise that with not waking him, she knows he has changed physically and in so many other ways, flaunting herself in front of him had felt wrong deep down. But he could read her so well. She thinks of Sam, not known for that, and can't imagine why she ever thought they were alike. I did love Sam, we had good times but I didn't realise there were different types of love, and my love with Matt is so different, but I know I was lucky to have been loved before, in a different dimension.

She and Matt have gained a closeness over the last twenty-four hours, she hopes that might help Matt to heal, it seems that is all they can do, hope, carry on building the blocks to help him, she hopes the closeness will prevent this awful insecurity, but thinks there will be some more issues, it is like a roller coaster, but if that is all she has to put up with then she's lucky.

She settles Bob, he is now back to the lounge for night times, giving some normality, as leaving him with the children might be a reminder of that awful scare, and both are happy he wants to stretch his paws and guard the whole house, she marvels at those two, she is so lucky. They are kind and thoughtful, they showed all their cards they made for Matt to him today, they put them into a box so he could keep them, each one made by hand, she knows how touched he was by their thought, they are now making cards for the homes, as they were asked to do, luckily Matt's old office seems to have a never-ending supply of paper and card, probably left over from his parents time.

She walks through to the bedroom, just checking on the children, who sleep soundly, Molly rarely waking in the night now, she ponders that, a different environment, not the old house, or the presence of Matt, although she did do it fairly quickly after the move, scary night and all. Matt is lying down, slightly lower than usual, another positive, she thinks he must feel a little more confident in his ability to breath. The side light is on and she gets undressed uses the bathroom and then gets into bed.

"Bob takes ages, it can't be age, he's only young."

"Bunny rabbit smells probably," he smiles at her, he feels different, more relaxed somehow, a slight niggle at having a gorgeous woman in his bed but not able to make the most of it lies underneath this though.

"I was thinking about Dave and Sue while I waited for Bob, he had some langoustine delivered from Nick at the Bugle to eat up at the summerhouse, he had it all planned. I was remembering our time there. Your thoughtfulness," she moves nearer and holds him to her, now able to hold him properly rather than worry about how his skin would be sensitive, gradually some symptoms were subsiding, but not all, energy was a worry. He wears a T shirt in bed, she feels this is because his body is so different but realises Matt will make his own decision about this, and in his own time.

The next morning, I am tidying away all the breakfast things, the children are in their room, they are making more cards, we found some old farming magazines too and they have been cutting out pictures to put on them, those old pinking shears make the edges look pretty. I put another load of washing in, just catching the news on the radio, they are opening a rehabilitation centre for the NHS at Hedley Court. I wonder about Arthur's fund raising money for Help for Heroes, that is where they started the care of the injured and rehab, how appropriate this new centre should be there, called NHS Seacole, after Mary Seacole who set up rehabilitation care for those injured in the Crimean War and named for her to represent the diversity of those working there, such a wonderful act, but then you hear the death rate, still very high and the new infection rate, and such a worry, thinking all of this I wander into our bedroom, as I approach I see Matt on the floor.

"Matt," I rush in, "Are you alright, what are you doing, did you fall?"

"I was doing my exercises on the floor and couldn't get back up."

"You idiot you are supposed to do those on the bed," she bends down to slip her arm through his when he pulls her down laughing, a deep wonderful sound, the first real laugh.

"Are you ticklish Annie," he starts to tickle her both floundering on the rug.

"No Matt," she says trying to stop him.

"What's going on Mum," Arthur says running in with Molly.

"We're being silly and trying to see if Mummy is ticklish."

"Can we try too," Matt nods and the children get onto the floor, tickling their mum, Annie laughing and all of them having fun, Matt joining in where possible.

"Can anyone join in," says a voice from the open patio door.

"Uncle Dave we're being silly and tickling Mummy."

"I can see that," both him and Sue are laughing too, a fantastic moment Dave thinks to hear that laughter in the barn.

"Is there a revolving door on this room, it's very busy," I say scrambling up, trying to get some order, but laughing, Matt's deep laugh reverberating deep inside her, "Ok you two go and finish your cards, and as for you Matt Abbot keep your exercises to the bed," oh I realise how that sounds and start laughing again. I kneel down and see the knowing in Matt's eyes as I help him up, he uses the bed to finish getting up, little power still in his legs.

"You tell him, Matron," Dave says.

"Haha, big brother, what can I do for you two?"

"Thought we'd just say a quick hello, but there was no one in the lounge so came round here, to socially distance and say that hello to Matt," they are outside both dressed for gardening by the looks of it, now that's a first for Sue, I think. "What I could do with Matt is some hose."

"Ose," I say and start giggling, "As in O's," I double up at my own joke, no one else catching it, "Two Ronnie's, O's," I'm on a hiding to nothing here I think, "I'll leave you to it," I walk out of the room giggling, hysteria, I think.

Later as Dave and Sue walk up to the garden, they have huge smiles on their faces. "That is the best thing I have seen for weeks, no months, laughter has been in short supply around here, perhaps you've bought us all good luck darling,"

Dave grabs Sue round the waist and they link and walk on, "Matt is still very weak but do I spy a light at the end of a long tunnel?"

"Fingers crossed, even if it is far off."

That was the best, the absolute best, feeling the vibrations of Matt's laugh go through me. I feel it is something I will never forget, it meant so much it lightened the atmosphere here. I know he has only been out of hospital 9 days, but I think there has been a slight upward turn. I try not to think too deeply because it is such early days, but if he does go back a bit, he knows how good it feels when he rests and gets back up those steps, moving forward. I go back into the bedroom and Matt is doing his exercises where he should have in the first place. I give him a knowing look, and get the towels from both bathrooms to put through the wash, although they will dry quickly outside, I will nip up to the house and put them through the drier later as I like them soft.

I find Matt outside under the parasol with Arthur and Molly doing cards on the table for the homes. I must get an envelope from the office and put the cards into and get them dropped off at the school post box by Don, good old Don, he and Phil are certainly kept busy with one thing and another. He wants to chat to Matt too, so I will have to get that arranged.

"Does sandwiches sound good for you lot, egg mayo, all round," approval from the three of them, lucky I plan ahead. I hard boiled eggs earlier. It is a full-on catering service here. We sit and have lunch and some chill time.

"What did Dave want with some hose," I smile at Matt.

"He's going to replace the perished hose in the greenhouse, Don has checked the tank and that is fine, all they need now is rain to run into it from the gutters and he can start using the watering system."

"He has to put holes in the hose, doesn't he?"

"Yes, so it can spray over the plants, if we don't get any rain, he can use some from the tap to fill the tank and at least it will reduce the amount of manual watering he has to do in the greenhouse, he sent that video over, didn't he?"

"Yes, I'll get my phone and you can see it," he puts his hand on her arm as she goes to get up.

"Sit down for a while Annie, enjoy the rest," she sits and he leaves his hand on her arm, circling his thumb round on her skin, soothing her, she's always rushing. The children gently chatter about their cards while eating lunch, then energised they go to play swing ball.

"Don't run yourself ragged Annie, we won't have this lovely weather for ever, so chill and stay here," she moves to sit in front of him on the bench seat, his arms come round her and she lays her head back on his chest, just being themselves for a while, laughing at the children, and Bob who hasn't worked out the ball flying around is attached to the pole, he sees it then runs down the garden looking for it and then turns and there it is again, and he runs back up to get it, repeat, they both laugh, "Not quite the full shilling our Bob eh?"

"No, but entertaining though," he kisses her neck just light butterfly kisses, something he can't resist doing.

"I will have inappropriate thoughts if you carry on with that," she turns her head, smiling at him, he kisses her mouth.

"Yuk, they're kissing again," shouts Arthur, stopping Matt and Annie who both burst out laughing. Annie thinks what a lovely day filled with laughter, "Mum can I have an ice cream?"

"Yes, sure love," she goes to get up.

"Do you know where they are Arthur," he nods. "Go and get you and Molly one, and make sure you shut the freezer," with that Arthur rushes off, "Is that ok?"

"Course it is, you're right I do too much for them, sometimes it's easier than clearing up the mess later."

"Chill," he stills her with his arms and they just pause, enjoying the moment, he places his hand on her stomach something coming back to him, something in the back of his mind a dream? The children come back out and sit under the parasol an ice cream each.

Matt goes in for a rest and I give him my phone to watch the video Dave took of the ground they are thinking of using. I go up to the house and put the drier on, as I check around and make sure everything is ok. I grab some clothes for Matt, he needs a few more T shirts and although a bit big for him they will have to do. I grab some more card for the children too and a few things from the big freezer to put in our freezer in the barn.

I carry the towels and food down to the barn a lightness to my step for once. I go inside and look in the garden, no children, where are they? I go into our bedroom and they are both sitting on the chair with Bob at their feet. I look at Matt lying on the bed, questioning him with my look.

"I woke to find these two staring at me, know anything about it," he says smiling.

It suddenly dawns on me I asked them to keep 'an eye' on Matt while I went up to the house. I laugh, "Sorry I think they took me literally. I just said keep an eye on Matt."

"We have Mum but he slept most of the time," Arthur says, "Can we go now?" I nod and they run off with Bob.

"I woke up and thought what an earth is going on, they both just sat there watching me, stealth ninja's," he is smiling, "Those two are a source of great merriment."

Dave and Sue are searching the outhouses for hose, Sue cannot believe the amount of stuff in all these hidden places, Dave shows her the boxes Annie had made for veg boxes and they talk about her ideas and Matt's.

"I could see a farm shop working here Dave, that old barn you said Matt had converted, and it wouldn't mean too much disruption for everyday life. I think you could sell more than veg and salad too, even flowers, the gardens are just wonderful. Matt's mum did most of this you said?"

"Yes, quite a talented lady, Ted said she quite often won at the local vegetable shows, and the sunken garden is lovely and inventive, and I know Matt thought of a café as well with the farm shop, that is a plan for a long time in the future though," they find some hose.

"How's this going to work then?" Sue says as they walk over to the walled garden.

"To be honest we need better and smaller bore hose than this, but with water in the tank we can just attach a hose lay it through the growing area, and then just turn it on, if I puncture the hose, it will spray water over the seeds and seedlings in the greenhouse, the greenhouse is quite old, and large, a newer system would be good but I don't want to suggest that as yet, it could be costly, if we can work with this great."

"You've learnt a lot haven't you," she says admiring his knowledge, and so pleased for him, he needed to move on, and this has given him the purpose he needed.

"Yes, I love it Sue, it has given me so much. I can't believe the change in me. I am coming up with ideas too, how we can promote what is happening here."

"What are you thinking?"

"Well, some YouTube films for instance to show 'how to,' it would be advertising for the farm and produce, Annie wanted a website, which I think would be great and when she sent the plans, she added some early pictures she'd taken, which would fit perfectly on it, showing how much has been done and also how traditional it looks, the inside of that amazing walled garden, the espaliered trees, the slate plant labels."

"That sounds great, by the way I gave my notice in," he turns to her and lifts her in the air.

"Oh, I'm so pleased Sue. I wasn't sure you would, but I didn't want to pressurise you, it had to be your decision."

"I thought long and hard about it and realised it was what I wanted, I've money saved and the money from my parents' house too. I don't want you thinking I'm living off you, or Matt as well. I want to contribute, and to our future, wherever that is Dave."

"We have a future, in terms of us, where that will be and what it will be I don't know any more than you my love. I just want to help Annie and Matt out and then see where it leads for us. I want to make the business profitable, or at least breaking even, but helping them is the main aim now," he hugs her to him.

"I know, and mine too, a huge priority before we plan our future, oh I just had a thought. I saw a couple of Gardeners World programmes trying to increase my knowledge," she laughs. "And you can send in videos showing what you are doing. I know this is grand and for selling produce, but you could just show how you only started picking and helping your sister, with no planting knowledge and see where that leads."

"Yes, it's worth a try," he pulls her to him, "We make a good team."

The weekend is very hot, my anxiety ramps up again. I can just imagine picnic areas in the Forest full, limited social distancing, and the beaches. I try not to watch much news. I know the government are concerned this is a dangerous moment, with easing of some lockdown rules, how would everyone cope with another wave of the disease, numbers aren't falling for newly positive cases, but you have to just get on with what you have to do, keep safe.

Fran texts me and I phone her back, it sounds like she's sitting outside, birdsong in the background. I mention this to her, "Well I am outside but my outside is in a car park," she says.

"How do you mean Fran?"

"I've been living in the hospital accommodation."

"What from the beginning of the lockdown?"

"Yes, there are a number of us, medics and nurses, it meant I didn't put the family at risk at all, so this car park is my garden, well a lot of tarmac but at least outside."

"Oh, Fran I had no idea."

"It made sense although I'm not sure how much longer, to be honest I am a bit fed up there are so many positive cases still and people going out, to parties, staying over with friends. I just think all that sacrifice all those lives and people are willing to put life at risk."

"Fran, perhaps we see it differently I don't know, but I am with you on this. I look at Matt and feel the risk, it is still rolling around, and people don't seem to care." I tell her about Dave giving up work to mainly come and help our business and his sacrifice at not seeing Sue. I also mention the fact Sue is here now, and they want to isolate, she feels that is over cautious but it is up to them. We talk about her children and how they are getting on, her husband managing everything on his own. I can see she feels very isolated, and she is. I worry about the impact on her in the future, what with the hugely high-risk work and not being with your own family to give you support.

I have seen the hospital documentary about the beginning of the pandemic at the Royal Free, and the work, the skills, the pressure, nearly running out of piped oxygen, the stress, was insurmountable, but everyone from top to bottom gave, and gave their all.

I feel restless that night, awake, thinking about so much, good things too, Matt's laughter, his smiles, which there are more of, but he is so lacking in energy still. I feel he might need more rehabilitation. I wouldn't want him to go anywhere though, is that selfish, possibly, probably, but I would worry he might get ill again, just as I am worrying about this, Matt jolts awake beside me, thrashing around, he sounds frightened. I go to hold him, but he knocks me away still in his dream.

"Matt it's me, it's ok darling, you are home, it's ok," I try to reassure him, "What is it?" I turn the bedside light on, he seems to come too then, his eyes wide, not knowing where he is, he sees me then. I see recognition, he relaxes back on the pillows. I hold his hands in mine.

"You're ok you're here now, what is it?"

Matt looks at her and feels terrible, he knows he hurt her, "I am sorry, sorry I hurt you."

"You haven't hurt me Matt, you pushed me away just now but you haven't hurt me."

"I did though I left you to struggle with the baby and what to do about it. I wanted it."

"What do you mean love, we haven't had a baby, we just have Arthur and Molly, my two," he turns and looks at me, shock in his face.

"You've had a bad dream Matt, it's just us four here and always has been, there's no baby."

"I let you down. I didn't use a condom and then it all went wrong, the baby and everything."

"Shush now, we talked about contraception after our first time. I still have my coil in, so there is no worry at all, we did talk Matt, there is no baby," I carry on saying the same things over and over, to try to reassure him, god you think we are moving forward then something comes back to terrorise him from when he was in a coma, "I wouldn't get rid of any baby Matt, if I had got pregnant I would with absolute joy have your baby, do you hear me?"

Matt looks into Annie's eyes, and hangs his head, he thought the dreams were going, this one haunted him. He remembered every word when he woke up out of the coma, the days following that were full of anguish, not knowing what was real and what wasn't, this one haunting him, he starts to breath more easily, he had a vague recollection of holding Annie's stomach and... God, he felt as if sometimes he was losing it, how many more times will he be haunted, dreams forgotten that disrupted his early post coma days, returning.

"Matt, look at me," she frees her hand from his and lifts his head. "You are the most wonderful man, no woman would not want you to father her child, and I am no different. I wouldn't harm any baby, it is a scary dream love, all those drugs, the virus causing so many different symptoms, no one knows about, that is all this is."

"I thought they'd gone, why come back today when it was a good day like the last couple?"

"I don't know Matt. I don't think anyone does, this virus has damaged so many different parts of your body, and this is one aspect, yes, we've had some good days, perhaps being tired is encouraging some of those dreams to the front of your mind, do you know I think if you recall them, like now, perhaps they won't come again," she prays silently for that.

"Ever the optimist, hug me Annie," I lay my head on his chest and put my arms around him, trying to give him the love and reassurance he needs, his arms come round me too. I feel him kissing my hair, holding onto me, for what feels like dear life.

We sleep fitfully. I don't want to go to sleep just in case he has another dream, and I guess he doesn't want to sleep in case he does. I get up and make some tea, coming back and sitting in bed with him, he looks exhausted this morning. I suppose I don't look to good either.

"John gave me his number. I think I might text him to give me a call today."

"Ok Matt, that sounds good," he felt more himself when he spoke to John last time, it might be what he needs just now. I feel for him because as he said we had a few good days and then this pushes us back.

Dave and I had hoped that I could take the landy up later after home schooling and look at the ground we were thinking of using, meeting him and Sue, but I'm not sure, I'll see how the day goes. Breakfast over, children settled at the table with some schoolwork. I get an opportunity to see Matt, he's had a shower and is sitting in the chair, looking a bit disconsolate. I kneel in front of him, resting my hands on his oh so thin legs.

"Have you done your exercises?"

"I'll do them later I think."

"How about a drink. I could do you a hot chocolate or a smoothie."

"I'm ok, you carry on I expect you have lots to do," he looks away from me. I get up hugely dismayed by how he is. I rest my hands on the arms of the chair and lean into him. I take my right hand and I lift his head, and kiss him, giving all my love to him.

"One step forward Matt, and as the saying goes a million back," I rest my forehead on his looking into those blue eyes that had started to shine but look sad now.

"What's the point, without the bad dream I couldn't give you a baby anyway, what… is… the…point…" he finishes slowly stringing out every word.

Something ignites in me, anger. I know I should keep my temper but, "Do you know Matt. I don't know what else I can say. I love you so much. I love you as you are now, how you were and how you will be in our future, but there is only so much I can keep saying," I don't have the words. I stand and walk outside.

Matt just sits, shocked by Annie's reaction, just then his phone rings, John. He just about manages to speak to him, guilt coursing through him, John realises something is wrong and coaxes Matt into telling him, which he does.

"Matt I don't know you both as a couple, but anyone who has someone in critical care with this awful virus, who can't be with them, who sees the news daily of the vast amount of deaths, who has to wait and see if you survive, keeping the home fires burning as they say, then support you on return home, will have moments themselves, moments that words can't explain, the stress for anyone and I include Annie in this is huge, in some ways some of my patients have said they were in a better place than their relatives not knowing what was going on."

"I'm not sure about that, but it shows how things at home were. You just have to work through it all, and as for the dreams coming back when things pick up, it could be that you are experiencing more brain activity and that triggers the scary dreams, tiredness, or just the virus biting back. Sorry to say this Matt but it is very early days."

John finishes the call and Matt sits for a while, he can't see Annie in the garden, and decides to go into the lounge, he must stretch his legs he must carry on. He walks through, the children are at the table still doing some home schooling, he looks for Annie and can see her outside wiping down what looks like shopping.

"What's your mum doing Arthur?"

"Oh she's cleaning the shopping, she does that every time we have a delivery, then she comes in and washes her hands then throws the plastic away, washes her hands, then washes all the fruit because we don't want the virus in the house, she says it's a military operation," Arthur says it in a matter of fact way that allows Matt to see how much he has missed, he didn't know she did this before he was ill, but then they didn't live together but he also sees how much protection is needed, not just for him but all of them.

"Does this happen every time?"

"Yes, but Mum looks a bit upset today, she doesn't usually throw the stuff on the floor, does she Molls."

"No," shaking her head.

Matt goes out to Annie and tries to catch her hand.

"Don't," she says and he pulls back, "No I meant don't touch, as I haven't cleaned everything and then washed my hands."

"Put it down and wash your hands, go on," he waits for her to come back then takes her hand in his and leads her round to the table at the back of the barn, he sits her down and then uses the table to ease himself down onto the bench seat next to her.

"You do that every time?"

"Yes, no one knows when it was touched, on plastic the virus lasts 72 hours, it's important to protect everyone."

"I know sweetheart, you were doing it with such vigour though, I'm sorry," he straddles the bench with difficulty but he wants to look at her face, she turns to him.

"So am I," she puts her head on her arms on the table, "It is too much, and I don't mean you, all of it, it feels never-ending, look I'm just having a bad day. I am so pleased you are home, and the last few days have been good, hearing you laugh," with that he sees the tears fall, "I'm sorry."

"Shush now," he pulls her towards him, "What are we like if it isn't me, it's you. I didn't know how difficult it was for you when I was in hospital. I didn't think. I didn't think about the effect it would have. I didn't think about what it was like at all. I just didn't know," he strokes her hair, talking to her quietly, wanting her to realise his mistake. "Perhaps I have focused too much on me."

"No, you have to, you have to get better, we are all depending on it," they stay like that trying to gain some balance, some calm, then they hear the children talking, "Oh what are they up to. I hope they haven't touched the shopping," they get up, Matt struggling, and go round the corner, there they are, looking at the shopping, hands on hips.

"So that lot looks like Mum has cleaned it, you take that in Molls, put it on the island, I'll clean this last bit, ok?"

Molly picks up some of the shopping and is taking it through when she sees Matt and her mum, "We are finishing the shopping and putting it away for you, Arthur is going to clean that stuff there."

"Oh, you both are so good, that's fine, you have the shopping I've cleaned Molly, I'll finish," but Arthur gets the wipes and finishes cleaning the few bits left. I throw the rubbish away and go and wash my hands. Matt goes back to the bench seat and eases himself down, going over everything, he decides that when he goes back in to the bedroom to get his laptop and look more deeply at what has happened over the last month or so, do some research, see what he's missed, although he and Annie talk, he needs to look at it himself.

He will read the children's diaries too, although they have read some of it to him, in those early days he couldn't take it in, and didn't Annie say she wrote something down too, he needs to know more, he needs to be part of this, John's words go through his mind, not just about Annie but about himself. They just don't know what might come next, this virus and recovery is a mystery tour to end all mystery tours by the sound of it, like firefighting unable to plan. He might not be able to plan but he can help by knowing what happened in that time he wasn't here.

Annie sees Matt gently walking along the patio and back several times, and then going down the lawn towards the fence and river as she works with the children on home schooling, going over their latest work, she feels pulled in so many directions, and feels she can't please everyone, she suddenly wants her mum and wishes they were up here, she'll give her a ring later and talk through everything, she hasn't had much time to talk and it would be good, a necessity she feels. she gives the children a drink and biscuit for their break time then goes outside with a drink for her and Matt, as he comes back onto the patio.

"You didn't have to do that," he says.

"The children are on break and I need a cup of tea."

Matt leans on the table for support, his walking burning his legs, "It is difficult times isn't it Annie, not just for us but everywhere. I want to get my head around it all and also what happened when I was in hospital, I'm going to look back on my laptop and read the children's diary, you said you wrote one too, didn't you?"

"Yes. I did, but you don't want to read mine. I mean…"

"What, not for public consumption?" he smiles.

"I said a lot of how I felt, and what was happening, so you might not need to look at past news. I was quite forthright."

"I can take it Annie, and I need to know what has happened and what is happening now, don't you agree. I can't shield from all of this forever. I know I had a bad night and I know the impact on us, but it feels right to do this, I'll sit this afternoon get my strength back and perhaps we can go up and see the ground Dave is talking about later, what do you think?"

"If that's what you want, ok," I worry that seeing everything that has happened might be too much for him, too much to take in, they did say limit some conversation and news, it isn't even two weeks yet since he's been out, but he seems determined. I might just text Fran and see what she says, he also hasn't said if John phoned.

"Did you speak to John?"

"Yes, he was as sound as usual, he helped me to see what you went through to be honest," he reaches for her hand, "This is all huge pressure on you Annie, and it has been before this too, not that I realised properly until today. I can see why Dave was so determined to come up here and help, he could see what I couldn't because of where I was, and I'm grateful to him for that, immensely so. I need to build on the good days, and yes, I might get more dreams but I have to cope with that, as much as you help me, I have to help you too," with that he stands and goes into the bedroom to rest but also to appraise himself of life while he was out of it.

I popped into Matt later and gave him some lunch, he seemed ok and was absorbed in my diary. I said a lot in there, shock of numbers dying and testing positive, fear, oh that came out a lot, fear for him, worry if something happened to me too, how would the children cope, and on and on, it originally started as a diary but became my journal, a way to express myself without talking to someone without tears all of the time.

Matt is shocked about what he reads not just for the country and the world with so much death, so much unknown, but how health services did or didn't cope, Annie's retelling of news stories, of documentaries which must have nearly pulled Annie apart to watch, but watch she did, so she knew what was happening in a place she couldn't get into, into critical care, where he was. The enormity of it was mind boggling. He witnesses first hand her anxiety for him and running the farm and business and for the children. Questioning what would happen if she became ill, that hit him hard, for the children her anxiety, yet carrying on.

It is a lot to take in, but he feels it is important that he does, there was a very much later entry after he was home, about him not needing to see how she was unchanged, in terms of physicality, and he obviously was, but he thought that she had changed emotionally, and he could now see the toll on her, she had changed contrary to what she thought, he can see she had lost weight, and he could see why their laughter of the other day had nearly turned to hysterical laughter and more because of the insurmountable pressure.

It did make him feel guilty but there wasn't much he could do to change the path that he had been put on, it did give him an insight into how she felt about him, he knew she had said how she felt and reassured him, perhaps he couldn't always hear the words, but seeing it in writing, made him feel overwhelmed by her love, and her comment about different types of love and how his love was everything. He had some lunch, not that he wanted to eat still, but he needed to try so hard to increase his strength, he felt he needed to be there for her a bit more.

Annie walked up to the house to bring the land rover down, at least she could practice her double de-clutching on the way down, she left the gate near the barn open but would have to open one at the top. The children were excited about going up and seeing Dave and Sue and a ride in the land rover, Matt was waiting outside the barn with Arthur and Molly, he hadn't said much since that morning. When all were strapped in, she drove up slowly circling around the house, the pond to the right below his office window, ducks waddling about, and then up and above one of the barns, she stopped and was undoing her belt, when Matt went to jump out.

"No, stay," she said jumping out herself.

"I'm not a bloody dog," Matt said indignantly, both the children in the back giggling.

When we stop at the field the children get out before us, as I shout social distance. I glance at Matt and like the children he is laughing.

"Sorry," I say. "I'll try not to be matron or chief carer, just me."

"It's fine, we'll have a good chat later, out of the way of young ears."

"Matt swore at Mummy," they could hear Arthur saying, "Matt said I'm not a bloody dog." Both him and Molly were laughing then.

As Matt and Annie approach Dave looks at them, they both look tired, not as jovial as the other day, a bit strained. He waited until they came as close as they could and started to chat about the ground, he and Matt walked away slightly from Sue and Annie, well Dave walked but Matt shuffled, his leg strength still poor.

"Alright mate?" he kept his voice low. "Is there something wrong, only you two don't look good today."

Matt let out a deep sigh, "Had a bad night Dave a very bad dream, that wakes you in terrors," Dave looks at Matt and sees shadows under his eyes and some light gone from the other day, "I realise how much she has had to do, and I don't seem to be moving forward, we had a few words this morning, since then I've looked at all that happened since I was away, news stories, Annie's diary, well journal really where she poured her heart out, she gave it to me. I didn't read it without permission, and it is emotional for me, and for her, so overwhelming. I can see why you decided to come and help her Dave. I am so grateful for that… I don't know how to ever thank you."

"Stop there, Matt, we are all pulling together as a family. I did it for Annie and you, and I am so pleased I did, because it is working for all of us. Annie has had so much happen over the last few years, not least your illness, but you are the best thing that has ever happened to her Matt, she loves you and would do anything for you, but everything that has happened impacts, I'm sorry about the dream or nightmare I'd call it, have you mentioned any of this to the consultant bloke?"

"Yes, I spoke to him this morning, the thing is they don't know why you might get something like that coming back to you, as I had it in the induced coma, could be the virus, information on recovery is evolving, he also made me realise that while I was in a coma what had been happening, and I suppose I haven't looked at all of it and thought it through. I just feel so weak and exhausted Dave. I can't even make love to Annie," tears well in his eyes, Dave wants to put a reassuring hand on his shoulder and has to stop himself, he bites his lip to stop the emotions, for Matt and Annie, his little sister.

"Look it is early days, Matt. I know you love her as much as she loves you, be patient together, and you mate are the most level headed man I know, calm, and brilliant for Annie, keep the faith bro," Matt surreptitiously wipes his face and they turn back, where it is obvious Sue and Annie have been talking, the two children running around the field, oblivious to all the emotion.

They decide the area is ideal, and that Dave will speak to Don about rotovating it himself, as they climb back into the land rover, Dave puts his arm round Sue, "Problems?"

"Yes. I think she's as exhausted as Matt is Dave, but you know Annie, won't give in, he had a very bad dream last night, and I think trying to reassure him Annie lost it a bit," he turns her into his arms and she rests her head on his shoulder.

"He's so weak and exhausted, worried because he can't make love to Annie. I get the feeling that was quite a big part of their initial relationship, although I don't want details," he looks at Sue and she nods, "He's not been out two weeks, he is quite different at times from the Matt I've known."

"This illness is hateful Dave, it puts the fear of god into you, yesterday some scientists were doubting the easing of lockdown, you feel you don't know where you stand."

"We'll be ok here Sue."

"Did you find out why Matt swore?" Dave asks Sue.

"Yes, when they got to the top gate Matt was going to get out and she said, Stay," she raises her eyebrows at Dave.

"Oh. I see, difficult, she's trying to help him and he's trying to help out, stalemate, by the looks of it."

I feel sick by the time we go to bed, the emotions of the day have been so high, what with lack of sleep, Matt's dream and our words, it feels it's too much to take in, and that is me. I don't know how Matt is managing, he joined us for some food, but I can see he isn't wildly keen to eat, his appetite still poor. I will look at him eating smaller meals and often or putting snacks in between meals, and increasing the nourishing drinks, and adding cream and cheese to food, to boost it, and although he needs to drink plenty he shouldn't before a meal as it can fill you up.

The weather is going cooler in a few days so I might do some casseroles, chicken, something lighter, fish pies, that would be good, all of this is going through my head as I have a late shower. I didn't get a chance earlier. I put on a little satin nightie instead of my shorts pyjamas for a change.

He is standing, well leaning on the wall by the door, with Bob mooching around, a few minutes of calm, he sees Annie through the window come into the kitchen to put a drink on for them, he smiles, she always looks so lovely even in bad moments, it's been a difficult day, so much to think about and that dream, he remembers being in HDU after being weaned off the ventilator, he vividly recalls the feeling of loss knowing the baby was no more.

He hadn't thought about that since those early days, even now it feels it is part of his history and not a horrible dream. Bob licks his hand to remind him why he is out here, and he lets them both in. His whole body feels heavy, it is such an effort, but he moves to the kitchen and puts his arms around Annie, she turns in his arms and lies her head on his chest, he pulls her in close, whispering words to her, of his love.

Annie carries two drinks through to their bedroom and gets into bed, Matt follows, she notes how his walk is more shuffle than walk. Today has taken its toll on them both, but Matt more so. They quietly drink, both lost in thought, Matt puts his drink down and turns on his side to look at Annie.

"I'm sorry," he says, she turns onto her side too and looks at him, this man who has suffered so much.

"Don't say that Matt, there is nothing to be sorry for, all of this is out of your control," she knows that is what he needs and thought it the other day, control, to control some aspect of his life, she'd hoped today going up to look at that land might have been a positive, but on the back of his bad dream, unlikely, she can't think of anything to say at that moment that will help him, tiredness overtaking clear thought.

"Turn round and snuggle in Annie," she does and he puts his arms around her holding her close, he feels her relaxing and begin to sleep, which helps him to relax, hearing her steady breathing, he tries not to think, tries not to let that dream re-enter his head, he gently strokes her leg lulling himself off to sleep, taking his mind away from dreams.

Dave and Sue work in the greenhouse, trying to put the hose line in, managing to do the job with what they have, Dave has moved the water butt away so any rain, he knows there is some coming at the end of the week, can flow down the greenhouse and gutters into the tank, and they can use that for inside watering, the butt has gone over to the lean too, where rainfall in the guttering had just been emptying into a drain, win-win, he thinks. And luckily the water butt was light as they had little rain over the last few weeks, so easy to move.

They both get so much pleasure being in the walled garden, it feels like a sanctuary, not huge like some stately home walled gardens, but no less magical, calming, which they love, it inspires them, they have been sowing and re-sowing, trying to make sure that there will be plenty of produce, moving young plants into the beds, bringing on seedlings in the poly tunnels and planting out in the beds near them. The peas and beans were beginning to grow up supports, and he's contemplating putting in squashes and possibly pumpkins, they would do well on the new planting area, now that Don had rotovated it, he and Sue were going up there later to divide into beds, using some old bricks to edge the beds with, and put some paths in if they can, so if it is wet, it won't be a quagmire weeding and generally working up there, Don had a couple of bags of gravel delivered to do this too.

"Are you ok?" Dave looks up at Sue, her glasses on, sowing seeds into paper pots, he smiles at the difference in his beautiful girl, ok not a girl really, but she is to him, "I can't believe you."

"What, oh gardening clothes, converse and sun hat. I know different from heels and suits, eh? I love it though Dave, all the last few months of stress have gone, work aren't too happy that I went so quickly but my notice period hadn't been put into the contract correctly so one week," she giggles, because she thought it would be at least a month if not three, but someone had written it in wrong, someone in her own department before she took over as head of human resources. She admitted to Dave she hadn't noticed, which was good now but didn't reflect well in her role then, but did she care, no, it suited her. She had never gardened before but she loved it, more so being with Dave, she'd known him a long time, but until that night in the pub had never really looked at him, something clicked and look where it had got them both.

"Shall we have a break?" Dave asks.

"Yes, that would be good I put some sandwiches and cold drinks into a cool bag, do you know I would love to look at the orchard, shall we go there?"

"Good idea. I wanted to see some of the soft fruit trees."

"Oh, here's me thinking you would enjoy my company," he pulls her too him and they walk out of the beautiful walled garden holding so much history, she knows how Annie and Matt came together here, she wonders at past generations, Matt's parents, and back before them.

The orchard was awash with blossom Dave tells her, through May. Now it is important to keep everything watered if in a dry spell, the trees will do their drop, to increase quality fruit, they wander round the orchard and he shows her the other fruit trees.

"There are some pear trees over here too."

"They look so old, what are these?" she asks pointing at fruit bushes.

"Gooseberries, mainly, but I think there are some redcurrants and blackcurrants, they should be ready next month, but the gooseberries look ready now, we could pick some and put them into the farm shop boxes, I'll email and check they want them." They sit down and look out over the farm revelling in the peace, feeling so lucky to be a part of this away from the outside world, but obviously aware of it all.

Feeling the peace flow through him Matt sits on the patio, he's done some exercises and is getting his strength back with a drink he made and one of the new snacks Annie had made for him, Arthur and Molly tucking in at break too, lovely bite size cheese scones, when he had finished his exercises earlier he went in and made drinks for them all, shaking his head at Annie when she tried to stop him, he could lean on the island and put the kettle on, that much he could do, he left her a drink, she comes out now to sit down with him.

"Lovely scones Annie," he takes a mouthful and savours the strong taste, unusual for him he thinks, "I can taste them too."

"Oh good. I used some strong cheddar to make them tasty. I thought having something small at intervals during the day might help you, and it's no hassle to do it as you know Arthur likes his regular breaks, and a nibble then is always welcome."

"I know you've done your exercises but do you fancy walking down to look at the river with me," It was easier to talk walking side by side, she thought.

"Yes, that would be good," feeling slightly revived he stands and they stroll down the lawn, his arm looped round her shoulder, but not leaning on her, "I know how much all of this has taken out of you Annie. I want you to know I am here for us. I hadn't entertained the idea of what had happened while I was in hospital, reading your diary, it woke me up to the toll on you. I needed to know it all and although I feel guilty at not being here, it wasn't a path I chose for myself, but I want you to know. I know it all now."

She stops and turns in his arms, knowing he has seen her deep emotions reassures her, she couldn't tell him all of that but for him to read it instead, that helped immensely.

"Reading how much you care, sort of overwhelmed me, in a positive way, it has helped me see things from your perspective, how hard you worked to keep it all going, but not being able to see how I was must have been so hard for you."

"It nearly tore me apart not being with you, you know me if I could I would have been there every minute of every day, making sure you were looked after and had me by your side telling you to get well. I and many others weren't allowed to, but having those wonderful staff to look after you and relay messages was so important to me and now, I realise for you," she thinks of his dream about his parents, or was it the brink, her words pulled him back, the enormity of that is too much to think about.

"You watched those documentaries too, on the Royal Free, filmed at the beginning of lockdown."

"I needed to know Matt. I needed to see what you were going through, and although so hard as you say, it helped me visualise your care."

"I do love you Annie. I know how deep your feelings are, and I want you to know mine mirror yours. I wouldn't be here if it wasn't for you, and since I've been home you've looked after me so incredibly well, even thinking about small things like snacks to try to improve my eating, those are so important, but I want to do more, to help you but also to be back as a human, and I know baby steps, well I'm going to start taking some toddler steps."

He grins at me, and pulls me into his arms, "Look we are going to have more up and downs. I know that, John said as much but we must make sure we talk to each other, tell each other how we feel, and I'm as bad, when we first got to know each other, we were open about how we felt, and that has to continue, so share and I will be doing that too."

"I will Matt, it's finding time isn't it sometimes, with all that is going on here, the home schooling, which I need to check on soon or they will go off piste again, but at least Dave and Sue being here takes some weight off."

"When I go in shortly, I'm going to email Dave and discuss the planting, and copy you in for your ideas. I want to see what he has in mind for that plot, and no we didn't really get into it much yesterday, and I need to touch base with Don too, are you ok me discussing the garden with Dave?" she nods emphatically.

It seems that even in the downs, coming out the other side makes us both try to move forward. I suppose part of me thinks to the next down, but I try not to be negative, "Ok I'm going to do a bit of cooking while I keep an eye on those two," he smiles.

"I know all about 'keeping an eye' Annie, those two are priceless sometimes," we walk back up to the patio and go back in.

The next morning is cooler as I let Bob out and start breakfast, so porridge then, no escaping I think and I add cream, the children come in for breakfast as I do them toast. I go through and see if Matt is awake, he had a better night last night in that again no dreams. I slept, but I feel I am only half sleeping wanting to be awake as soon as he has any problems. He's coming out of the shower as I pass the bathroom door to make the bed. I look at him, there is a slight change in his body, he has a little more meat on his ribs I think, but as I don't see him without his customary T shirt it is difficult to tell. Tucking the towel around his waist, he holds her to him and kisses her with longing, "Oh Matt," she says into his mouth, holding onto him.

"Sweetheart," he smiles a genuine smile, and looks into her eyes, he sees what he has wanted to see, although she says she loves him, to see lust and longing in those eyes has done him so much good, he tells her.

"Don't doubt me, you are everything I want," she says and disappears out of the bathroom. Annie stops before going into the lounge and lets out a breath, what it must feel like to be him currently doesn't bear thinking about, to feel that he couldn't make love and be the vital man he was before. Matt comes in for some breakfast, there is a lessening of his shuffle this morning, that's doing his exercises, resting and eating she thinks, as she stands next to him, he softly draws her to him and she kisses his head.

Dave and Sue have taken a wheelbarrow of tools up to the top plot, and are pegging out the beds they want, it is easier to work today as the weather is a bit cooler, a flask of tea with them not cold drinks. They work methodically having discussed the size of the beds needed, and the size of paths in between. Sue eyes the huge sacks of gravel she knows they will have to cover the paths with, not something she is looking forward to, but it had to be done.

"It will be good to get this done today and tomorrow as Friday looks wet and as for the weekend it will be raining most of the time," Dave says, "We might have to use some edging boards if there aren't enough bricks, but it will look nice. I was thinking when I emailed Matt back as this area has access, perhaps we can do pumpkin picking for Halloween, that's to say if we will be able to that is, who knows."

"It's so up in the air isn't it, although if you look at Europe you can see easing and they are a few weeks before us."

"But look at our deaths Sue, what country will want any English citizens visiting, which makes me think there will be lots of holidays taken in this country and days out. So, the pumpkin picking might work later in the year, and when we are able to get the barns up and running income for Matt."

"Has he spoken at all about finances or Don?"

"He vaguely mentioned it in his email, saying how good income was from produce and how pleased he was we were getting some meat into the farm shops as well, but nothing else, he's given me the bank passwords and asked for me to look at the produce income and outgoing, so could do with your help on that one," she laughs, although Dave has shown how good he is with the gardening side of the business she knows from their conversations that the financial side of that isn't going to be his area, at least she has some experience of that.

He digs a narrow edge along the pegging string to put either bricks or wood edging in, and Sue starts raking over what will be paths, they both stand back leaning on the fence and get a drink taking in the mornings work.

"It's really taking shape, isn't it?"

"Yes, I think this spot will be ideal for a number of things to be honest, might put the pumpkins nearer the fence and gates and then other produce the other side. We could put in swedes, maincrop carrots and squash there and some winter cauliflowers," he said pointing at the beds away from where they were standing.

"We have them growing on don't we in the greenhouse?" Sue asks drinking from her mug, enjoying the togetherness of their lives.

"Yes, and we'll sow some more, same with some salad to keep a good turnover for the farm shops, come here love," he opens his arms and she steps into them turning and looking out over the farm, feeling the warmth of him and feeling just so happy as he wraps his arms around her.

"I'll pick some of the flowers from the sunken garden later, as they will be ruined if we have heavy rain, the roses particularly, I'll leave some at the barn for Annie too," she turns around giving him a long lingering kiss. "Can you believe how much has changed for us Dave? When you passed over the phone last night and I was talking to your mum it really hit me, she is pleased for us, but so worried about Annie and Matt."

"I know she is I could hear her smiling when we spoke, but as for Matt, it is slow progress, he was so devastated about that dream on Monday, and they both looked worn out, although I was pleased, he emailed and is looking to take some leads on the farm and garden, that will do him good, but…" She finishes his sentence.

"Baby steps. I know, to be honest if I hear that again I will go mad, god knows what Matt thinks," they smile at each other and carry on working.

Later Annie gets some food for the children while cooking a lasagne for her and Matt, and quickly doing some sausage rolls for tomorrow for snacks, thank goodness for frozen pastry she thinks, she also needs to replenish her freezers soon, she needs to email Dave for the next order, and ask about meat as that is low in the big freezer, but Dave will sort it out. As she's just contemplating a shower, she hears a knock at the door, and sees Dave and Sue place something down then step back, she goes out and has a chat with them, touched by the flowers, she puts them in a jug and onto the dining table.

She and Matt sit in the lounge eating, he only had a small portion but he has had more today overall with little and often, she put some spice and chilli into the lasagna, the dietician who phoned had suggested that might help his taste buds, adding herbs and spices, as the symptoms of COVID-19 can make eating and drinking less enjoyable, it doesn't take much to do a few bits of cooking while the children are home schooling. The children are sitting on the floor watching TV, Matt's hand reaches for hers and they eat with their fingers entwined, feeling slightly normal for once.

"These flowers are lovely," Matt says.

"Sue dropped them off earlier with Dave, she picked them from your mum's garden, they smell divine, they said they had been very busy up at the top plot, pegging out and dividing up the land for beds, they started putting down the gravel and want to finish it tomorrow if they can, Dave said that a weather front is coming in with a lot of rain Friday and the weekend and much colder."

"Yes, he sent a couple of photos of progress, they work hard those two don't they, just never would have Sue in that setting though," he smiles at her.

"No, nor me."

A day for staying in as the cool weather continues, home schooling isn't going too badly. I feel out of my depth quite a bit though, but the teachers are wonderful and give us plenty to do, the children still love Joe's PE, which we had to explain to Matt, they do some bitesize on the BBC too, so it adds to a varied day, by afternoon though they need to kick off the traces and they go outside. I start to take the bins up to the gate.

Matt hears a scream from Molly, he struggles out of the chair opens the patio door and goes into the garden, Molly points to Arthur down by the river.

"He's gone to get his ball," she shouts sounding frightened.

"Stay here Molly," Matt walks as quick as he can towards the fence, stumbling, knowing running is out of the question, trying to take the shortest route, he has to get over the fence. Somehow, he manages to stand on one leg while supporting himself on one of the posts, he can see Arthur in the distance and calls to him, he swaps hands to get his other leg over again supporting himself, although the post is wobbling a bit. He gets to the other side of the fence and stumbles again, he goes down the hill and shouts for Arthur to stop, he can see him near the bank, just at that point he sees Arthur trip and fall down out of sight towards the river, he increases his pace, his legs are pumping but he feels he's going know where, his breathing stuck not coming out, he gets to the bank and sees him lying on the shore. He scrambles down the bank, mainly on his bottom, he manages to get to Arthur, please god let him be ok, it's quite a drop.

"Arthur, Arty," Matt falls to his knees, he's not in the water but lying still on the shore, Matt places his hands on Arthur's back careful not to move him, "Arty," he uses the pet name he has for him, as he does a breath suddenly comes out of Arthur and he lifts himself, winded trying to catch his breath, he sees Matt and flings himself into his arms crying with fear and relief, Matt himself now being able to breath.

"It's alright Arty, you're safe, that was quite a tumble it's a long way down here, it's alright," he holds him tightly, just moving his own legs to sit from kneeling as the exercise had his thighs screaming.

"I only went for my ball," he looks down the river and it's gone, fresh tears erupt.

"Hey there are plenty more footballs, but not plenty more Arthur's," Arthur lifts his head and looks at Matt, his face smudged by tears and dirt, "You shouldn't go near the river, you are so important to all of us matey, we couldn't do without you, you might have been hurt or not been able to get out of the water."

Arthur takes what is a combination of a breath and a sob and says, "Would you miss me?"

Matt goes to reassure him when he says, "I miss my daddy," he leans his head on Matt, crying still.

"I know you do; he was a good Daddy and I know he misses you too, have you told Mummy you miss him," Arthur shakes his head, "Why not?"

"She might get upset, and I'm the man of the house and have to look out for her and Molly."

"She'd want to know, she could give you hugs and talk about Daddy, look at his medals and all the photographs, remember all the good times, and make you feel better."

"Will you stay Matt?"

"Of course, I will Arty."

"Will you get better, you won't die, will you?" he asks anxiously.

"I hope not, I'll do my best to get better and then we can do loads of things together, with Mummy and Molly, like the beach hut holiday."

"I love you Matt. I want you to stay you make Mummy happy, and Molly loves you too," all of that takes Matt's breath away, "will you be able to get me another football?"

Matt recovers enough to reply, "I love you both too Arthur and yes definitely I'll get you another football, in fact knowing your mum I bet she has a spare football somewhere," he smiles at him, as Bob who has been circling them both, worried, put's his paws on Matt's lap and licks Arthur's arm.

When Molly screamed Annie was part way up to the gate with the wheelie bin, she heard it, abandoned the bin and raced to the far side of the barn, realising she couldn't get over the fence she called Molly and shouted she'd meet her by the front door while she ran round the barn, she had seen Matt trying to get down to the river in the distance and realised with Molly shouting that Arthur had gone down there, Bob was barking and eventually jumped the fence to go with Matt. Annie gets to Molly who tearfully tells her Arthur had gone after his ball, they set off.

As they run down, she now couldn't see either Matt or Arthur and felt dread deep inside her, she stops Molly at the trees and tells her to stay there and runs to the river bank, which is high here, she looks down and with relief sees Matt holding Arthur, with Bob nearby.

She bends putting her hands on her legs to steady herself, taking deep breathes, as she gained control of her panic and breathing, relief mixed with concern about both of them, Arthur stood and looked okay, it was at this point she knew Matt wasn't going to be able to get back up, he hadn't moved, he was sitting hands kneading his thighs as if he was trying to restore muscle power for the return trip, Annie stood up told Molly to stay where she was and reached down to help Arthur up the bank.

"Alright darling," she hugs him to her, reassuring him, "Go and stand with Molly I'm just going to have a word with Matt, stay together." She scrambles down the bank, and crouches down next to Matt, "Have your legs gone, Matt?"

He looks at her and nods, "I might need help, my legs are burning up."

"Ok, I'll put my arms round you and under your arms do you think you can see if you can bend your knees and push up," she's thinking this is not going to be easy, she places her arms under his and stands with a leg either side of him both of them slipping on the gravel bed, Matt tries his best to push up as Annie pulls him, he just does it and starts to topple back when she manages to stop his backward fall, they stand like that for several minutes getting their breath back.

"You're not going to get me up that bank Annie," Matt says looking at the steep bank, Annie turns her head and looks at it and then further downstream.

"I know, come on let's walk a bit downstream and up the shallow bank, can you move?"

"Not with you attached to me, no," I had forgotten I still had my arms round him.

"Oops sorry," I release him and we walk with small steps further down the river, and then somehow go up the shallow bank. I would suggest he sits on that bank to catch his breath but I don't think I will get him up this time, the children come over and are obviously very upset, we both reassure them as Bob runs along with us, it takes some time but we get into the barn, and stop, Matt getting his breath back.

"I just needed to get to him," Matt says looking exhausted.

"You did darling," I tell the children to sit at the breakfast bar, Matt stands leaning on the island. I get a cloth, wipe Arthur's face and hands and get them a quick drink and biscuit, all the time quietly reassuring them.

"I'll go through to the bedroom and lie on the bed, if I sit on the sofa I'll never get up."

"Ok, I'll sort Arthur's scrapes out and then put him in the bath, and come and help you if you want a shower or bath," both are filthy from the river bank, but as I say I'll help Matt into a shower or bath he raises his eyebrows suggestively. I give him a stern look but a ghost of a smile plays on my lips, although exhausted he has some light in his eyes.

"I don't want a bath…" Arthur stops as I look at him.

"Firstly, Arthur you are filthy dirty, secondly you do as you're told and that includes not chasing after your football outside the garden."

"You tell him Mummy. I told him too and he wouldn't listen to me," I turn and see little Molls with her hands on her hips, mimicking one of her brothers poses, looking cross.

"Good girl, you should listen to your sister, she knows better than you, right you finish your drinks and biscuits," I go through to the bedroom Matt sits on the edge of the bed.

"My legs feel terrible," I bend down and take his trainers off and then lift his legs onto the bed pulling a throw under them, he sits propped up and opens his arms for Annie.

"Oh god Matt, what if the river had been high, what if you hadn't got there. I was only behind the barn taking the bin up."

"Shush now, you can't talk what if's, it wasn't high and I got to him, and you had to do what you had to do, luckily he was only winded, but he could have been more seriously hurt, but he wasn't darling, things to be grateful for."

"Thank god for you, those legs got you there, look I think you need to do some stretches before they stiffen up and you can't move them, I'll just give you a gentle massage," he leans forward to stretch as Annie goes and gets a cloth to wash some dirt off, then she strokes her palms up and down his legs, gently kneading the muscles up his legs.

"I'm ok you better get Arthur into the bath," he kisses her on the head and continues with his stretches and massages his legs himself, feeling good that he was able to do something, contribute to their life at last, whatever the eventual toll on himself.

He can hear Annie chivvying Arthur along with the sound of the bath filling further down the corridor, and knows she will give him hugs and reassurance along with a quiet talk to them both, not in a cross way but telling them what should happen when they are in the garden, no breaking of rule one, he knows she will feel bad later that she wasn't there, but you can't be everywhere, Molly then walks in steadily carrying a drink for him, he smiles at her concentration as she puts it down on the bedside table.

"Mummy told me to bring this through for you Matt. I didn't spill any," she smiles her beautiful smile, so like her mum he thinks and has always thought, "Can I sit at the bottom of the bed?"

"Course you can Molls, are you ok?"

"Yes, but Arthur was naughty he frightened me," she draws her knees up to her chest and rests her head on them, he can see some moisture at the corner of her eyes.

"Do you want a hug sweetie," she nods and he indicates for her to move up the bed, she rests under his arm and nestles in. "You were a good girl, and yes some things are scary, you tried to get him to stop and stay in the garden, but it all worked out, didn't it?"

"Yes, he won't do it again will he?"

"No he won't," no doubt Annie will be drilling it into Arthur that he can't, but he feels that it scared Arthur, he hopes he's telling his mum how much he misses his dad, he won't say anything it would be better for Arthur to say, his words touched Matt beyond believe, and the fact even with his illness and everything, they had noticed how good he was for Annie, he reaches for his drink, feeling good for once, and immensely relieved, hugging Molly to him he quietly talks to her and tells her he loves her.

"Bob jumped the fence like you, and he went near water," Molly says incredulous.

"Well, he knew he had to get to Arthur to stop him, he's a good dog isn't he," she nods and hugs him back.

Later Annie is putting the children to early bed, both tired out from the day, and the shock and tears, Matt's taking a bath, washing off the dirt of the river bank and letting his legs ease, they had begun to stiffen up even with massage, but now feel better, he even thinks he can get out unaided.

"I've some chicken casserole if you want some, shall we have it in the lounge, I've put a light to the log burner, as its cooler?" she looks at him leaning back in the bath, and feels an incredible love for him, she has listened to Arthur and he told her what he said to Matt and Matt's word too, he said how much he and Molly loved Matt, although she had never needed their approval it was so wonderful they felt like that, as perhaps they all had a future together, but baby steps, she thought, she knelt down by the bath and leant in to him, taking the lead and kissing him with such love, Matt could feel it different from their lust and need, love.

"What was that for?"

"For being you, for everything," he sat up, "Do you need a hand?"

"No, I'm fine I can get out," he takes her face in his wet hands and kisses her back. She stands, legs jelly and goes and has a quick shower.

They sit eating, lost in their own thoughts, "This tastes great Annie," she turns and looks at him surprised and pleased.

"Oh, I'm glad it's good, Matt," she sees he's eaten virtually all of it.

"I probably won't be able to move tomorrow," he grins, "But whether it's adrenaline tonight I feel like there has been a change for me today. I think being able to help and not feel I am a burden has helped me, and I am so glad I got there for Arthur," although buoyant she can hear the tiredness in his voice.

"You've never been a burden Matt, Arthur told me what he said to you, and what you replied. I feel bad not talking about his daddy recently, and reminding them about the anniversary, it feels selfish somehow, but so much has happened since we've been here, but it is important for him, both of them, to remember him."

As we both gaze into the burning logs, I am so pleased I didn't have my phone with me, as the first thing I would have done was call Dave, and this has given something to Matt. I hope long term it doesn't affect his recovery. I will tell Dave and Sue at some point, and will chat with Matt first though. But not now, all I want to do is enjoy this moment, my two children safe and Matt by my side.

"I'll put these dishes in the dish washer and clear up. I think I've got some deep heat cream in a box somewhere, when we moved, I think I just shoved all the stuff out of the bathroom cabinet in it," she goes to stand.

"Stop, and enjoy quiet time," she sits back and holds his hand, revelling in family and them all being safe.

The next morning Matt is regretting one or two actions from yesterday, the 50-yard dash being one, his legs are so stiff today he can barely move them, he starts to think of various things John has told him, clots being one of them, he leans forward and starts to massage his calves, pulling his foot up towards his knee on one leg then the next. He did all the things he wasn't supposed to yesterday, lifting, bending, reaching out and twisting, he lowers his legs out of bed and places them warily, feet flat on the floor, some stiffness going up his calves, he tries his best to walk to the window and look out, the weather is wet today, rain falling, he thanks god the rain didn't come before today, as he knows this water course well, it fills quickly and that exposed river bed Arthur landed on would be covered in water.

"Morning," Annie comes up behind him and puts her arms round him. "How are you today," she sees his face, "Regretting the run then?" but smiles at him.

"You could say that," he manages to catch her off balance and kisses her, again surprising her, feeling better in himself, "Better have a shower then, coming?"

"Haha, it's porridge for you first, I'm going to get the iPad out this afternoon, which has some of Sam's photos on it and sit with Arthur and Molly and have a chat about him, do you think that would be good?"

"Of course, I do, while you do that, I'm going to phone Dave and talk to him about their work yesterday and see how they got on, also I'll see how I feel later and if needs be phone John, well text and hope he is free to talk."

Alarm bells ring for her, "Why, don't you feel well?"

"Annie, I feel ok just muscle stiffness, actually I'll text the physio who has been allocated to me, that might be better," she comes up to him.

"Are you sure you are ok?"

"Yes, now get on and I'll eat my porridge and drink my tea, and I'll have a shower, don't worry sweetheart."

I decide to go up to the house and put all our clothes now washed from yesterday in the drier as it's too wet to dry outside, and see Dave and Sue, Matt was happy with that and both children are on the bed with Matt having a rest and reading to him. I texted Dave and they are going to stand in the front porch as it's raining and I'll be in the hall.

When we get together, neither of them can believe what happened, how Matt got down to the river, and although he is tired today and his muscles ache, he isn't too bad, I'm relieved to tell them. Dave is incredulous I didn't phone him, and I explain for the millionth time I didn't have my phone and it all happened so quickly.

I see them both looking at me. I look tired today, not surprising really, with everything that's happened, and yes. I haven't been eating as much as I should especially as I am using so much energy. I feel worn to be honest, although yesterday was terrible I think it helped Matt. Dave begins to talk about the plot they have been working on and I say Matt is going to give him a ring later and they can catch up, we finish off with me promising to keep a phone, fully charged with me.

As they go off, Dave turns to Sue, and mouths a load of expletives, and shakes his head, they go back into the walled garden to continue their jobs, they sit in the greenhouse, welcoming the warmth and shelter and have a hot drink.

"I can't get my head around what is and has happened round here, it seems as if bad luck is following them," Dave says obviously anxious.

"Dave, everything worked out ok, Arthur was fine, Matt managed, and it probably did his confidence the world of good."

"Yes. I know. I just worry so much, Annie looked worn out, when I speak to Matt later, I'll see if he has noticed."

"Don't interfere Dave, I'm sure he has they appear closer from what Annie said."

"I wish we could do more, have the children, take some weight off them."

"Dave we are doing all we can within all of the rules aren't we. I don't know perhaps we are being over cautious but Matt is sort of being shielded, so what choice is there?"

"Yes, I know," mulling it over, "I might give Tom the Force Medical Examiner a ring to double check."

I get back and can hear voices coming from the bedroom where I left them all, it's cooler again today and wet, thank goodness yesterday was cool, imagine the effects on Matt if it had been one of those hot days we had been having, it doesn't bear thinking about, I get some drinks and go through, they all look happy and Matt looks ok, dark smudges under his eyes but ok. The children sit on the floor with drinks and biscuits and Bob, of course. I nudge Matt up and sit by his side. I got us both a warm homemade lemonade, sweet and tangy.

"Dave phoned," he says.

"Bloody hell that was quick," then realise what I said as two little people take a sharp breath, "Sorry," the way we are going I am going to have to get a swear jar, just for me, snacks finished the children run into their room Bob in pursuit, although the weather is cold. I don't see them asking to go outside, which they normally would, hot or cold, "What did he have to say?"

"Lots. I mainly had to listen and make noises," I smile, "Which was useful as those two were in here, he told me about the beds they've made up at the top plot and they must have worked like mad yesterday as the paths are down too. I think they are hoping to dig in some well-rotted manure too, but might be a bit wet for that."

"Wow."

He finishes his drink and goes to put it on the bedside table, Annie taking it from him, he takes her hand then, and shifts sideways looking at her, really looking at her, not with the mists of longing or his own issues hiding anything but properly looking, worried what Dave had said to him, and he knows Dave was right, Annie looks thinner, he sees how tired she looks too, his heart goes out to her, she tries to cover up how she feels so much.

He feels that is a throwback to her relationship with Sam and also after he died with anyone who was around, part of him knows they should be more open with each other, about how each is feeling, not about their love, that is a given, but physically and mentally how they feel, he has covered up to a degree but she has more, later he thinks, when they won't be interrupted by Arthur and Molly.

Waiting for Annie to put the children to bed Matt thinks on what was going through his mind earlier, no she hadn't hidden her feelings from him before he was ill, in fact he remembers how she showed him her feelings, told him how she felt about them in their relationship, and she had told him how she felt since his return, but that was love and now he needed to know how she was day to day, to not hide those things worrying her and obviously pressing on her. He'd read her diary and that gave him huge insight, but they did need to share.

He wonders if yesterday was a sort of watershed, although it had nearly killed him, he feels he must take a positive from it. He leans back and thinks to those times in the past that had filled their brief lives together, and feels something inside him waking too, it was difficult to put words to what he suddenly felt, he knew he loved her and he knew he found her so attractive, but perhaps he might be everything to her in the end, he so wanted to be the Matt who she had fallen for, don't dwell he thinks, then the lady in question comes in, although tired, still his and still as beautiful.

"You look gorgeous," he says as I walk into the bedroom. I look at Matt.

"Well, I think that run has gone to your head as I certainly don't look gorgeous. I look like an old…" Before she can say what, he pulls her into him, she hops onto the edge of the bed, curling her legs under her, and next to him, his arm around her, rubbing her back, through her nightie.

"You are always gorgeous to me Annie," he rubs his thumb over her cheeks and gently caresses her face, "But as we have said truth, yes physically I feel like shit today, and am not surprised, but I have slightly improved over the last couple of days in terms of food and how it tastes and if I want to eat, the dream earlier in the week took so much out of me, but again a little lighter today, now you."

"What do you mean?" she asks guardedly.

"This is where you tell me how you feel, why you aren't eating so much, you don't always sleep I know and that is the same for us both, how you feel up here too," he points to her head, "Truth, we share it all, ok?"

"I do look bad then?"

"No, but you have lost weight and yes you do look a bit worn, so work with me on all of this."

She takes a breath, "I don't feel like eating sometimes, that is bit of a throwback to being on my own, cooking for the children but not always eating myself, but I feel sick with worry for all of this, 40,000 dead announced today, wearing face coverings outside, what world are we in Matt? I know I never stop either. I try but you are right I do it for ease, perhaps for control, so if Arthur gets an ice cream out of the freezer, if I do it, I know it will be shut, but I do need to delegate more."

"Would it be easier if we were up at the house, you go a lot, for the drier the freezer?"

"Not yet," then I realise what I said. I don't know our future, living together, we sort of fell into the current arrangement. I look at him and he looks at me.

"Now I can see your mind whirring want to tell me?" He holds her hands to encourage her, knowing how sharing is problematic for her with her past, before she says he continues, "I would have expected by now that we would have been living together don't you. I know circumstances have dictated where we are now, but I like to think in my lucid moments that I would have asked you to move in," or more he thinks.

"Although it was forced, it feels right. I couldn't be without you, you do give me strength, you do remind me to slow, you are so calm. I know some of your famous levelheadedness has drifted away with the virus, but I see more of my Matt coming back, and I will slow, share and tell the truth, and ok eat more."

"And sit when you eat, instead of rushing it, because otherwise I am putting you on my diet," he laughs, "Come and get into bed, you feel cold, the weather is going to be poor this weekend, but it would be good to go up and see what Dave and Sue have done on Monday." She jumps off the bed and gets in the other side.

"Why didn't you clamber over?" he asks suggestively.

"That's why, come to bed eyes Matt, and you know I might have hurt your legs, have you massaged them again?"

"Yes, constantly today, and that deep heat helped, you can do them tomorrow though," he lies on his side, more confident now about his breathing, not frightened, he knows it has only been just over two weeks since he came out but he does feel there has been some very slight progress. He looks at her and they both just lie there, "How did it go looking at the pictures of Sam?"

"Ok, so many memories, good ones and obviously painful ones, but they're memories are on the whole good, quite a few questions, which made me think I haven't been in touch with Stewart at all, since all of this. I did drop him a line about us moving here, but I never heard back, all the post has been coming here anyway, so don't know why."

"Do you want to hear from him?" he's very perceptive she thinks.

"Part of me says no, but he is the only link the children have to Sam, well apart from me, but, and I am being truthful here," she looks at him nodding, reassuring him. "I don't know if I want the past in here at the moment, there is enough to cope with, without that rearing its head, but then I think how selfish, he's only ever been nice to me, if a bit misguided at our last meeting."

"Very misguided," Matt says.

"Saturday, a lie in," Dave says.

"Yes, sure, it's 7 o'clock Dave, and you would have been up if it wasn't throwing rain at the windows," she moves closer, "It feels cold, this is the first time I've felt cold in here."

"I will put the heating on for an hour or so, to take the chill away, and dry yesterday's coats," he chuckles, they had worked hard through the day although wet and managed to get some of the large beds dug through with manure, he knew that what he wanted to plant up there needed good conditions.

Bacon sandwiches eaten Dave sat planning, and as Sue noticed happy, he seemed so different from the man she first met, but not different from her friends brother from years ago, she admitted to him she had taken a shine to him in her late teens, but then life moved on and they went separate ways, but now she felt he was who he should be, she wasn't sure of their future in terms of where it would be, she knew it would be together.

"That top plot is going to be so useful. I will put in pumpkins, and hopefully we can sell to the public later or sell to the farm shops near Halloween. I was thinking of putting in sprouts and cabbage up there too, but Don mentioned the rabbits, so it might be better by the polytunnels, or in them, otherwise I might have to put up low fencing around some of the beds wouldn't it be lovely to go and pick sprouts on Christmas Day."

"Blimey you're getting ahead of yourself," she smiles at him. "Are we going into the walled garden and greenhouse later?"

"Yes, I think so are you up for it too?"

"Definitely I love it Dave. I wanted to look at the peppers, they were coming along really well the other day, and I want to plant out some more of the chilli's, Annie's did well in the greenhouse and I can put them into one of the beds in the garden, and I am going to plant the purple sprouting broccoli too, what do you think?"

"I think that would be a great idea, some of those might go in the farm shop boxes in a few weeks, that would be a good addition, with the herbs as well, and that kale will be so useful that we put in, oh I was thinking you know that old sink you found," she nods, "What about if we plant it up as a herb garden for Annie and Matt at the barn, she hasn't got anything but lawn down there, and that needs mowing again."

"Yes, that would be good. I don't think the children have been up to see their produce for a while. I must double check but I think their radishes are ready, we could pick them and take them down, and what about a second sink or pot for them to plant up themselves?"

"Hey good idea. I saw a galvanised tank that might work, we could put compost in and then give them some seeds and small plugs of various things, the weather will improve next week. I might make up some pots with flowers too, I've some left over from putting by the beds you know the ones I used to attract insects, and there are also some French marigolds left."

"Those are lovely dotted around the walled garden and beds by the polytunnels, and the Calendula, what do they call them, is it companion planting?"

"It is, you are learning something new every day, come here you lovely girl," he reaches over for her and thanks whatever god that is up there that they have each other, he worries for Annie and Matt, he spoke to his parents the night before and shared his concerns but knows there is little they can do, he is glad he spoke to Matt, and hopes it wasn't interfering as Sue said, Matt seemed pleased he'd told him.

Although still raining they make their way into the walled garden, looking at the brimming beds, strawberries to pick, there were many plants also in the polytunnels on raised platforms, and they had picked packs full for the farm shops, just then Dave's phone goes.

Sue leaves him to his call and goes into the greenhouse, lovely and warm and dry, taking her coat off she starts on the tomatoes, pinching outside shoots, checking the flowering and hoping for further crops, she's about to start re-sowing some crops when Dave comes in.

"Everything ok?"

"Yes, fine that was Bill at the farm shop, they could do with some kale and carrots, as the weather is colder he thinks his customers are going to need Sunday lunch produce rather than salad, so am going to pick a load and run it down to the gate, he'll pick it up in half an hour, can you put it into the books, so he doesn't end up getting something for free," he smiles and then gets on with the picking, now so much quicker than when he first started.

Matt gets up, not as buoyant as yesterday, he stayed in bed until lunch time, his legs still ache and are stiff and he feels a bit disorientated, a bit spaced out, perhaps it is the tiredness he thinks, and yes will probably keep it to himself, and then curses himself for doing what he told Annie not to, but he doesn't want to worry her, he wants to be her fully fledged Matt again, he just sits himself on the edge of the bed, getting his breath, and that's when he becomes worried, he felt breathless, fear grips him, he starts to shake, which doesn't help his breathlessness, he feels hot too…

Bob jumps off the bed and runs barking in to the lounge, Annie sees him, and he goes back into Matt barking still, she follows quickly.

"Matt," he is breathing very quickly.

"I can't get my breath. I don't feel right," he heaves his shoulders, "Is it coming back, Annie? Oh god please no, my arms and legs feel…"

"Matt, just calm down," she looks at him assessing his breathing, "You are having a panic attack sweetheart, hold on," she quickly runs back into the kitchen and rummages in the cupboard and finds what she's looking for, "Stay here for a minute you two and keep Bob, Matt's feeling a bit sick that's all."

She runs through to the bedroom where Matt is still sitting on the edge of the bed, his breathing terrible, she hopes she's right, "Just breath into this bag Matt, slow your breathing, breath in slowly through your nose and then out slowly through your mouth, that's it, I've got you darling, just ease your breathing down, it's fine, slow down now, the tingling in your arms and legs is from the over breathing, close your eyes focus on your breathing, in through your nose and out through your mouth, that's it," she could feel his breathing gradually getting back to normal, she takes the bag away and says, "Has the tingling gone away a bit?" he nods concentrating on his breathing, she just rubs his back trying to help him.

"Oh god Annie I'm sorry," he says barely audible.

"Shush now, you've nothing to apologise for, did you not feel too well, you said you were just tired earlier," she looks at him, facially he looks ok, tired yes, but not that terrible colour he was when she had to call the ambulance.

"You're fine love," she puts her hand on his forehead and he is warm but not too hot.

"I didn't feel right, a bit spaced out, off, you know, yes tired, oh Annie when will I have days and days that are good?"

"I don't know Matt, I'm not sure anyone does, but to quote everyone, take each day as it comes, Thursday was tough on you, and yes you felt ok that evening and not too bad yesterday but it has to take a toll for all you did for Arthur. I don't think anyone would have expected you to do what you did, and if you spoke to John, he would reassure you that what you feel is normal for such an exertion on your depleted resources, come on put your legs on the bed, and lie back for a bit, your breathing is fine now love, I'll put another pillow behind you,"

"What am I going to do it's such a rollercoaster, for all of us. I analyse it all, perhaps I'm too pleased when I have a good day and do too much, but then I look at the good days and I don't feel I do too much," she can see the despair in his face and hear it in his words, he's searching for answers, and at the moment there aren't any.

"Perhaps we celebrated too much with your marathon. I don't know. I just don't know. I think we have to be patient," I hold his face in my hands and look at him, what I do know he is the love of my life and I will do anything to help him because of that, "I know you are such a patient man Matt, you waited for me Matt with little or no hope, you kept your faith in us being together, especially the last couple of years, you held back until you knew how I felt, you put so much into making us a couple, so I know that patience is there and that's what we both need isn't it."

"I suppose, but I don't know why I'm… I feel stuck."

"You are moving forward. I tell you what we need, we need a chart to show you, the days just go one into another, so it's difficult to see it, so when you get a dip that's all you see, but what if that dip isn't as low as previous dips, and your highs are higher than earlier ones. I know I'm not making sense, but me and the children will draw you one, they can keep it up to date too. Matt, think of us."

I take a deep breath stumbling over my words, feeling tearful but trying to hold it in, "Think about what I said, you waited and waited for me, and I'm so grateful you did, no matter what we've been through and what happens, I'm so glad you persevered and waited for me to catch up to your feelings, waited for me, you have given me courage, love and everything."

"Oh Annie, don't get upset, please, those words mean the world to me."

"I've a couple more," I whisper what I say to him next, "You are the love of my life, no doubt at all," the tears flow then, overwhelming her, and she is pulled into his chest.

"You're lucky Matt," I jump up and wipe my eyes, "Mummy makes us have a bucket if we feel sick, doesn't she Molls?"

"Yes," they are both standing in the door Bob between them, oblivious to the drama unfolding. I turn to Matt to explain quietly, showing him the paper bag.

"I told them you felt sick, so as not to worry them too much," I whisper, he smiles and wipes his damp face too, "Right let's get some lunch, Molly can you get the tomatoes and lettuce out of the fridge, and ham, Arthur get some crisps out of the cupboard, and I'll come in and get some celery soup for Matt."

"I hate celery soup," mumbled Arthur as they go into the kitchen.

"And me," says Matt. I must look horrified as he then says, "Only joking, you know it's my favourite," he sits a bit higher in the bed.

"Do you want a shower first?"

"No, I'll get some strength back then think about that later, come here Annie," she moves into his arms, it is a struggle for him to lift them today but he just manages to put them round her. "Thank you. I know it's not easy, but you give me so much. I wouldn't be here without you," she looks into his eyes and kisses him lightly and goes to help the children.

Annie just feels like she could lie down and never get up, the emotion is so overwhelming, it feels like it is taking every bit of her, she will text John, but is aware it is the weekend and it isn't fair to expect an answer, but she needs to get some food into Matt, he didn't eat breakfast this morning.

Arthur and Molly have put their ingredients on the island and are sitting expectantly for me to put together a miracle sandwich I think. I put the oven on knowing I have some savoury cheese puffs in the freezer. I know everyone will enjoy them, while that is heating up, I get out some celery soup and put that on for me and Matt.

I don't feel hungry, my appetite gone with all of this, it doesn't help my mood today with rain lashing down outside and it's cold too. I had put the heating on low earlier, an extravagance and June too, but hey I'm not going to feel cold and I certainly don't want Matt or the children to be either.

Arthur and Molly take their sandwiches through to our bedroom, I'm thinking of putting a table and chairs in there, but realise I couldn't as I want Matt to come to us really, those times are few as yet, cheese puffs cooked I take a tray through with our food on, and set Matt's soup down and offer him one of the appetisers. I can see he is reluctant, but he takes one.

"You'll love these Matt," says Molly diving into one with her sandwich.

"I'm sure I will Molly," I help him sit a bit further up and put another pillow behind him. I can feel how worn out he is, everything is an effort.

"We're going to make a poster this afternoon kids," they both look up, "It's going to be a chart showing how well Matt is doing."

"Will he get gold stars Mummy?" Arthur asks.

"Well, some days he will but remember he might not feel too good other days, like today so might go down a…"

"A ladder," a light bulb moment. "We could do it like snakes and ladders," says Arthur warming to his idea, "What do you think Molly, so yesterday he is far up our chart but today as he felt sick, he goes down a short snake, then we can see how he will be tomorrow, Mum, can we start it from when Matt came out of hospital."

"We could but we might not remember it all."

"We do don't we Molly."

"Yes, we put it in our diaries, so if Matt stayed in bed, we wrote it down and when he had a walk and best of all when we all went out in the landy."

I am so surprised that they have done this, they must have continued their diaries long after he came home, Matt looks pretty stunned too. Molly jumps up and goes over to the bed and Matt.

"The thing is we can show you getting better, because Mummy said that's what we wanted, so Daddy," she hugs him, and realises her words, smiles, and goes, "Whoops, but Mummy he feels like a Daddy," she clambers onto the bed and sits next to Matt, who looks over at me with a huge smile on his face.

"We weren't going to say yet were we Molly," Arthur stands now.

"What weren't you going to say Arthur?" I ask.

He lets out a big sigh, "We were going to make Matt a Father's Day card," he comes over to me as I sit in the chair. I put my arms round him and look over his head at Matt and Molly, my wonderful kind children I think, looking at Matt's face I hope this gives him more strength. I think it will.

The whole weekend was a wash out, weather wise and cold but it gave the children time to put together their poster. I only hope we have loads of ladders as I don't want too many snakes for him to slither down. I want him going up and up. I cook and make food that is tempting and nourishing, interspersed with snacks and nutrition drinks, and although that is what I have done constantly Matt hasn't always eaten or drunk them, but now I feel like standing over him and making him.

Dave would call it my matron attitude, but I know what it is. I've only spoken briefly to Dave. I know they've been very busy, and by the sound of it enjoying every moment. I can't wait to get back to gardening and knowing Matt is on the farm busy himself, part of me doesn't want to think too far ahead, but human nature isn't always reined in. There are anti-racism protests all over the country and world. I worry about everyone getting the virus and the spread, but realise they feel so strongly, quite rightly so. I pray all will be safe.

Monday, PE with Joe and home schooling begins, they have some work to get on with and I look in on Matt, as they start their school day, he is having a shower. I look in and he's standing or rather leaning on the sink having a shave, I'm pleased as he hasn't at all this weekend, his hair is longer and quite thick. It needs cutting, but I won't offer as I know he will echo Arthur's thoughts, as I take the bed linen off and head into the kitchen my phone goes, it's John. I had texted him yesterday with an update, and although he said he was at work and would call he obviously was busy and didn't have time.

"Morning John, how are you?" I wander outside it has stopped raining and the sky is cloudy and it is slightly warmer.

"I'm fine Annie, sorry to hear Matt had a setback, tell me more," I tell him everything, how he had been improving and then about the run or fast walk to get to Arthur, his exhaustion, as I do I walk down the lawn a bit, looking back I can see both children sitting doing some work. I glance at the river and can't believe my eyes, it's so high. I splutter on my words with John, feeling slightly sick.

"Annie. I think it would be good to do a Skype with Matt if possible, to go through some questions and also, I can see him, can you set that up for say, 15 minutes time," I say yes and go into Matt, he's sitting by the patio doors, dressed, and has his laptop open and is checking emails.

"John just called, he wants to do a Skype chat with you, is that ok love?"

"Yes, of course," I tell him when and leave him to it. I feel that Matt must be honest about how he feels and talk to John, he doesn't need me looking over his shoulder. I have confidence he will be honest with John.

As I help the children with their work, my mind wanders a bit to what Molly said to Matt, he mentioned it when we went to bed that night and last night,

Saturday night he fell asleep before saying too much but last night he said how much it meant to him and did I mind. I don't mind. I know he isn't their father and deep down they both know that but he is a strong presence and if they want to call him that then it is ok. I think it is more Molly as she didn't really know Sam that much. I will have a chat with Arthur, but no doubt it was his idea about the card. I hear Matt call me, so pop back into the bedroom.

"John wants to feed back to both of us," I sit on the arm of the chair with the laptop showing us both on screen. I can see John.

"Annie glad you can join us, I've told Matt that I want to check some bloods, peak flow and blood pressure, so will arrange for someone to come in and take them, just to see if there have been any changes since he left us. I want to make sure about his immune system and look if iron levels are ok too, anything that might be a cause for his lack of energy. But I am only dotting the I's and crossing the T's as I feel it is this virus, everything might be ok but we know so little about recovery that we just have to roll with the punches and take what comes. I do think your uhm, run, to use that term has contributed to the last few days of lack of energy, you haven't got a temperature, which is good."

"So, I don't feel this is a relapse, but we have to be mindful that doing too much might cause extra symptoms, so gradually increase exercise, a pacing approach as discussed, eat well, and drink plenty of fluids, make sure you do the exercises, you know that blood clots are a side effect, so again try to keep active. I will get the physiotherapist to call you, she saw you on the ward and can look at progress. Annie how do you feel Matt's normal mobility is, we won't consider since the other day but before that?"

"It has been improving John, he has been walking fairly well, but not fast, he has been getting a bit of power back into his legs, but over the weekend both legs and arms had no power at all, he could barely lift his arms, which from what you are saying is due to his exertion."

"Yes, definitely Annie, that took a lot out of you Matt, and I can understand you felt you had to, but it is a setback, so gently increase everything, and emotionally, we have discussed this briefly Annie so I know how Matt has felt, again this lack of energy and what he feels about lack of progress is impacting on how he feels emotionally, but you are sleeping Matt, and that is not always present post COVID-19 and for me that is a huge positive, not only mentally but it helps you regroup physically too, you could talk to one of my team about the emotional effect if you want, have a think about it and then text me your answer.

In terms of a re-scan, to check on lung damage, we can wait for that as I don't really want you in the hospital at all currently. Ok you will hear from the district team to sort out your bloods etc, hopefully for tomorrow, is there anything else."

If all of that wasn't enough, I think, we both say no and John signs off. I put the laptop down and look at Matt. "Has that helped?"

"Yes, it has. I suppose I just want to be better now, and as John points out that is not going to happen as quickly as I thought and hoped, but then he also points out how very ill I was in hospital, until he talks about it all I don't go there too much as being near death is a very, very scary thought, and I feel if I do go there, it won't help me mentally will it?"

"No love it won't, but if you do want to talk more about it then we can, can't we? Or you can talk to one of his team, I'm not pressurising you one way or the other," I kiss him and get up, "Coffee time or tea break, what do you fancy?"

"Well, that's a stupid question," he says and grabs my hand and kisses it, a slight smile replaced by a cheeky grin.

I go in to the kitchen and get drinks and biscuits all round, as it is school break time too. I might be able to put the sheets out, I do have a whirly thing round the side of the barn, kindly put in by Don. I don't fancy going up to the house. Matt has a high protein cholate drink, I'm in determined mood, as all I want is him back too. We all have jobs on our minds, the children once school is finished look at their poster, putting in all his ups and downs, and leaving blanks areas to add. I hope, ladders, and no more snakes, it's very clever I think, Matt comes through and sits in the lounge, he had a rest after lunch and has a little colour in his cheeks, he is looking at emails.

"Hey Dave has had a good idea about that top plot, he wants to plant out pumpkins and then all being well either sell direct to the public near Halloween, either just there outside, thinking about social distancing, we don't know what it will be like by then, or utilise the part finished barn shop up there, and obviously use the access road I thought of for it."

"Yes, that is a great idea and a beginning if we can for your farm shop, and here as you know we wouldn't be treading on anyone's toes."

"No, we wouldn't. I did some research before making the decision on that. I don't think my idea for a cafe is on though, that we will put off for some time."

"I think Dave's popping down in a bit. I had a text."

"That would be good to catch up with him."

Just then we hear the quad coming down the hill, we all get up, some quicker than others though, the children and Bob go and run up and down the fence, Matt and I just stand by the door, Matt leaning on it, they have the trailer attached and it looks full.

"What you got there then Dave," Matt asks.

"We come bearing gifts," he jumps out and Sue does too, she looks well and very tanned, that's working outdoors all the time I think, "We've filled this old sink for you, Annie, we thought it would go by the door and it's full of herbs, so you can dip in when you want, then we have this old trough that the children can plant up, when we've put it down we'll fill it with compost, then Arthur and Molly can plant up some of these lettuce plugs and some more radish seeds, and some spring onions, then I've put some flowers into some different pots so you've got something nice to look at."

"You've been busy," Matt eases himself into a chair by the door. I notice Dave looking concerned. I haven't had time to tell him how the last day or so has gone but he can no doubt guess.

"Dave, Sue, that's lovely, so thoughtful," we all make sure we are well back and they unload and put the sink and trough into place, fill the trough and then go back to the quad, "Children, you two can plant out some lettuces now if you want, I'll come and supervise in a second."

"Can I put my fairies into our garden?" Molly asks, "They can keep an eye on the seeds and make sure no birds get them."

"Of course, you can Molly," she dashes past to get some of her collection. I go down the side of the barn to where Dave has put the trough and show Arthur how to plant the lettuce and then I was going to show him how to put his seeds in. But he tells me he's done that at the walled garden, "You sort it out yourself then love, we could label them too."

Molly's standing next to Matt holding his hand and telling Dave and Sue about his snakes and ladders chart, she runs in and gets it holding it up for them to see.

"What we want," she explains, "Is for Daddy," she giggles, "Matt to go up and up the ladders and not come down any snakes, don't we Mummy?"

"Yes, we certainly do, are you going to put your fairies in and help Arthur?" she is like a fairy as she flits between groups lightly skipping as usual. I can see Dave is dying to ask about the 'Daddy' name, we need a good catch up without little ears. I think.

"We found an old bird table in one of the outhouses, I've repaired it and Sue has painted it, we thought it would be good down there towards the trees, and the birds can be seen from all the back windows and doors, we'll bring it down tomorrow or Wednesday if you like?"

"We have a district nurse coming some time tomorrow to do some bloods and stuff for Matt, and I don't know what time yet," Dave raises his eyebrows questioning me. I start to walk down the fence to see where they could put the bird table and Sue follows, well away from me, Dave stops to chat to Matt.

"Is everything ok? Actually. I don't know why I'm asking I guess that adventure has taken its toll on Matt?"

"Yes, John the consultant phoned today so Matt's had a thorough check up, John says the exercise has set him back and that he needs to take things at a more gentle pace, it was reassuring to be honest, and although I knew it probably was the extra exercise that didn't help him, coming from John helps. Matt's been so drained, it is so difficult for him."

"And for you Annie," I look at Sue. I think that is how I looked a few months ago, tanned, healthy happy, now I feel a shadow. I feel drained too, but don't want anyone's sympathy. I just want Matt well again. We walk back up towards where Dave is updating Matt, "We heard from Ted, Iris is doing well after her hip surgery a few weeks back," Dave says, "Ted is coping well with it all, he sent his love to you both."

"I'm glad she's ok, I'll give Ted a ring myself when I get a chance, did you tell him about the garden and everything Dave?"

"Yes, he can't wait to come up and see it all, you could do with a tour too, how about all of you come up later in the week, we could get the landy down here again and it should go up to by the polytunnels shouldn't it, Matt?"

"That would be good Dave, then I haven't got too far to walk," he smiles and pushes his hair out of his eyes, "I could do with a haircut so the sooner we can all get closer the better, and no don't worry Arthur," he sees him jump up, "I'm not letting your mum near me," I pull a face at him and Arthur, who shows his still very short fringe.

"We'll see you later in the week then."

Matt gets up and wanders into the barn and waves at Dave and Sue, as the children make their way to me.

"It'll be Wednesday, won't it, kids? at cake o'clock," they jump on the quad and go off laughing.

"Yes," Arthur gives him the thumbs up and they go. I look at them both.

"What's happening, Wednesday?"

"It's Matt's three-week anniversary Mum since he came home, we thought we could make a cake."

"Yes, one we like too, perhaps chocolate," Molly says.

"With three candles on it."

"So how does Dave know?" I don't know why I'm asking as I know it has something to do with my phone. I might as well give it to Arthur anyway.

"Well," Arthur looks sheepish, "I did mention it when I spoke to him yesterday."

"Ok, it is a good idea and we can make the cake early Wednesday before Matt gets up," they look excited, and I shush them to keep the surprise from Matt.

What a palaver getting the district nurse in, not from her side I might add, but too many gates and complicated instructions on where to find Matt, eventually she comes in through the patio doors and all kitted up takes his bloods, does his blood pressure and peak flow, and then disappears, gates locked behind her down to her car by the road. But luckily Don sorted most of it out and then popped back to talk to Matt from a distance.

While they talk about everything farming. I check on the children, and make some sausage rolls, adding a bit of spice to ours and just ordinary ones for the children. I make sure they don't get mixed up, there would be some complaints then. I must email Dave with our list for shopping, he has sorted out the house freezer and has put some meat in now, as a lot of it had gone down, the weather still hasn't picked up much, it's slightly warmer but grey, no sun.

We have our little party for Matt the next day, he was completely surprised, we sat outside with Dave and Sue on the other side of the fence, candles lit and blown out, Matt assisted by the children of course, somehow, we managed the handing over of cake without any contact and without Bob getting his jaws around the cake too. I can't believe it's three weeks, some days have felt like a lifetime, other days have flown by. I look at Matt, he needs more good days and certainly more weight on him, he turns and looks catching me weighting him up, he grabs my hand and kisses it.

"It'll be alright," he says nodding at me reassuring me, he has a bit more energy today, and that's all we can hope for that he gets more each day, no more setbacks. I hope.

That night we catch up in bed on the day we've had, Matt still slightly raised on his pillows again, some confidence gone, we both turn on our sides and talk, whispering.

"You were sizing me up today."

"I was. I was thinking how we need loads more good days. I don't want to plan though, we just have to take it easy, don't we?"

"Yes, we do. I caught the news, so no reopening of primary schools then, your decision to keep Molly at home was completely the right one."

"Definitely, it was too much of a risk for you and would have been so wrong to separate her and Arthur, they are so close aren't they, and they both love you so much."

"Do you know, that is the most wonderful thing, to have that love from them," he looks into her eyes, stroking her face and then leans forward and kisses her longingly, pulling her too him, running his hands up her warm skin, he keeps his T shirt and boxers on, something somewhere inside him still not willing to give all of himself, to show how different he is, but loving being with her anyway.

The next couple of days are spent cooking and schooling, chats with Matt in bed at night, he has come out of the bedroom some more and sits in the lounge, he's exercising every day, and he's had some food with me. I just want so many more days of this, the children have put the poster of snakes and ladders up on the wall, we have a short ladder for each day, showing progress. I wonder how much longer everything will be like this. I don't mean me and Matt I mean everything. There is talk of not going into lockdown early enough, infection rates are dropping, but not quickly, yet we are moving on towards new measures, bubbles. I can't quite get my head around who can see who.

John phones as I stand there contemplating. I take the phone through to Matt and we put it on speaker.

"Matt, Annie, everything is ok, pretty much the same as on discharge, so that is good, one thing I think would be an advantage though is for you to start taking vitamin D supplements, it will help with immunity, which is important here. I also think it wouldn't harm you Annie to take some, all of this takes it out on those closest."

"Ok, is it prescription or can we get this over the counter or online?"

"Over the counter or online is fine, I'll email you all of this with the correct dose too, we'll check bloods in three weeks Matt. I want you to think as well about energy conservation techniques, pacing yourself, so if you intend to sit out or walk, think about reducing your exercises beforehand and if you feel ok do them later. I will send some information for you too."

While John was on the phone, I ask him about more close contact with Dave and Sue, although they have been isolated from the outside world for some time, he felt Matt needed a run of days when he was well or a week, to continue an upward trend and then review, in a sense he was shielding, and that might change soon from government.

I get a few missed calls on my phone. I don't keep my phone with me as I did when Matt was in hospital, to be honest it is a relief not to have it by my side, just looking at the phone would make me anxious, so that's why I missed them. I phone the number back but no reply and no message service, eventually Matt has my phone with him when it rings again. I hear him talking and when I take through a drink, he finishes the call.

"That was mystery caller, someone called Esme," I look at him and haven't got a clue who that is.

"A call centre?"

"No, a neighbour of Stewart's, she says that Stewart is in hospital, she is unclear why but wants you to come over and sort it all out."

"What now?"

"That's the impression I got, she wasn't exactly polite and wasn't too keen to speak to me," he doesn't add the woman was rude when he said he was Annie's partner, insulting Annie getting another man so soon after losing Sam, harsh Matt thought, but he wouldn't share that, perhaps Esme was a bit confused, although with what else she said he doubted it somehow, he was trying to be generous, "I think you will have to phone her back sweetheart, and try and get some sense out of her," he watches as he sees worry etch her face. "Come here we'll do it together," she comes and sits on the floor at his feet, leaning into his legs, he hands her the phone.

Annie puts the phone on speaker as soon as Esme answers, she can't remember an Esme if truth be told, and Stewart always talked about his neighbours, the call was very one sided, the woman wouldn't listen to Annie saying she couldn't go over there and couldn't go to the hospital either, Esme was very put out, leaving Annie feeling the only course of action was to go. Matt cut the call and switched the phone off, they needed a few uninterrupted minutes to talk and work out the best plan of action, he knew he had to help her with that decision, as she was obviously pulled in two directions, loyalty for Sam's only living relative and for all of them at the barn, she wouldn't think of herself at all.

"Right are you ok?"

"No. I…"

"Sit up here or we can sit next to each other on the bed and talk," they moved to the bed and sat leaning on the rails at the bottom, "As I see it from what the woman said, it sounds like he's had a stroke, she wants you to sort everything out there, and look to sort out Stewart. I don't know in what way as she was very unclear. For what it's worth I think we need to phone the hospital, do you know which one he is likely to have been sent to?"

"Yes, Newsome probably."

"Ok I'll get the number and phone, he doesn't have a mobile himself does he," he looks at Annie and she laughs, he gets the feeling Stewart was a bit of a luddite, "I don't seriously think there is anything you can do by going over there is there? And I doubt you would be allowed in anyway sweetheart, when we find him, we can make decisions after that, are you happy with that love?"

Annie feels a weight lifted, she has had to make so many decisions about so many things over so many years, she feels she is at the end of a very long tether, and it's looking to break, and she feels she doesn't know how she will be or anyone else if it goes.

Matt can see her and he knows how much she has dealt with for so long and for everyone, he makes the call finding the number and luckily it is the correct hospital, they get through to the ward and Annie speaks to the nurse in charge, who doesn't have particularly good news, saying it is just a matter of time, he scribbles next of kin on a piece of paper and puts a question mark as unclear as to why she wasn't contacted.

Eventually the call ends and Annie sinks into his arms, "Tell me what was said. I couldn't grasp all of it."

"Well Stewart is very ill and likely to die soon, he is comfortable they say and well looked after, about the next of kin it is his other neighbour who I know, Alfred Roberts, he knows all that is going on, and Stewart only went in yesterday. I didn't bring up Esme. I thought I'd ask Alf when I get hold of him. I think I've got his number in my diary; Stewart gave it to me once."

Annie jumps up and gets her diary and she calls Alf, who said he was about to give her a ring, he apologised for interfering Esme, he was most upset, she moved in to one of the cottages last year and had been a nuisance all round, he said Stewart had asked him a few months ago to be his executor and also next of kin, he hadn't wanted Annie to have any more pressure with death or dying, as Alf tells her this, she starts to cry.

Matt takes the phone and chats to Alf, he was aware of Matt and new that they had ended up on his farm, he didn't know how ill Matt had been though, the call ended with Alf saying he would ring when he knew more.

"I feel terrible, Stewart thought of me with his arrangements, it is so kind. I feel bad with everything that happened, perhaps I misconstrued some of his words. I don't know. I think I am over sensitive to what happened with Sam."

"No, I think as we discussed his words were misguided, he meant well and what he put in place shows that, how did he know about the move and me?"

"I wrote to him when we moved to the barn, he was a letter man, no email or phone. But his words that day set off a chain of events allowing me to tell you about what he had said and what Sam did. I think that was important, it was like a release."

"I agree," he kisses her head, he still found it unimaginable how any man could hurt Annie, or cheat on her.

"Thank you for sorting everything out, I would still be stumbling around listening to Esme and thinking I ought to go over, you took the weight off me."

"That's my job, it's about time I did something for you for a change isn't it?"

"We help each other Matt, that's what love is about, isn't it?"

"Millionaire shortbread moments."

I smile at him and he folds me in a hug, remembering that day at the summerhouse and many other times, he kisses her deeply, she slides onto his lap, he wants so much more but knows he must be patient.

"They're kissing again Uncle Dave," a voice calls from the door. I jump up and go into the lounge, followed by a guilty looking Matt, and I am sure I am blushing too. Dave is at the front door leaning on the door jamb, he laughs at us, and raises his eyebrows, "Feeling a bit better Matt?"

"Funnily enough yes," Matt walks carefully over to the door and he follows Dave outside, Dave goes through the gate and walks down the garden stills distancing himself from Matt, he breathes in the air as he gets outside, stretching a bit and feeling ok, knowing he needs many days of feeling ok, they catch up.

"Are you all coming up to the gardens tomorrow?"

"Yes, hopefully. I feel so-so, you know, but take each day as it comes, Annie just had some bad news about Sam's uncle," he tells Dave about the whole thing missed calls as well, and what they sorted out.

"How come he didn't put her down as next of kin and used his neighbour?"

"I think Stewart felt Annie had done so much in the last few years he didn't want to pressurise her with one more task, and doing what he did was meant well, to perhaps heal a slight rift."

"How do you mean, they always got on so well didn't they?"

"Some crossed wires last year, and something about Sam, but it's not my story to tell I think Annie needs to tell you herself," Annie looks out the door and sees them in deep conversation, she walks up to Matt, and quietly asks him to tell Dave about Sam, he looks at her.

"Are you sure?"

"Yes, it's time and I don't want to have the conversation, do you agree love?" he nods and Annie goes back in.

"You'd better sit down, mate, this could be some time," Matt walks back to near the door and sits on the chair and Dave sits on the grass the other side of the fence, Matt keeps his voice as low as the distance allows to ensure the children inside don't hear anything, he proceeds to tell Dave about Sam's affair and the subsequent chat with Stewart.

Dave cannot believe what he is hearing, he didn't think Sam would do that, he feels winded, and hurt for Annie, and bubbling to the surface, anger.

"She never said anything to me, how did you find out?"

"It was about January and I went into the garden, she looked upset and eventually she told me what Stewart had said when they were at the grave, and then about Sam."

"At the grave, you mean his birthday?" Matt nods, "But that would have meant she was thinking about this for months, upset by it all and that's only what Stewart said."

"I know, the years of hurt, the unfinished business, and Sam never apologised, just rushed his leave and went back, and we all know what happened then."

"Jesus, she keeps a lot inside doesn't she, and perhaps how she reacted to his death was coloured by that affair, the unfinished business as you say, the news of his affair must have taken so much out of her and then before they had time to sort issues out, he died," Dave is shaking his head, he is stunned and so hurt for his little sis. "If I'd known, well I probably would have ended up in a cell for my trouble."

"I know Dave that is how I felt, Annie did keep a lot inside, we are a work in progress about that, it is getting better, we did have a long chat about it recently, everything was so hard for her, with me, the past, she wasn't eating as you noticed and well you know what she's like, so now we share, truth. I still find it, well words fail me… well incredible that anyone could hurt Annie, or even want another woman when they had her, she's a precious gift. I tell her that."

Dave looks at Matt and knows how good he is for Annie, and now even more so, he hopes Matt can get himself well, he knows that is a huge ask though, she needs that level headed calm man, who obviously loves her immensely.

"Can you do me a favour Dave, next time you put an order in can you order millionaire shortbread, or see if there is a local shop doing homemade," Dave looks at him.

"Annie's favourite," Matt says, nothing else was needed to be said.

Matt has a rest, and then joins all of them for something to eat, sausage mash and onion gravy, but not for Arthur, he has sausage, mash and tomato sauce.

"What no gravy Arthur?" Matt knows his aversion to what he calls 'wet food' anything with gravy or sauce, or casserole, he hates it all, he loves tomato sauce and mayo though and does have the occasional curry, so I am hopeful for a non-wet food future.

"Stop teasing him," Annie smiles and listens to the little conversations around the table, glad Matt could stay up for food. "We'll go up to the gardens then tomorrow, I'll drive the land rover, and no comments from either of you two," she points at Matt and Arthur, both keep quiet, wisely, "If we go about 11, we can take a flask and drinks and cake, there's still some chocolate cake left."

"No school then Mum."

"No, it'll be alright this once."

Night time catch up for Matt and Annie, she asks him how Dave took the news.

"Flabbergasted, what made you decide he needed to know," he lies on his side looking at her, breathing her in, the shape of her, he feels something stir in him, and wants her there and then, but he waits, wait Matt, get even better, don't hurry what they both want, don't have a setback, he lets out a breath he hadn't realised he had been holding, a smile playing on his lips. She notices all of this, but doesn't say or ask, she sees the need in his eyes, and hopes he is waiting, she doesn't want him to have a relapse, doesn't want him to fail, it would hit his confidence.

"I don't know, it felt right to have everything out in the open, no secrets."

"I agree. I think it was a good decision, and I was happy to tell him on your behalf, he was hurt and angry for you, as I am and was. In terms of no secrets look we could all be living here for some time to come, and I think the less issues lying around the better."

"Do you really think we'll all be here some time?"

"I do, in one form or another, look we don't know how I'm going to be, and I get the feeling that Dave and Sue are happy and want to do something like they are now in the future, where I don't know, but it is something we need to think about long term."

"Yes, I can see that, it will be good to go up to the garden tomorrow, are you sure you are ok with that."

"Pace myself, John said so, if we drive up as you said and then I can have a walk around and then sit and rest as I do here."

The Future?

It's good to go up to the garden and see what Dave and Sue have been doing. I miss gardening it has helped me mentally, so many things are sorted in your head by easy tasks such as weeding, hoeing, sowing seeds and planting. I hope to be able to do all that again, but life has changed so much, when I think about it all I can't believe how our lives have taken so many turns over the last few years, not to mention the last months and weeks.

Matt has taken his time with tasks and exercise this morning so that he can enjoy the trip without feeling tired. I look at him and see he looks slightly better, perhaps padding out a bit, he hasn't strength in his muscles yet though, the children are happy to miss school and see Dave and Sue, socially distancing.

I've looked at the bubble, that was announced and with John's permission when Matt is a little better it would ideal for all of us. I would love a hug from my brother, that is a given and I know the children are itching to spend closer time with Dave, their beloved uncle.

The walled garden looks how I envisaged. I am so proud of all of us, me starting it, Matt allowing me to use the garden and Dave and Sue for the biggest part. It looks alive with growing, everything blooming, small apples on the espaliered trees, broad beans ready to pick, runners on runner beans climbing the framework of canes, flowers showing, and on peas, although the day was grey it didn't feel grey it felt bright inside. And if that is how I saw it Matt must be really shocked, as it certainly wasn't like this before he went in to hospital. I turn and watch him taking it all in, then he puts his arm out and I go over to him, Arthur and Molly are running down to their plots and Dave and Sue stand near the greenhouse.

"Oh, Annie it looks fantastic, so like when Mum ran it," he pulls her into him and kisses her head, "Well done, it's transformed."

"Well, I can't take credit for all of it, Dave and Sue have worked wonders here," they come a bit closer and Matt exclaims to them about the garden, his mum's pride and joy, and how pleased he is, Dave chats then about other planting. I know he has more runner beans growing in the patch by the polytunnels and brassicas and leeks, he has started sowing some pumpkin seeds and is going to plant them in the new plot.

"You certainly had a good idea Annie when you started this, and your other plans are worth moving forward with," although Dave says this sentence lightly, I can see he is excited, "There is great potential for the Ash Farm produce, as you originally thought, and not all going off the farm eh Matt?"

"You're right Dave. I think using the barn to sell pumpkins later in the year is great, rules allowing, and then build on it, as I wanted to do, did you chat to Don about any of this," Matt asks.

"Yes, when we started the top plot we chatted, he agreed it would work in terms of somewhere to sell the pumpkins and he knew your vision for the farm shop, you might need to put some hard core down for parking up there, but he felt little else, not sure if we have to apply to the council for a new business venture or if it is just an extension to the current business, will need to check."

Matt sits on one of the raised bed walls. I can feel his enthusiasm for all of this igniting, it is what he needs. I stand back and although my baby originally, I am happy to share it, as it has given us all different things at different times. I thank god for it too as it bought me closer to Matt. I think of the first feelings I had for him, experienced here, telling him about Sam's affair and him saying I was a precious gift. I look at him and feel such love for him, it still takes my breath away. I hope we can move forward without further bumps in the road. I walk down the garden to Arthur and Molly, feeling a lump in my throat at all that has taken place in the last year, nearly a year, the holiday, my confidence growing and Matt.

"Mum, can we pick some of these?" Molly asks pointing at the quite large radishes and some lettuces doing well in their beds, "And some strawberries," I notice one or two might have gone in their mouths already. I saw Sue pointing some out for them.

"Yes, of course, but don't eat it all," we spend some time just picking and I find a basket to put them in, "We can have the salad tonight," they don't look enthusiastic, they enjoy the picking but not necessarily the eating especially Arthur. I go and get drinks out and sit myself on one of the raised beds, passing the children then Matt a drink. I notice he is looking up towards the house, the top two floors in view.

"What you thinking?" I ask Matt.

"The house needs to be lived in Annie, it shouldn't be empty," he is mulling this over I can see, "But not for us yet, not long," he turns and looks at me, sending me a loving look.

I've not really thought about us living in the house, living together was thrust upon us and yes Matt said he felt he would have suggested it at some point. I hadn't thought about the future, there is too much present to deal with, but I can see he would want to be back up here, and I would go where he was. But; and I feel it is a big but, would he be capable of climbing the stairs, the house is on different levels, oh I don't know why I am going over this as I feel it is still many months before this should be discussed.

We go out the small gate into the sunken garden to return to the land rover, the garden looks lovely, the water gently trickling through the mill stone, cooling in hot weather, it feels humid today though. I pick a few flowers while Matt walks towards the house, he wanted to collect some paperwork from his office, wouldn't let me get it. I worry that going up the kitchen steps will be too much for him. I look over and yes, he is struggling up the steps but he is so obstinate, eventually he comes back carrying papers and a folder.

"Shall I put it in this basket, I'll try not to crush the produce," he agrees and I carry the basket, we walk past the house and outside of the walled garden, Matt spots the front lawn.

"What happened here?" he asks, as the wild flower seeds have taken hold of the old lawn, uhm he doesn't sound too happy.

"I didn't want the lawn growing and the lads having to mow it so I threw some wild flower seeds over it, and by the looks of it they've grown," I go in and pick some cornflowers. I turn and look at Matt, "What do you think?"

"Uhm well. I can see your thinking, but not sure, it can be reclaimed I suppose."

"It's good for the bees and pollinators and good for all of the produce, you philistine," I say as he laughs.

"Ok you win, in retrospect I love it, like I love you," he puts his arm around her waist, and they all walk back to the land rover.

"Can we run down to the barn," Arthur asks, they run off down the hill, Dave and Sue stayed in the walled garden, we watch the children go leaning on the land rover, taking in the beautiful farm, river and land below. We are lucky to have this. I think, Matt puts his arms round me and I lean on him gently.

The next morning Matt wakes early, and for once before Annie, he is on his side and looks at her with her left hand curled and tucked under her cheek, she looks so relaxed, no stress, beautiful. He can see her ring finger, and sees that the white mark from her wedding ring has gone, he never mentioned the fact all those months ago that she had removed her ring, he noticed straight away, but he knew it wasn't something to highlight, but it gave him hope.

He watches her, his Annie, he can't believe it after wanting her from a distance for so long, their passion which was so abruptly halted, their love now, he wants to offer her the world, or perhaps he thinks with a wry smile, not this world as who wants to have it as it is now, no he wants to offer her his world, more than the one they currently inhabit, but he knows he has to pause, not run at it, he knows that if he ran he would go backwards again, and that is not an option for him now.

He wants to be back in the house, he quickly cast his eye over it yesterday, it's a family house, he wants a family, and he knows Annie and the children are that family, but he wants to be better than he is to get there. The house is large and on different levels, as his climb up the kitchen steps and then down into the hall yesterday found, he knows he can't do that yet, and although he feels ok today after yesterday, that was with an afternoon of rest and a good night's sleep.

Slowly Matt, don't race and don't let the demons spoil it, he feels they are just waiting for him to stumble and then they will cast doubts on everything. They give him doubts about them as a couple, and himself and what he can achieve, give him insecurities, but he must hold on to her love and be patient.

He quietly gets out of bed trying not to disturb Annie and goes into the kitchen putting the kettle on, standing at the sink, or rather leaning, to bring his legs alive for the day, he sees the house further up the hill, he knows that whenever they move, he will have a lot to do to bring it up to date, but he also wants Annie to know it is their future. He makes the tea and then just about manages to take two mugs through on a tray, not realising that with his hands occupied he can't hold onto door jams and furniture, which shows him he has a way to go yet, but he makes it and gets back into bed, waking Annie.

"Oh, what time is it?"

"Shush it's early, drink your tea."

"You made me tea in bed, and oh Matt how did you get this?"

"Special delivery. I asked Dave to sort some out and yes, I have a piece too, so come and snuggle up to me and we'll enjoy our tea and millionaire shortbread," he bites into the biscuit savouring the richness and taste, enjoying the fact he can taste, at least that has improved.

They talk quietly, discussing Arthur's joy about an alternative trooping the colour at Windsor, rather than none, Matt had explained what the colour meant and about the different regiments to him, while they sat and had sandwiches after their trip up to the garden.

The children are still charting Matt's progress, trying to think how best to show his current plateau, which he has reached over the last couple of days, Arthur doesn't like the short ladder but got all excited about a travellator, like at airports so they were drawing that on to the chart in the afternoon.

Matt reaches out for Annie's hand and kisses her ring finger, "I noticed you know?"

"Me leaving my wedding ring off?"

"Yes, but never said anything, it gave me hope darling, a lot changed after you told me about Sam's affair."

"It felt like the right time, the right thing to do, do you know that day stayed with me for a long time, and even now. Why did you race off. I know you kissed me, although I thought afterwards did he, or was it me dreaming that light kiss," she smiles at him?

"I was so angry, angry with Sam and with Stewart, you must ring Alf later," she nods, "And you carried that without telling anyone else. I was in awe of your strength too, although it did worry me that you forgave him, we've talked about that, but I was angry with anyone who could hurt you. I love you, you do know, don't you?"

"How could I not Matt, and I knew back then how much I was beginning to have feelings for you and I think that subconsciously that is why I took my ring off too."

Precious time together, he knew he eventually wanted to give Annie more, to see a ring on her finger, but he felt he needed to be more himself. Matt went into the lounge later and spent the morning sitting at the table looking through the documents he collected from his office along with the millionaire shortbread. He is so glad he got Dave to get some for Annie, he liked to surprise her and opportunities were few and far between, he wanted to cook her a meal again, but he would need to plan that with care, mainly so he could achieve it himself.

"What's that Matt, is that the farm?" Annie leant over him and looked at the plans spread out on the table.

"Yes, it shows the whole farm, the cottages dotted about, Don's cottage, and the ones at the top of the farm that were sold for conversion, allowing me to continue Mum's work with these barns and buildings down here." He pointed to the diagrams down by the river, you could see the walled garden and the perimeter of the house and outbuildings near the house. It was quite a sizeable farm, she thought.

"I never realised it was so big, and it goes further than I thought looking at the markings for the perimeter, it's broken into fields as well, isn't it?"

"Yes, it helps when we are planning planting or animal grazing, also we need to do rotation so we are not always planting the same crop in the same field, to give the soil a rest, which Dave has to look at too in the garden and other plots."

"You've learnt so much since taking over."

"I suppose I have, although I think being here with Dad and Mum it seeped in over time. I got the plans out as I just wanted to bring myself up to date, Dave mentioned about renting the holiday cottages out at some point, although I am not wildly keen, but there is no date set for reopening anyway, but I think we might forgo that this summer, we'll wait and see, but if we did, then we have to think about Dave and Sue, but," here he hesitates, "I don't know about you but I don't think I feel comfortable having people on the farm, perhaps I feel a bit vulnerable... What do you think?"

"I agree with you love, I'm not sure I would be comfortable for some time. I can't even visualise going out shopping at the moment, let alone sharing here with visitors, but if finances drive what you have to do, fair enough."

"No, that wouldn't be in the assessment. I sold the barns to finance all of this down here, so it didn't have an impact on the farm, it would be nice to have the income, but not if it puts us at risk and we would have to service the barns for visitors so extra work too. I think not for now is the right decision."

There is a lot to think about, and from what Matt has said he wants us to be together, so I suppose I should sell my house at some point. I don't want to think about it, if I'm honest. I just want to see some more good days for Matt and see him improving, although looking at the children's chart he isn't going down, or hasn't for some days.

Unanimous decision, trooping the colour food should be hot dogs, so I sort those out to eat before the repeat programme starts. We're sitting round the table eating the requested food, spicey sausages for me and Matt, he is being able to taste so much more now, but I try to keep up with food that has strong taste.

"Mummy do you think…" Arthur starts.

"Do you remember the rules, Arthur?"

"Rule one, don't go near the river."

"Thank you, Molly," Annie says, Matt is smiling as he can see Arthur is going to dig himself in deep here, especially as he tries to talk again.

"I'm thinking the one where you shouldn't eat and speak at the same time."

"What number is it Mummy?" Molly asks.

"2001."

"What's 2000 then?" Arthur asks, sailing close to the wind.

"It's the one that says not to check your mum," Matt says, hiding his laughter.

Eventually they sit for trooping the colour, Arthur talking about Sam's medals and asking Matt if he had medals, he has and spoke briefly about them, he's quite a modest man. I reach over and curl my hand in his. Seeing the majesty of Windsor Castle and the beautiful blue sky above with no vapour trails takes our breath away, it all looks so normal. Arthur wants to go to London and see Buckingham Palace, and the changing of the guard, you wonder at the children's future, you can't hold them back but how will everything return to normal; it just seems insurmountable.

"Are they having horses, Mum?"

"I don't think so love."

"I don't think so too, because it would mess up the lawn and the Queen wouldn't be too happy." He watches the Guards intently. I think he might want to be one of them tomorrow.

We can feel the weather closing in, the heat feels intense. I think there will be a storm as forecast, later as Matt lets Bob out, "It feels oppressive you can smell the storm coming can't you," Bob shoots back in as we shut windows, "I think he can feel it coming too, are the children, ok?"

"Yes, although I would like another window open as it's so warm, but they might hear the storm more," in some respects she found having the bedrooms on the ground floor difficult, it was probably associated with the initial problem with trespassers.

"What are they like with thunder, and you love?" he wraps his arms around her and brings his mouth down on her drawing her into him, he has felt better today and has had a few good days, he feels her response her breathing quickening, he kisses her probing her mouth, slowly, languorously, she groans in his mouth, then a flash brings them up short.

"I'm not too good with thunder and lightning, 3, 4, 5, ..."

"What are you doing?"

"Counting how far away the storm is, the children will probably come through to us, we'd better get to bed."

"Oh yes!"

"Oh, shut up you," she slaps his bottom as they go through to the bedroom, she draws the curtains as a huge flash of lightening and a clap of thunder happens, she jumps and gets into bed, just as two worried children come through clutching their favourite go to bed toys, Molly sucking her thumb, Bob follows, blimey a bed full.

"Can we get in bed Mummy?" Arthur asks.

"Yes, come on."

"I want to be next to Matt," Molly says.

"And me," says Arthur.

We position them one either side of Matt, Bob on Matt's lap, "Mr Popular," I say as we hear another clap of thunder and lightning flashes everywhere around us.

"I want to be next to Matt," I say laughing, he extends his arm drawing me in.

"Alright everyone it's only the angels tap dancing," Matt says.

"With hob nail boots on," I bring the duvet up and over us as we all snuggle down.

"Will the cows and sheep be ok Matt?" Molly asks taking her thumb out for a minute.

"Yes, sweetheart they are very brave."

The storm goes on for a few hours, coming and going mainly lightening, we sleep a bit, Matt stroking my face and sometimes squeezing my shoulder, little Molls between us, it's so reassuring for me and for all of us.

"Are you alright?" I whisper, worrying about his position with his arms stretched, all he says is.

"Family, wonderful," and smiles, which I see in a flash of lightening.

I'm glad there is no more as my eyes are glistening with tears, family. I swallow and a tear trickles down my face. A very disturbed night, but Matt felt good, it was as he said to Annie, family, he felt part of something for the first time in a long time. His parents had been wonderful, he had a brilliant childhood, but going away as an adult to work broke some of that up, coming back to his mother's death and his father's illness was even worse.

He'd thought it the other morning, family, Annie, Arthur and Molly, he'd never really considered having children himself, and he wasn't sure whether that was an option for him and Annie, his body needed to mend, and would any drugs he had effect his fertility, whether Annie could or would, but his memory goes back to her words after his dream and he smiles, but so much was up in the air, life, him, how he would be in the future, but he felt better, god so many questions.

So much whirling through his head needed to be said to Annie, they needed to discuss their future. They all felt tired the next day with poor sleep, particularly for the adults as although the storm had raged the children had slept well, wrapped in love.

Annie wanted to cook but hadn't been able to make up her mind yesterday what to cook, Sunday lunch didn't float her boat as it was too humid, she decided to spatchcock the chicken she had rescued from the freezer, with loads of her new herbs and herby potatoes too, with fresh garlic, some she had planted in the walled garden so long ago, dried out and bought down by Dave and Sue. She hoped last night hadn't been too much for Matt with lack of sleep, but he'd got up showered and came through for breakfast, he did his exercises and was sitting resting on the sofa looking through a farming magazine, Arthur was drawing Army stuff he said, involving a lot of cutting and colouring, and Molly was making bead hair ties for her dolls.

"Matt, can I do your hair?" she asks.

"What do you want to do to it Molly?" he looks slightly alarmed. I used to do that to my dad sometimes, play hairdressers with his glossy hair. I smile at the thought.

"Comb it like I do my dolls."

"Ok," he says, oh dear I hope she doesn't put slides in it. I carry on and see her sitting on the arm of the sofa combing his now thick hair, not too long but certainly thicker than it was. I remember it quite close cut with his startling blue eyes and shadow on his chin, that was the first time I had seen him in so long, on our holidays, did he open my eyes then I wonder? He sees me looking at him and smiles that special smile, ours, exclusive, and so sexy.

I nip out and pick parsley for the potatoes, then some thyme, which with garlic, chilli and lemon juice I will make into a butter for the chicken. I look up as I come in and poor Matt has got clips in his hair and a small pony tail at the side. I snigger and go to get my phone.

"You dare," he says, and waves a finger at me.

"Oh shame, you look lovely doesn't he Molly?" she smiles and agrees and steps back.

"Can I get you a drink or a magazine?" she asks, playing hairdressers then.

"Molls I've got the mascot outfit sorted; shall we parade?"

"Ok Arthur, I'll be back soon," she says to her customer, they go outside with Bob, I've a feeling Bob could have a new role, yesterday Matt told Arthur all about mascots in the Army and showed him some on his laptop, mainly goats.

"Do you want me to free you from your hair ties," I laugh and go over to him, knowing Molly will be absorbed by her next role.

"Yes, please, and you can stop laughing," as I kneel on the sofa to untangle his hair, he pulls me into him. "Oh, perfect position," as he rests his face between her breasts.

"Matt stop it," my phone rings. "Saved by the bell," I pick up my phone, "Oh it's Alf."

I guessed his call would be bad news, and it was I am so sorry for Stewart, he was such a character, so eccentric, a man for earlier times. I could imagine him riding his beloved motorbike where and when ever he wanted now, and greeting Sam, as I think that I get up quickly and nip into the bedroom and sit by the windows. I regret our last meeting, and feel very responsible, he was a lovely man, a good uncle to Sam. My eyes fill and I just sit there remembering, Matt walks through, he took the phone from her as he could see she was upset.

"I'm ok, just a flood of memories, including Sam. I had this vision of Stewart on his motorbike waving to him, up there together now, bloody life, eh?" I rub my eyes. He knelt in front of her and holds her face, "Don't hide it Annie, if you want to cry then cry, I'm here, and you can talk about Sam you know, to me."

"I know," she takes a huge breath, "I'm alright Matt," she looks into his eyes and sees his calm reassurance flowing towards her, and yes, she was alright with him by her side.

"Mummy, Matt, look at this," Arthur and Molly with Bob in tow are outside the patio doors, we get up and open them, and watch, they are in line, but to make it straight they put an arm out to straighten the line shuffling into position and in front on his lead with a sort of coat on is long suffering Bob.

"The mascot?" Matt asks, picking up his phone and beginning to video, he put his arm round me and we watch and laugh at their version of trooping the colour, saluting and turning their head towards us as they pass, the children lightening another moment.

I arrange a Skype call with Mum and Dad, we sent the video of their trooping the colour to them and they chat with them both, they show Bob's mascot coat to my parents too and then go outside and we sit and tell them about Stewart, it's the first real time I've been able to sit and talk to them, Matt by my side, they say he looks improved and we talk for ages until I remember I haven't put the chicken in.

While we're clearing up after lunch Matt at her side, Annie suddenly turns to him and says, "You stood up."

"Yes, I'm standing now," he replies.

"No, I mean when you were with me in the bedroom, you were kneeling and stood," trying to get the right word, "Fluently, no, seamlessly, no, oh with no problem, Matt," she stands in front of him smiling a beaming smile.

"God yes. I never thought about it. I did. I just did it, wow, Annie that is such an improvement, and I know I shouldn't go mad, but it shows I have some power in my legs."

"Oh Matt, just keep doing the exercises darling. I think you deserve a ladder for that," she tells the children who get the poster down, again, and draw in a ladder.

Just then my phone goes again, Dave. "Hi Dave."

"How come me and Sue missed out on trooping the colour Arthur and Molly version."

"Mum and Dad phoned you then?"

"Yes, in fits of laughter, so we want a full performance, not the video."

"Pop over tomorrow and you can see their version, was everything ok with you two and last night's storm?"

"Yes, no worries, the tank in the greenhouse has filled with all that rain too. I might have to put another water butt back by the greenhouse. I don't want it over flowing as we have a load of rain forecast this week," he says enthusiastically. I hand him over to Matt to chat.

We all go to bed early that night, we have our little catch up, and I can tell Matt is feeling a bit more his old self, he seems lighter, just realising one simple movement shows some advance. I know he is eating more and can taste, but some more strength in his legs is so positive, and I am not going to say to him, baby steps.

The next day is humid and grey with thunder lapping the edges of the county, home schooling starts again, Matt does his exercises and speaks to Don, they chat about barley, will there be a market? And about the rape seed crop and sale of some of the stock.

Dave and Sue come down after school and Arthur and Molly put on their trooping the colour, Bob not as happy this time to be mascot, Dave tells me about the garden again and how we are doing, and offers his condolences for Stewart, him and Matt have a walk down the fence catching up.

As Dave and Sue walk off still laughing, Dave says, "I thought Matt looked slightly better, did you?"

"Yes, I did. I know it's only a couple of days since we saw him but he looked a bit stronger, Annie said he got up from kneeling by the chair without leaning on anything, just using his own power, that's good, isn't it?"

"It certainly is sweetheart."

"Do you think they will move up to the house at some point?"

"Yes, eventually but he has got to have all his stamina, that place has so many levels and stairs, and three storeys too, Matt said he felt the holiday accommodation would have to be on hold for some time, even when opened up by the government, he said it felt weird thinking about having people around on the farm, but as he said, that might change as he felt improved, so we can stay where we are."

"That's good, isn't it?"

"Yes, love, but he did say that whatever, we had a place here, he didn't just mean work, if we wanted it, but a future, he said he felt he wouldn't be right for a long time, and if we did rent out the barns, he said he had an idea for somewhere for us."

"Did he, wow all of this sounds brilliant, what do you think?"

"I think in a few weeks or so we all need to get together and sort the future out, I agree with him he isn't going to be well enough to farm and run everything for quite a while, he said he hasn't said as much to Annie, but he will."

After tea I walk down the lawn where the children are playing swing ball and gather them to me in a hug and we sit on the slightly damp lawn and I tell them about Uncle Stewart, they only know him as someone distant, although he had been to our house for Christmas, since Sam's death, Arthur talks about his motorbike and how he knew Uncle Stewart had driven through France on it, they want to pick some flowers and put them at the bottom of the garden.

Then Molly remembers how they had started painting stones, and wanted to add those too. We go up to the sunken garden and pick flowers and they pick up the stones from the table in the walled garden, they make their little shrine to him and stand looking at it, then they run off and play swing ball again.

Matt comes out and we sit watching, "Don't you wish you had a child's ability to move on to a game of swing ball after some relatively bad news."

"Yes, it's not completely understanding, especially as they rarely saw him, they are so thoughtful though, aren't they?"

Matt wraps his arms around Annie, "Just like their mum," he drops a kiss on her neck loving the feel of her against him.

Later they catch up in bed, some slight rumbling of thunder can be heard miles off, both hoping it doesn't come their way, mainly to get a good night's sleep for them and the children.

"What were you talking to Dave about?"

"We just chatted about the farm, he could see my point about not wanting anyone on the farm from the holiday accommodation, whenever the government allows. I also said to him they have a place here for as long as they want it, to live and work," he waits for her to ask the inevitable question, she raises her head off the pillow.

"You don't think you will be well for some time, do you?"

"No, not to run all of this and the garden and any subsequent business, don't get upset Annie. I might be wrong, but recovery is slow and I can see that now and I don't want to rush and find I have setbacks. I think it is only right for Dave and Sue to be aware of that."

"But why didn't you say to me?" he pulls her to him; she resists a bit.

"Shush. I hadn't meant to say too much to Dave but we started talking about the holiday lets and I wanted to reassure them that whatever happened there was a place for them here, that we need them. I have to acknowledge it will take some time, and your patience has shown me that…"

"Matt…" he kisses her questions away, "I will try my best but all I can say is it might take some time to get all my strength back, and in the meantime," he doesn't finish as Annie interrupts.

"I don't want anything to happen to you."

"I'm not going anywhere. I just know I may not be fully well for a long time."

"Don't leave me," her tears flow as Matt kisses them away, him saying he won't be well for some time has ripped her apart, she knew, but wouldn't accept it, won't accept it, she watched every day for small improvements like the children and their chart, she kisses with desperation, trying to make him well, for life, her kiss is deep, it pulls Matt along, she puts her hands under his T shirt and pulls it over his head, and starts to kiss his body, she can feel his hands on her cupping her bottom to him, he slides her on top of him.

They are both so carried away by the emotion of his words that their passion is like a hunger, they don't think about the weeks and months in the past, just now, kissing so deeply feeling their mouths full of each other, he turns her onto her back, forgotten are the barriers that have held him back and he goes with her. The passion and all that happens unbalances him, makes him dizzy, his limbs feel weak, they lie there for some time before either of them can speak.

"Matt. I didn't mean for that to happen, I'm sorry…"

"What? Don't be sorry, that was… Jesus Annie," his breathing is laboured, but inside him he feels it is a good laboured, not the virus, he holds her close, "I never thought I would be able to do that again."

"I was in agony at your words Matt, and I wanted to kiss life back into you. I didn't expect my desperation would make that happen," she giggles, and that starts him off, relief at some form of normality in this world where what ought to be right was so skewed. They hold each other quiet laughter rolling around like the thunder of earlier, whispering to each other, they both knew that there might be a payment to be made with his strength after this magic, but for now they make the most of those moments lost in passion and desperation.

Annie wakes and sees Matt lying next to her, no T shirt, and she drinks in his body, feeling such pleasure at both him and last night, shocked that they came together in such a way, longing and needing overcoming so much, especially for Matt, she smiles.

"I can hear you smiling," he says opening his eyes and pulling her to him, his confidence brimming, but knowing too how he might feel today or tomorrow, but to do that last night, "My little shy Annie, if I remember rightly."

"Wow," is all I say.

"Well, I wouldn't give myself high marks but hey better than none," he smiles into her mouth, enjoying his feeling of confidence, he has no expectations that his stirring of passion might be repeated soon, but he was content he had been able to do something.

"So, what you said last night about it taking some time to be better…" She leaves the question hanging in the air.

"Yes. I have spent a long time thinking about my health and I now know I won't be able to manage everything for quite some time, be who I was, and I don't want you to have to struggle, Dave and Sue are content here, so let's go with the flow, and my aim is to be back up to some type of normality, but time wise I've no idea when. Look darling I might feel terrible in the next couple of days, but I know I can…"

"Yes, so I gather," she goes to get up, "Just don't be too cocky," she bursts out laughing and the tension of so long dissolves, and she falls back on his chest, feeling his warm skin next to hers, so good.

They spent the day doing home schooling, exercises, paperwork and cooking, each to their own jobs but with secret smiles on their faces, both knowing that there might be consequences, but realising how wonderful it felt to have some form of normal back, even if it was temporary.

Annie eased the fish pie out of the oven and put it to cool, she could see the weather getting darker outside, heavy rain was forecast and some electric storms, Matt was with the children, telling them a bedtime story, and for once they were going to eat on their own, she put the news on the television, she hadn't caught it all day, it was a mistake to watch it sometimes, as the numbers of deaths sent her into a spiral, not just in this country but worldwide.

But for once the news was good, talk of a drug that had helped to lower deaths, Dexamethasone, a drug she had seen herself in the past, good for inflammation and helped the immune system, and fantastically cheap. She stood completely still taking in this news, something tickling her memory but unable to grasp, a randomised controlled trail, some drugs unproven, control groups, Oxford University, fitting into NHS settings, then it hit her, Matt, she knew he had been on a trial and wondered if it was this one, she turns as Matt comes in.

"Dex."

"What."

"Oh my god. I signed you up for a drug trial, and never told you. I don't know if it was this one or what," she continues speaking quickly. "I should have told you."

"I know," he stills her and holds her face between his hands, "I know about the trial, John told me, obviously I don't know for sure if I had 'Dex', but John mentioned that you had signed me up for a trial, and what a huge decision it had been for you on your own, but if it was this one and I had 'Dex' then good. I have no doubt I will find out at some stage, come on, let's eat and we can talk more."

"You're asking to eat," she laughs, and puts the food on the table, both of them start and then gradually talk about the drug trial, "There should be some paperwork with your things from hospital."

"Yes, there is but I haven't read it."

"I'm going to read up on all of this tomorrow, wow, its brilliant news, the cost is so low too as it's out of patent. What wonderful scientists we have, Matt, and if it saved your life then even more so."

"Slow Annie, calm, eat," they both eat the fish pie savouring the flavour in his case particularly so, enjoying his food, it had been for a couple of days that he had felt that food tasted good, he didn't want a lot but it felt good to enjoy it for a change, also sitting with Annie and enjoying food together. As they take in the shared moment, lightning flashes, around, and the heavens open.

"Gosh look at this rain," Annie stands and goes to shut the windows, hoping there is no thunder, she goes through to the children's room they are tucked up and asleep. Having cleared up they sit watching the rain and fork lightening streak across the sky, glad they are not directly under the storm.

"Both Dave and Don will be pleased with this, filling water butts and the reservoir. I know Don was slightly concerned as he had to water a lot earlier in the year, that's another thing."

"What," she sits close to him.

"He thinks part of the hose on the irrigation system is going, so might have to get someone in, which understandably he is reluctant to do. So, I've said give them a call and see what we can do from here with their guidance."

"The river will be filling, won't it?" suddenly anxious, Annie asks.

"Yes, but it won't flood up here, don't go back to Arthur's escapade, we are all ok," he kisses her head and draws her closer to reassure her, she does get moments of worry, he supposes that is about all that has gone before, bringing up the children on her own and having to make so many decisions has coloured her old self with this layer of anxiety. He can't begin to think how she dealt with everything when he was on a ventilator, and the decision about the drug trial must have been so difficult for her.

"I did a will before lockdown."

"Oh, why then and not before?"

I saw a future, he thinks to himself, but says, "My solicitor had been on at me to do it, so with everything that was happening with the pandemic I felt it was the right time. I made sure Don was looked after and," he hesitates here, "I left the farm to you." She slowly turns in his arms. "I know it would have been a huge undertaking for you but it felt right, it would have given the children a future too, and I know Dave would have stepped up to the plate."

"Matt. I don't know what to say, other than I never want to hear that will read," it bought to her the fragility of their times, not just for them as a couple but for the children's future and the world.

Matt lifted the weights gingerly, they weren't heavy, in fact he was sure Annie could lift these easily, he needed to put strength back into his arms and just doing these carefully was his way, he'd asked Dave to bring them down from one of the outhouses where he had some gym equipment, he sat at the edge of the chair and allowed himself to think as he did his exercises, his confidence had grown, but he was all too aware he had a million miles to go to become the man he had been before COVID-19.

Talking to Annie had been good, not least that it had kick started their physical relationship, and yes it might be some time before a recurrence of that, but it had added another layer to them, the depth of their relationship was evident and he wanted to take that further, but fought against his own wishes knowing he couldn't do it quite yet. He did not want a relapse, that he dreaded, he'd been there with the dreams and the lack of energy and just didn't think he could do it again.

As he lifted the weights, he remembered it was a month today when he had come home, the last week had seemed quicker than the previous three, presumably because he had felt so ill back then. As his mind went over the time in hospital he thought about just before he was ventilated, he hadn't told Annie about it but he saw this frequently, both asleep and awake, the fear, not being able to get his breath and the medics telling him what they were going to do. He couldn't say what he was thinking, and that was, will I make it? He had also wanted to say tell Annie I love her but wasn't able to, it wasn't just his fear he felt but he saw it in the eyes of those around him, that was all you could see, eyes, and they did come back to him, he took a deep breath to steady the flashback, the image, to get rid of it, and realised he was sweating, he put the weights down and slowly put it behind him as best he could, he breathed in the fragrant air coming through the patio doors, and focused on the colours spread out in front of him, alive.

This too shall pass. The words come to him as he sits back, he has a memory of a voice, at his bedside, soft, she said, "This too shall pass," to remember the happy when he was sad, he sees it in his mind when he was in the terrible scary times, and saw it with Annie's love too. He lets the words settle around him, and gently drifts off to sleep, Annie walks in and sees him sleeping, she takes a good look at him and is pleased he looks better, some colour in his cheeks and his face isn't as hollowed as it was, she sees the weights and realises how hard he is trying. But knows he tempers this, pacing himself as John had said. She rests herself on the edge of the bed and allows herself some time, just looking at him, remembering the other night, absolutely thrilled for him, and blushing at the thought of her passion, she draws her knees to her chest and wonders if this is a beginning, a month today he came home he was still so ill, and yes there was a long way to go, but for the first time she thought there might be some hope.

The children ride their bikes down the road towards the gate as Matt and Annie walk along behind slowly, Matt has improved over the last few days, on top of his other good days, but his walking is still a bit laboured with limited muscle power, as they catch the children up they turn and look up at the farmhouse, they could see the pond below the kitchen window and Matt's office, the lounge window hidden with the trees and front garden, as his mum called it, although at the back of the house, with the yard and kitchen ending up the main entrance. Matt leans on the gate and holds Annie's hand.

"I was thinking, if we ever moved to the farmhouse we could do with a brighter and more open plan kitchen," she looked at him quizzically, "I think the layout of the barn has got me thinking, it is lovely to have us all together, the kitchen in the house was made in the past and is isolated from the living aspect of life isn't it really?"

"Well yes, it is," wondering where he's going with this.

"Would you like to live up there at some point, is what I'm asking Annie?" he puts his arm around her shoulder and looks down at her.

"Only if you are well. I don't want you saying let's do it and struggle."

"It would be when I'm well, it's a family house and I would love our family to be in it," he continues to look into her eyes.

"Then I would too."

"It would need some remodelling I thought, and this is the fault of too much day time TV being on," we laugh, because he knows we don't have it on, but sometimes when I'm cooking I will put Escape to the Country on for light relief, but only when Arthur and Molly are outside, "So I thought that if we had a garden room coming off the kitchen where the window is, half glass and coming quite far out, there is room, it would overlook the pond, it could have the long kitchen table in it width ways, and some window seats on the main window side and chairs the other, the children could sit at the table then doing homework or whatever, and you would have to decide this, perhaps an island by the aga, which gives an area for preparing food. I think the rest of the kitchen is ok, but I might have blinkers on, what do you think?"

"You have been watching too much TV," I grin. "Yes, I think that would work quite well, it would give more light to the area, and wouldn't look out of place. I like the idea darling."

"The only other thing I thought initially was to update the bathroom next to the main bedroom and make it en suite, everything else could wait I think."

"I agree," her spirits lifted further, plans, and good ones. He pulls her into him, so wanting to ask her something but feeling he needs to wait for that question. They stroll back towards the barn and talk about the shops opening, pubs, bars and restaurants, they both, like Dave and Sue feel that it feels early, but they have been so cocooned here the outside world is difficult to contemplate, the talk of moving the 2-meter social distancing was something Annie thought was early, and although a couple of weeks away it was frightening and new cases in factory settings too, it was a worry, as the children and Bob go past yet again, Annie voices her concern for them.

"What will life be like if this virus recurs, and not just once more but every few years, if they can't get a vaccine made. I worry. I know just worry about today."

"No, don't worry at all, about today or tomorrow, we have to take each day as it comes as that blessed saying goes, they are happy, and soon we can see Dave and Sue and be one family, then think about your parents too, they've missed them I know that, and it might all come together for Molly's birthday then Arthur's, and that is what is good."

Matt has had over ten days of good, well, better health, the ladders are all over the chart. I am pleased to say, he has paced himself, and isn't likely to run anywhere, but what he has been doing has been good, but it means we can see Dave and Sue and have our own bubble, Dave wants to do a celebratory barbeque, we haven't told the children yet, but it looks like tomorrow after home schooling they are coming over and cooking up a storm, the weather is going to be brilliant, so make the most of it. Just then Dave and Sue come into view going down the hill to their barn, he gives massive thumbs up and I jump up and down. I can't wait for a hug from my brother and my best friend Sue, it will be so good.

I am preparing chicken kebabs, Dave has sausages and burgers to keep certain people sweet, and he said some prawn kebabs too, so much food and I reckon there could be bubbly for our bubble, how can something we used to take for granted be so incredible, and so welcome, then my song comes on the radio, and I have a mixture of happy and sad tears flowing.

"What's the matter?" Matt says coming into the room, she puts her head on his chest crying.

"It's this song Times like these, it played the day you went into hospital, about love and hope, it resonated with me, as the ambulance came, I knew I wanted to tell you how I felt, and when I hear it, it brings it all back, but it is mixed with happy tears too."

The children run in, "Mummy," they both say, and join the hug, "Why's Mummy crying, she used to a lot but doesn't now you're here," Matt smiles at the simple words that carry so much.

"It's this song," Matt says.

"Oh, is that all, well don't play 'we'll meet again'," Arthur rolls his eyes and drags Molly off for swing ball.

"We'll meet again?" he asks.

"Yes, the Vera Lynn classic, they played it a lot for the VE day commemorations, and it was very moving, and the Queen used those words too."

"Has VE day happened," he can't quite get his head around everything that has taken place.

"Yes, love, you missed so much," just then we hear the quad and Dave and Sue appear, with barbeque and food and drink, they let themselves in through the gate as Arthur tells them off for not socially distancing.

"It's ok love we are allowed to now, we can all hug," as I say that Dave gives me the biggest hug in the world, and yes tears start but such happy tears, we all hug, the children, Matt, Sue and of course Bob. Dave manages to get the barbeque set up and started, which gives us time to sit and take in the pleasure of their company, Dave comes over and gives me another kiss and hug and I hold onto him. What I would have given to have this in those dark hours, with Matt on the brink, it makes this feel so special.

The children are overwhelmed at having Dave and Sue so close, Dave has to play swing ball obviously, but we sit down to eat and the food tastes wonderful, we have a glass of bubbly and the toast is "family." How appropriate. Although we've all talked as best we can through all of the lockdown, it seems we have all missed aspects of life in our brief conversations, so the chatter was overwhelming and good, even the children running up and down asking Uncle Dave questions, they missed him too.

"Have you got some clippers Dave, as you see I could do with a good haircut, and I think Arthur wants one too."

"Yes. I have, do you want me to pop up tomorrow and I can cut it for you?"

"Yes, that would be great."

"Do you think while you're doing that I can go and do a bit of gardening," to see the garden and take in all of it on my own would be tremendous, it's not that I don't want Matt and the children around but I would just like a bit of the past and me time in the garden.

"You don't have to ask sweetheart, if that's what you want then go and do it," he takes her hand and squeezes it, knowing she needs that time.

The next morning is very warm and humid, Matt after his exercises sits outside, Arthur and Molly doing a bit of schoolwork at the table by his side, Dave comes down and sets up his hairdressing kit.

"Nice shorts Annie," Matt looks appreciating her lovely legs and that cute bottom on show, he winks at her, Dave notices the chemistry and is pleased for them, he just hopes they have better days now.

"Are you coming with me Molly?"

"No, I'll stay and watch the haircuts Mum," I thought she might, she'll be handing out coffee and magazines next, "You won't be able to put anymore hair slides in Matt's hair after today."

"What?" says Dave.

"Unfortunately, no pictures Dave, they were banned," I smile as I go up the hill and hear Matt say.

"Fortunately."

I breath in the warm air as I walk up to the walled garden. I use the double gates on this side of the garden and go in, no Sue, she must be on her way I think. Then I slowly walk round what was my baby, looking at how well the growing is going, the beds are full, the runner beans growing well up their stakes, with orange flowers on one variety and purple on another. I step into the greenhouse and take in the lovely smell; the vents are open so Dave has probably been up already. I go over to the peach tree, espaliered on the warm wall, and fruit is evident. I lean over and smell the sweet smell and gently cup the fruit, that lovely soft downy skin, not quite ready yet. I must mention to Dave if Matt can have the first fruit, thinking of his mother.

As I come out, I stand and take in all the memories, going back to how it all started in September, not a year yet but so much has taken place since then, good and bad, the first time I looked round and Matt came in, catching me in his arms. I remember feeling a shiver of something then. Attraction, yes, I think so, but I didn't recognise it then, the growing closeness, the kindness, the thought, and then us, together, the joy, followed by uncertainty in the world, the fear, but all of this here helped to get me through. I look up at the house. I know Matt wants to come back and I do too, it does feel a while off though, he's got a review with John later in the week. I hope he sees Matt's progress. As I contemplate all this Sue comes in.

"Hi. I thought you'd be up here when I came in."

"I assumed you might like a bit of your own time," we hug and turn looking at it all, "I love it here."

"So do I Sue, it gives so much doesn't it?"

"Yes, I feel it has some magic about it, it's in the air, just there, hard to put your finger on it, but I think it is all the people who have walked through here, all the memories."

"Yes, I agree, and thought that in the past too, so some weeding, it will be good to get my hands in the soil, and what needs picking? You tell me what you want me to do."

We settle into a rhythm, and get loads done when Matt, Dave and the children appear, Dave bringing lunch. I hadn't realised the time. I look up and see Matt, he looks more like the Matt who belongs here, his hair as it was when I met him, much shorter, his lovely blue eyes shining, it catches in my throat, this is the first time he has looked remotely well. I go over and hug him close to me.

"Love the haircut."

"What about mine, Mum?"

"Oh, yours looks great Arthur," shorter, to match his not so growing fringe I think. I give him a hug and ruffle his new haircut, the children run off as Dave starts to put some lunch on the table.

"He wanted it to be like Matt's," Dave smiles. "So, I did it a bit shorter, but it matches his unfortunate fringe," we all laugh, it is so good to hear and lovely to have Dave and Sue with us.

"You have both done so much in here. I can't believe it and it's growing so well."

"It has slowed over the last week but the warm weather earlier has helped so much and this week will encourage it all, the farm shops are doing so well too, it's hard keeping up some times with all the produce they want, but we do."

"Are people preferring to buy in those shops rather than supermarkets?"

"To a degree. I think the social distancing has been an issue, in a farm shop it is smaller so I think it is mainly the fact you know where the food comes from. I think people feel it is safer in that respect."

General chat circles round the table once again, about produce, the farm, the new plot and sowing of seeds, the children coming and going as usual, sitting to eat then running off, Bob has been allowed in, and he is enjoying new smells.

We walk back down to the barn, the weather still humid. I think Matt needs a rest soon, and I can see he is slightly struggling, the children settle to some school work, and Matt goes for a lie down. I rinse the lettuces and tomatoes and radishes I have picked to make a salad with steaks tonight. I supervise a bit of schoolwork and feel the best I've felt in quite a while, just a sandwich at lunch but again food prepared by someone else, it makes my life better.

I take a cup of tea through to Matt, he is awake as I saw him stir when I was outside watering the pots, the children are playing swing ball now. I don't think that will last as it is warm for them. I put the tea down and kiss his forehead and run my hand over his now shorter hair. He looks into my eyes and I see some more of the man I knew before. He sits up and puts his legs over the edge of the bed, pulling me into him, and giving me a kiss that has promise. I think, grinning into the kiss.

"What are you smiling about?"

"I thought that was a kiss with real promise."

"What do you mean I always kiss with real promise," he smiles at me, holding my face with both of his hands. "It's been a good 24 hours, hasn't it?"

"Yes, life has been different and I mean a good different. It is good to chat and share with Dave and Sue and not have barriers between us. How do you feel?"

"Not too bad, but I needed that rest, I'm going to do some emails now and check some stuff with Don," he gets up and takes his tea over to the chair, but stands for a moment and looks at the children. "It would be nice to get them a paddling pool wouldn't it, although knowing this country as soon as we buy one it will rain."

"Yes, they'd love that, not sure that Bob would though."

Matt sits and opens his laptop, he'll see if Dave can organise one for the children, he knows he's good online and quite quick, as he opens his emails and sees one from Alf, he looks at it as Annie comes in through the patio window followed closely by the children.

"I'm just going to put some more sun protection on these two," she's about to follow them into the far bathroom, when Matt calls her back.

"There's an email from Alf here you need to read," he shows her the contents of Alf's missive.

"Bloody hell," I stop myself saying any more as little ears are nearby, Stewart had left the children his cottage to do what they want with it, "That is so kind I can't believe it, and Alf has said he will sort out the contents and get a house clearance company in, to deal with everything except that which Stewart has gifted to others," I get up and put the sun cream on the children and go back to speak to Matt.

"Blimey, it's quite overwhelming isn't it all of this, and so, so kind."

"Yes, do you want me to get my solicitor Geoff to sort this out?"

"I think that's a good idea, he can liaise with Alf, and then we can think what to do with the money, invest it for their futures. It's a lovely legacy for them, it means if they wanted to go to university, it is there for them. I know that is a long way off but, it will be their money to spend as they want."

I sit outside a couple of days later drinking my tea and watch the children as they check their plants, and give them some water, what we didn't talk about the other day and I think it sort of hung in the air was my house. I know that Tim who is using it won't be for much longer, given that there are changes to everything including shielding in the future, so do I look for a tenant or sell. I know that Matt has said we have a future together, am I worried about relying on someone else, no, that does not come anywhere near this decision.

As I trust Matt with my life, it is just moving on from the past, that final tie, and as I look around, I know that is what I want, to break that tie, the children have a tie to Sam's family in the legacy they have been left, but for me I don't need that tie any more, of the house.

Arthur suddenly calls out, "Mum there's someone in the river," I jump up and Matt must have heard to as he is by my side from the bedroom in a flash. I breathe a sigh as it is someone in a kayak, in fact two kayaks.

"Have you got your phone," I nod, "Call Dave quickly, they have trespassed to get this far, and we don't want contact."

I ring Dave. I think the best course of action is to let them carry on down river as we don't want anyone near us, but I am not sure how the river is for kayaks further down, Matt takes the phone from me, and him and Dave talk. We watch them go further down and out of sight, that possibility of contact has unnerved Matt and me. I usher the children in for some work, and I go too, Matt continues to monitor the river and walks down to the end of the garden. I see him take a call and then he walks up towards the barn. I go out to him taking a cold drink as the weather is hot today.

"Don's gone to check up stream as to come this far they must have climbed onto land or cut the fence that is across the river to stop the cattle wandering off, and he said there are hundreds of people on the river bank and in the river down by the village, his wife phoned and you can't park for cars everywhere, people walking around with inflatables and barbeques, apparently it was like it yesterday too, and the mess they left is beyond belief."

"But why?"

"Don't know. I know it's been popular for locals in the past but not to that extent, and nothing is open, no pubs, no café's, no facilities."

We learn later that it isn't just by rivers, the beaches are absolutely heaving. I am frightened there was already talk of a second wave, but this irresponsibility is dreadful. Later we catch the news, and see Bournemouth beach, you cannot see a grain of sand for people. I know everyone feels stir crazy for being inside for months, but many have gardens and can go out walking, but going down there and being so close, yes, it worries me sick, perhaps they need to rerun the films of hospitals and staff struggling to save lives, and remember those who died and whose lives are altered forever.

I wake next morning feeling off colour, the heat got to me yesterday but in reality, I know it's not that. I feel anxious, it unsettled me those people kayaking down the river so close and that made me nervous, we've decided to have a brief meeting today with Dave and Sue about the future. It's still warm, but cloudy, so we sit outside the children running around the garden playing one of their made-up games, it looks slightly like trooping the colour to me, but Bob is keeping a low profile.

We talk about how we all want the garden produce to go well, and about the farm shop barn, we decide to go and have a look at it all over the weekend, even if initially we just use it for pumpkins at Halloween.

Dave says that he has lost some crops in the polytunnel, he thinks a rabbit is enjoying himself in there, Matt volunteers Bob for any tasks in there, as he speaks, he seems to pause and loose his way.

"Are you ok Matt?" I put my hand on his, he is just staring ahead.

"Yes, where was I, oh uhm," he looks pale suddenly, Annie looks at him anxiously, "I'm fine love don't worry, we all get senior moments, and that was mine."

Then it is the discussion that if the farm shop is open to the public, who will front it and what are the risks, it seems so far away to be discussing this, return to school is before that. I have no doubt that schools will reopen completely in September, what are the risk for Matt, with the children attending and me ferrying them to and fro. I know some families are contemplating home schooling for their children for the long term, not via their original schools either. But I feel the children also need to socialise with friends, and although they have each other they do need that contact with friends. In terms of Matt. Will he still be an infection risk, but what about second waves and further lockdowns, which appears to be happening in some places worldwide already. Everything is running round inside me, trying to work out all the problems, not least Matt's momentary pause mid-conversation, he appeared slightly confused.

We decide between us to prepare, and just keep an eye on the news constantly for changes, Don's wife is coming back to the cottage on the farm and so we talk about Phil, he is keen to stay on, and we must think where he can live, if he wants to live on the farm, then Matt tells Dave and Sue how he is giving the cottage to Don. All of this is going through my head, and as Dave and Sue leave. I walk into the barn and feel a bit dizzy, then don't remember another thing.

"Annie," Matt sees Annie slump and he gets to her as she faints, he manages to put her on to the sofa, instructing Arthur to put some cushions under her feet, elevating her legs, she looks deathly, he quietly murmurs to her but she is still out, "Arthur get your mum a glass of water and Molly wet a towel and I'll put it on her face," the children are obviously anxious, "Annie," she stirs and opens her eyes as he wipes her face, she still looks so pale, Matt is worried he feels this isn't just a faint, as he thinks this Dave and Sue come in.

"What happened, Arthur texted me?"

"Annie fainted, but she took a while to come too, and is still a bit groggy." Matt lifts her head and she takes a sip of water, "It's alright sweetheart."

"Did she bang her head."

"No, I caught her, it's ok Annie," she tries to sit up, and he gently pushes her back, he gestures for Sue to take the children outside.

"I'm ok go and play you two," she manages to say, they look reassured and go out with Bob.

"What is it love?"

"I don't know. I felt anxious earlier after our meeting. I have felt light headed now and then too."

"Why didn't you say, right we'll phone the surgery, perhaps you can have a telephone consultation with one of the nurses or doctors."

"No."

"Yes," he settles her in his arms and strokes her face, he was so scared she looked awful and took a long time to come round.

"Come on you need some rest, and I'll get you a drink and a biscuit, to bring your energy levels back up," he lifts her in his arms, thinking this could end badly but he does it, pleased with himself and puts her on the bed, and lays a throw over her, she feels cold too. He gives her the phone and goes to get her a drink, having a quiet word with Dave.

She gets a call back from the advanced nurse practitioner, and as Annie thought when she told her all her symptoms, she wanted to see her and examine her, she hadn't told Matt but she had been experiencing intermittent bleeding over recent weeks, she knew she should have said but felt shy on top of all the other worries, she was also worried what it could be, as if they didn't have enough going on.

Dave takes Annie to her appointment, she was petrified, not least about herself but about wearing a mask, gloves and being in contact with people, she had explained about Matt, and the nurse had tried to reassure her, but what could she do, they wanted to see her but what if she bought something into the house and made him ill, she was so worried.

Matt was beside himself; he knew deep down there was nothing seriously wrong, or was there, but to not be with her, it hit him how she must have felt seeing him go in the ambulance, "This bloody virus." Molly tugged at his hand as they saw Annie driven off, "She'll be fine you two, she's just going to have a blood test, and then she'll be back."

God, I'm turning into anxious Annie she thought as she came out of the surgery, relief flooding through her, she felt sick, all of this, what a way to live now, but she took a deep breath relieved she had been examined, she thought she had something awful, but she was ok, probably anaemic, and was told to look after herself more.

Before she got back in the car, she took off her gloves and mask and put them into a bag she had with her, then washed her hands in the hand sanitiser also in her pocket.

"What did they say?"

"Nothing major, woman's problems," she thought if she said that Dave would stop asking questions, "And probably anaemic, she told me to look after myself too."

"Yes, well that sums it up doesn't it, and I bet you didn't tell Matt the problem either?"

"No, he has enough to worry about, I am frightened though Dave," he pulls her into a hug, she tries to stop him, worried what she might have on her clothes, but he still holds her, "I love him so much, it's been difficult for all of us, but for Matt more so. I know he is improving but John's call earlier in the week and Matt saying to you then me he knows his journey to where he was before is going to be a long one, sort of broke my resolve, nearly broke me again I don't know the details but it can't be good."

Dave knew about the consultant call, by the sound of it he was making sure Matt were aware of more possible side effects from this virus, heart and other organs, although the consultant reassured Matt that probably wasn't something he needed to worry about but he did say his lung function might never be the same. And of course, Dave was aware Matt felt his route to full recovery would be a long one. Dave and Sue found that hard to come to terms with, especially as Matt had been so fit so vital, but what it must feel like for Annie he couldn't imagine, but he needed to reassure, be there for her.

"I know little sis, but he'll get back there, he is so determined, you've been a worrier for far too long, Matt is good for you, and he is taking this in his stride now, you need to absorb his calmness and you have to be open. I know you made so many decisions in your married life and since, but share with Matt, he said you were, but do even more sis. I think you two need a few days on your own, just looking out for each other, not worrying about the children, the farm, the garden and certainly not the rest of the world."

When we get back Sue has taken the children up to their barn for tea, not overnight I say, and she has left us a lasagne to reheat, Matt comes over. "Go and lie down and rest, you still look pale."

"No, I just want a shower. I need to get the outside world off of me," literally she thinks, throwing all her clothes into the wash basket.

Matt looks at Dave, "How'd it go?"

"She's ok, run down I think, just have a chill together and a chat, you know she's a worrier and I've said she needs to lap up your calm levelheadedness, if there is such a word," he grins and goes, hiding his worry for both of them.

I come out of the shower, I'd slipped on some pink joggers and matching zip up top, a present from Sue when she was in her high powered and highly paid job, Matt is sitting in the chair looking out of the windows.

"Come here love," he beckons me over and indicates for me to sit on his lap.

"Are you sure?"

"Very. I can take your great weight," he smiles and wraps his arms round me I rest my head on his chest.

"I thought it was something nasty."

"What do you mean?"

"I had some bleeding in between periods and thought… well it's not, she thinks I'm anaemic though, and a bit run down."

"Why didn't you tell me about the bleeding?"

"I don't know, everything goes so fast, the changes daily I can't get my head around, the outside world getting nearer it frightens me, your health, the uncertainty of it all, and just trying to cope. I know I do keep some things in, but forever I have had to make decisions on my own, you know what it is like in the Army, limited communication with home. So, I just got on and did things, not always popular but I had to arrange them. I virtually built that house, so it's hard to let go, help me, help me give more and let you in."

"You do sweetheart, you just don't realise, you give so much and you have let me in. I understand keeping some things in is to protect yourself, but you don't have to I'm here."

"I was so scared you weren't going to be though Matt, that time still haunts me," Matt takes a steadying breath and thinks, and me, "I thought I'd lost you."

"I'm not that easy to get rid of you know," he kisses her head. I put my hand on his chest, it feels hard and more substantial somehow now.

"I had to have my coil taken out, as she wasn't sure if that was the cause."

"It doesn't matter we'll sort something out; I've got some condoms somewhere."

"Probably out of date," she laughs.

"Is that saying before you I had very few dates, cheeky girl?"

"It seemed so simple didn't it when we first got together, although the storm clouds were gathering, but you just can't get your head around how our small world has changed, wearing masks Matt, in the village, it looked so wrong."

"I know Annie, but we have just got to get on, we will think about school and all the risks later, come on. I need to put Sue's lasagne in the oven. And yes, I'm cooking."

They go through to the lounge and realise Dave must have put the oven on and the lasagne in, as it is bubbling away, "Shall we eat at the island, we can see the house from here," it would be good to see the house, it sits solidly looking down on them, a beacon. He was feeling stronger and felt he could manage the stairs in the not-too-distant future, but was also aware that this barn felt very much like home for Annie and the children.

"I've never sat here."

"What, where do you eat or did you before I came home."

"Well, I would eat at the table with the children, breakfast, but other meals I generally stood, until you came home, but even now I eat lunch standing."

"Well, that's going to change I can tell you."

"You're very masterful," he comes over and kisses her, "Mmm very."

"Now eat up," he sits next to her and they enjoy the rarity of peace and food, and not rushing.

"That was lovely," Annie pushes her plate back, "So nice to not have to cook too."

"I'll clear, is that your phone ringing?" She jumps up and answers it. The call was very brief and one sided as Annie barely said anything.

"That was Dave the children want to stay the night."

"You didn't say much."

"I didn't have any choice they railroaded me."

"Rest then and I'll cook tomorrow. I was going to anyway."

"Were you. I didn't know."

"It was supposed to be a surprise."

"What's on the menu?"

"That's a surprise, do you think Arthur and Molly will stay up with Dave and Sue all weekend?"

"Very possibly as its novel, they might need clothes though."

"Stop worrying, Dave is a grown up now having Sue with him, so they will work it out, let's just enjoy ourselves and chill out," he comes over and sits on the sofa next to Annie, they talk about each other, laughing about childhood, and games up on the farm, the shared times, and then talk about their likes and dislikes, times when life was good, his parents and her parents, as with everything that has happened to them there was never time to get to know the details of life, other than they loved each other, he pulls her close never wanting to let her go.

They sleep in the next morning, he gets up and gets Annie breakfast in bed, they take a moment for themselves, although they both love Arthur and Molly, and of course Bob, who has accompanied the overnighters, it is nice to have time for each other, he would love to make love to her, but how he feels and how Annie is means not now, but having affection and talking has made them closer, if that is possible.

Dave brings the children down mid-morning, mainly because they need clothes, but he wanted them to see how Annie was, she looked better this morning, not back to her usual self but certainly better than yesterday, there is much chat and Arthur tells them he's been helping collect eggs, and how they've seen the pigs, but they smell, and on and on, Annie thinks it is good for them to have a different perspective, with other people, it has been very enclosed here, perhaps claustrophobic for them. Dave surreptitiously gave Matt the couple of bags he had promised him, with all his ingredients in.

"I think it will be dry tomorrow, Dave, any chance of getting the golf buggy down. I thought I would take Annie round the farm and show her more of it, I'm fairly sure I can drive it ok."

"If you're sure, yes no problem, I'll let Arthur and Molly have a lift in it to bring it down, so you two can do your own thing, come on you lot, things to do," with their bags they all leave.

"What was the whispering about," she goes over and puts her arm around his waist as they wave everyone off.

"I thought we might have a golf buggy ride tomorrow; we can have a look round the farm and I'm cooking tonight."

"Again, this is becoming a habit, a good one." Over mussels and chips, or Moules-Frites, they chat and enjoy each other's company, "What made you decide on this?" pushing her bread into the lovely juice surrounding the mussels.

"The children said it was a meal you loved on holiday when you went out one night, so it thought I would have a try, it is easy to do, not much standing at the cooker."

"How do you feel?"

"A bit worn, it was lifting you the other day," he smiles.

"Yes, yes, very funny, but with all this lovely food you won't be able to lift me, what did John have to say we've not really talked about it much."

"We don't have to now," he looks at her and realises she feels now is a good time. He recalls the phone call and tells her the details, John asks how he was.

"I'm having a run of fairly good days, but pacing myself, some exercise and the exercises, but I still get fatigued, although I think not as much. I don't feel as fragile." He asks Matt about dreams and mental health, "Uhm I seem to get like a repeat image, so I suppose it's a dream, eyes, fear, my fear and fear in other people's eyes, and I see them in daytime too."

"Transposing images, do they feel intrusive?"

"Not too bad. I do get a bit anxious when it happens and it seems to pause what I'm saying, it has happened a few times. I remember some words spoken softly and repeated," John asks what those are. "This too shall pass."

"Dolores, one of our nurses," John laughs. "It is her favourite saying, she says it often to remember happy when in sad times," John continues. "The dreams are lessening then, have you put on some weight?"

"A bit I think my face isn't as hollow."

"Good, we just need to have a chat about further symptoms that might occur, you know as I've said this situation is evolving so we are learning on the job," he goes onto talk about effects that are manifesting, his biggest concern is fatigue, lung issues and mental health for Matt, but there are other organ effects that might arise, but he didn't suffer these in hospital so it might not be a future issue.

"We'll get a home visit or telephone consultation from the physiotherapist, just to assess strength, any questions?"

"What about the future John. I have tempered my improvement with caution for the family, for Annie, but I know inside I won't get back to how I was for quite some time."

"I think you're right Matt, some people have moved from critical care and regained physical health quickly, as yours was initially slower I'm with you on length of recovery and pace, it is not something we can be certain of as yet."

"The physio would be good as at some stage we would like to move back into the house on the farm, which has many levels and stairs."

"She'll certainly help and advice Matt."

As Matt stops talking, he didn't say how the conversation finished when John asks after Annie, he told him she was "running on empty," he hadn't said to John how she was rocked by his estimation of recovery, although she knew deep down, hearing it was difficult, but he reiterated how they had talked and were supporting each other.

"That was quite a chat then," she hadn't interrupted but let Matt talk. "So still some kind of dreams but in daytime," she realises that was what happened in the get together to discuss plans with Dave and Sue, "He was pleased overall though Matt?"

"Yes, he was. I told him about the children's snakes and ladders chart, which made him laugh, it will take time like I said but we can make some plans can't we?"

"Of course, we can, but steady plans no rushing, we don't have to rent these out and we can live here, the house will wait for us love."

"I know. I see it as a goal though and one I want to achieve, but I have to slow down, as you say the house will wait," but could he?

The next morning the rain had stopped and although the day was grey it was warm, it felt like a strange freedom, not from the children but from the life that had been there for months, the worry, the anxiety. Although Dave had said they both needed a rest from the farm, business and other worries he needed to do this, see his future. Just driving round the farm at an early hour, the peace was wonderful, the sound of birds being the only chorus. They stopped for Annie to pick some flowers, and then went over the farm to an area Annie had never been to before, at the top of the hill she could see the square tower of a church, St

Hilda's, she'd not seen the church from this aspect, as when she came to Matt's father's funeral, she approached it from the actual village.

They left the buggy in a field and crossed the lane to the church, through the open lychgate and over to the end of the graveyard overlooking the farm. There was the new stone for his parents, it was the first time Matt had seen it, it was very simple showing them both together now in death. He knelt with Annie behind him resting her hand on his shoulder, he placed the picked flowers on the grave and then went to get up, he struggled but more from emotion than lack of strength. He hugged her to him, looking out over the farm.

They walked back to the buggy, Annie was about to get in when Matt stopped and beckoned her to him, "I love it up here, it was always my favourite place on the farm, with it all spread out below, everything Mum and Dad made and that I love now, it's so peaceful," he kisses her gently on the lips, "I love you, Annie."

"I love you too, Matt."

"Life isn't going to be the same for a long time, if at all. I mean for me, us and everyone. I feel it's about seizing the moment and making the most of what we have," he took her face in his hands, "As you know it is going to be a long time before I am well, if I ever get that fitness back, we don't know whether my health will suffer in the future, they don't know yet, but I want a future, and I want that future with you, if you will have me, will you marry me Annie?"

"Oh Matt, I don't need marriage to be with you forever, but I'd be honoured to be your wife."

"I haven't got a ring, which sounds very cheap when I'm asking you to marry me. I did look the day I went to see Geoff, my solicitor before lockdown, his office was next door to a good jewellery shop. I saw something as beautiful as you and thought I'll pop back in, but life took over, so I feel bad now."

"No, don't feel bad, because it is our secret Matt. I want to hug it to me, if I had a ring on everyone would be talking weddings, bridesmaids and on and on. I don't want that, for me it is sealing the love we have, not frippery, unless you want the morning suits etc," she looks up at him smiling.

"I agree, it is ours, you have my heart Annie," he places her hand over his heart and she puts her other hand on top of his, sealed.

Just then the church bells ring the hour, he turns and looks at the church an idea coming to him, "What would you think about a simple blessing, just us two, or the six of us, Arthur, Molly, Dave and Sue and a small party afterwards," she turns in his arms and looks at the lovely church, a shaft of sun coming through the grey morning, and shining down, "I think it would be lovely Matt all of us. I think we leave telling them until the last moment. I just don't want fuss and I feel it might be too much for you too."

"Yes, no running," he kisses her lightly on the lips, "I might need to ring the vicar then," he looks at her and see she's crying, "Happy tears I hope."

She nods and he gently strokes the tears away with his thumbs, looking at her with such love. "How do you think the children will take it?"

"They will be happy Matt, Daddy Matt, they see you as part of the family now."

"I'd love to have a family together Annie but I don't know if I can…"

"And I'm too old."

"No, you're not."

"I'd love to have your children, Matt," she remembers his terrible dream and hopes she can give him what he wants, and what she wants too.

"We'll have to try, try and try again, and enjoy doing it," he picks her up pressing her body to him, she bats his arm smiling up at him as he takes her mouth with his, kissing her deeply letting her know he meant every word of what he said.

"Did your parents get married here?"

"Yes, they did, full circle for them and lovely if we could get married here too, I'm not sure whether weddings can go on yet, and I would like to get married soon, what do you think?"

"I would too, so give the vicar a ring and see what he says. I wouldn't be surprised if they are allowed services soon if pubs and stuff are opening," they get into the buggy clutching their secret to themselves, smiling at each other, as they go down the hill Annie points at a building set at the back of one of the fields.

"What's that place?" Matt stops the buggy, "That was one of the two buildings I sold for conversion to fund some of the holiday lets, but from an email I had from Geoff the buyers have backed out."

"It's a lovely position, and huge potential."

"What are you thinking?"

"Dave and Sue?"

"Yes, I wondered that to be honest. I know they are happy working here, but do they want to settle down here too, they are keen to garden and I know Dave said they had thought about buying a business when they first started, but if they wanted to stay then this place would be ideal to do up and give them space, and if they stayed, we should look at some sort of partnership, what do you think?"

"I think that's a great idea," Annie was pleased he had thought about them and their future.

"Shall we just pop into the house then?" They did, they walked into the kitchen and Annie could see immediately how Matt's idea would work in there.

"Oh, there's a text from Sue, do we want to join them for Sunday lunch."

"That would be good, what time?"

"Two."

"That's ok it would give me time for a rest. I think I'll probably need one, with all this excitement," he smiles, and they hold hands looking round.

"It's a lovely home Matt. I noticed the day I cleaned…"

"When did you clean and why?" he's so surprised, didn't she have enough to do, he sits down at the table and she sits with him.

"After you had gone to the hospital, I thought it would need a deep clean, because of the virus, so the next day I came and scrubbed, washed bed linen, towels, sofa covers, and cleaned everywhere, well surfaces, with alcohol cleaner. I didn't know if you would need to come back to the house and it needed to be infection free."

"You did all that?"

"I had to Matt, admittedly I might have gone a bit OTT, but for me it needed to be ready for you."

"Sweetheart, another job you took on."

"For you, for us, to make sure no infection went anywhere, it was what it was."

"Come on let's go and have a cup of tea and a chill before lunch," they jump back in the buggy and drive down to the barn, enjoying the secret that would be out soon, but just keeping it to themselves. Matt takes his tea and goes to lie on the bed, resting, Annie follows a while later, he is dozing already, she pulls the throw over him and just watches again, checking his breathing and colour. Something she knows she will probably do all their lives.

How does she feel, marriage, she thinks briefly of her wedding to Sam, it wasn't elaborate, it wasn't church but there were a lot of people there, her wish for simple with Matt came from their love not from previous experience, it felt right to just be the people closest, she knows her parents would love it, but when she said she didn't want fuss having them there would just add some fuss, whereas they had a solid unit, the children and Dave and Sue, and also from what Dave had said her mum was very scared of going out. So, travelling up north as she called it, might be a step too far. As they had gone out so early that morning, they had plenty of time for Matt to regain any used energy, he had improved but like her was cautious, he would feel tired tomorrow with being out early and then going to lunch, as she lay next to him thinking she felt his hand find hers, he lifted it to his lips and kissed her ring finger.

"A promise Annie."

"Another one."

"A ring to cement our future."

"A simple wedding ring is all that is needed Matt, don't start worrying and making plans, we just need to keep this modest, and it will be beautiful because of us."

He rolled onto his side and pulled her to him, kissing her fully on the mouth a sudden need in him, lighting, he wanted her so much after his proposal, he felt he needed to seal it, bond them with that proposal. He leant over her, running his hands up her body feeling her breathing change knowing how she was feeling.

"Matt we shouldn't."

"Why, why not, there is only us, and we'll just take it easy. I want to finish that proposal, unless you feel it might hurt you sweetheart," she smiles and shakes her head, wanting him too, but gently, he took her face in his hands and kissed her, they made love slowly, in no hurry, just enjoying themselves and their love, the feeling of his love and body just beyond anything Annie had experienced—the slow love making increasing the physical feelings for both of them, emotions and love, knowing how close she had come to losing him overwhelmed her, then worry.

"Are you alright Matt? Was it too much?"

"No sweetheart it was the best," he put his arms round her, "It should be me asking if you are alright. I probably shouldn't have done that should I?"

"I don't care it was perfect."

"Oh, higher marks than last time then," he joked. They just lie there letting their heart rates return to normal, he could feel his legs complaining, but it was so worth it, he thought smiling to himself.

"I can't tell you how glad I am I got to know you, thank you for waiting for me to catch up, all of those years you loved me from afar, and thank you for asking me to marry you."

"No problem, as long as I can have sex like that all the time," here's hoping he thinks. He did want so much more, greedy for something he thought he wouldn't have again, her, he remembers his head resting on the kitchen table as he told her not to come near, seeing her go, his consciousness going, those mixed-up days in hospital, no weeks, nightmares, images, trying to get her in his mind but driven out by horrors, then home and too weak to do anything, unable to even kiss her. That is what had driven him, to be able to kiss her, make love, the bonding of the two of them had been emotional. They were joined in the fight against all the illness that had changed them both, no words are needed as they both get their breath back, Matt breathing deeply, but so happy.

How they get through lunch, they don't know, particularly Matt, as yes, he does feel fatigued, and he knows they shouldn't have, but life needs to be lived and it felt so right at the time, they think it doesn't show. But they are both happy if not tired, Dave and Sue can see a difference in them, hoping time on their own has helped them both, with colour in her face Annie looks better, her eyes are shining, they all laugh at stories, especially the swear jar Arthur and Molly have produced for them.

"We don't swear," Annie says indignantly, the children point out the exact time of said swearing, so two deposits for Annie and one for Matt, who also denied swearing until Molly told him he said, "Bloody virus," when Mummy went to the doctors, then got told off herself.

They walk back to the barn with the children and Bob, giving Dave and Sue some peace this time, Matt is tired and shuffling a bit but is beaming. The next morning, Annie is up with the children as Matt enjoys some time to recoup. He sits up in bed thinking of yesterday; all of it, his marriage proposal and them together, his legs feel tired today as do his arms, there is fatigue, but inside him there is joy, a slight feeling of normality, progress.

"Here you are scrambled eggs on toast. I thought you might need to build your strength back up," she kisses his head and gives him the tray.

"Thanks darling, that's so kind, I'll be up in a bit and get some exercises done, and give you a hand, then a few thoughts on what we all said at lunch yesterday."

Dave and Sue were interested in Matt's idea about a partnership and about the building at the top of the farm for them, they intended to go up later and have a look. In the meantime, they had jobs to do in the garden, having the children did hold them back a little at the weekend but seeing how Matt and Annie looked was worth it.

"What are you still grinning at, oh I know those two in the big barn, yes well I don't want to go into it, but obviously all his bits and bobs are working again, from their faces," he puts his hand up as Sue laughs and tries to start yet another conversation about them, "No she's my little sis, too much information," but he's laughing, he shakes his head if ever two people had fully enjoyed some time on their own then those two certainly did, it was written all over them, good, enjoy he thinks.

"So, jobs then, shall I water the fruit trees in the orchard. I know we've had rain but I thought they looked a bit dry the other day, then some sowing and picking."

"Yep. I saw your day plan. I was going to put in those maincrop carrots, turnips and then lift and dry off those shallots, onions and garlic."

"Annie was all for the flavoured oils, so later I'll order that oil with the company I approached and get the bottles ordered, although we ought to check one of Matt's mum's cupboards or outhouses, as she was a bit of a hoarder and there might be some bottles about we could sterilise."

"Good thinking, it will go down well with the herbs, once I've dried them, garlic and chilli's too, just need to sort the labels too. Shall we wander up to the top for lunch, we can have a look at the top field to check on drainage and then look at those buildings Matt mentioned."

They do that, a busy morning followed by a lunch of soup and sandwiches, both in their layers as it had gone cool, with rain forecast for later. They stand back and look at what was once a cottage, and both turn and enjoy the views, the lane could be seen behind hedges, and the top of the house lower down and barns by the house.

"This is lovely, isn't it?"

"It is," Dave stands next to Sue taking it all in, "Who would think our lives could change so much, and for us for the better, but I am cautious saying that. I don't want bad luck coming our way, there's enough of that around or there has been. But sometimes I have to pinch myself at where I am, where we are. I love it, all of it the work, the place, it feels idyllic."

"I know I said to Annie the other day that garden is such a pleasure to work in. I might change my mind when we are doing all of this in the winter but I don't think so. And I like where this cottage is, it will need a lot of work, but it gives us some space, we can't all live on top of one another can we."

"No, we can't and it is good, a good position, I'll get someone in to give us an idea of what could be done and then chat to Matt about price, he was intimating yesterday that he didn't want much. So, I'll get it valued too, what do you think of this partnership he mentioned?"

"It sounded good to me, it's an opportunity Dave too, are you going to talk to your dad about it?"

"I don't think so, he's got enough on his hands with Mum at present," Dave and Annie's mum had struggled at times during lockdown and had lost two close friends, she didn't want to go out and she was also finding it hard that Annie had managed through all of this with minimal input from her mum, "She can't quite get her head around Annie's independence either."

"No. I know Annie's aim when she started gardening was to have that independence from her parents, although they had been brilliant for her, she wanted to strive on her own, have her own money, and as you said when Matt became ill Annie didn't need her mother worrying she would lose again. It's difficult from afar though Dave, and, you've kept in touch regularly. I wonder if her friend's deaths have both impacted in her confidence in terms of going out, but also for her mental health and that is why she can't quite understand some things like Annie's need to go it alone a bit."

"You could be right, when I catch up with Dad later in the week I'll see if he has thought of that and thought of the GP perhaps, also Mum doesn't seem to realise how ill Matt was and the struggle here, Annie didn't have a minute to ring, that's why I did it, but perhaps we are all to blame for that as we haven't necessarily told them everything, have we?" He then blanches a thought coming to him, "You don't suppose all this change and being low has bought something else on, like Matt's father had," they look at each other and a cloud dulls their day.

Cooking for once, she thought, having enjoyed a weekend of being cooked for, homemade chicken goujons and chips for the children and chicken stroganoff for them, she could easily adapt whatever Dave ordered into lovely food and whatever was around too. She did feel lighter and clutched the proposal to her, their secret, she stops and looks out of the window up towards the farm dreaming, suddenly Matt grabs her round the waist.

"All I could hear when I walked in was sighs from you, good ones, what were you thinking?" he raises his eyebrows, and even that is not easy today, yes, he was paying for their activities yesterday, but inside wow he felt good and by Annie's sighs she did too.

"Good things, yesterday, our secret and everything. I feel good Matt, and I can't remember the last time I felt like that."

"I know," he says, she turns and looks at him, she can see he is tired though.

"You feel tired?"

"Yes, and a bit worn if I'm honest, but it was worth it, hopefully with a quiet day like I've had today I'll get some strength back and feel less tired tomorrow. I got hold of the vicar," he looks to check Arthur and Molly aren't within hearing, "He said weddings are going forward from the 4th July. Like you thought, there is a maximum guest number but that doesn't concern us, and he has given me a couple of dates, he was aware I have been ill as Geoff mentioned it when liaising with him about the grave stone. He says he will ensure we will be COVID Secure, he said he'll email me to follow up our conversation," hearing the children coming, he says, "We can chat later."

They do catch up later, they talk about everything, what they spoke with Dave and Sue about too, rain is falling again, it can be heard on the barn roof, the children are settled and asleep, Bob too, although he wonders why they are going to bed in the light, both Matt and Annie wanted an early night, he more so as he did feel tired, but good.

"Dave sent me a text, he said they were keen on the old cottage and he's texted a builder mate to give him an idea of what could be done, and a mate who does valuations, does he have mates in every profession?"

"More than likely, he always made friends with people and kept phone numbers just in case."

"He mentioned about the valuation, I'm not bothered I know what price we had it on for before, so I've emailed Geoff to get in touch with Dave about the price, but I asked him to lower it, considerably, I'm not over charging my future brother-in-law, don't want to get on the wrong side of him."

"What dates then for our wedding? Oh, that sounds strange, but good strange," they are lying facing each other as usual on their nightly talks, holding hands.

"How about the 11 July, it's under two weeks away. The vicar is going to apply for us to have a Common Licence as the banns won't be able to be read, especially with everything that is going on now. I thought late morning, then if the weather is nice lunch in the garden, what do you think?"

"That sounds great. I am excited, never thought I would say that word again, it will be lovely. I will look for a dress, and one for Molly too, and something nice for Arthur."

"Talking of Arthur do you think he would be my best man. I know I should ask Dave but I think it would mean so much to Arthur, and I know there is only us, so Dave could give you away if you wanted."

"I think Arthur would be overjoyed at the job, and I don't want to be given away. I want to walk down the aisle just me coming to you waiting for me, but knowing Molly she will have seen something where the bridesmaid scatters rose petals in front of me, but it will be so much us as a family doing this, however it is, with Dave and Sue at the front too."

They have a busy few days, and have arranged to go up and look in the barn by the top plot after home schooling, Matt has kept activities and exercise to a minimum, he did feel tired after Sunday, but feels now he can recoup with pacing as John had told him, Dave and Geoff have emailed and agreed a price for the old cottage, Dave of course phoning Matt and berating him his generosity. Dave's builder mate is also coming onto the farm to look at the cottage and also the two pieces of work for the house, Dave is going to point him in the right direction, socially distancing of course. With Annie's permission, Matt has asked Geoff to put her house on the market, a final piece added to her own jigsaw, allowing her to fully move on, he hopes so, but inside he knows she has already. He sits at the island having a protein drink looking at his laptop, "Have you seen the website?"

"You mean ours for the farm?"

"Yes, the farm and gardens, Dave told me to check it over, it looks fantastic, the pictures of the original garden showing what Mum and Dad had done is just so great, with some of her prizes shown too, shots of the farm you unearthed and then the designer has put in the modern ones of the garden and produce, it looks really good," she looks over his shoulder and realises it has captured everything they wanted, the past and the present, and the future, however unclear. She looks at Matt's face and sees emotion and pleasure at what has been achieved here, she kisses his head, and hugs him.

"God. I can't believe so much has happened and we are here now," alive he thinks, "I think some images of the barn if we go ahead with it would work too, and didn't you say we are still supplying produce for the Bugle," she nods, "That link should be on here too, especially if Nick is reopening."

"Dave will know if Nick is reopening on the 4 July. I do know he is doing some cook chill meals as take out, and that is very popular, they can just reheat at home then, it's amazing how so many people have diversified during this to keep going. I hope Nick is doing well."

They get in the landy later to go up to the barn, Matt driving, this will be a test for him as it is heavier to drive than the buggy, but he gets them all up there, it is warmer today, so any walk up there would be out of the question. Sue and Annie are out the front viewing the area as Dave and Matt chat inside, the children are with their mum, looking down into the fields and looking at the sheep seeing if they can recognise their lambs.

"Are you doing anything on the 11th mate?"

"Well chance would be a fine thing nothing except for gardening etc, why?"

"Annie and I are getting married," he sees Dave's shocked look, "I know sudden, but seize the moment we both thought, it will be just the six of us, I'm going to ask Arthur to be best man, would you mind too much."

"Oh Matt, I am absolutely overjoyed for you both, and no I don't mind at all, me and Sue will just be so happy to be there, oh where is there?"

"St Hilda's church and then we thought lunch in the walled garden or up by the summerhouse or anywhere here to be honest, we haven't given it much thought. We don't want fuss, it is just us all, and for Annie and me that is the most important part, we're going to tell the children tonight," they both look up and see that Annie has taken the opportunity to tell Sue too, they are hugging and Sue has tears in her eyes.

The children are sitting on the sofa waiting for their tea, Matt and Annie sit near them.

"We've something to tell you," they both stop and look at Annie looking worried, "Matt and I are getting married."

"About time," and "I told you," rings out from Arthur and Molly respectively. Matt and Annie burst out laughing.

"But don't ask me to be Paige boy Mum," says Arthur hands on hips, Molly comes to Annie and says, "Do you want me to be a bridesmaid Mummy?"

"Definitely sweetheart," she gives her a hug.

"Arthur," Matt reaches for him and sits him down next to him, "I have an important job for you, no not Paige boy," he says quickly as he can see Arthur's brain working, "But would you be my best man? You must look after the ring and stand by me and give it to me to put on Mummy's finger."

Arthur is nodding his head in agreement, but I know him he is thinking of adding a dimension to this, "Yes, cool, can Bob hold the ring too, he could have it in a packet attached to his collar or…" I'll nip this one in the bud I think, Bob has been reluctant to dress up since trooping the colour made him the mascot, and do we want Bob there too, but Matt steps in.

"Lovely as Bob is Arty. I think only guide dogs are allowed in church, so you are in charge of the ring, how does that sound."

"Ok Matt. I would be happy to as long as no fancy clothes," bargaining done, they go into their room for a catch up, I think.

"What is that lad like," Matt is shaking his head laughing.

"Well done, nipped in the bud, you know Arthur that could have become very complicated," she hugs Matt to her, learning the ways of her two, just as they come back in.

"Are we going to church on the quad, Matt?" Arthur asks hopefully, then sees the shake of Matt's head and they disappear again.

"Me and Arthur could walk up to the church."

"It's too far from here Matt."

"Well, I thought I'd stay at the house the night before."

"Oh, I'd rather you didn't, not yet, and not without me," she is fearful of him falling on the stairs, some anxiety floods through her.

"Annie. I won't. I just thought it would be nice to go from there, but I know where you are coming from, it's only two weeks away, or less than that, and I might not have the strength, I'll stay with Dave and Sue, and conserve my strength for our wedding night," he says lightly, drawing her towards him, he would have liked to stay in the house, remembering his parents, but he knows it would literally be a step too far, yet. Perhaps they could have a few days there when the renovations are done, before they move in as a family, he voices this to Annie.

"I think that is a brilliant idea darling, are you alright with me saying don't stay there?" worried about ruling him like she tries to do the children.

"It's fine. I know I was pushing it to be honest. I don't mean with you I mean how I will be. We're a team now sweetheart, we look out for each other, and I can't wait to make you my wife," he kisses her with the heat coursing through his body.

Epilogue

Matt turns and sees Annie walking towards him down the aisle, Molly had walked down before her and was now standing with Sue, in the left pew, Dave in charge of Arthur was at Matt's side. Annie looked radiant, her ivory strappy wrap around dress falling to mid-calf, opening slightly to reveal her legs, he remembered how she looked when she came up to the house for the barbeque, so reminiscent of now. She carries a small posy, flowers picked from the sunken garden and beams at him as she gets near, her mum had sent her a hand worked belt that she had worn round her wedding dress when she married, the stitching picking out flowers in silver thread, so appropriate and her something old.

He is overcome with emotion, and feels it is all too much to take in, he leans on the pew, he came so near to death and now he is to marry the woman he has loved for a good part of his life, he says a silent prayer to thank whoever is looking down and looking after him, he realises how lucky he is to have survived and now to do this.

The vicar starts the ceremony socially distancing, it is an intimate ceremony though, as it is just the six of them. Arthur handed the ring to Matt, heavily supervised by Dave. As Matt slips the ring onto Annie's finger, they both step forward to watch, Arthur turns to Dave and says, "Why are you crying, Uncle Dave?"

"I'm not Arthur, I've got something in my eye," but Dave looks over at Sue and can see her crying too, it takes his breath away, he prays that this will last, that nothing will pull them apart and that the future holds wonderful things for these two incredible people, who mean so much to both him and Sue. They walk up the aisle to "Times like these," the song that meant so much to Annie, no organist, but the music filled the church and resonated for them both.

Outside with the sun intermittently shining they see Don and his wife with Phil waving from the other side of the road, just asking the others to wait a minute before they go through the lychgate, they take Annie's posy and place it on

Matt's parents grave, stopping a moment. Annie although tremendously happy feels tears making their way out of her eyes, for it all, for getting to marry this wonderful man.

"I love you so much, Matt."

"And I you, Annie, thank you for being my wife. I will always love you and look after you." They walk back and go through to the waiting landy, Dave is driving them down to the walled garden. Sue, in charge of Arthur and Molly, went before them to get the garden just right.

They get out of the landy, and Dave disappears into the walled garden, giving them a moment on their own. Matt holds Annie to him and kisses her deeply, longing for her as always, unbelieving of where everything has ended. Walking hand in hand they go through the double doors, which has flowers garlanded across the top, going in, they see wedding bunting along the greenhouse and balloons attached to six chairs, the table set with flowers and riotous coloured plates and glasses and napkins, Annie guessed that was more Arthur and Molly than Sue.

Dave snapped photo after photo, all of them looking and feeling happy, not knowing what the future held for them all, just enjoying each other's company at such a momentous occasion, that no one thought or dreamed would happen, given the circumstances, in times like these.

Milton Keynes UK
Ingram Content Group UK Ltd.
UKHW022216091024
449475UK00006B/103